ON THIN ICE

On
THIN
ICE

A Novel

Cherry Adair

BALLANTINE BOOKS
NEW YORK

A Ballantine Book
Published by The Random House Publishing Group

ISBN 0-345-47579-8

Manufactured in the United States of America

Text design by Susan Turner

To my darling husband, David.
You and Max the Wonder Dog are my inspiration.

Acknowledgments

To the Bears, Peggy and Bill of *Bear Air,* thank you for your time and patience; the wonderful people at Rainy Pass Lodge for letting Derek and Lily spend the night there; the Iditarod Committee and dedicated volunteers for sharing their expertise; the friendly people at Alaska Airlines; the helpful individuals at *Alaska Men Magazine.*

Thanks also to my wonderful editor, Charlotte Herscher; my terrific agent, Nancy Yost; my darling assistant and friend Amber Kizer; and to my fabulous friends—Maureen Child, Kelsey Roberts, and Myrna Temte.

Your help was invaluable.

ON THIN ICE

One

THE NEWBORN CALF LAY CURLED IN THE STRAW AT ITS MOTHER'S feet while the proud mama started licking it clean. Outside the glowing warmth of the birthing barn, night pressed icy black fingers against the windows, and snow lay thick on the ground.

Exhausted but triumphant, Dr. Lily Munroe tried to ignore the itchy, someone-was-watching-her sensation on the back of her neck, a creepy feeling she'd had off and on for several hours. She patted the cow's russet-colored rump. "You have a beautiful bouncing baby boy. Good job, Peaches."

"Peaches?" a familiar husky voice said behind her. "She's not a pet, Doc."

The straw at her feet rustled as Lily whirled around, hand to her throat. "Damn it! You scared me to death!"

Tall, dark and annoying.

Derek Wright.

With one shoulder resting against the planked wall, he looked as though he'd been there awhile. His physical presence was like a hard punch to Lily's chest, and her stomach did its usual betraying flip-flop at the sight of six foot four inches of pure, potent male. His lean, handsome face was ruddy with the cold, his glossy dark hair mussed sexily by the wind she heard howling outside.

Beneath her fingertips she felt the hard pounding of her heart, and hoped to hell Derek couldn't hear it. And if he could that he'd attribute it to the fright he'd just given her. The adrenaline rush made her feel light-headed. She ruthlessly tamped down her body's visceral reaction to the sight of him as she started cleaning up her instruments and other birthing paraphernalia from around the stall.

"Sorry," he said, voice silky. "Didn't mean to spook you." He didn't look the least bit sorry, and she shot him a dark look. His lips twitched. "You're hell on a man's ego, Doc."

"There's nothing wrong with your ego. It's healthy as a horse," Lily told him. The breathless, heart-stopping feeling would fade if she took deep breaths and got a grip. "Maybe you should wear a bell around your neck when you skulk. Or whistle. Or stomp or something." She bent to pick up the obstetrical handles and chains she'd used earlier and sealed them in a bag to sterilize later.

"I wasn't skulking. I was waiting for you to finish what you were doing so I didn't distract you."

Oh, he distracted her, all right, but she wasn't going to give him the satisfaction of knowing it. Had it been the subconscious awareness of Derek watching her that she'd felt for the last few hours? She couldn't imagine him staying quiet for that long. She met his eyes. *Zing* went the strings of her heart. She wished her heart and brain would get into sync.

"I'll have you know I have a reputation for being very light on my feet," he told her, suave as always. His dark blue eyes twinkled beneath midnight brows.

"Have to be to sneak out of all those bedrooms, huh?"

He shook his head and smiled. A smile, Lily noticed, that didn't quite reach his eyes. "No sneaking. No bedrooms. I dance like Fred Astaire," he told her immodestly.

He probably did. For such a big man he did move with surprising grace. "Good for you. Could you dance back a bit? You're spooking Peaches and the baby."

They both looked at the cow and calf. Neither had noticed the two humans invading their space. Derek gave her a slow, assessing look. "Feeling crowded, Doc?" One corner of his mouth lifted and Lily told herself to ignore his sex appeal.

He always made her want to fidget. With her hair. Her clothes. Her personality. Everything about Derek was attractive. Exciting. Larger than life. Being around him made her feel like a small brown bird. He was Technicolor. She was sepia.

Nothing wrong with sepia, she told herself firmly, annoyed that she felt this way when she was around him, and not quite sure how to fix it.

"I always feel crowded around you," she told him honestly, tossing a spare pair of surgical gloves back into her bag. She resisted his charm with the same determination she'd used for years. It wasn't easy. She felt his pull. Her tide to his moon. Which was fanciful non-sense. Her hormones misbehaved because he was a hottie. Chemistry. Nothing more.

"Why is that, I wonder?" he asked softly. His voice always re-minded Lily of dark chocolate. It was smooth, rich and had a slight huskiness to it that abraded her nerve endings like a cat's tongue.

She straightened and gave him a firm look. "Give it a rest, would you? I'm not up to your sparring weight tonight. I'm exhausted, hungry and absolutely filthy. If you want to flirt with someone, go inside and make a call."

"It's midnight."

"Poor baby." She bent to pick up her jacket, then gave it a good shake and hung it over the rail. "All your lady friends turned into pumpkins?"

"Might as well have," he groused.

Lily shook her head. "You're incorrigible." And charming, and funny and unhealthily appealing.

"What's the baby's name?" Derek asked, white teeth flashing. He always teased her about naming the animals. He seemed to enjoy teasing her, period. He also seemed to know exactly how far he could push her, and then he'd cleverly back off. Devious man. "Pit?"

"Brad."

He smiled, and not being made of stone, Lily smiled back. "Only you would name a potential prize-winning bull after a movie star."

He got it. Of course he did. Lily bit back a sigh as her smile faded. Unlike her husband, Derek had a wicked sense of humor, and an agile and clever mind behind that handsome face. All of which made resisting him damn difficult. "It's a talent," she told him modestly, turning back to her task of tidying up. "What can I say?"

Tucking her T-shirt hem back into her jeans as she straightened up, Lily wondered if resisting him would become easier over the years, or if it would always be such hard work.

Still, he was a pleasure to look at. No matter what the circumstances, he appeared darkly elegant and cultured. And tonight was no exception. As always he was appropriately dressed for tromping in the barn on a cold winter's night. Jeans, boots, and a thick, cream-colored wool turtleneck under a bulky shearling jacket. Appropriately dressed, but somehow looking as though he'd stepped out of the glossy pages of a men's magazine.

Conscious of her gunk-covered jeans, shit-covered boots and sweaty face, Lily forced her hands not to fiddle with her God-only-knew-what-was-in-it hair. "How long were you standing there, anyway?"

"Couple of minutes. Need a hand?"

"I'm good, thanks." What she was, was sweaty, filthy and worried. They needed to talk, and talk soon. But a woman needed to be at her sharpest to match wits with Derek. And Lily wasn't nearly up to locking horns with her partner tonight. On either a personal or business level.

Besides, she needed to have all her facts together before confronting him, and damn it, *she* wanted to pick the time and the place. He made her jumpier than anyone she'd ever known, including her late, unlamented husband, and she was sure he did it on purpose.

His tone changed as he said softly, "You're skittish tonight."

The man was way too observant. Her instincts around him had always been primitive; Lily felt the need to raise the drawbridge, man the battle stations and drag out the big guns. "I'm not skittish," she lied. "Just tired. Peaches and I have been at this for sixteen hours."

He gave her an assessing look that made her blood feel as effervescent as champagne as it zipped through her veins. "You look good tired."

She snorted and shook her head. He really was incorrigible. "Sure. And wearing Eau de Bovine is downright tantalizing, too."

"On you, yeah."

She huffed out an amused breath and crossed her arms, then, realizing her body language practically shouted that he made her nervous, uncrossed them and stuffed her hands into the deep pockets of her rubber apron. He didn't need to know he made her feel a little like a rabbit squaring off against a cobra: scared, but fascinated nevertheless. She cocked her head as she looked at him. "You're wearing an earring."

A small sapphire glinted in his left earlobe. It made him look like a chic pirate. The dark hair brushing his collar did nothing to soften his face. His eyes were a dark, almost navy blue, and thickly screened by black lashes. His mouth was frankly sensual and he had a playbill of smiles for every occasion. This one was both mocking and enigmatic and, annoyingly as hell, sent a fresh shiver down her spine. "Like it?"

She shrugged; what she'd like was to nibble it right off his ear. Absolutely disgusted with herself, Lily scowled. For pity's sake, just how tired was she? "Not many ranchers I know wear gemstones," she mocked. "Not the guys anyway."

His chuckle, low, throaty and filled with implications that had nothing to do with the conversation, made Lily's mouth go dry. "Are you casting aspersions on my masculinity?"

Not just no, Lily thought, but *hell* no. Derek Wright was all man. He had a magnetic personality, and men and women alike were drawn to him. The earring would make him even more attractive.

Women made fools of themselves over him already. He was wickedly attractive, wealthy and charming. And he burned with a smoldering sensuality that had females turning to mush at the mere sight of him.

All it took was a certain look, a suggested arch of his eyebrow and a crook of his finger, and susceptible women with no sense, no self-restraint and no willpower fell at his feet like puppies waiting for their bellies to be rubbed.

Like Sean, Derek was a high-maintenance guy.

No thanks. Been there, done that.

The trick was to keep him at arm's length at all cost. "What are you doing here anyway?"

"I live here," he told her mildly.

The original ranch house where Derek lived was a hundred feet away. The ostentatious house Sean had had built for their marriage was five miles away. The ranch house had charm and character. Her house had expensive *things.* She'd switch any day.

"Here, in the barn, at midnight," Lily said patiently.

"Sounds like a song." He smiled charmingly when she arched a brow. "Okay, okay. To see you."

Lily yanked on the tap and waited for the water to get warm before scrubbing her clean hands . . . cleaner. She glanced at him over her shoulder. "I thought you were in New York seeing that new Neil Simon play with what's her name." Derek liked, actually *enjoyed* opera, the theater and even ballet. He also liked sports and country music. Mostly, though, he liked *women.* He was a dangerous man.

"Christine. I was. We did. Flew back an hour ago."

How many men flew to New York for the night just to catch a play? A man with way too many sides to his personality. And a different lady friend for every activity, too. Which is why Lily tried her damnedest to keep some distance between them. Usually she succeeded. Clearly, Derek wasn't going away, so stalling the much-needed conversation wasn't going to help her any.

She was in no shape to be doing this now, she warned herself. But if not now—when? Might as well get the small bone of contention out on the table and over with. The other, major one could wait until she'd armed herself with facts and figures.

"I had an illuminating conversation with Angie Blaylock yesterday," Lily said casually as she looked around for something to dry her hands on. Angie was an ex of Derek's and the personal assistant to the town attorney, Barry Campbell.

"Sweetheart, if you want to hear about my love life, come to me directly." The words were spoken as much with his eyes as his voice. His smile was lazy and more than a little arrogant as he finished smoothly, "I'd be happy to te—"

A woman could drown in those somnolent blue eyes— She blew out an exasperated breath. "Don't be an ass." It made her insane the way he flirted with her. As if he needed the practice. "Angie told me you deeded half the Flying F to Sean three years ago when he was diagnosed as terminal. Is that true?" Lily's skin felt hot and tight with equal parts embarrassment and annoyance. *Damn you, Sean. How could you?*

Derek tossed her a towel. "So much for client confidentiality."

His flippancy made her hackles rise. "Damn it." She dried her hands and watched as the calf, after several unsuccessful tries, wobbled to his feet and started rooting for nutrition.

She straightened, meeting his gaze again unflinchingly. God, she didn't do confrontation well. Unfortunately it was one of Derek's stock-in-trades. "For once be serious. Is it true?"

"What if it is?"

Lily counted to ten, then eleven, then gave it up. "The only way you could have given Sean half was if you had the whole to start with. I thought you were equal partners." She shoved her hair out of her face. She needed to cut her bangs.

What a hell of a mess Sean had left her. One more lie, she thought. Stacked onto the mountains of lies her husband had spent his life building. And millions of dollars changing hands like playing cards was just one portion of the current mess that still had to be addressed.

"I own half. You own half. What's the big deal?"

"Sean told me— No, never mind."

"Sean told you what?"

He might have been a liar and a cheat, but Sean had been passionate about his family's ranch. "He was embarrassed that he had to bring you in to help with the financial aspect of buying the ranch."

"That works for me. Let's leave it at that."

"But it's not true." She knew it wasn't. Down to her bones, she knew Sean had lied. If the truth would have helped, he'd still have fabricated some wild story that made him either the hero or the victim.

"What do you want me to say, Lily? That I bought the ranch six years ago and let Sean claim ownership?" Derek shrugged broad shoulders. "Made no damn difference to me, and it made him happy. What was the harm? Half the Flying F is yours. That was always the plan."

Whose plan? Sean's? Lily would like to believe her husband had been that far-seeing, but it was pretty damn hard to swallow. Hence the name the Flying F. A finger to his dead father, who'd let the ranch go to hell in a handbasket rather than leave it to his only child. She shot a look at Derek. "Then why—"

"Jesus, Lily." His eyes flashed and his mouth went tight. "Who cares, for God's sake? No one. Let it go. What difference does it make in the grand scheme of things how it came about? None. Sean and I both wanted you to own half the spread. It's a done deal. Live with it."

Fighting back waves of fatigue, Lily stiffened, and gave him a glare equivalent to pitchforking him to the wall. "You might be used to giving orders that everyone jumps to obey, but news flash, Ace: I'm not one of your employees. I don't jump when you say jump."

"Don't I know it," he said ruefully. He gave her a studied look. "Then fight me for the other half, and boot my ass out."

"That does have a perverse appeal," Lily told him. "Thank you, but no thank you." She leaned her butt against the sink and stuffed her fingers in her front pockets as she watched him prowl around the stall.

Peaches mooed as he walked around her to pick up a couple of small wood figurines sitting on a post. "These are incredible." His long fingers caressed the detail in her three-inch-high carving of Diablo.

She shrugged, ridiculously pleased, and acutely aware of the way his thumb moved in almost a caress over the wooden bull as he turned the carving in his hand. It was so like him to home in on the one thing she was most proud of and neatly change the subject.

"Just something to while away the time while I'm hanging around waiting for my patient to do her job. About the ranch . . ." Few people knew about her hobby, and she liked it that way. Woodcarving was personal and hers alone. It seemed strangely intimate to have Derek Wright of all people touching—fondling—her work.

"Don't make any hasty decisions; live with it a while and see how it goes." He held the carving up to the light and twisted it this way and that. "My God, the detail is amazing. Look at the expression on his face. This guy is pissed and ready to charge." He looked over at her. The lights reflected in her eyes, making them glitter. "You could sell these, Lily, you'd make a fortune."

"It's just a hobby, and I already *have* a fortune," she reminded him dryly. Despite Sean's failings, he'd left her a very wealthy woman, which was why she'd been taken by surprise at the news that he hadn't had even part ownership of the ranch. "So the ranch was the secret Sean was keeping, huh?"

Derek's eyes narrowed. "The—what?"

And maybe it wasn't. Damn. "Nothing." Suddenly, the barn, the ranch, hell, *Montana* felt crowded. Lily couldn't wait to leave for the Iditarod trail. Alone. Just her and the dogs. Miles from anywhere and anyone who had the power to hurt her. She was sick and tired of pretending to everyone, including herself, that things were hunky-dory. She wanted honest emotions and no more pretenses. She needed to be away from the ranch, from memories of Sean and from the discomforting presence of Derek Wright.

What she needed was solitude, miles of it. She'd get that in the next few weeks.

"I knew Sean was up to something before he died." Lily folded the damp towel and draped it over the edge of the sink, looked around for something else to occupy her hands. She could toss the wood carvings into her bag—but Derek stood between her and the little group. "I guess this business with the ranch was it. Thanks for saving his pride by pretending it was half his. But I really have no interest in being part owner of a ranch." She put out a hand. "Here, give me those."

"I'll buy this carving of Diablo from you," Derek said easily, his thumb moving back and forth over the tiny bull's back. "You should have a showing in New York or somewhere. Seriously, Lily, these carvings are magnificent. People would clamor at your door to have your work. It'd be a viable source of income for you."

Lily dropped her hand, and jerked her gaze from his long, tanned fingers, and that slowly moving thumb, back to his face. "You can have it." Nobody had anything she'd made over the years. Not even her father. She tried to tamp down the little glow inside at the thought of Derek owning something she'd made. *Silly. It's just a piece of wood.* She had dozens, hundreds of them at home.

"Flattering, but no thanks. It's just a hobby and I like it that way. Besides, I could retire tomorrow if I wanted to. Which I don't." She suspected the obscene amount of money in her name in a Cayman bank had been illegally obtained by her husband. She'd give it back as soon as she figured out who it really belonged to. "I love what I do, thank you very much. And I have my dog-training income. By the time I get back from the Iditarod, if I come back, Barry will—"

He stopped stroking the little carving to stare at her. "What do you mean *if* you come back?"

"I might stay in Alaska, open a practice there. Train sled dogs on the side." Okay. *Not* something she'd thought through yet. But a possibility. She had to learn to become more proactive about her own life, damn it. She'd spent most of her twenty-seven years blowing in someone else's wind. Her father was a vet. She became a vet. Sean—

"You do that here."

"Maybe I need a change of scenery." The idea was gaining momentum like a snowball rolling downhill.

"For God's sake, Lily." He shoved the little carving into his pocket. Heat poured off his large body as he stepped closer and, typically Derek, invaded her personal space. "You're overreacting. What does it matter how the split of the estate happened? Half is yours, legally, fair and square. It's a done deal. You can't just pack up and leave." He looked around, as if looking for someone to agree with him. But the cows couldn't care less. And the calf's little sides heaved as he nursed, oblivious to the humans.

"You've lived here your entire life." He scanned her face for— what? "You have friends here. Family. Hell, what about your father?"

Lily shrugged. "I'll call him often. Besides, he has Paula and Matt." Her dad had married Paula Kruger eleven years ago. Her son, Matt, was Lily's father's veterinarian assistant and partner.

In the last few years Lily seemed to have been squeezed out of everybody's life with no regrets. Even her own dad had moved on, building a new life that didn't include his daughter. It didn't matter how adult she was, she missed the closeness she and her father had shared since her mom's death in a plane crash almost nineteen years ago.

She had nothing against Paula and Matt. They were lovely people. They were just lovely people who'd unintentionally driven an ever-widening wedge between Lily and her father. But she had to admit, if only to herself, that she'd allowed it to happen. All part of that "getting blown around by other people" thing she was so determined to fight her way out of. It wasn't too late to salvage a relationship with her father, and Lily was determined to find her way back to *herself*, too.

"Not the same as working with his daughter," Derek muttered.

Lily smiled, a part of her appreciating the knight-errant comment. "They manage the practice fine without me. Look, Derek. This is a waste of time. I don't understand the legalities of what you did or how it even came about. That said, I won't accept charity from you. You and Barry will have to work this out."

"It's complicated—"

"Yes. Things with you and Sean usually are—were." She shook her head and stared up at him.

There was good reason not to tell Derek what she'd learned about Sean over the years. She'd like to believe she didn't want Derek to know about his friend out of a sense of loyalty to the man she'd married. But the reality was, she didn't want anyone else to know because she couldn't take the pity—or the humiliation of having everyone know what an idiot she'd been. And even if it didn't matter to Sean anymore, Lily wanted to hold on to whatever tattered threads of dignity were left to her. Sean might've been a philandering jackass, but he had been her husband.

The other, even more powerful deterrent was that as long as she could convince Derek that she still cared about Sean, there was a faint possibility he'd eventually take a hint and stop flirting with her. Unfortunately, he had a skin like a rhinoceros. It didn't matter how many times she told him she wasn't interested, he just loved to flirt.

It had been an ego-bashing realization—that to *Derek* the flirting wasn't personal. He just . . . did it. It was in his DNA to flirt.

The first time she'd met him, six years ago, she'd taken one look and it had been as if a bomb had exploded. His impact was total, and complete. His looks first, then his charm, but the physical impact, that chemical reaction that said *I can't wait to get my clothes off and feel you skin to skin,* had shocked Lily to her toes. Shocked and, God help her, scared her to death. Anything that powerful, that intense, had to be dangerous.

Anything a person wanted *that* desperately could be taken away. A person could go from euphoria to despair in a heartbeat.

Unfortunately she'd wanted to sink her teeth into him, she'd wanted to lick and taste his skin, she'd wanted to grab great fistfuls of his long dark hair in both fists and draw his mouth down to hers. She wanted to throw caution and common sense to the winds.

After one date with him she'd wanted a whole lot of things, Lily thought crossly. All of them bad for her. So she'd run from Derek, straight into his best friend's open arms, and found herself in a whole different sort of mess. And if that wasn't a sad, sorry statement for a widow to make, she couldn't think of one.

And the reality, the ego-bruising reality, was that Derek had let her go. He'd done nothing to make her change her mind. He'd toasted them charmingly at their engagement dinner, and he'd been Sean's best man at their wedding, laughing and joking, flirting with every woman present.

So that heat, that fire, had been completely one-sided. Fool me once, she thought ruefully.

He'd never by so much as word or deed, or glance, done anything while she'd been married. But afterward . . . the heat had been back, like a smoldering fire under dry leaves in the fall. Just waiting to ignite into a gigantic bonfire. If she stuck around, she'd be burned to a cinder in no time flat.

"Do me a favor," Lily said quietly, yanking off the apron and tossing it with her things in the corner. "Don't run the race this year." The grueling, thousand-plus-mile Iditarod race from Anchorage to Nome was brutal and challenging enough without having Derek along. She already had too many questions, and too little information circling around in her mind. She wanted to sort the wheat from the chaff without Derek around clouding the issue.

He raised a brow. "Why the hell not? Scared I'll beat you again?"

Lily had trained him and sold him his dogs. He was an excellent musher and had actually beaten her race time twice. A powerful adversary, he was determined, competitive and focused. Before, she'd enjoyed the competition. But for some reason this year was different. "I'd like to run the race without having to watch my back."

"Don't flatter yourself, Doc," Derek said smoothly, a glint in his eyes. "As attractive as you are, when I'm in the race, I'm there to win. Hard to watch your *back* when I'm way ahead of you on the trail."

"In your dreams," Lily scoffed, torn between amusement and irritation. "I want to run the race with my full concentration. If you're there—"

"Well, bless your heart, are you saying I distract you?" He gave her a slow, lazy smile that touched off a response somewhere in her aching body. This was why, she thought, this was *exactly* why she didn't want him on the trail this year.

She could handle Derek Wright just fine. Didn't mean she *wanted* to. She twisted her wedding ring deliberately around her finger. As soon as she noticed his gaze there, she stuffed her hands back into her jean pockets. She could be as subtle as Mata Hari. Sean's wedding ring was her body armor, and she used it ruthlessly to hold back the enemy at the gate.

"Don't you have a serious bone in your body?" she asked crossly.

"Oh yes," Derek assured her, blue eyes alight with wicked humor, apparently not in the least put off. "I have several bones that are very serious."

Two

T HE BITCH HADN'T TOLD HIM.
        Yet.
        He'd been up here in the loft for hours, sweating like a pig, and dying of thirst. The hay prickled him through his sweatshirt and made his skin fucking itch. Good thing he'd taken his allergy meds. Christ only knew the hay made him sneeze. And just thinking about the bugs and shit that might be *in* the hay made him desperate to scratch.

Maybe he'd get a bonus for his troubles and the doc and Wright would fuck. At least it'd be something interesting to watch. Had to make for better spying than the revolting spectacle of a cow giving birth.

Maybe he could pick up some tips, he thought, getting hornier, but also angrier by the second. Casanova had nothing on Wright, and he hated him. Hated his easy familiarity with women, his charm, his good looks and all his fucking money.

Wright deserved a fucking bullet in the brain just because. *Because* was good enough reason to blow the asshole's brain from here to hell.

He grinned in the half dark of the hayloft. Now wouldn't they be surprised if he fell down and landed at their feet, guns blazing?

Of course, he mused, stroking the barrel of his H & K and half listening to the conversation below him, he *could* take them *both* out now. No muss, no fuss. From this angle, a shot to the top of the head would be pretty damn immediate and final. He had the silencer screwed on . . .

But a bullet was a bullet. And two gunshot deaths would mean the big redneck cop in town would be all over the place like a fly on shit. Hard to explain the deaths as an accident.

No. This wasn't the time to be overt. Subtlety was called for, he reminded himself firmly. Subtlety.

In a couple of days they'd all be up in Anchorage with thousands of other people at the start of the race. There'd be miles and miles of pristine forest and open land.

Strangers all over the place. There'd be lakes and rivers, opportunities for death by avalanche, by drowning, by . . . The possibilities were endless and appealing.

So varied, so creative. So *accidental.*

"I'M GOING TO CHECK SOME OF THE OTHER MOMS," LILY TOLD HIM. Sounding a lot more brisk than she looked. "See you whenever."

Derek leaned back against the rail and crossed his ankles. "I'm in no hurry. Take your time." He bit back a grin at her exasperated glance.

"Whatever."

She looked beat, and he frowned with concern as she went into the next stall and murmured to her bovine patient there. He wanted to wrap his arms about her and let her rest her head against his chest as she slept. But Lily being Lily would be more apt to beat him about the head with a blunt instrument, or that sharp little tongue of hers, than let him touch her right now.

Soon . . .

He heard her soft murmurings to one of the new babies nearby.

Every cow bred with their prize bull had had problems giving birth. Diablo was two thousand pounds of prime Red Brangus. The bull had weighed almost a hundred pounds at birth himself, and his calves were chips off the old block. Good for Derek's breeding program, but hell on the veterinarian who had to assist Diablo's extensive harem with every difficult birth.

The lights in the building combined with a heater made the interior of the birthing shed downright balmy. Outside the temperatures had plunged to well below freezing. Lily had stripped off her outer clothing and tossed a sweater here and a shirt there as she'd worked, leaving her in jeans, cowboy boots, and a thin, much-washed pale blue T-shirt. While she checked on her patients, Derek shrugged out of his own shearling coat, tossing it over the picnic hamper he'd brought in with him.

She'd ignore him until the job was done.

All he had to do was wait.

God only knew, he was a master at *that* game.

In a few weeks he'd have her undivided attention, and she'd have to deal with him, whether she liked it or not. Instead of bulldozing through her resistance as he'd very much like to do, this time he was going to take it slow and easy.

His flirting made her slightly uncomfortable, Derek knew. But damned if he'd stop. She needed to lighten up. Needed to relax and not take life so seriously. God only knew, the last few years had been hell for her. No humor there.

But this was a new beginning. And he was here to make sure she got what she wanted. What she deserved. Even if Lily herself didn't know what that was, he thought with dark humor.

With Lily he was never quite sure what was a smokescreen and what she truly believed. He suspected a lot of what she spouted about Sean was a shield to keep him at bay. The thought that she found it necessary to erect a buffer of any sort between them made him smile a tiger smile of satisfaction. It meant she wasn't immune.

He'd deal with whatever rhetoric she threw at him until he could show her that that particular barrier was unnecessary. Hell. *Any* barrier between them was unnecessary. Like a kitten batting away a pesky bee, Lily either took swipes at him or tried to ignore him.

One thing she wasn't was immune. Bless her sweet, stubborn little heart, she fought herself as hard as she fought him.

She would have to learn that this time he wouldn't let her go without a fight.

The only reason he'd let her go before was because he'd believed Lily loved Sean, and he'd been fooled into believing that Sean truly loved her in return.

They'd all been wrong.

He turned the delicate carving of the bull over and over in his hand, enjoying the feel of the smooth, cool wood beneath his fingers. She was so worried about pleasing the people she loved, that Derek wondered when last she'd done something for herself, just for the sheer pleasure of making *herself* happy.

In a few weeks she'd be a very happy woman. He'd make sure of it.

He'd bet she'd taken her sweet time checking on the new mamas, but there was only so much she needed to do now that the babies were born. Within ten minutes she was back.

"Still here?" she asked pointedly, picking up her flannel shirt and shaking it out.

"Nowhere I'd rather be," he told her honestly, admiring the muscles in her slender arms, and the way the soft fabric of her T-shirt molded to the gentle swell of her breasts. Her silky, light brown hair was a mess. Half in the braid and half out. Her bangs brushed her eyelashes. Unself-conscious and sexy as hell. She looked as though she'd just climbed out of bed, sleepy-eyed and tousled.

"How about Tahiti?"

He imagined Lily, golden and naked, spread out on a sun-bleached beach. "I can have us there in ten hours."

She shook her head. "Some of us work for a living." She absently twisted her wedding ring as she looked around to see what else needed doing before she left. "Why don't you go on ahead," she told him, shrugging into her shirt and shooting him a wicked glance. "I'll meet you there."

"When hell freezes over?"

"When pigs fly," she said at the same time.

"Your loss," he told her, smiling.

"I'll sob into my pillow tonight," she assured him.

Light glanced off the plain gold band on her left hand as she buttoned her shirt. Inside it, Sean had had engraved *4 ever.* Derek knew, because he'd gone with Sean to pick out the ring, then stood beside him as it had been engraved. And all the while Sean had regaled him, and the three salespeople nearby, with the story of a waitress he'd picked up and spent the night with only the day before.

Derek'd realized then that Sean's judgment was screwed. He could never trust this man. But by then it was already too late. Derek was by no means a prude. If his friend wanted to screw every woman in Montana and beyond, that was his business. But the fact that he was screwing everything that moved and sliding a ring onto Lily's finger was enough to make Derek want to pound his lying face into the ground.

"Flip the lights, would you?" Lily told him, clearly ready to leave. The overhead lights in the birthing shed were brilliant enough for him to count the freckles across her flushed cheeks. He hit the main switch, and the cavernous barn was plunged into a soft amber glow.

"Now that we got that out of the way, I brought you dinner." He moved his coat and picked up the basket he'd brought in with him.

"Did you?" Lily's hazel eyes, always slightly wary when she looked at him, widened. She looked around for her coat. "Thanks. But I'll grab something at home."

"No, you won't. Come on. Take an extra ten minutes and eat with me. I'm starving. If you don't want anything, just stay and keep me company." He herded her over to a picnic table. "You're the one who instructed *me* to bulk up beforehand. Better eat something and practice what you preach." At first he'd become interested in the dog races because they were Lily's passion, had given him a chance to spend time with her. But the more he'd learned about the sport, the more he'd enjoyed it. Enjoying something with Lily had made it that much more attractive.

She stopped in her tracks. "Damn it, Derek. You're going to race anyway, aren't you?"

"Damn straight." He maintained an easy, taunting smile, knowing it would piss her off.

He was delighted to hear her robust laugh instead. That laugh was seldom heard these days, so he enjoyed it. That and the sharp intelligence in her eyes as she shot him a half-amused, half-exasperated look. "What *am* I going to do with you?"

He wiggled his eyebrows just to see her grin. "How many suggestions can I make?"

"I'm going to hit you if you don't stop flirting with me."

"Will you tie me up first?"

She shot him an inquiring look. "Have you— Never mind."

Derek laughed. "I have my own handcuffs, wanna play?"

"I have my own sticks, wanna be staked out for the coyotes?"

He shook his head and grinned. "Different game. But I'll be happy to play." It took everything in him not to wrap his arms around her and taste that smile. She shook her head back at him and gave him a mock scowl. Lily had guts, and a wicked sense of humor. She was also prickly, argumentative and fiercely loyal—and a royal pain in the ass—and he wanted all of it. All of her. In his life, in his bed.

He was done waiting.

And by race's end, it would be mission accomplished.

But first things first. "Sit," he told her, flipping open the lid of the basket. She circled the table and plonked herself down on the bench seat opposite.

"Feed me then."

"Yes, ma'am." He started unloading Annie's offering.

Lily didn't stand a chance. All the Wright men were warriors, and Derek was no exception. He was a lover *and* a fighter. A tactician and a foot soldier. She was under siege. She just didn't know it yet.

This time things had to be done in the proper order, so as not to scare her off again. Friends, then lovers. He'd waited six years. What were another few weeks?

"Fine." Hands in her lap, Lily watched him spread the contents on a blue-checkered cloth. If he'd thought he'd get away with it, he would've brought candles and wine. Another time.

"If you insist on entering the race," she said, eyeing the selection of foil-wrapped packages on the table, "I can't stop you. Just promise you'll do your own thing and leave me alone."

Hard to do when she *was* his thing, Derek thought with an inward smile. "Not only am I going," he told her cheerfully, "I'm going to beat your time. Again."

"In your dreams," she scoffed. "What did Annie send me?" She fisted her hands in the small of her back and stretched out the kinks.

Her nipples were hard little pebbles beneath the thin cotton T-shirt that she wore under the flannel shirt. Derek felt an answering twitch in his groin at the sight. God knew, he never got used to this intense physical reaction he'd always had to her.

"Here." He scooped up her sweater, shook out bits of hay and handed it to her. "Since you're not moving around, put this on before you catch pneumonia. That shirt's not enough. And how do you know Annie put the basket together? How do you know I wasn't the one to fix our meal?"

She shrugged into the sweater without comment, a silken filament of hair clinging to her cheek. Derek resisted reaching out to brush it away.

"Because this isn't an amorous encounter, Wright. Because this is me. The widow Munroe. That's why."

Derek finished setting out the food. His housekeeper had thrust the filled basket into his hand when he'd paced, one too many times, across her kitchen, glancing through the window toward the barns.

"Who said this isn't an amorous encounter?" For a second, he saw in her eyes something that stopped the fog of his breath, and then the look was gone.

"Could we resolve this flirting crap once and for all?" she snapped, reaching for a foil-wrapped packet without knowing what was in it. She frequently forgot to eat, but when she finally did, she more than made up for it.

"We both know you're not really interested in me. And even if you really *were,* and I know you're *not,* it's way too soon—what's this?—it's only been six months."

"Crab. Try it, you'll like it." In Sean's case, six months in mourning was too long. Derek watched her take a cautious bite. "Six months is plenty," he told her, wishing she'd look at him like she was looking at the crab sandwich. "Time you started dating again."

She made a rude noise. "What would be the point? I'm never marrying again— God, this is good . . ." She paused to chew and swallow. "Besides, who would I date around here? Pop Skyler? What is he, eighty?" She shook her head. "Six months is hardly a decent mourning period. Besides, who has the time—other than *you,* of course?"

"There's the solution right there. Go out with me. That would solve that problem."

"Oh, please." She shook her head. "We've done this to death. Don't waste your time. I'm immune. We tried that once, remember? Didn't take." She uncapped the Thermos and poured two fragrant mugs of Annie's great coffee. "Thanks, but no thanks. I'll leave you to spread yourself thin on the state of Montana's female population."

"Scared?"

"Of you?" she mocked. "Try *not interested.*"

"Sure you are," he said easily, his dark eyes glinting in the amber light as he glanced at her neck. "I can see the frantic pulse right there at the base of your lovely throat."

Lily rolled her eyes, and resisted, with admirable restraint, covering the telltale pulse with her hand. "That's the superior vena cava, found in most humans," she told him, cool as a cucumber. On the outside. "Not something you'd find in one of your blow-up Party Pattys."

Derek laughed. "Party Pattys? Is such a thing?"

She gave him a patient look.

"Come on, Lily, give me a break here. Test your self-control. Go out with me before we leave for Alaska. Hell, you might even enjoy yourself."

"I wouldn't."

"Why not?"

"Because I don't want to date. Not you. Not anyone," she said quietly, watching his face for a reaction.

"You had dinner with Don Singleton on Wednesday."

Talk about the bush telegraph. She didn't bother asking him who his informant was. It could've been anyone at the Dipsy Diner. "I went in for a piece of pie after going to the feed store. He was there. We shared a table. Hardly a date. After Pop, Don would be my second choice as date material, however."

Derek's expression went several degrees cooler.

Game, set and match, Lily thought with satisfaction and took a sip of rapidly cooling coffee. Time to go home. "It's been a long day." She rose and walked over to pick up her coat. "Are you home for a while, or do you have somewhere else to run off to?"

He ignored her question. "I know you loved Sean, Lily. But someday soon you're going to have to start living your life again."

"My life is exactly the way I want it, but thanks so much for your concern." Lily let her impatience color the words. The man was as damn relentless as Mrs. Simpson's bull terrier, Beasly. "Sorry if your enormous ego can't stand rejection. But there you are. Put me in the *Guinness Book of World Records* as the only woman to ever tell you *no*."

Even when she was pissed off, Lily had beautiful eyes. A rich hazel, long-lashed and luminous. And Derek spent way too much time thinking about them.

"I need to tal—" She waved her words away with a brushing gesture of her hands and shake of her head. "Never mind."

Derek stood. "No. What were you about to say?"

"It'll wait." Lily covered a yawn. "I'm too tired for another confrontation with you tonight." She leaned over and picked up her sandwich from the napkin on the table and bit into it, barely chewed before swallowing.

"Sit down again and finish that before you dash off. When are you leaving for Anchorage?"

She didn't sit, but she took another bite. "In the morning."

"Tomorrow morning?" he asked with a frown, and at her nod, said, "Why so soon? The race doesn't start for three weeks."

"I'm driving, first of all. And second, I want to get in a couple more weeks of training before the race starts."

"Jesus, Lily. *Fly.* It's a hellishly long drive from Montana to Alaska. Especially at this time of year." He handed her another sandwich as soon as the first was finished. "I can fly us both up to Anchorage when I get back at the end of next week."

Lily peeled off the foil and bit into the sandwich. "You're going on another trip? You just got back."

"Business."

"I'm sure. Monkey business. No thanks. I don't want to wait."

"Then let me have one of my people take you."

"No thanks," she said around a mouthful of— *Hmm. Ham on rye.* "You don't want to fly."

"That's right. I don't. . . . I'm surprised Annie had time to make me a picnic while she's so busy with the wedding preparations."

"She has plenty of help." Derek didn't want to talk about his housekeeper or his father's upcoming nuptials. He knew Lily was afraid to fly. She'd been in the plane crash that had killed her mother when she was a child. "Flying is perfectly safe," he told her gently. "Come up with me a few times—hell, let me teach you to *pilot* a plane. I guarantee if you felt in control the fear would go away."

"It's not fear," Lily told him briskly. "It's a phobia. I'm dealing with it." She took another big bite of her sandwich, barely swallowing as she changed the subject again. "There can't possibly be enough help for a woman pushing sixty who's preparing for a hundred wedding guests to descend on her in six weeks." She tilted her head, making the long silky rope of her braid fall over her shoulder. Derek wanted to wind that shiny, honey brown skein around his hand and—

"Why's he getting married in the dead of winter anyway?"

Because it was the only time his sons could shake free at the same time. "You'll have to ask him."

"You could bow out of the race and stay to help," Lily suggested, reaching for her coffee mug.

It was his turn to snort. "And let you win?" Lily wasn't going to talk about what else was bothering her until she was good and ready, apparently. So they might as well get this settled. No way was he allowing her to head off to Alaska without him being close by. And no goddamn way in hell was he going to let her freaking *move* to Alaska. Not without a fight anyway.

He made a rude noise. "I'm going to win this year. Why not save yourself the embarrassment?"

It was a pleasure to see her cheeks pink and her hazel eyes sparkle as she got caught up thinking about the race, forgetting Sean for a while.

"You are so going to lose," she laughed.

"Come around here and give me your hand."

She narrowed her eyes. "Why?"

Derek reached across and pulled her around to his side of the table. "Sit."

Lily's butt hit the bench seat beside him. "Woof."

"It always amazes me," he said, sliding his fingers through hers and then using his thumb to deeply massage her palm, "how such small hands can be so amazingly strong." He ignored the initial pulling back of her arm, and kept massaging until he saw her eyes lose focus and her lashes flutter to her cheeks. He tamped his sigh of satisfaction down deep, and continued the spontaneous massage.

The woman worked too hard. He rotated her wrist, worked through the resistance and manipulated her fingers between his. Her skin was as pale and fine-grained as a baby's, yet she sported some serious calluses across her palm and dozens of fine white scars, presumably from the whittling knife. Her hands were as slender and strong as her body. Her nails were cut short, no polish. Lily's fingers curled against his hand and the sensation shot directly to his groin.

"God. That feels amazing. If this is what you do for your girl-friends, it's no wonder you have to beat them off with a stick."

Keep it light. "I only do hand massages for partners who've spent the night pulling a calf."

"Mmm." Lily let her eyes drift shut, then pretended to snore.

"Okay," he said, releasing her hand reluctantly. "When the lady starts falling asleep during a sensual hand massage, it's time she went home."

He was right. It was past time for her to go. But oh, she really didn't want to leave the cozy warmth of the barn for the frigid wind and the long drive back home.

"Go home and get some sleep," Derek told her quietly, hating to ruin a peaceful moment between them, but seeing the lines of ex-haustion on her face.

"Um-mmm," Lily agreed, not opening her eyes. "Still going to beat you."

"Dream on, Doc."

Lily opened heavy-lidded eyes. "You're right. I need some sleep."

Derek rose when she did, snagged her heavy parka out of her hand and shook off the bits of hay before holding it out for her to slip on.

"Thanks." She pulled her braid haphazardly from the neckline and tugged up the zipper.

"Spend the night. Why waste time driving when you could be sleeping?"

"It's only five miles. I'll be fine. I'm camping out with the dogs anyway." She slanted him a look. "And so should you be."

He gave a mock shudder. "I prefer the comforts of a nice warm bed for as long as I can get it. Plenty enough time during the race to sleep with a snow blanket."

"You're a high-maintenance guy, Mr. Wright," Lily said with a small edge to her voice.

"I like my creature comforts," Derek told her, absently pulling one side of her collar straight, and tugging her braid all the way out of the back of her coat. The long rope felt cool to the touch, and, God—

sleek, soft, sweet-smelling. His fingers lingered before he dropped the silky length.

While meticulous in her care and treatment of animals, Lily barely spared a thought for her own. There wasn't an ounce of vanity in her. No makeup, no perfume. Just the clean fragrance of her soap and the incredible texture of her skin. Her eyes gave off more bling than a thousand diamonds.

He walked beside her and pulled the door open wide enough for them both to step through. The still, frigid air hit them like an ice pick. "You sure—"

"Positive, but then . . ." The snow lay thick and crystalline on the ground. Icy-cold air made Lily's words visible. She frowned as she glanced round. "What happened to my truck?"

"In the garage."

His foreman, Ash, had moved it. Lily, being Lily, had arrived in a spray of snow and gravel and left the truck parked—barely—and still running outside the barn. If it had been left sitting outside, it wouldn't have started.

The snow had stopped an hour ago, and the moonlight sparkled on the banks of bright white, shimmering like diamonds.

Their boots crunched and the rhythmic beat accompanied them to the side of the house where an eight-car garage housed Derek's collection.

"Boys and their toys." Lily shook her head as he opened the side door and she preceded him inside the heated garage.

"But there's always that one toy you can't have, isn't there?" Derek said quietly behind her.

Three

EVERYTHING WAS PERFECT. OR IT WOULD'VE BEEN IF DEREK HAD stayed in Montana.

Lily glanced at the crowds while a reporter and her television crew set up their cameras and equipment to interview her. She'd drawn number twenty-nine at the start line, and so far Derek was nowhere to be seen in the churning, cheering mass of humanity lining the streets.

"Ready?" the attractive blond anchorwoman asked Lily, while a gaunt-looking man followed her with a blush brush in one hand and a comb in the other. "Stan, thanks, I'm done. No—thank you. My hair's great. Lily? Could you stand near the sled? We'll pan down the line as we talk."

"Sure," Lily said obligingly, waving to several people she knew. She'd much rather be talking race than standing conspicuously before a camera crew from the San Francisco station. But there were relatively few women running the race, and although she wasn't comfortable with a camera pointed at her, the publicity was good for the sport.

"Seventy-three teams are gathered in Anchorage for the start of the race," the KPIX anchor said smoothly. "As you can see, excitement is pumping through the crowd." She smiled, "With us is Dr. Lily Munroe, a veterinarian from Montana who has run the race—how many times?"

"Five," Lily said obligingly.

"Dr. Munroe has won the Iditarod once, and placed in the top twenty twice. An amazing accomplishment. Historically more than half of the eager teams gathered here on Fourth Avenue today have no hope of reaching the finish line. Isn't that true, Lily?"

Lily smiled at the little red light. "It wouldn't be called a race if anyone and everyone could win, or even complete the race," she said easily. "Forget *not winning,* very few of us will even make it to the top twenty cut. For most competitors, the main goal is simply to complete the grueling race. Crossing under the famous burled arch at the finish line in Nome with our dogs will, for many of us, be victory enough."

Lily answered most of the reporter's questions by rote. The noise level made a lengthy interview almost impossible. Fans, volunteers, photographers, radio broadcasters and television crews focused on the start line beneath the fancy banner fluttering overhead. Raised voices coupled with the crush of thousands of onlookers, and the keening and barking of hundreds of dogs eager to get started, gave the whole event a circus feel. Adrenaline was the drug of choice and everybody was high on it.

The reporter and her crew went down the line of Lily's dogs while Lily identified tug lines, gang line, and parts of the sled, and introduced her dogs. Hooked up to the sled in pairs, her team stretched more than eighty feet from the noses of her leaders, Arrow and Finn, to the back of the sled. Longer than an eighteen-wheeler. They were fired up and rarin' to go.

Lily couldn't wait to test her own ability and get out there and see what her dogs could do.

The fragrance of coffee and hot chocolate floated tantalizingly on the crisp air as she walked around her dogs, murmuring encouragement and checking gear for the millionth time as the camera followed her. While she smiled and answered the reporter, her mind was already fixed on what lay ahead.

"Tell us a little about the race. What do you think you'll encounter? Is it really as dangerous as we've heard?"

Lily smiled. "The race, from a logistical viewpoint, is practically *impossible*. Yet most of these same mushers enter year after year. A team starts here in downtown Anchorage and has to make it all the way to downtown Nome—a distance of over eleven hundred miles—in about ten days."

"That's an incredibly long way for a dog to run. And that sled weighs what? Upwards of four hundred pounds?"

"About that." Lily glanced around. Where was Derek, for goodness' sake? She'd seen him briefly last night at the banquet, and not since. Had he left? Gone on another of his mysterious trips? Good.

"The dogs—?"

Lily brought her attention back to the reporter. "The care of the dogs has to be constant," she said smoothly. "They have to be snacked every hour, and the musher must take frequent rest stops. The dogs have to be nurtured, have booties put on their feet, fed full meals every four hours, and the injured have to be flown back to Anchorage, where prisoners care for the dogs until their owners claim them, sometimes weeks later. Harnesses have to be fixed or replaced, the sled repaired—the list's endless."

"It sounds exhausting for the musher. When do *you* get to sleep?"

"When we can," Lily said with a smile. "Sleep deprivation is an occupational hazard on the trail. Hallucinations are quite common."

"Have you had hallucinations?" the reporter asked eagerly. Expecting, Lily thought, that she'd reveal something salacious.

"I had a little blue puppy ahead of me last year," Lily told her, straight-faced. "He turned into a talking donkey at some point."

The woman laughed. "Say anything interesting?"

"That I needed a nice long nap." Lily's tone was dry.

They spent a few more minutes chatting about the trail and the race, and the woman and her crew went off to interview someone farther up the line.

"Are y'all a movie star now?" a man asked, coming up behind Lily. She turned with a smile, which slipped a little when she saw Don Singleton. He looked like a linebacker, with broad shoulders and no neck and a square head, dressed as he was in a heavy coat and hat. Lily turned to face him fully. She'd dated him a couple of times before Sean and Derek had bought the Flying F six years ago, but there'd been no sparks. Even though he'd tried to start up a more-than-friendly conversation last month when they'd bumped into each other at the diner.

"Hey, Don, how's it going? All ready?"

"Had to go and drop two dogs," he said dismissively. "Didn't see y'all last night after we pulled our numbers, little girl. Where'd you get to?"

"I went back to the hotel. Too much partying gives me a head-ache. Hi, Susan. Tom." Lily greeted friends from last year, and the four of them chatted for a while, before Don, seeing that he wasn't going to get Lily alone, ambled off.

"Snowmobiles had to come in again this year, I see," Tom McGuire, a three-time winner, said easily, glancing down at the six inches of snow covering the road. Snow-removal-equipment opera-tors had reversed their normal operations, dumping tons of snow onto Main Street the day before.

"Snow and freezing temps predicted, though," Susan said with relish. "The dogs will be happy." She crouched down to give Ding-bat an ear rub. "Hi there, big boy, ready to do some running?" Ding-bat butted her knee with his head. He'd run until the cows came home if Lily'd let him. "You guys want some coffee?" she asked Lily and Tom.

"No thanks," Lily said. She'd trained all year for this. She just wanted to *go.*

"I'll come with you," Tom told Susan, and the two said, "See you later," and wandered off together.

Lily shivered and pulled her hat down more firmly over her ears. It was bitterly cold. She was dressed much as everyone else, in polypropylene underwear, layers of Thinsulate, Gore-Tex outergarments, wolf-skin gloves and sealskin mukluks. Her numbered bib capped off the outfit. High fashion it wasn't. But she wouldn't freeze.

"This year," Lily told the dogs as she dragged in a deep breath of the bracing, cold air, "we *are* going to win." She felt it in her bones.

"Feeling pretty confident, are you?"

The too-familiar deep voice sounded way too close. She imagined she could hear the theme music from *Jaws* as the bottom dropped out of her stomach.

A muscle in her cheek ticked as, steeling herself, she turned around. "Just when you think it's safe to go back in the water . . ." She tipped her head back and stared up into Derek's eyes.

He feigned insult. "Lily, you wound me."

"There's an idea. Hang on while I get my knife." She actually *did* have her whittling knife tucked in her boot. He smiled. "Go away."

"It's a public street," he pointed out.

"It's also crowded. I'm trying to psych myself up."

"You have plenty of time." He gave her a once-over. "You left early last night."

"Are you by any chance looking out for me?" she asked suspiciously. Lord, did she have a spot on her face? He was looking at her hard enough to count pores. "Because if you are, it's unnecessary," she assured him, resisting the urge to swipe her hand across her cheek. "I've run this race more times than you have, and I can take care of myself just fine." She turned to make unnecessary adjustments to the straps, already taut across her supplies.

"Yes, I am looking out for you," he told her mildly, and when she turned around to say something, said, "And yes, before you bite my head off, I know you're perfectly capable, competent and knowledgeable enough to take care of yourself."

"Then clearly I don't need you, do I?"

"That remains to be seen. I enjoy watching out for you. Hell, I enjoy looking at you, period. Ignore me if you like."

Ignoring him would be impossible. "I'd *like* you to go away."

His eyes locked with hers, then he reached out and pushed a long strand of hair out of her eyes. Lily shivered as his gloved fingertips briefly brushed her skin. She jerked her head away—*after* he'd tucked the strand back under her hat. Goose bumps formed on her skin. Even his absentminded touches were potent. She so didn't need this. Didn't want this. Derek was already too deeply commingled with her life for comfort.

"I'll be going soon enough," he said placidly. "But I won't be far."

Great. "I don't have time for chitchat. And neither do you. Shouldn't you be with your dogs?"

"They're fine. Just came by to say good luck."

"You too. Bye." She tightened the cinch on Finn, and the poor dog looked over his shoulder as if to say, "Hey! It was fine just the way it was." Lily loosened it and apologetically scratched the dog's floppy ear.

"What number did you pull?" Mr. GQ wasn't wearing his numbered bib. Seventy-two, she hoped. Let him be as far back as was humanly possible.

"Seventeen." His smile told her he knew exactly what she'd been thinking and was pleased as hell to disappoint her. "Your eagerness is transferring to the dogs."

Only twelve teams between them? Not nearly enough. Still, he'd be well on his way with that much lead time. *"Settle!"* She told the dogs uselessly. "It's not *my* eagerness getting them pumped. They're doing that all on their own. And hearing all their fans yelling and screaming is just adding to what they're already feeling. This is one of the worst parts of the race. The waiting."

The announcer yelled out, "Number *twelve*. Ten-nine-eight—"

Derek smiled, his teeth white against his tanned face. "Ever impatient, Doc. Good things come to those who wait."

"So speaks the King of Patience," Lily scoffed. Derek had the attention span of a water newt. He'd be home at the ranch for a couple of weeks and then off he'd go, to return days or weeks later with no explanation. He'd look either tanned and fit, or as though he'd been to war. Had to be rough, being a millionaire-playboy type. All those women really took a toll on him.

He'd just recently returned from yet another of his mystery vacations. He'd blown off some of his training to go and indulge himself—probably with some busty bimbo named Bambi. Clearly, he'd been somewhere hot and sunny, Lily thought, annoyed all over again by his tan. He'd been gone almost two weeks, and had arrived back yesterday, just in time for the party. And just in time to pop her little balloon. She'd about convinced herself that he'd blown off the race. But he'd disappointed her. Again.

Here he stood, ready to take part in a race that everyone else had been killing themselves getting ready for. Derek, though, did the least amount of work with superior results. No matter *what* he did. While mere mortals trained relentlessly with their dogs, and stretched themselves to their own physical limits month after month, Derek coasted. And because Lily loved his dogs, she trained his with her own whenever he was gone.

If he won, or came anywhere *near* winning this year, Lily would— She didn't know what she'd do. But it wouldn't be pleasant.

"You'd be surprised just how patient I am," Derek said tightly.

"Since you've never waited for a single thing in your entire life," she said sweetly, "how would you know?"

"Honey, there are plenty of things I'm still waiting for."

She chose not to notice the dark gleam in his eye or the swirl of something liquid and hot spearing through her stomach.

"Patience doesn't count when all you have to do is lie on a beach and have hot- and cold-running waiters cater to your every whim."

"You don't have a very high opinion of me, do you, Lily?"

"Do you care?"

"What if I said yes?"

Then she wouldn't believe him, Lily told herself. No way was Derek interested in her. It was just second nature for him to flirt. The danger came if she were ever stupid enough to fall for his baloney. What he felt was more than likely pity. His best friend's widow. Poor lonely thing. Let's be nice to her and boost her ego with a little harm-less flirting. For some reason, today particularly, the thought that he hung around out of pity or sympathy really annoyed her. "Look, Derek, I know you're just being nice to me because you think I need a friend right now. Fine. Terrific. Thanks. We're friends. I really need to concentrate now, pal, so would you mind?"

"Nice . . ."

The word faded out, as if he couldn't believe she'd said that, but Lily didn't care. She gave him a pointed look and went back to her unnecessary checking of the dogs.

"Is there a particular reason why you're so eager to get rid of me?" Derek asked mildly, leaning against the handlebar of her sled and in-vading her personal space to an uncomfortable degree. He stuffed his hands deep inside the pockets of his thick shearling coat and watched her, as if capable of reading her mind.

She needed this solitary time—this open space where it was just her, the dogs and survival—to clear her head. To try to find the woman she used to be. Before Sean and trouble had wiped away everything she was, leaving a stranger to look back at her from a mir-ror.

Sighing, Lily turned and looked up at Derek. "Look, do I have to draw you a picture? I don't want company. I don't want to visit. I don't want—"

"Me?" He finished the sentence for her and his eyes fired even as his features tightened, darkened. He nodded, but didn't move. "That's plain enough, Lily. I'll leave you be."

There was a flash of something in his midnight blue eyes. Hurt? Disappointment? She sighed. Whatever it was, it couldn't be either of those. Her instinct was to reach out and touch him; she resisted. This was Derek. He was neither hurt nor disappointed. He was thwarted. "You do that."

"For now," he tagged on relentlessly, "I'll give you the race, then we sit down and have a serious talk."

Lily's spine stiffened. Was he going to admit that he was involved with the whole bull-sperm scam? She tried to read his thoughts, but as usual with Derek, his expression was closed. "About what?" she asked suspiciously.

"Your future."

Say what? Her eyebrows rose. "*My* future?"

"The thing that comes after."

"For heaven's sake, Derek!" Lily couldn't help but laugh. "Are you determined to be cryptic as well as annoying? What are you talking about? After *what*?"

"After the race. After Sean."

"Well, I hate to break it to you, Ace, but you're the last person I'd discuss my future with," she told him hotly, annoyance banishing amusement.

"We're partners, Lily. So that makes me part of your life. Whether you like the arrangement or not is moot. What *kind* of partners is really the question, and you know it."

Lily's heart leaped into her throat and her mouth went dry. Matt Kruger, her stepbrother, had warned her not to say anything to anyone until their investigator could discover who was involved in the scam. Was Derek—? "Are—are you threatening me?"

His dark brows rose. "Did that sound like a threat?"

"You know it did." The thought of the elegant and sartorially magnificent Derek Wright locked in a jail cell had immense appeal. Try me, Lily thought, mentally rubbing her hands.

"Brave words from a woman who took the low road because she was afraid of too much passion."

Lily balled her fists in her pockets to keep from slugging him. "I married Sean because I *loved* him. Not that it's any of *your* freaking business."

"You were mine first," he said mildly.

Utter and complete astonishment blinded her to the cold, the crowds, the smells and the race. "You egotistical ass! We had three dates! *Three.* And just so your inflated sense of self is clear, I dated Don Singleton three times before that, and that didn't work, either. Sean swept me off my feet. Something you didn't do."

"I didn't try," he said in a deep, low, emotionless voice. "And tell the truth: Sean was merely the path of least resistance."

"My God." Lily stared up at him, stunned by his unsubtle attack. "How can you say that? He was your best friend."

"Was he, Lily? Or were you just too blind to notice what was going on right under your nose?"

Three years of resentment spewed up like lava. "You want to know what I noticed, Derek? I *noticed* it was hard to tell between the two of you who did the least amount of work. I *noticed* that it wasn't until Sean got sick that you curtailed your social activities enough to help around the ranch! That's what I noticed! So don't come telling me I didn't notice things. *I noticed!*"

"I'm guessing this would be the wrong time to tell you how beautiful you look when you're angry?" he said, straight-faced. "No hitting, sweetheart. The camera crews are just looking for something nice and juicy to beam back home."

"I've never hit anyone in my life." Lily said through clenched teeth. "But there's always a first time." She took a step back, out of his reach, her chest heaving with fury.

She cast a brief glance around and saw the milling crowd giving them a wide berth. Her cheeks scalded with embarrassment. "I've never hated anyone as much as I hate you right now," she told him, lowering her voice, her throat tight with tears of anger. "Just go away and leave me the hell alone."

"I will for now. But we're not done. Not by a long shot." He pushed away from the sled and stuffed his hands deep into his pockets. "Flip a coin and see what's on the other side, Lily. You might be surprised." And he sauntered off.

Damn you. Lily watched him walk away and her gaze locked on his broad back until the crowd swallowed him. If looks could kill he'd have been toes-up on the ice. "Grrr. Arrogant bastard."

A few deep breaths and an equal number of possible methods to aid in his demise restored her sense of humor, and gave her a small measure of calm. She even managed a smile.

"Happy thoughts?" Matt shouted as he came up beside her. With the noise of thousands of raised voices, loudspeakers blaring and dogs barking, she hadn't heard him step up behind her. Lily forced a real smile, pushing disturbing thoughts of Derek out of her mind. She was *not* going to waste any more time thinking about the man. "Why not?" she asked, her breath fogging the air. "It's a glorious day, the kids are tugging at the lines to get going, and unlike some people, I left the party early enough last night to get some sleep." She eyed her stepbrother sympathetically. "You're looking a little rode hard, and put away wettish."

As one of the veterinarians who'd volunteered to care for the dogs involved in the grueling race, Matt would go ahead to wait at the checkpoints for the mushers to arrive. Until then, he was sharing the runners with her on the big sled. Acting as her handler, he would help her carry supplies to the first drop-off and the restart of the race the next day. After that he'd either fly to the checkpoints or ride one of the snowmobiles available.

He laughed. "That's just how I feel. It's damn bright out here."

Tall and lanky with thick brown hair and a crooked smile, Matt was good-looking, but best of all he was a hard worker. Luckily for all of them he'd wanted to stay in Montana to be near his mom. Matt's skills as a vet were an asset to Lily's and her father's practice. Even though there wasn't really always enough work to warrant three vets in such close proximity.

Still, her dad was crazy about Matt, and Lily was delighted to have a brother. Just because the child in her resented his closeness with her father didn't mean the adult in her didn't welcome him as a brother. Plus, Matt had been a godsend at the ranch when Sean was so sick. Lily would always appreciate the way he'd stepped in to help her.

"Where are your sunglasses?" she asked.

He felt the bridge of his nose, grimaced and pulled dark glasses out of his pocket. Shoving them on, he nearly sighed at the relief from the glare of sunlight bouncing off snow. "Now if you could just get the roar of the crowd to turn down a couple of hundred deci-bels . . ."

"Mother Nature will help you with complete silence in a couple of hours," Lily told him, unconsciously scanning the mushers for a familiar dark head. She should probably apologize for losing her cool like that—or not, she thought, irritated at herself. Take control, Lily Marie, she told herself sternly. Just take freaking control of your life. If I want to get flaming mad, I'm totally allowed to do so.

There. Proactive. She felt better already.

In the narrowing corridor of onlookers, her dogs lunged and danced in their traces, crazed with excitement. They were all eager to take off, to do what they did best. Lily felt the same urgency, the same frantic pull tearing at her to get started.

Her heart raced with excitement, her fingers flexed on the handlebars. *Let's go.*

"One more thing," a smoky voice said. Lily whipped her head around to find Derek standing beside her sled again. Oh, for God's sake! Couldn't he take a hint? Her heart sped up a little. Damn it. "Not again."

His deep blue eyes twinkled. "Miss me?"

"No."

"Hey, Matt," Derek shouted in greeting, still looking at Lily. He dug something small out of his pocket and handed it to her in a tangle of thin black wires. His hand was tanned. And huge, well shaped and masculine. A hand, Lily thought bleakly, that was probably capable of exerting tremendous pain or giving a woman exquisite pleasure.

Lily had caught a glimpse of the man behind the lighthearted flirt last year when Derek's sister and husband had visited. Lily had walked into the barn to find Derek stretched out in the hay with his two nieces as they observed a cat and her newborn kittens. She'd stood in the shadows and watched them, as a lump formed in her throat.

Her first thought had been a sickening envy at the sight of the two little blond girls with their sweet giggles cuddled up to the long, hard body of their uncle, whom they worshipped. The sight of their tiny coveralls and cute little cowboy boots made her heart twist.

She'd never have children. At the time she'd been trapped by Sean's illness into a loveless, sexless sham of a marriage.

Derek had reached out absently and tugged at the littlest one's ponytail. The child had given a war whoop and thrown herself onto her uncle's back. Sophisticated Derek Wright had rolled about in the straw, heedless of his black cashmere sweater and designer boots, his enormous hands gentle as he tickled and cuddled the little girls.

He'd been so gentle, so sweet with the kids, it had made Lily's heart yearn and ache.

Another time, she'd heard the frost in his voice as he'd implacably told off a hired hand who'd treated one of the horses roughly. The man had been drunk and belligerent and Derek had him packed up and fired without raising his voice. The expression on Derek's face had chilled Lily to the bone. She'd never seen anything as unforgiving or cold.

Would the real Derek Wright please stand up? Lily thought dryly. The glimpse she'd had of him with the children had made her want to know more. She'd driven back home as fast as possible, all the while giving herself a firm mental kick in the pants.

She kept her hands stuffed in her pockets. "No thank you."

"You don't even know what I'm giving you."

"Neither do I want to. Go away."

Lily watched him untangle the wires with an amazingly delicate touch.

"This," he told her, snagging the front of her jacket with one large hand to keep her in place, "is a lip mic. I want you to wear it from tomorrow until the end of the race."

"Well, damn, and I thought a smart guy like you would know girls prefer jewelry to electronics," Lily said sweetly. Damn it. He was too close. His breath smelled of the coffee he'd drunk, his skin smelled of soap and his hands—what the hell were his hands doing?

"Cut it out! Don't take off my ha— Damn it, it's freezing! Hey! Don't stick that thing in my hair." Lily slapped his hand away. "I'm not wearing it." That's all she needed, Derek in her ear as she was trying to find peace. She yanked the small headset free and stuffed it back in his warm hand. "Thanks for the thoughtful gift, but I don't take presents from people I don't like."

His lips twitched. "At least clip it to your collar. Here, see? You don't even have to turn it on if you don't want to. Just for emergencies. Please? For me?"

"Take it, sis. It's a good idea."

Lily shot a glare at her stepbrother. *"Et tu, Brute?"* She spun around to Derek when Matt gave her a sheepish smile. "I like silence just fine. Having you yakking away in my ear for a thousand miles will drive me nuts."

"I asked nicely."

"Yeah. Which makes me suspicious as hell."

"Come on, Lily. Do I have to say it?"

"Say what?"

"I'd feel a hell of a lot safer knowing you were nearby if I have any problems with the dogs."

She gave him a suspicious look. He appeared sincere. And was still considered a novice . . . "Okay," she said, against her better judgment. "Show me how it works and I'll keep it in my poc—"

"Clipped to your collar. Here." His hand brushed her throat, causing Lily to shiver from the soles of her feet to her hair follicles. He clipped the small mic to her collar, then handed her back her gray and white fur hat. She tugged it on, glaring at his back as he strolled off into the crowd.

"Wow. That was some intense interaction," Matt said, giving her a curious look. "What was that about?"

Snagging her attention away from happy homicidal thoughts, Lily shrugged. "Just a Derekism."

"Ever wonder what it would've been like," Matt asked, "if you'd chosen Derek instead of Sean?"

"No." She'd made her bed all those years ago. And if she *had* thought about it—occasionally, briefly, *fleetingly*—it was always with relief she *hadn't* continued seeing Derek. Sure, Sean hadn't been perfect—not by a long shot. But Derek wasn't without issues, either. Just different issues.

"He's far too rich for my blood, for one thing," Lily told him.

"I thought all women believe you couldn't be too thin or too rich. Nothing wrong with being loaded."

"Not that kind of rich," Lily said. "Rich as in too much dark chocolate in one sitting, rich as in one too many wool blankets on a cool night, rich as in—"

Matt wiggled his eyebrows and gave her a teasing eye roll.

Well, hell's bells. She wasn't about to tell her brother Derek was too darn hot to handle without an asbestos shield.

"I always thought you were a little in love with him."

"What? No way. That wasn't love. It was pure irritation. The man would flirt with a *rock* if it had eyelashes and boobs."

"Hey! I've dated women like that."

Lily grinned. "You have not." If Matt dated it was rare. There weren't that many single women in Munroe. "Why don't you start a practice somewhere like Seattle, or Boise? Somewhere where there are women?"

"Happy as a pig right where I am. But thank you for trying." He touched her nose. "Scared?"

"Only a fool wouldn't be," Lily told him absently. "Believe me, I have a healthy respect for wild animals."

"I was talking about Derek."

She grinned. "So was I."

"He's the most *un*wild man I know."

"Have you ever looked into his eyes when he wants something?"

"Um, no." Matt's lips twitched. "But I do know," he said seriously, "if I was ever in a crunch he'd be the guy I'd want at my back."

She gave her brother a startled look. Yes, Derek could look frighteningly menacing at times. But it was an illusion. "You must be kidding me. He's almost as unreliable as . . ."

"Sean?"

"Yes."

"Wrong."

"How can you say that knowing as well as I do that when he's needed, he's off on some exotic vacation?"

"Not every time. And when he's not there he has excellent people in place who *are*. Ash, Sam, Joe."

Lily scowled. "He owns the damn ranch. *He* should be there."

The noise level was suddenly so high she could barely hear herself, and she realized their voices had been getting louder to top the crowd. "Hold that thought," she shouted, then made a hand gesture to indicate she was focusing on the race.

She didn't want to *see* Derek, or *talk* about him or *think* about him for the next week or so.

"Fourteen," the announcer yelled before beginning yet another countdown. Every two minutes another team advanced to the line, dogs straining against their handlers, the mushers riding the break. The crowd went nuts, screaming and shouting encouragement, clapping their gloved hands and narrowing the dog-run corridor as they pressed in for a closer look.

"Settle down, kids," Lily yelled at her impatient team, her breath crystallizing as she made one last check. Anticipation reared its head and roared through her body like a freight train run amok. She was as eager as the dogs to get moving. "Almost our turn."

Four

His heart raced with expectation, even though it would be days before he dared do what he'd been instructed to do. It'd been a while since he'd killed anyone. Still, once you got past the whole moral thing, killing someone was nothing more than an especially interesting exercise. And killing a woman, particularly *this* woman, held a certain morbid appeal. Not that he had much choice. It was kill Lily Munroe or be disposed of himself. And there was no doubt in his mind at all which of them was going to win that contest.

It had to look accidental—which shouldn't be difficult at all. But there was nothing saying he couldn't have a little fun first.

Derek had broken down the initial three legs for his first day on the trail. An hour and a half to get to Knik—a Lily sighting there. Three, maybe six hours to Yentna Station and the second Lily sighting, then another six to Skwentna, where he planned to stop and sleep for a few hours to rest the dogs and arrange a third Lily sighting. By then, she'd be too damn exhausted to fight with him. Time with Lily. That was the goal he would focus on during the first twenty-four hours.

How the hell was he going to pull this off? Derek wondered, on automatic pilot as his dogs, all trained by Lily, followed an invisible trail in the snow. It was bitterly cold. He hadn't caught sight of her in several hours, but thanks to his GPS he knew exactly where she was. He forged on ahead of her.

He was on a roll, comfortable, easy, as he let the dogs do their thing.

Now the race was really on.

The only reason he was here, the only reason he'd taken any interest in the Iditarod at all, was because of Lily. They'd never been friends, Derek thought. He'd taken one look at Lily as she'd loaded bales of hay into her dilapidated truck at the feed store six years ago, and he'd wanted her more than he'd wanted his next breath.

Every scrap of finesse had been shot when he'd glanced up and her eyes had widened. Thank God, he'd thought, she feels it, too.

But his heat had frightened her and she'd run. Run straight into Sean's open arms. Sean Munroe, who wanted to *be* Derek. But that was then. This was now. Derek wasn't planning on skipping any of the courtship stages *this* time.

He was just going to accelerate them to warp speed.

She was going to have to learn to trust him, and since there was nowhere out here for her to run from him, she was going to have to learn fast.

He'd given her six months. More than enough time to mourn Sean. Derek was done waiting. It was time to tell her some truths.

"Hello?" *Click-click.* The sound of a fingernail tapping echoed loudly in his ear. "Damn it, how do I turn this frigging thing— Hello? Hey! Derek?"

She'd slipped on the headset. Pleased, Derek's lips twitched at the annoyance in her voice. "Hey, Doc. How're you doing?"

"I just wanted to see how this thing worked. Amazing. You sound as if you're whispering in my ear."

Not yet he wasn't. "Everything okay?"

"Fine."

"Call me anytime you want to talk."

"I don't," she said, already sounding as though she regretted contacting him in the first place.

Derek grinned as he heard the crackle when she tried to turn off the small electronic listening device.

It didn't work, and for more than an hour he'd eavesdropped on Lily praising her dogs.

"Ah, hell."

"What?" she yelled, clearly startled by his voice right in her ear.

He drew his custom Baer from his pocket and clicked off the safety. "Moose."

A male, easily six feet high at the shoulder, stood silently in the tree line up ahead. Its enormous antlers indicated it was young and had yet to shed them even this late in the season. A young bull could be territorial, protecting its mate— Jesus, there were any number of reasons for it to be pissed. It turned its massive head slowly back and forth as if using its ears as a nature-made radar system.

Lily hissed a curse in Derek's ear. "Don't mess with it!"

"Trust me, sweetheart," he whispered to the woman who was miles away, "I want nothing to do with him. But he's blocking the trail."

There was no telling what a wild animal might do if it thought its territory was being invaded. And a damn moose could tear a man to bits with its hooves and antlers. Perfect. Dodge bullets most of your adult life and get killed by Bullwinkle.

He was going to try to slip by, as silent as a ghost. "Gee! On by!" he told the dogs, keeping his tone matter-of-fact and even. Eyes forward, Derek kept a peripheral bead on the giant in the trees for any sign of aggression. So far, so g—

The moose laid back its ears, the long, coarse hair on its rump raised as if electrified. It tossed its head and stepped purposefully out of the trees on long spindly legs. Long spindly legs that could easily kick the hell out of anything as puny as a human and sixteen dogs.

"Shit."

Braced and ready, Derek held the weapon easily, balanced for one-handed shooting since his left was needed to control the dogs. A gunshot was sure to freak them out.

The huge beast started its gangly run toward him. It was coming flat out, snow spraying in its wake, head lowered, eyes white and wild.

Derek took one shot, aiming high and right to scare the animal off. In the eerie quiet the sound echoed off the snow and trees. The noise didn't faze the moose one iota, but it scared the shit out of the birds. In a flurry of flapping wings and squawks, twenty or so small gray birds cannoned from the nearby trees and took off like buckshot into the sky.

"What's going on?" Lily demanded in his ear.

"Give me a minute—"

He got off another shot. Snow sprayed up in a white froth at the animal's churning feet. That one was closer. The moose stopped on a dime, raising its head, then stood its ground. Derek admired its steely nerves.

"Come on, pal, shit or get off the pot," he said softly, running out of options. The next would have to be a kill shot. And he was reluctant to kill the magnificent beast just for protecting its home. But given a choice between the moose and protecting his own ass and that of his team, the moose would have to go.

The animal moved restively, ears flat.

The dogs, aware of the danger, yipped and snarled, straining against the lead dogs, Max and Kryptonite, who seemed focused on getting the team past the threat.

Clark and Twit started barking madly; several of the others chimed in their two cents' worth. The moose's ears rotated like satellite dishes. One step forward, head lowered.

Derek pulled on the lines. *"Come haw!"* He reined them to pull 180 degrees to the left. "Quiet, boys," he told the dancing dogs softly. "Just go on by and don't look at him."

Clearly royally pissed at the invaders, several tons of moose charged again.

Snow sprayed behind those lethal hooves as the animal raced toward Derek, head positioned for maximum damage on impact, close enough for Derek to see the whites of its eyes.

"Ah, crap. Damn it to hell."

Derek got off another shot, but the sled tipped at the same moment and the shot went wild. The moose kicked out with its front feet, hit the side of the sled—*BAM!* A fully packed sled was no match for a pissed-off Bullwinkle. The sled rolled, then fell on top of Derek with a shuddering thwack, spraying wet snow against his goggles. The sled was heavy with supplies, and for several moments he was in a protected spot as the furious moose rammed and battered a genetically choreographed attack.

"I see you." Lily's voice was an urgent and welcome sound in his ears. "At least he's not after your dogs."

Her words came directly in his ear. Thank God she wasn't the object of the moose's attentions. And at least the animal wasn't stomping his dogs into the snow. Not yet anyway. *He* was another story. Those hooves were sharp and lethal as the enraged moose repeatedly kicked the shit out of the sled.

There was a flat, familiar *crack* and the smell of cordite on the crisp, clean mountain air. Another shot. And another. The moose bellowed, turned tail and ran like hell back into the trees.

"He's gone." Lily's relieved and mildly amused voice came through loud and clear as Derek shoved the sled and fallen supplies off his body.

"My hero," he said dryly, brushing clumps of wet snow off his pants and coat as he watched her approach. A rancher through and through, Lily knew what she was doing with that gun, thank God. She looked like a bundled-up Amazon. An ancient warrior in a long fleece coat and furry boots. And he was damned glad to see her.

She brought her team alongside his. The leads, Arrow and Max, immediately, and happily sniffed at each other. Derek wanted to do the same to Lily, but he was just a little afraid she might use the gun again.

Lily gave Derek an up-and-down look. "Are you hurt?"

"Only my ego."

"Then you may never recover." Setting the brake, she hopped off her sled. Without offering, she put some muscle into helping him right his, which was top heavy and unwieldy. "Good job securing everything."

"Thanks, teacher." He looked off into the trees where the snow had been violently churned and branches broken as the moose had made its way. "Think our friend's gone?"

"Probably. I didn't hit him. But I scared him enough to deter him a bit. Why? Want to break?"

"Let's go a few miles on before we do. My new friend might be lurking behind the trees waiting to jump out again."

They continued on for several miles before deciding they were clear.

Derek was actually quite pleased to take a break. And God only knew, Lily must be just as exhausted. The last several years had been hard on her. Little sleep and a lot of stress. The years nursing Sean, followed by the funeral, had taken their toll on her, although he'd never heard her complain. After Sean's death, Lily had put everything she had into her dogs. There must be at least a hundred of them by now. Training the dogs and then staying up all night for weeks on end helping the cows give birth, then training herself for the race day and night would exhaust anyone. But she'd rather be boiled in oil than admit it.

He at least had the advantage of his T-FLAC training and could subsist for weeks on very little sleep. But he saw the lines of strain on her face, and knowing Lily, she'd push herself until she dropped. A break of even an hour would do her good. And since there seemed to be a silent truce, he'd take what he could get when he could get it.

Of course, telling Lily he was stopping for her own good would probably get him shot.

"Are you pleased about your father remarrying?" Lily asked, keeping it casual as she checked the dogs' booties and gave scratches behind ears as she moved down the line. Talking about the upcoming wedding was safe. It kept her blood pressure down, and it was a finite kind of conversation. His father's wedding was going to be held at the ranch a couple of weeks after they returned from the race. She'd met his father a couple of times when he'd visited Derek at the ranch. She'd also met his sister, Marnie, and her family. There was a twin brother out there somewhere, and another couple of brothers. If they were anything like Derek, Lily shuddered to think of the trail of broken hearts they'd left in their wake.

She promised herself she wouldn't bring up anything inflammatory. Not now anyway.

She kept a professional eye out for injuries as she went down the line. The dogs were barely breathing hard, and rarin' to go with excitement, yet they needed to pace themselves. So did she. They'd barely started and there were a thousand grueling miles to go.

"I am. Yes," Derek said, answering the wedding question as he added a few dry branches to the small fire he'd started. "Sunny is good for him. He was alone a long time before he met her."

Lily automatically checked Derek's dogs too before joining him at the fire. "Kodi's favoring his right foot. We'll keep an eye on it, although he's done that since he was a puppy to get extra attention, so I'm not too worried." She drew off her gloves and rubbed her hands as she stood over the flames. She noticed with appreciation that Derek had set a pot on the fire filled with coffee. Her taste buds salivated.

"Your mom died when you were pretty young, right?" She knew they had that much in common.

"Yeah, but my grandmother was there. Here." He handed her a steaming mug. "Be careful, it's hot."

"I'm feeding the dogs first—"

"Drink your coffee. I've got it."

Lily scowled. "We're not supposed to help each other."

Derek poured out food into bowls and started taking them down the line. The dogs, still harnessed and standing, dug into the high-fat, high-protein snack. They didn't care who handed it out as long as it was there. "Stupid rule since we're both in the same place. Hungry?"

"No."

"You'd better remember to eat on this trip. Since you took care of the moose for me, I'd feel obligated to backtrack to check if you've fainted from starvation somewhere along the trail. Think of it as tit for tat, especially since very soon I'll be so far ahead of you, I won't be able to repay your assistance. I'm winning this race." He was not talking about the Iditarod.

Lily gulped the last inch of scalding-hot coffee. It must've burned like lava all the way down her esophagus. "I've never fainted in my life. And for the record, *I'm* going to win."

He let that pass.

They were *both* going to win.

She rarely thought about food for herself, but coffee was essential. "In case you haven't noticed, I'm not one of the thoroughbreds you usually date. We mutts have way more staying power than the show dogs of the world."

She poured the last couple of servings of dog food into bowls and walked down the line to place them in the snow in front of Derek's wheel dogs.

"Nothing wrong with a good, faithful mutt," he said, laughing. "That said, you have an erroneous and completely false idea of my love life, Doc. Though you know you're always welcome to ask. I don't mind telling."

"Really? Wow." She gave him a mock admiring glance. "Thanks, but I think I'll pass on that. This mutt isn't interested in that particular treat."

"Not even if I promise to pet you?"

She stilled, shot him what she hoped was a quelling look despite the rush of something hot and luscious deep inside. "Want to pet something? Try one of your short-lived girlfriends. Here's an idea." Lily struggled to keep the sarcasm to a minimum. "Have her meet you at the next stop. Assuming she can find Alaska on a map."

Then she straightened, unsettled by the catty turn of her own thoughts. "Are you done resting? Because I am. I want to make Skwentna before dark." Only if she were jet propelled. But let him sweat thinking about it.

"It wouldn't kill you to take a full hour."

"I am taking a full hour," Lily said, peeling back the layers of

clothing at her wrist to glance at her watch. "See? Thirty-eight minutes. Almost exactly an hour."

He shook his head and bit back a smile at her impatience. "We
need to get you a watch without Mickey on it, Doc."

Lily was so tired she couldn't see straight. Almost in a trance,
brain turned off, she arrived at the Skwentna checkpoint on autopi-
lot, well after dark.

She'd come one hundred miles.

Skwentna was a small village located on the river by the same
name. This would be the busiest and biggest checkpoint because all
the teams hit here at some point during the first twenty-four-or-so
hours of the race. After tonight the teams would be straggled all over
the countryside.

The Delias—Joe, the local postmaster, and his wife, Norma—
generously fed close to four hundred people every Iditarod, helped
by an army of local volunteers called the Skwentna Sweeties. The
smell of their famous stew scented the crisp air and made Lily's mouth
water.

The area around the two-story cabin was already a beehive of
noise and activity. Lily blinked at the lights, which were far too bright
after traveling so long by moonlight. The noise, too, seemed extra
loud to someone accustomed to nothing more than the sounds of her
own breathing and the soft swish of rails on snow.

Exhausted teams were scattered on beds of straw on the ice.
Nearby planes landed and took off, a diesel engine roared constantly
and newly arrived dogs barked, ready to go again.

Lily checked in, snagged the straw bale they gave her, tossed it
into the sled and went on to pick up her food bags. Matt was there
to check her team, and she stood by silently, too tired to move.

"You made good time," he told her, checking Deny's feet.

Lily grunted. There were already at least twenty teams resting,
which had made it in better time than she had.

"How was the trail?" Matt asked, handing her a candy bar.

Lily tore into it, barely getting the wrapper off before her teeth sank in. "You're a prince. Oh, God, this is good. Thank you," she said around a mouthful of glorious, thick, dark rich chocolate. Second only to coffee. Food of the gods. "Other than a moose spotting, uneventful." She polished off the last half with enthusiasm. The sugar hit was welcome.

Matt gave her a hard up-and-down look while she chewed. "Are you okay? Did she attack?"

"He. Yeah, he lit into Derek's sled and kicked the beejeebers out of it—" She interrupted herself to yawn. "The dogs are all okay, his sled's fine and Derek wasn't hurt. Fortunately," Lily gave him a devilish grin, "I came in, guns blazing, and saved the day."

His eyes narrowed. "You're carrying a gun?"

"Of course. Isn't everyone up here? Hey, I was lucky not to have to kill the big guy."

"Derek?" Matt said with a smile.

"Don't put ideas in my head."

"I'm glad you weren't hurt, Wonder Woman. Although Derek's pride must've taken a hit having you charge in and save his bacon."

"Well, yes, there was *that* nice perk," Lily said, enjoying the memory.

"Did you have any time to talk to him?"

"About what?"

"Any of it," Matt said absently, picking up Adam's back leg and removing the bootie to check the dog's foot. "Diablo specifically."

The bogus bull sperm business. Lily frowned, following Matt's movements as he inspected each dog. He was thorough. She leaned against the sled, satisfied that he'd find anything she might've missed. The vet inspection had to be done officially and reported, no matter that she was qualified to do it herself. "No. But I will."

"When?"

"When we get back and I have all the facts. Now's not the time. But honest to God, Matt, I thought he was going to say something yesterday in Anchorage. He didn't. And frankly that conversation went badly enough for me to be grateful we didn't have to bring Diablo up, too."

"Good. Wait till after the race. And I want to be with you when you do," Matt told her grimly, pausing from his inspection of the dogs to look at her. "Seriously, Lily. Promise me."

Fatigue clawed at her, and she fought it back. "Why? Do you think he'd hurt me in some way because I found out? To be fair, which in this case chaps my hide, there's an outside chance that *he* doesn't know anything about the illegal sales; have you thought of that?"

"Yeah, I have. But I know Derek would never hurt you. This is an important race, so it probably isn't the best time. We've got someone I trust looking into how involved this is. Wait until all the findings are in. And for God's sake, just promise that I'm there when you do broach the subject."

"I will. Thanks, Matt." She wasn't sure who to trust anymore. Who else knew about the sales of bull sperm being made under the table? Diablo's sperm was like gold, highly prized and incredibly expensive.

From what Lily had been able to piece together, the illegal sales had been going on for years. Sean had been eyebrow deep in it, using her expertise and qualifications to legitimize what he'd been doing. All without her knowledge. The thought made Lily sick to her stomach. The money from Sean's illegal activities sat untouched in the bank in the Caymans until she and Matt and the investigator could go to the authorities with all the information necessary.

God. What a mess. She had no idea how many cows had been inseminated by fake Diablo sperm. Could be thousands.

The question that had been going around and around in her head for the last six weeks was, was Derek involved in the scam?

She'd overheard the conversation between two of the hands five weeks ago. She hadn't confronted them, but she'd started piecing together what little paper trail she could find. The more she'd discovered, the bigger the scam appeared. Sales of "Diablo" sperm had been made worldwide. Japan, Korea, Europe—the list and magnitude of the illegal operation was staggering.

She hadn't confided in her father. But she'd told Matt. He'd cautioned her not to report anything to the authorities until they could ascertain if what she thought she knew was fact. He knew a private investigator and had put him on retainer to track down who was involved before Lily made any accusations.

Stud fees for a prize bull like Diablo were big business. Fortunes were made and lost on the strength of a herd. And a bull like Diablo could guarantee big, healthy calves. The profits from the sale of his sperm were in the millions. Someone was selling inferior liquid gold and labeling it as Diablo's. As randy as the bull was, he had only so much sperm. There were fake little test tube bulls out there with false pedigrees.

Lily had been a lot more observant of late. Who suddenly had a lot of money? And what was sudden, after all? As far as she could figure out, this had been going on for years. Derek had made a good point the other day about her not noticing things. In her own defense she was not a rancher, she was a vet. Sean had done the books, and after he died, Derek had taken over.

How was she supposed to know the ins and outs of the ranch when both men had made a special point of leaving her out of the daily working of the business end of it? And the reality was, outside of her passion for working with the animals, she had had absolutely no *interest* in running the ranch. Derek clearly had money. He'd come from wealth and was easy with it. His lifestyle hadn't changed since she'd known him. Unlike Sean, he'd never thrown his money around. But then, Lily thought with irritation, the man took a hell of a lot of exotic vacations. He also owned his own plane, and several very nice vehicles.

But Sean . . . Sean had lived a lot higher on the hog than Derek ever had.

"You must be thinking about your dearly departed."

Lily blinked. "What?"

"Must be thinking about Sean. You have that I-want-to-dig-him-up-and-kill-the-son-of-a-bitch-all-over-again look in your eyes."

Lily forced a smile. "I do not."

Matt gave her a sympathetic look, which made Lily feel even more guilty. Because some secrets were meant to stay just that. Secret.

"One of these days," her stepbrother told her gruffly, "you're going to meet a great guy and live happily ever after."

"Not even if Brad Pitt proposed would I put myself through that again," Lily assured him cheerfully, pushing all thoughts of virile males, bovine and human, aside. "Thanks but no thanks. I have my family, my dogs and a Shower Massage. All is right with my world."

Matt gave a laughing grimace and raised a hand. "Information overload. Okay. I get the message. The widow Munroe will turn into old lady Munroe. You know, the one with all those dogs."

"That'll be me."

"Things can change . . ."

"Nah. Why mess with a good thing? Let's concentrate on finding *you* the perfect woman."

"How about a bunch of *im*perfect women first?" Matt teased.

Several more teams clustered behind them, waiting for the vets to check them. The time for private conversation was over. Instead, Lily was forced to make nice with several people who came to offer their condolences about Sean's death and to chat about the start of the trail and what they anticipated up ahead.

As tired as she was, Lily wanted to get out of the crowd and back on the trail.

"When did you eat last?" Matt asked as a couple of mushers dragged themselves up to the house for a meal and some shut-eye. "Stew's real good tonight," he added, as he continued down the line, checking legs and feet for trouble. The kids were still amped up and rarin' to go, though. And as long as they were fine to run, she had no complaints and wasn't stopping. She could sleep standing up on the sled. Lord knew, she'd done it before.

It was way too crowded here for her tired brain, and her stomach was growling. Along with the scent of cook fires and diesel she could smell the savory stew on the cold air. "I'm quick-stopping. As soon as I'm done sorting my food bags. It's too *too* here."

Matt raised a brow. "Too?"

Lily rotated her neck. "Too noisy, too bright, too frenetic." She was starting to use Derekisms herself. *After.* After Sean. What did that mean?

"Don't go too far," Matt cautioned. "You and the dogs all need sleep. And for God's sake," he said sternly, touching a gloved finger to the tip of her icy nose, "don't forget to eat something yourself!"

"Yes, Mom." She smiled. "That chocolate will hold me for a bit." It was nice having a big brother. "Are we good to go?"

"Yeah. Travel safe. I'll check your food bags through for you. See you at Finger Lake."

"With bells on," Lily assured him. "Thanks." Maybe she could push on another four hours and beat the rush to the next checkpoint.

She checked her lines one last time, hugged Matt good-bye and notified the checker she was leaving.

"Let's go, kids." The dogs took off as if spring-loaded. Lily laughed as the chill wind slapped her face and snow sprayed out in a rooster tail behind the sled as they headed back into the wilderness.

It was a perfect travel night. Crisply cold, bright with moonlight, the snow packed and fast. If she could catch a few hours' sleep while mushing behind the sled she'd have it made.

FULL OF BEEF STEW, HE LAY AGAINST THE WALL OF THE LODGE WRAPPED in his damp sleeping bag trying to defrost his extremities. He hadn't been that late, and it pissed him off that all the choice spots near the fire had already been taken. Losers.

The floor was hard. He rolled over to find a more comfortable spot. There wasn't one. He wanted his own bed with an intense longing. Hell, he wanted his own bed, a fifth of scotch and a soft broad. Not necessarily in that order.

But here he was. In the middle of fucking Nowheresville.

She'd looked exhausted. Well, fuck! Who wasn't?

He closed gritty eyes. Opened them again. She'd have to stop to sleep. Even as driven as she was, she'd have to fucking stop, at least to rest the dogs.

He tossed the sleeping bag aside, glanced around the firelit room. Lumps under sleeping bags as far as the eye could see. Everyone was catching z's. No chatting, no socializing, no watching the nonexistent fucking TV. When these assholes stopped it was necessity, not a vacation.

It had only been one day. But what a fucking day. He was sick and tired of the noise of all these freaking damn dogs yipping and barking. He was sick of all the goddamned *snow.* The landscape was nothing but white and green, white and green, white and green, as far as the eye could see.

And goddamn it, he was fucking *sick* of being cold all the freaking time.

He hefted himself out of the bag and sighed. Honest to God. This cat-and-mouse game was supposed to at least afford him a little fun. But this was purgatory. He wanted to be done with it. He wasn't interested in a good time anymore. All he wanted now was the bitch dead and his ass on a nice warm plane home.

"I hope you appreciate that I'm now going to make this quick, Lily," he said under his breath, pulling on his still-wet boots with a grimace.

Nobody stirred as he tiptoed around the snoring, snorting, farting lumps scattered around the room.

"Losers," he muttered under his breath as he opened the door to blackness and cold. Cold so fucking icy it felt like tiny ice picks attacking his eyeballs and freezing the snot in his nose. "Fuck Alaska."

Five

DEREK SLIPPED THE HANDHELD SCREEN OF THE GPS OUT OF HIS pocket. He'd had a small side bet with himself that Lily wouldn't stay at the last checkpoint for one second longer than it took to check in, get the dogs inspected and be on her way again. He'd been right on the money.

"Get up!" he yelled out to encourage the dogs to pull harder and pick up speed. He needed to head two degrees southwest to intercept Lily. He'd detoured from the trail because of the rough terrain caused by the Ice Dog snow-machine race, which had occurred several weeks before. Lily, being Lily, would take the direct route, even though she'd have to travel over the heavy-duty tracks left by the big machines.

Just as he'd heard her greet her stepbrother for the check-in, he'd had to turn her off to take a call from his sister. Marnie had questions about their father's upcoming nuptials. Her call had then been interrupted by a call from his T-FLAC control.

He'd been only too pleased to talk business instead of wedding. As much as he loved his sister, there was only so much a man needed to know about canapés and coral-colored napkins. Still, there was a lot to be said for all the new technology that made talking on a phone, at least *this* phone, possible no matter where he might be. As much as he'd rather talk business, Derek scowled. He could've done without this second call from HQ.

T-FLAC, or Terrorist Force Logistical Assault Command, the anti-terrorist black ops organization he worked for, had been alerted to a possible act of terrorism in the northern section of Alaska. He was closest. *Closest* being relative in such a large state. There was nothing T-FLAC was aware of that would make the Iditarod, or any of its participants, a target for any known terrorist group. But they were looking into possible scenarios, and he should keep his eyes and ears open.

Yeah, he'd do that. But right now an encounter with Lily was a hell of a lot more appealing than dealing with some nebulous tango threat. Not that he wouldn't keep an eye out for anything untoward, and he sure as hell would keep his sat phone on for further updates. But unless his other life intruded, and he hoped to hell it didn't right now, he had a serious op of his own. Something a lot more personal.

Derek readjusted the ear bud and clicked over to the other chan-nel so he could hear Lily breathing. Then he set a steady pace to a point where she would have to stumble over him to go any farther.

The problem with keeping his two lives separate was that Lily only saw him through Sean's skewed point of view. And while the playboy persona was part image, and he'd fostered that image inten-tionally, now it no longer suited his purposes.

Lily knew she'd traveled an hour past sensible.

Time to stop.

She'd taken the route over the huge moguls, big ruts and bare hills left in the wake of hundreds of snowmobiles and four-wheelers after their big race. No problem if you were in a vehicle. But the Iditarod teams tackling these man-made obstacles had a much tougher time of it.

She could've gone around the tracks and bare spots. But it would've added several hours to her time. Instead, she put up with the less than fabulous conditions and considered a bitten tongue and a headache well worth the miles she'd made up on the miserable, aggravating route.

She'd been traveling by moonlight, admiring the monochromatic, black-and-white landscape through gritty eyes. Time to stop and rest the dogs and herself. A few hours were all she needed to revitalize.

She had to force herself to keep her eyes open, and even then, the world looked blurry. Suddenly seeing an orange sparkle through the blackness of the trees up ahead was almost surreal.

She blinked. Still there. For a moment or two she thought the orange-red glow of a fire might be a hallucination. The dogs didn't. Seeing what she did, and probably smelling wood smoke long before she could, they suddenly got a renewed burst of energy and raced toward the glow like kids on the last day of school. Lily let them have their heads; knowing the sport as she did, they'd be welcome at the other team's fire. The closer she got, the stronger the fragrance of wood smoke and hot coffee became, and something else: a smell savory enough to make saliva pool in her mouth.

"*Whoa!* Hello, the fire," Lily caroled, pulling on the brake to slow down the team as they approached the campsite with noisy enthusiasm. Her arms and legs quivered from the continuous motion of the sled and the strength required to guide it.

Sleepy dogs lifted their heads from beneath their tails and yipped hello as Lily's team pulled into the shelter of the trees. A large figure, backlit by the fire, rose to greet her.

"You made good time."

Crap. *Derek.*

Anticipation snuffed out in a heartbeat. She was too tired for this. Lily yanked off the brake and pedaled like mad, keeping one foot on the runner and pushing with the other. "*Mush! Haw!* On by. Coming through."

So much for a hot cup of coffee and a few hours' rest. She felt a spurt of guilt that she'd told the dogs to stop and then immediately instructed the poor, tired animals to do exactly the opposite. But she wasn't staying. Not here. Half an hour away would be much more comfortable for everyone.

"Whoa!" Derek told her team, snagging Arrow's neckline as they tried to pass him. "Whoa!" he repeated, with no room for negotiation. The well-trained dogs stopped on a dime.

Derek walked purposefully toward her. "Nice try, Doc." One-handed, he effortlessly hefted the heavy straw bale out of the cargo bed and tossed it on the ground near his own dogs. "I've got some of Annie's beef Burgundy heating up, and hot coffee. Chow for the dogs is ready, too."

Lily smelled the rich, heavenly fragrance of food and coffee and her mouth watered. Her body still felt as though she were in motion even though she was no longer moving. Like a sailor too long at sea, feeling the ocean beneath his feet even while on land. "Let go," she said tightly.

"No." His bulky coat and black fur hat made him seem as big as a mountain and just as immovable. He gave her a penetrating look. "Don't be an idiot, Lily. *You* let go," he told her roughly, grabbing her arm before she could do—what? Hit him? Run? *"Now."* His tone was implacable.

Screw you, she thought belligerently but without much heat as she tried to shake him off. It would be a nice trick if she *could* let go.

Deliberately, he let his gaze roam over her face. Lily gave him a stony look in return. "What are you trying to do?" he demanded. He frowned, apparently not liking what he saw. "Kill yourself?"

"Did you ask that ridiculous question of any *other* musher as they came through?" Lily snapped, trying without success to release the handlebar so she could step off the runners and move out of his range. Her stiff, cold fingers were locked in place. She couldn't even use one hand to pry off the other. Much longer in this position and she'd be petrified. They'd have to bury her standing up on her sled.

Only Derek Wright would have specialty meals prepared and waiting for him at each stop. The rich, savory fragrance of Burgundy and the image of succulent, tender chunks of beef drenched in thick, dark gravy seduced her. Her stomach growled so loudly and for so long that several of the dogs turned around to look for the source of the noise. Derek swore under his breath. They were nose to nose. Far too close for Lily's comfort. His face was almost completely in shadow, yet she could clearly see the devilish sparkle in his midnight blue eyes. Her breath caught in her throat as he reached out—

For her hand. He pried her gloved fingers loose until she could release the handle. She sighed with pleasure. Liberated, and feeling strangely as though she'd escaped some unseen peril, Lily flexed stiff fingers and stumbled off the back of the sled. Derek or no Derek, it felt good to move.

"Go eat. I'll take ca—"

She mustered up a glare. "And have me disqualified? I don't think so."

"Fine. Take care of your dogs. But at least save time and use the food I heated up. There's plenty."

Stupid to refuse. And frankly, she wasn't sure she could wait long enough to heat anything up for herself. She might just start gnawing on whatever first came to hand. "Fine. I'll feed the kids and be right there."

She started removing the dogs' food and a large pot.

Derek took both items out of her hands. Lily didn't put up a fight. Just watched him through glassy eyes as he stashed the food and pot back under the sled bag in the cargo bed.

"I'll trade you," he said quietly, his features hard to read. "There's food ready for them. Just feed the dogs so you can feed yourself."

"But—"

"Do it before you collapse face-first in the damn snow, for God's sake."

"Thanks." Numb with fatigue as she was, Lily went down the line and fed and watered the dogs, feeling the heat of Derek's gaze on her back as she performed the tasks by rote.

Done, she examined the animals' legs and feet for injury, then bedded down the dogs on the straw Derek had spread.

By which time she could barely put one foot in front of the other. The first day on the trail always seemed to last forever. Once she got a momentum going it wouldn't be quite so bad. Or so she assured herself at this point every year.

"Why do I always forget how bad the first day is?"

He laughed shortly. "Probably a lot like childbirth. My sister insisted the only reason she had more than one child was because she'd forgotten how hard the delivery was. After five my mother probably felt the same way."

Lily glanced at him. He looked a little less ferocious now that he'd gotten his own way. "Difficult to imagine you as a child. Or having a mother."

His mouth quirked. "What? You figure I dropped full-grown out of the sky?"

She gave him a half smile. "I was thinking more like slithering out from under a rock."

"Not up to your usual pithy standards, Doc. You usually do better than that in cutting me down to size."

"It's the best I can do when I'm this tired. Tomorrow is another day."

He laughed, his teeth white against the darkness of his face. "Poor baby. Get some sleep and a better perspective."

His low, deep *seductor's* voice sent shivers up and down her spine. Annoyed with herself, she wandered over to the fire to warm her hands. Derek sat off to one side drinking a steaming cup of coffee as he watched her. Minutes ticked past. The teasing done, quiet reigned. His silence unnerved her. A world of words hung almost visibly between them in the darkness. Each razor-sharp accusation suspended in the frigid darkness like laundry on a line. As merciless and cruel as the icicles bowing the branches around them.

She wanted to trust him. She really did. But she'd been so badly burned by Sean and his lies that it was hard for her to give a man so similar the benefit of the doubt. And while it might be unfair to tar Derek with Sean's brush, she didn't know how to change it.

There was no reason for her to presume that Derek wasn't the head honcho in the illegal sperm sales. God only knew, he was smart enough. . . .

Derek had spread his wide sleeping bag on a bed of branches. Lily tried not to be jealous. She was tired enough to beg him to share. A thought that wouldn't have crossed her mind unless she was desperate. Still the idea sent a welcoming heat through her so it served a purpose in some convoluted way. She'd been relatively warm while she'd been on the sled, but her body temperature was lowering the longer she stood around.

She tried to figure out how to get from upright to flat with a small amount of dignity. Her sleeping bag was way over there, strapped to the sled. All she had to do was put one foot in front—

"Snap to it before you keel over, sweetheart," Derek said grimly, not moving from his position.

Right. She really, *really* needed to do that.

Lily looked at him through eyes glazed with exhaustion, then stumbled away from the meager heat of the fire and unstrapped her sleeping bag from the sled. She glanced around for a decent spot to lay it, out of the path of any other mushers coming through. If she didn't do this before she ate she might very well be tired enough to lie down in the snow for her nap.

"Over here."

She suddenly noticed the second bed of branches beside him. *No freaking way.* Even exhaustion had its limits. "I don't think so."

"Me or the snow."

"Snow's safer."

"Don't be ridiculous."

"That's too close to you," Lily told him. "Way too close."

"I won't bite," he said, his eyes on her mouth. "At least not very hard."

Lily's heart did that weird flip-flop in her chest. Ridiculous. "I'm presuming," she said as coolly as she could manage while swaying on her feet, "that you're practicing your seduction skills on me because there isn't another female humanoid around for a couple of hundred miles. News flash, Romeo: you're wasting your breath. I've been vaccinated. I'm immune, remember?"

"Are you now?" he asked, his voice silky. He rose and went to the

fire, where he poured a mug of steaming, fragrant coffee. He came
back to her, his large, booted feet crunching in the snow, and handed
her the cup. "Sit down and drink this."

"I don't want—" She met him glare for glare, then shook her
head. Why was she arguing? He held the elixir of the gods in his
hand, and her legs were about ready to collapse anyway. She sat down
on his sleeping bag and reached for the mug, careful not to touch his
hand as she did so. And ignored the little thrill of excitement in her
tummy as his fingers brushed hers anyway. Not excitement, she assured herself. *Annoyance.*

"If you're immune, you're okay to take coffee from the enemy."

"You're not the enemy . . ." *Exactly.* She took a scalding sip of coffee.

"That's my girl," he said with approval as she took another sip.
"Sometime when you're not falling over exhausted, you'll have to
elaborate on that one for me."

She bit her tongue. "I'm not anybody's girl." The heat of the mug
warmed her hands even through her gloves. "You're flogging a dead
horse. *Again.*"

"Drink it," he instructed harshly, standing over her, the light of
the fire flickering on his face. "Because you're a widow?"

"Because I—I loved my husband, and he's only been dead six
months." She took several more sips of the hot liquid and it burned
all the way down her esophagus. Oh yeah. Just the way she liked it.
Then Derek spoke again and ruined a perfectly good coffee rush.

"Sean was sick for years before he died. You didn't have a husband. You had a patient."

She stared up at him, appalled by his callousness. "That's a terrible
thing to say." True, but callous.

"It's the truth and we both know it. It was a terrible thing for you
to go through."

"Not me. Sean."

"He's the one that got all the attention and sympathy. What about
you?"

"I wasn't the one dying."

He gave her an enigmatic look. "Weren't you?"

"My God, Derek. That's low. Even for you."

"*You're* still alive, Lily. When are you going to take something for yourself?"

"I have everything I need. I'm perfectly fine, thank you very much."

"You're going to be a hell of a lot . . . finer, believe me."

Her heart started pounding erratically in her chest and her mouth went arid. She licked dry lips as she stared up at him. "What does that mean?"

"Think about it," he said softly, his eyes focused on her mouth. "And while you do, let's get you settled for the night before you fall asleep sitting right there." In seconds he'd spread her bag and unzipped it. "Get your boots off and climb in. Unless you want to share mine with me. We'd both be a lot warme——" He gave a short bark of laughter. "Jesus, if looks could kill I'd be a smoking ember right about now. Okay, move onto your own sleeping bag then. Now, where are your dry socks?" His eyes tracked her features and he shook his head. "Never mind, I'll find them."

He strode over to her sled and rummaged around for her duffel bag. He didn't look up from what he was doing, and she stared at his broad back with glassy vision as he pawed through her personal items. "Outside left pocket," she told him, feeling cranky and out of sorts and . . . *itchy,* for God's sake. The man would drive a saint to drink.

Lily shifted over the two feet separating the two sleeping bags, and started unlacing her boots. She put up a hand to take the ball of socks from him.

He shook his head and crouched down beside her. "If I were so tired I braided my shoelaces, wouldn't you help me?"

Lily glanced at her gloved hands on her left boot. Instead of untying the laces, she'd twisted them into a rope. She was loopy with exhaustion.

He tucked the clean socks inside his jacket. "Lie down," he said briskly, shoved her useless hands away and untied the laces of her heavy boots himself.

No way was she going to lie do— He solved that little problem by yanking her leg up to remove the boot. Lily fell backward onto the soft, insulated bag. It felt incredibly wonderful to be flat. She closed her eyes and stayed where she was. In a second or two or three, she'd protest that he was removing her shoes as if she were a sleepy two-year-old. Soon. Very soon, she'd tell him just what she thought of his caveman tactics. In fact, any minute now, she'd fry him with a scathing comment.

The second he removed her boot, cold air took a searing bite at her clammy foot, making her jerk back her leg. Derek pulled off the sock and wrapped his warm, bare hands around her foot to keep it in place on his rock-hard thigh. For several seconds he massaged her icy toes until warmth seeped back into them. She wasn't sure which felt better—the heat or the foot rub. And for one glorious minute, she forgot all about killing him. He removed one of her socks from beneath his jacket and tugged the warm wool up her foot.

He touched the small knife she had tucked into a pocket inside her boot. "You think there'll be time to whittle out here, or are you planning on using this on me?"

"You never know." At the moment she couldn't imagine moving, let alone whittling anything. As for carving a slice out of him, she'd need a bit of energy first.

"I've never seen a woman who hates to sit still as much as you do."

"Hey, check me out now. I can't seem to take off my own damn shoes."

"I kinda like having you malleable and acquiescent under my hands."

Lily closed her eyes as he removed her other boot. "Opportunist. I'm as limp as a dish rag with exhaustion."

She was confounded by his gentleness and care. Nobody had taken care of her since her mom had died when she was eight. Her father had always been busy with his veterinary practice. And he'd reminded her enough times that she was a big girl and didn't need babying. He'd been right. She was quite capable even then of preparing her own meals, bandaging her own cuts and scrapes and making her own dentist appointments. She'd even called the local volunteer fire department for help when Cinnamon had thrown her and she'd broken her arm.

She certainly didn't need a man to help her put on clean dry socks. But, oh, Lord. His warm hands on her cold foot had a soporific effect and felt so good she decided to give him another ten minutes before she reamed him out.

"Explain how you came to Montana with Sean and bought the ranch." Her own voice sounded distant to her ears as she fought sleep.

He hesitated. "Were you aware that Sean was my foreman in Texas?"

Lily frowned up at him, her pretty eyes glassy with fatigue. This wasn't the time or the place to bring this up. But if not now, when and where? Derek thought with frustration. She'd erected the Wall of China between them long ago. It was either break it down stone by stone, or take a bulldozer and do it fast and dirty.

"You and Sean owned the ranch in Texas together?" Lily asked, voice as hazy as her eyes.

"No. Sean worked for me for a couple of years. When he discovered that his father's spread in Montana was for sale he asked if I'd be interested in buying it." Begged. Bartered. Tried to blackmail.

Lily stared at him, clearly trying to wrap her brain around something that was the complete opposite of what she'd been led to believe. Derek knew what Sean had told her: After Sean's father had disowned and disinherited him, he'd gone to Texas and eventually bought a small successful ranch there. When he'd heard that his father's ranch was being sold off by the state, he'd come back home and bought it. Inviting his previous foreman, Derek, to join him.

Sean had been one of the most accomplished liars Derek had ever encountered. And he'd encountered many. Both as an antiterrorist operative and as a rancher. Derek had always prided himself in his ability to size someone up within minutes of meeting him or her, but in Sean Munroe's case he'd been wrong. Dead wrong. The man had been a pathological liar and, God only knew, charm personified. Sean could run a scam with all the innocence of a choir boy and it wasn't until your wallet was gone that you realized you'd been had.

Sean had wanted wealth. His father had disinherited him, eventually giving the bulk of his estate to cancer research. The ranch hadn't been worked in years and wasn't worth a whole hell of a lot. It had suited Derek's purposes to be in just such an isolated area. He'd made the state an offer and moved his main operation from Texas to Montana.

It hadn't taken long for the blinders to fall from Derek's eyes. But by then it was too late to scrape Sean from his shoes. He'd met Lily.

But if he, a professional bullshit barometer, hadn't figured Munroe out, how in the hell could a woman in love see through the man's lies?

Lily rubbed her forehead. "But he said—"

"Sean said a lot of things that weren't true." God only knew he'd managed to snow Derek for several years. He'd been that good. Christ, he'd been *unbelievably* good. Sean Munroe had had the face of a fallen angel, and could sound so sincere, so absolutely convincing, that even when Derek had known the son of a bitch was lying, he'd been hard-pressed to believe it.

Conning a woman who loved him as passionately as Lily had loved Sean must've been a piece of cake. Sean had laughed about it. Worse, he'd mocked and taunted Derek with it. And for once in his life Derek had been powerless to control the situation.

It killed him to wonder if Sean had only claimed to love Lily because he'd always known how Derek felt. And by the time Derek realized just how many lies he'd told and what subterfuge his "friend" was perpetrating on Lily, Sean had been diagnosed with terminal cancer.

"Then how did—"

Derek tipped her face up with a finger under her chin. "We can talk more about this tomorrow. Right now you can't keep your eyes open and I want you alert and listening when we talk. You need to eat before you sleep, though." He brushed his thumb along her jaw. Her skin was cold but heated up under his touch. He dropped his hand.

"I'm not hungry."

"You're a lousy liar." He put a taunt in the words. "You just don't have the energy. No matter. You have to make the effort. How can you beat my ass if you're anorexic?"

She scooched into the bag and pulled it up over her shoulders, zipping it all the way up from the inside, and closed her eyes. "Tomorrow."

"You've got to eat something. Can't go to sleep just yet."

Lily drifted. Arrow snuffled as she always did just before she dropped off. Rio yawned, straw rustled. A branch snapped under the heavy weight of snow and made a soft plopping noise. Firelight danced on her eyelids.

She knew she should eat. She had to take care of herself or she'd be no good to her dogs. But damn it, she was comfy. And warm for the first time in hours. Her breath warmed her throat and lower face; just her eyes were visible between her fur hat and the bag. She'd let the dogs rest for a couple of hours, perhaps four, then up the team, grab something to eat and slip out while Derek was sleeping.

A smile curved her mouth as she welcomed the grayness of sleep.

"Oh no, you don't. I slaved over a hot stove to keep this warm for you. Sit up."

"Derek, go away," Lily groaned. "Tol' you, not hungry." Her stomach cramped with hunger at the smell. God only knew, she'd eat the bowl and the spoon with it if she had one gram of energy left. Unfortunately she didn't.

"Up and open."

Derek hauled her to a sitting position by grabbing the head of the sleeping bag and yanking her upright.

"Bastard," Lily slurred without opening her eyelids, which were now leaded.

"Open."

"I'm n—" She got a spoonful of warm stew shoved into her mouth.

"Chew."

She chewed. It was good.

"Swallow." He sounded amused.

Lily swallowed, then opened her mouth again like a baby bird.

He laughed. Stubborn little pain in the ass. He fed her the entire bowl. All she'd been required to do was open her mouth, chew and swallow. The sleeping bag was gently lowered so she was once again lying flat.

"Had enough?" he asked, setting the bowl aside on his own bag. She didn't answer. Out like a light. Derek shook his head as he rose.

Throwing a few more logs on the fire, he went down the line and gave all thirty-two dogs a quick once-over before removing his boots and climbing into his own bag beside Lily.

He reached over and pulled her fur hat lower on her brow, then tucked the thermal bag tightly around her head.

He gazed up at the sky. The panoply of stars, unfaded by city lights, looked brilliant, and close enough to sift through his fingers. Through the black canopy of the trees sheltering them, the moon shone a brilliant golden white.

He turned his head to watch Lily as she slept. Long lashes shadowed her cheeks, and her lips were slightly parted. Derek suppressed his raging desire and maintained a tight control. Common sense ruled that he must. For now. He dare not rush her, though her response to him earlier had been encouraging. Unable to resist, he used a light finger to brush a silky strand of hair off her smooth cheek, then whispered softly, "You're going to be a hard nut, aren't you, my darling?"

Six

LILY'S DREAMS WERE FILLED WITH FLEETING IMAGES. SEAN. DIABLO. The house she'd hated from the moment her new husband had carried her over the threshold. Derek's mouth on hers, as soft as a breeze. The gentle touch of his hand against her cheek, the slide of warm fingers against her neck and down her throat. Lips followed his hand. His mouth brushed hers. Once, twice, a long pause filled with anticipation—and then again. A more lingering foray.

Instinctively, she opened her mouth to his. He'd kissed her before. All those years ago.

He'd kissed her outside the movie theater. His body sandwiching her between the cold metal of his truck and the furnace heat of his large body. The kiss had rocked Lily to her core. Admit it. She'd been scared of all that passion. Terrified that it would burn her to a crispy critter before the smoke settled and he'd be long gone. Taking her heart with him.

Sean had been the safer bet. Or so she had thought at the time. But this was a dream, and Derek's passion didn't scare her at all, here where she was safe and it was just make-believe. She opened her mouth and welcomed him in.

She gave a helpless moan of desire. Heat flooded her body as her tongue met his. The same as before, just the same, and yet better. His taste was familiar. The passion banked but just as compelling.

Lily gave herself up to the glory of it. The danger and comfort of it. If she fell, she knew he'd be there to catch her. Her body arched against his as he held her cradled in the safety of his arms.

Safe? No—she frowned in her sleep. Derek wasn't safe—Sean—no, God, no. *Sean wasn't safe—*

She didn't want to be afraid. She didn't want to think. This was her dream. Dreams weren't real.

He kissed her again, a slow, sweet, drugging kiss that rocked her to her core and made her body ache. Her heavy clothing seemed like a prison. She wanted his hands on her aching breasts. Between her legs, where she felt hot and damp. She wanted to lie naked with him and feel his mouth move down her body—

"Take off—" she said urgently against the mouth of her dream Derek as she tried to yank open her coat.

"Not here. Not now," he said with gentle amusement, pushing her hand aside with ease. "You certainly know how to test a man's forbearance, don't you, sweetheart?" he added dryly, brushing her cheek with his thumb. Like a kitten, Lily butted her head against his hand. She ached. She yearned. She wanted.

"We'll resume when you're awake enough to participate more fully. And that's a promise." Lips brushed hers once more before she felt the warmth of her sleeping bag being tugged up around her throat. The loss of his touch was devastating.

She whimpered from the loss. A gentle hand brushed a strand of hair off her cheek then lingered. "Woman of my dreams, what am I going to do with you?"

Wait, she wanted to say. *Wait. I want—I want—* But sleep rolled over her in an overwhelming rush.

LILY WOKE RELUCTANTLY BEFORE DAWN, THE DREAM STILL A FUZZY memory. Nightmare was more like it. It didn't matter that she'd enjoyed the dream. *Any* dream that included kissing Derek was classified as a nightmare. She glanced around their campsite, delaying getting up and determined to put the dream out of her mind.

The landscape was stark black and white. Ew, she didn't want to get out of the warm bag. Other teams had joined them during the night, she noticed. She hadn't heard a thing. Dogs and sleeping bags were gathered around the fire, which still burned brightly and gave off some warmth.

Derek lay facing her, asleep in his own sleeping bag several feet away. He had long lashes, she noticed. His black fur hat was pulled low over his brows, but his face was open to the elements. Didn't the man feel the cold?

She let her gaze drift from the long black lashes resting on his cheeks to his aquiline nose, his sharp cheekbones and then linger on his mouth.

She remembered the feel of those lips on hers. Remembered the taste of him. The feel of being held against his body. What she'd felt six years ago, the sexual energy between them, had scared her enough to make her retreat at a full gallop. That kind of heat could only be fleeting. Nobody could stand that kind of passion and survive. Not for long.

Part of the attraction she felt for him was the physical. He was so . . . *big.* He exuded power and strength. She'd feel completely safe from the world sheltered in his arms. It had been a long, long time since she'd felt completely safe emotionally.

And God only knew, just once she was tempted to give into the passion he always created in her when she was with him.

But the reality was, she was too intelligent to be fooled into thinking that she'd be safe for long. She knew herself too well. She'd sink into that heat, that power, and when it was withdrawn, as it would be eventually, she would have forgotten how to stand on her own two feet.

The reality was, she had only herself to rely on. Safety and security could disappear between one breath and the next.

Lily knew she had trust issues. Her mother's death had hit her hard. Her father's remarriage hadn't helped, and of course her marriage to Sean had capped off what seemed to be a losing streak. Nothing was forever.

She'd work through it. She would. And one day she'd start dating again. But this was neither the man nor the day.

Tempting as that proposition might be, she thought, wanting to sink her teeth into his lower lip as he slept. She gave herself a mental shake. No wonder she'd dreamed about Derek last night. Sneaky bastard. It was very, very rude of him to invade her dreams like that. And trust him to do it in Technicolor. The rat.

She still had sleep in her, and there was time to grab another couple of hours, but her bladder wasn't cooperating. And if she had to get up to answer the call of nature, she might as well be on her way. The sun would be up in another hour or so anyway.

She eased her way out of the warmth of the bag, careful not to wake the man sleeping so close to her. Geez, did he have any sense of personal space?

She pulled on her boots and slid out of her bag. She stowed it away, then with a quick glance around slipped into the trees above their camp.

Her butt was about to get a horrible shock, she thought with a grimace. No matter how many times she had to do this, she never got used to it.

The diffused chiffon gray of the sky cast soft, velvety shadows in the snow. Lily gazed up. It was going to be a snowy day.

A cup of coffee, a snack for the kids and they'd be on their way. She'd noticed a couple of the other mushers wandering into the trees to take care of business too. She'd like to beat them onto the trail.

The dogs hadn't stirred earlier. As her boots crunched in the snow, she checked them, deciding to wait until the most tired dog showed signs of waking. That would be Dingbat. He was always the last to get his little doggie act together in the mornings. A faint fragrance of last night's coffee and stew still hung in the air, a reminder that she would kill for a cup of coffee this morning.

Lily slowed down, enjoying the stillness of the morning and the anticipation of the day ahead. The back of her neck prickled as though someone was watching her. Silly. No one would be rude enough to watch her. They all had to go to the bathroom sometime.

While she mentally mapped the trail between here and Finger Lake she inhaled deeply. The air smelled intoxicatingly clean, of snow and pine and wood smoke.

Far enough from the others to ensure a little privacy, Lily found a handy tree and went about the unveiling ceremony with great urgency and grim reluctance. Geez, it was cold! Icy air radiated up her bare butt, and she tried to hurry.

A sharp crack shattered the stillness. A small flock of sleepy birds squawked out of a nearby tree a split second later, almost giving Lily heart failure. She held on to her garments and grabbed a spiky branch for balance. A bullet slammed into the shrub beside her, spitting bits of bark and snow into the air.

My God.

Someone was *shooting* at her.

Out of the blank stillness of the morning, another sharp crack split the air. The sound ricocheted off the mountains, then echoed eerily around her.

PIIING. Piiing. Piiing.

Lily looked around wildly. Where were the shots coming from? And what moron was shooting? Morning shadows still lay deep and impenetrable around trees and in the dips and valleys of the snowy monochrome landscape. The sun hadn't yet risen beyond a mere promise over the mountains behind her. Only the most meager of washed-out illumination bathed the tips of the peaks like weak spotlights gradually reflecting the bright white of the snow.

A bullet whizzed from behind her and slammed past her upper arm. A startled scream burst from her throat. "Hey!" She tried to rise, to run and hide, but stumbled against the pants still bunched around her knees. She tipped over sideways like a Weeble.

"Aaargh!" Her bare bottom smacked the snow. A mixture of blind fury fought a battle with tangible fear. Cursing, she kneeled, then got her bare behind out of the cold by pulling up her pants—all the while keeping her head lowered and her body crouched protectively.

"Damn it to hell, you moron!" she yelled at the unseen hunter as she continued with her battle against recalcitrant clothing and intimately clinging snow. Slapping layers and layers of shirt, sweater and coat out of her way with hands that shook, she swore. Where the *hell* was the zipper? Layers were great protection from the elements, but they were a bitch when one was running for her life and trying to find her own waistband. She must have pulled up seven garments and she still couldn't find the small tongue of the zipper.

Two feet away, snow sprayed up in a mini-explosion.

"Dammit to hell! Do I *look* like a freaking deer?"

Slithering and sliding, Lily tried to get her feet under her while attempting to zip up her pants with thickly gloved hands. *Come on. Come on. Come on.*

The weasel dog, whoever he was! He'd probably been watching her the whole time— Oh, God. That meant that he *knew* she wasn't an animal. The jerk. This was some sick game. She wished she had her own rifle so she could turn the tables and fire off a few rounds, and scare *him* to death.

Lily's face burned with frustration, her behind burned with cold. When had she lost the ability to dress herself, for heaven's sake? Pretty much about the same time someone had started taking potshots.

She grabbed the fingertips of her left glove with her teeth and yanked it off so she could at least get her pants done up.

As she dipped her head to see what she was doing, Lily noticed her sleeve. The blood drained from her head. The shot had torn through two thick layers. The hide of her favorite sheepskin coat sported two neat round bullet holes.

The stupid son of a bitch. She stuck a finger in the hole the bullet had made and stared at it. Had he hit her? She didn't *feel* any pain. . . . *Move!* What the hell was she doing? No time to sit and assess the damage.

She was a sitting duck out here in her dark coat on the pristine white snow. She might as well paint a red bull's-eye around herself. The only tree or shrub within fifty feet of where she'd been was her little toilet bush. Clearly no match for a bullet. Her footprints stretched down the hill behind her like twin arrows pointing to where she now stood.

Moron or not, she wasn't sticking around to argue with the anonymous and clearly deranged hunter. She wouldn't waste time looking for him either. She started running like a chicken with its head cut off back toward camp.

It was heavy going. The snow was deep and wet. Her thigh muscles ached and her lungs were about to burst with the effort it took to draw in each frozen breath.

Another *weeeeee* of a bullet.

This one slammed into the snow several feet to the front and left of her. A renewed and urgent fear rippled through the irritation burning inside her. She was in the open.

How far had she walked to find the perfect private spot for her bathroom? A hundred freaking miles? While she'd been in the bushes the shooter could have mistaken her for a deer, but now that she'd reached open ground there was no mistaking her human, two-legged form. Someone was after her.

Another shot. This one zipped past her, barely. *Way* too close for comfort. Breath a white plume, Lily put on more speed, not wasting time looking back.

Another shot. Her hat flew from her head.

"Damn it to hell! Stop shooting!" Lily screamed at the top of her aching lungs as she ran. Surely to God the people back at camp— *Derek*—could hear the shots? Where was everyone? Fear muted her hearing as blood rushed into her ears. Somebody up there was aiming directly at her. Deliberately.

Impossible. Ridiculous. But fact.

Safety was a hundred yards up ahead behind a thick stand of trees. Yet the snow here was too deep for running.

The dark bulk of a man came barreling out of the trees up ahead, running straight for her. Lily turned around and beat it the other way.

"Lily! Down! Get down."

Derek. Thank God. She needed no further urging. She dropped where she stood. Face-first in the crunchy snow. It hurt like hell, but she kept her face mashed in the icy surface and covered her head with her arms. Like that was going to stop a bullet from entering her brain.

She tilted her frosty face to yell a warning to him: "Watch out." A volley of shots followed in quick succession. A minute, an hour, a year later, Lily heard shouting through the blood pounding in her ears. The other mushers to the rescue. Yeah! The cavalry had arrived.

Coats flapping, hats askew, the mushers came charging up the hill toward them.

"What's happening?"

"—heard shots."

"—Who—"

"What the fuck—"

Derek was on her before Lily could stagger upright.

"Are you hurt?" he demanded urgently, wrapping a large hand around her upper arm and hoisting her to her feet in one smooth move. In his other hand he held a rifle.

"Where are you hurt? Did he get you?" He turned her around to inspect her back, her front. Saw her sleeve with the entry and exit holes and went white and tight-lipped. He started yanking off her coat.

"Wait. I'm fine, I'm fine!" Lily yelled as he ripped off her warm coat and started tugging at her sweater to draw it over her head. It was freezing and he was trying to get her clothes off. "Whoa, big boy."

She slapped at his hand, but he was so intent on seeing if she was hurt he didn't hear her. Eventually she grabbed his gloved hand and held it. "It's just my coat. I'm okay. I'm okay."

His dark scowl and grim mouth said he didn't believe her. "Sure?"

"Yes. I lost my favorite hat, and my coat looks like a moth with an attitude dropped by, but I'm okay."

"Rob. Don. Sandy," Derek called over his shoulder, scanning her features with eyes like laser beams. "Get her back to camp, check her for bullet holes and stick to her like white on rice." The frighteningly remote expression on his face made the hair on the back of Lily's neck stand up. His eyes looked flat and light-absorbing, his mouth grim.

This wasn't the suave, charming, laid-back Derek Wright she knew. This man, this *stranger,* was a warrior.

The three men came huffing and puffing to join them. "I can get myself back to camp," Lily told them urgently. "Go with Derek."

"Stay with *her,*" he told them, removing a small handgun from beneath his coat. He then turned and ran toward the trees to the left and above them, gun in one hand, rifle in the other.

"Holy shit," Rob Stuart said with awe as he watched Derek disappear over a berm. "Is he a cop?"

"N-no. A rancher." She buttoned her coat with shaky fingers. She'd never, in the six years she'd known him, seen Derek with that expression on his face as he'd hauled her to her feet.

Intense. Murderous. Terrifying.

Then . . . nothing. Blank. Cold. Merciless.

Lily shuddered, cold right down to the marrow. And it had nothing to do with the snow slowly melting inside her pants.

Don Singleton came and put a beefy arm around her. "Were you hurt? Did you see the guy?"

"No and no," Lily told him uncomfortably. She stepped out of his hold as casually as possible. What was it about the men she knew? Oh, Lily, get over yourself, she thought, suddenly amused with her own ego. Better a little female vanity than thinking about what had almost just happened. *That* made her knees feel like jelly.

The three men gathered protectively around her, rifles in their hands, but they were a lot more interested in watching Derek racing toward the tree line above them and speculating about the shooter.

"Let's get back to camp, little girl," Don said. "Get some hot coffee into you and you can tell us what happened up there."

"Sure," Lily agreed. "Let's." Everyone around her carried a rifle.

As she should have been, damn it. She knew better. But it wouldn't do any good to berate herself now. Now she could only think of Derek plunging off to do battle with . . . *who*? How many rounds did he have in his rifle and gun? How many had he started with? And how many were left? And where had he come from? He'd been ahead of the other mushers by minutes.

Lily felt a little foggy now that it was over. Surely *Derek* wouldn't be shooting at her? Nah. That was ridiculous. Embarrassment and an icy butt had addled her brain. The shots had come from behind her, Derek appeared in front of her: couldn't be him.

"Just kids out trying to bag a moose or something," she told the others with conviction. She listened halfheartedly to the wild speculations, and pushed aside the ridiculous notion that the shooting had been intentional and aimed at her.

Definitely, positively not accidental. There'd been too many shots and they'd all been close together. *Had* the shooter been aiming for her? Or had he been aiming for any musher and she'd pulled the short straw?

Some environmentalists or an Iditarod detractor? They could be a bit extreme. But would they stoop to shooting the mushers?

She couldn't imagine anyone wanting *her* dead. Unless . . . Lily felt bile rise in the back of her throat. Unless someone knew she'd been in the barn that day. Unless someone knew she'd overheard them talking.

God. Was it possible?

Could this be connected to the bull-sperm sales?

Lily tucked her hands into her pockets and hunched her shoulders to keep her ears warm. "Thanks for coming to my rescue, guys. I'm more than ready for that cup of coffee. If that kid's smart he'll high-tail it before he gets busted."

"STUPID FUCKING BITCH. DID YOU SEE THAT? FLOPPED AROUND LIKE A flounder and made me miss her by a goddamned country mile." The sniper didn't lift his cheek from the rifle as the other man walked up behind him.

How had the fucking sniper known he was behind him?

"Are you out of your fucking mind?" He couldn't believe they'd sent someone else to do his job. "What the fuck are you thinking, dickhead? How will *shooting* her look like a goddamn accident?"

The sniper shrugged, then squeezed off another shot. "Who gives a damn? Could be a hunter or something."

"Could be a fucking *moron* or something. Get lost. I have the job under control. Go back and tell the bosses that." He'd heard the first shot from down below and raced up here in the snowmobile, dreading who he might find. Of course it *would* be this soulless asshole. He'd do anything or anyone for a buck.

How had he known they'd send someone like this to check up on him? Because he was smarter than the average ranch hand, that's how. "Did anyone *tell* you to fucking shoot her?" he demanded when the sniper kept right on shooting as though he weren't there. "And what the fuck are you doing messing with my job anyhow?"

The sniper squeezed off another shot. "You've had plenty of time to do your job. I'm insurance. Stand still, Leaking Lily," he told her. He'd watched her pee through his up-close-and-personal scope. Nice ass. Of course she'd made him miss that prime shot, doing all that wiggling and squirming and getting him hot. And now having numbnuts behind him breathing down his neck didn't help matters.

"Back off, would ya? You're making me miss my shot, and your breath stinks like you just ate rat turds." He continued to aim and fire. It was like trying to shoot a lab rat in a maze. Irritating and time-consuming. And ultimately a waste of good bullets. Not that that was stopping him. There was a chance he could still get her.

"Know what I think? I think I don't like you pissin' in my pond." The man had been paid ten large to off Dr. Munroe. It was a matter of fucking pride. He slid the knife out of the scabbard at his hip, and with a quick, violent movement swiped the blade across the bastard's throat.

The shooter gagged and gurgled; his warm blood gushed out over his hand and the knife. The man's wet glove slipped a little on the hilt of the knife, but he slashed again at the sniper's throat. A little lower this time. Blood spurted out in a showy arc and splattered the snow in red confetti-like droplets. His heart raced. Fuck. This was cool. Really. Amazingly cool. He slashed again. And again.

The moron gurgled, choking on his own blood, but continued struggling in his hold. "Shut up, dickhead. Just shut the fuck up. This"—he slashed again—"is for pissin' in my pond. And this is for giving me a load of shit about it." Adrenaline raced through his body like the speed he'd taken that time. Fuck. He was invincible. This was un-fucking-believable. He loved it.

He'd found a new hobby. Better than money. Better than drugs.

"Woo-hoo, bro," he chuckled, dancing around while still hanging on to the man slumped in his hold. "I am *diggin'* this. I surely am."

The sniper's knees buckled—*'bout time, goddamn it!*—and almost pulled him over. "No fight left in you now, is there, you dickhead?

"As much as I'd enjoy hangin' around and playing some more, I think you prob'ly pissed off the boss man. He's gonna come up here to wup your ass." He laughed out loud at what Wright was gonna find when he showed up. Man. This was startin' to be an interesting adventure. That's for sure.

With an upward thrust, he buried the knife to the hilt in the dick-head's kidney before he knew what was happening. A neat little trick he'd learned in Nam. The shithead crumpled to the ground without a peep.

He stripped off his sodden gloves and wiped his hands on the dead man's coat. Then casually slipped on the nice clean fur-lined gloves the other man had conveniently stuffed into his pockets. "Thanks, man."

He picked up the rifle. Nice. He didn't have one of these. He hefted it in his gloved hands. Yeah. Real nice. The spoils of war. He'd keep it as a memento.

He held it up and looked through the scope. Oh, yeah. The shit had hit the fan down there, all right. *What a dimwit!* Here came Wright to the rescue. He turned the barrel of the rifle to the left and scoped out Derek Wright's face. Man, he'd love to blow *that* all-knowing, all-seeing dick away. He looked at Wright through the high-powered scope. Looked like the son of a bitch was looking right back. Man, his eyes were cold.

Fear coiled in his belly. He resented the fuck out of it even though he couldn't quite shake the sensation. Wright *couldn't* see him with the naked eye.

But he wasn't being paid to off the rancher. Still, maybe later, he'd toss Derek Wright in as a freebie. If he felt like some real sport—

Time to book.

NOT A HUNTER, DEREK KNEW WITH UTMOST CERTAINTY. HE RECOG-nized the sound. Only a high-powered, fully scoped rifle made that kind of echo.

A sniper.

An *inept* sniper.

He frowned. Jesus. He didn't know anyone like that. The people in his line of work, and the tangos they dealt with, were, on the whole, damn accurate. So what he had here was an amateur sniper?

Who'd he pissed off lately in his civilian life?

He bit back a smile. Besides Lily.

He smelled death before he saw it.

Sam Croft. Derek recognized the man immediately, and frowned as he crouched down to feel for a pulse. There wasn't one. Not sur-prising. This was a bloodbath. His marrow chilled at the sight of such horrific violence. Not that he wasn't used to seeing scenes like this. Not in his line of work. What chilled him was how close this violent death had come to *Lily*.

His two worlds were colliding.

For one of the few times in his life, Derek tasted fear. Croft had worked for him. Sean had hired him about a year ago. The guy was quiet, and kept pretty much to himself. He was a decent hand, and there'd never been any problem other than a couple of fistfights on a Friday night after payday. Not uncommon.

What the hell was Croft doing in Alaska? Was he the one shooting at Lily? It didn't make sense. Derek rolled him. A blur of red marked where the man had been stabbed in the kidney. Jesus. Talk about overkill. The killer had sure as hell enjoyed his work.

But whoever had killed *him* sure as hell knew what he was doing.

But why kill Croft? Because he'd taken a shot at Lily? Or because he'd missed?

Derek rose to his feet, taking in the scene. Croft had probably been the sniper. He'd stood right here. . . . Derek scanned the valley below from the sniper's vantage point. He followed Lily's zigzagging footprints down the hill, imagined her panic and terror. He remembered her white face and frightened eyes.

"Son of a bitch." He turned to look back at the body, and at the footprints behind it to try and reenact what had occurred before he'd arrived at the scene. "Someone crept up behind you, didn't they, asshole? Someone you knew?" Derek narrowed his eyes at the footprints.

"Yeah. You knew each other. He didn't scare you. You never turned around, did you? But he stood right there behind you. Talked for a few minutes, perhaps. Then he grabbed you from behind and slit your throat." He looked at the spatter pattern. "Over and over and over again.

"To stop you from shooting Lily?" Derek asked, still sorting out the footsteps imprinted in the bloody snow, trying to figure out who did what. Trying not to think of Lily, but instead to think like the operative he was. Cold. Methodical. Detached. "Or as a warning to me?"

He crouched again and searched the dead man's pockets. Nothing. The sniper's rifle was glaringly absent. Nearby, a pair of red-drenched leather gloves. Nothing else was on the hill but the body and the churned-up boot prints of the two men. No shell casings, no indication of who the other person was or what he'd wanted.

"Let's you and I have a chat, pal," Derek said grimly, turning to track the widely spaced steps leading away from the scene of the crime and deep into the forest. The second guy had walked in, run out. Judging by the spacing and depth of his footprints, the man was probably medium height, about 150 to 160 pounds. He tried to place anyone of that general description hanging around Croft back at the ranch. No one came to mind. The hand had been a loner, as were many of the men that worked for the Flying F.

Dawn turned the snow a milky pink and lightened the chiffon gray of the sky to a pale, soft smoky blue. The air was cold enough to slice a man's lungs, but it smelled of pine and was as fresh and intoxicating as the scent of newly mowed grass on a summer morning. Derek was used to snow. Enjoyed it in fact. He'd spent a brutal couple of weeks last year in the Ural Mountains to the east of Belarus tracking a high-profile terrorist, and had enjoyed the hell out of pitting his strength and intellect against a man who'd been born in that unforgiving landscape.

He'd not only captured the tango, he'd hauled his ass all the way back to Minsk for extradition. No, the cold didn't bother him. Truth be told, he found ranching in Montana's arctic winters to be a damn sight more challenging than anything he'd faced in the field.

The question here was, why had Croft been shooting at Lily? And was Lily the one he'd been aiming for? If so, he was, thank God, a lousy shot. Still, she could've been seriously hurt. Intentional or not.

Croft wasn't a professional hit man. Not even close. He'd missed too many times. Still, Derek's blood ran cold. Dressed as Lily had been, and from this distance, it was possible she'd been mistaken for a man.

For *him*?

Possible, but not probable if the guy had been using a scope, which at that range he would've done. He would've seen exactly who his target was. Croft worked for him. He knew who Lily was. He'd've recognized her almost immediately.

Besides, the idea that anyone would want to hurt Lily was illogical. She was a country vet. She didn't *have* any enemies. Everyone loved her. She was gentle, and God only knew, kind to a fault. She'd rather bite her tongue than hurt anyone. He was, apparently, the exception, Derek thought wryly.

Croft couldn't possibly have been shooting at her. He let the cold ball of fear dissipate from his stomach. No. For some reason Croft had been trying to smoke *him* out.

Lily'd been the bait.

But who had killed Croft? And more important—*why*?

Seven

DEREK FOLLOWED A FAINT TRAIL UP THE MOUNTAINSIDE. HE tugged his fur hat more securely over his ears as he tracked the second man's footprints straight up and over the rise. It was a steep climb to the ridge. The guy had slipped here, indicated by the running steps and churned-up snow. Fleeing the scene of the crime. "Yeah. You were in a hurry," Derek said harshly. "Weren't you, you bastard? Did you get off on the stink of blood? Did you watch his eyes as he died?"

He tracked for twenty minutes before reaching the summit of the hill and coming across the treads, narrow, sledlike ruts made by a high-powered Polaris XL snowmobile.

He stopped. No point continuing. Narrow-eyed, he visually followed the tracks of the vehicle until they disappeared over the next rise. Somewhere down there, another vehicle must be hidden by the trees. He'd send a team in to pick it and Croft's body up later.

His sat phone vibrated against his chest just as he turned to go back down. He paused to take the small phone from his breast pocket. "Talk to me."

"Elevated to code three," Darius, his control, said briskly, sounding as though he were standing right there on the breeze-swept hillside beside Derek. More than an alert, T-FLAC was now taking the Alaskan terror threat to the next level.

"Four *w*'s?" Derek asked Darius as he continued walking, indicating *who, where, what, when*. He slung the strap of his rifle over his shoulder, but kept the Baer firmly in his left hand. He hastened his steps. For all he knew the killer would double back and show up at the camp in the valley below. And while he knew Lily and the men with her all carried weapons, he would be a hell of a lot more confident if he was there with her himself.

"The who is Oslukivati," Darius told him. "All we have right now is that they've been sighted in your neck of the woods."

Oslukivati was a Serb group known for their expertise with dirty bombs. They particularly enjoyed blowing things up. They'd blown up the Zimbabwe airport at high noon on a Friday before a holiday weekend, killing several thousand people. They were responsible for the bombing of the South African consulate in London and the total destruction of a train station in Prague. Usually they wanted their people freed from some prison somewhere. But in most cases, it would take years to track down and round up the prisoners, and they were some of the most dangerous tangos on the planet. Their freedom was nonnegotiable.

"What are their demands?" Not that Derek gave a fuck, but he was mildly interested to know.

"Haven't made any. Yet."

Unnecessary, but a given: Whatever they wanted, they wouldn't get.

It would now be a race to see who won before something went up with a big, spectacular bang and hundreds of people died.

"Alaska Pipeline?" Derek asked, interest sparking. He thrived on the chase. God only knew, he was already on the most important one of his life. A terrorist warning would be the whipped cream on his sundae. There was an outside chance that the two were interconnected. But he doubted it. Very few people knew he worked for the anti-terrorist group.

"No," Darius said in his ear. "Not even in the neighborhood of the pipeline. Word is something bigger, with more of an 'Oh my God' factor. Your old pal Milos Pekovic is up to his ass in this one. Personally."

Pekovic. Just the bastard's name made the scar over Derek's kidney ache. The terrorist's group was large and far-reaching. Derek's most recent run-in with Pekovic had been seven months and almost one lost kidney ago in San Cristóbal. The man liked to be hands-on, and he enjoyed getting his hands dirty. It was a wonder he ever got the blood off. The terrorist was brutal, soulless and unstoppable. Known as the Butcher because that had been his profession before he started amassing large groups of rabid followers to his cause. Milos Pekovic and Derek had been dancing around each other for nine years. And they both had the scars to prove it.

Derek didn't flatter himself that the leader of one of the top-five terrorist groups was up here in Alaska just for him. But he bet if Pekovic knew he *was* here, it would add that extra fillip to whatever the hell the man was hell-bent on doing.

Their association had long ago gone from business to personal.

Off the top of his head, Derek couldn't think of a damn thing the terrorist group would want to annihilate way the hell up here in Alaska. If not the pipeline, then *what*? "My neck of the woods is pretty damn vast at the moment. Can we pinpoint a location?" he asked Darius as he followed his own tracks back to camp.

"Working on it."

"Timing?"

"Imminent."

"Jesus, Dare, you're not exactly a mine of information, are you?"

"We're sending your brothers to the wedding a bit early, with a detour to you. By the time we've gathered all the intel, they'll be there to have your back."

"Nice to know," Derek said dryly. Since Michael, Kyle, and his

twin, Kane, were coming at the end of the month anyway, they'd get
a free trip. Not that any of them needed it. Since they all worked for
the anti-terrorist organization, they'd covered one another's backs on
several assignments. Derek was pleased at the news.

"Intel is on this twenty-four/seven," Dare told him. "Keep you
posted."

"Anything else?"

"Not yet."

He'd have to be satisfied with the nebulous threat. For now. He
quickly filled Dare in on the shooter and the current situation.

"Doesn't sound like your pal Pekovic."

"The knife business gave me pause. But Pekovic is more controlled. He likes to get up close and personal with his kills. This was
done with relish, but not with Pekovic's attention to detail." Pekovic
better not come within a thousand miles of Lily, Derek thought
grimly.

"Watch your back." Dare concurred with Derek's assessment of
the situation.

They concluded the call, and Derek continued down to camp,
feeling a sense of urgency now that he knew his archenemy was
somewhere in Alaska. Big state, but at the moment, not nearly big
enough when Lily was in the same neck of the woods. Couple that
with a vindictive killer and it was a recipe for gut-wrenching worry.

This damn sniper thing bothered him. It just didn't make any kind
of sense.

He'd report the incident at the next checkpoint, and warn other
mushers that someone was up here taking target practice on the trail.

As for Lily, Derek promised himself, *he'd* be keeping a tight rein
on her. Whether she liked it or not.

"I bet the little boogers were long gone, weren't they?" Lily
rose from behind a fallen log. Clicking on the safety, she put the
nine-millimeter she'd been holding back into her pocket. Derek was
pleased to see that not only was she armed, she'd positioned herself

with her back against a broad tree with an unimpeded view of the clearing.

"Didn't see anything." His gaze swept the snow-laden landscape around them.

"Couldn't have been kids," Lily muttered, more to herself than to him. "Locals are smarter than to hunt so close to the race trail."

"Definitely not kids," he said, handing her her hat, which he'd picked up on the way back. "They'd've left tracks."

His gaze shifted to the worry-etched lines between her brows and he could have kicked himself. But if she hadn't already thought of everything he'd just said, she soon would have. Stupid, she wasn't.

Her cheeks were pink and shiny with cold, which made her long-lashed hazel eyes brilliant in contrast. She looked like a poster girl for the benefits of outdoor living. Healthy and natural. Beautiful in a subtle, understated way that made his mouth water and his heart do calisthenics whenever he saw her.

Every time he saw her, whether a month or an hour ago, he always experienced the same punch to the gut.

"Thanks for this. My ears are frozen." She tugged on the hat. The soft gray and white fur framed her face, and the silky length of her honey-brown braid fell over the front of her thick coat. He'd had some intense dreams about that spill of rich pale brown hair gliding across his naked body. The anticipation might very well kill him.

He dragged his attention away from her. Both sleds were neatly packed, the dogs ready to go. Nobody else was in the clearing. Fury, not far from the surface for the past several hours, rose up inside him.

"Where," he said dangerously, remembering that her coat had two freaking damn bullet holes in it, "are the others?"

Oblivious, Lily poured a steaming mug of coffee from a Thermos and handed it to him. He took it with a frown. "I told the men to stay here until I got back."

"I believe the general consensus was that they don't work for you."

"You were *shot* at," he reminded her.

"They *missed*," she reminded him. "Besides, I have Wayne here," she said mildly, patting her pocket and the nine-millimeter she'd tucked inside. "I told them they might as well get a jump-start on us." She drank from her own cup, then cocked her head. "You said yourself you didn't find anyone out there, right?"

"That's beside the point." He wasn't going to tell her about Croft. No point scaring her just now. "And *they* weren't privy to that information." *Jesus*—he pulled his temper back a couple of notches. It was futile getting pissed. The three men were relative strangers and, as Lily had pointed out, not under his command. Still, they didn't know if the shooter would double back and use Lily for target practice again. He'd thought Don Singleton at least would stick to Lily like glue.

"Most likely some stray jerk trying to make trouble for the racers," Derek lied. He wasn't going to lose sleep over Croft.

A flash of fear backlit her expressive eyes, quickly masked as she went back to sipping her coffee. "We'll keep an ear and eye out for them just in case, and report them, him, at Finger Lake."

Damn it. She shouldn't have to be afraid. *Ever.*

"I see you're ready to go," he said briskly, tamping down an unfamiliar and toxic combination of fear and worry. Darius was looking into the Croft situation, as well as his possible killer; in the meantime *he* would stick to Lily like oil on a gun barrel. "I'm surprised you didn't take off ahead of me."

Lily made a rude noise. "Oh, please, like I'd have to cheat to beat you."

"No. You wouldn't cheat, would you, Lily?" He walked over and cupped her cheek. Her skin felt icy cold under his hand. They were close enough for their breath to touch in the frigid air.

She licked her lower lip, a smooth, sensual swipe of her tongue that was totally without guile, but that sent a spurt of fire to his groin.

"Don't be too nice to me right now." Her voice was husky, her pupils large as she stared up at him. The fact that she wasn't backing up as she usually did when he got this close was a gift.

He stroked her cheek with his thumb, a light, controlled caress when what he needed was to pull her hard against him and crush her mouth under his. He brushed her smooth skin again and took pleasure in watching heat seep into her cheeks as her eyes started losing focus.

"Why not?" he asked.

She gave a small frown, as though she'd just now realized they were standing a breath apart and he was caressing her face. But she didn't move away. Instead she shot him a familiar I-know-what-you're-doing-and-it-doesn't-affect-me-in-the-least look.

Except when their eyes met, they clung, and that brief glance sizzled with electricity. They stood staring at each other, breath visibly commingling in the cold air. "I've had enough of an adrenaline rush for the day," Lily told him, and there was a faint tremor in her voice.

Oh, he couldn't resist *that* challenge. He used both hands to cup her face and took no satisfaction at her small jolt of surprise. He bent his head and kissed her. A sweet, drugging kiss. Not too much tongue, just enough to have hers come out tentatively to play. She tasted of coffee and winter-fresh toothpaste.

He'd kissed her harder and longer that night he'd taken her to dinner and a movie all those years ago. It had been summer, and as busy as he'd been on the ranch, he'd made time to see her. She'd worn a pale mint-green sundress, her tanned, toned arms and legs bare. Just seeing her feet bare, in strappy sandals, for the first time had given him an uncomfortable hard-on. He'd pressed her against his car out in the parking lot of the movie theater like a randy teenager. She'd given just as good as she got. Wrapping her arms around his neck and pressing herself flush against him, she'd given him tongue and with a little time, she would've given him her body.

Instead she'd avoided his calls for days and then gone out with his best friend.

No. This time he was going to pace himself. Give her time. He lifted his head using every ounce of control he possessed.

"I hope you appreciate my restraint," he said gently, dropping one more feather-light brush to her mouth before she could say anything. Then he gently took her shoulders and gave her a little push toward her waiting sled.

Without looking back, Lily stalked off, but not before he saw the bewilderment, desire and conflict play across her expressive face after he'd kissed her.

He laughed ruefully to himself as he mounted his own sled. It was going to be a battle, but hell, he'd fought harder wars and won. And this time, the battle was all-important.

"Hike!" they said in unison, and their teams lit out of the clearing as if jet propelled. Neck and neck.

Derek laughed with satisfaction as Lily streaked off ahead of him. "Frustrated and confused is just the way I want to keep you, sweetheart," he told her retreating back. "Frustrated and confused."

LILY GLANCED UP AT THE LOW CLOUDS OVERHEAD. IT LOOKED LIKE more snow. She'd made good time, leaving Finger Lake early enough in the day to travel the worst parts of the trail in the daylight. Going over the ridge to Red Lake, then continuing on to Rainy Pass was always extraordinarily difficult. Traveling it in the daylight, such as it was, was difficult enough. She sure as hell didn't want to do it at night. Not when the trail climbed wooded shelves interspersed with patches of muddy levy and decaying foliage.

After that, there'd be a steep drop down to a series of forested benches toward Happy River, then onto the frozen river itself via the dreaded Happy River steps. It was going to be another long day.

Right now it looked more like dusk than noon. The dogs liked the weather well enough, though. For them, twenty below was just right.

"How're you doing, Doc?" Derek asked in her ear. It was strangely intimate, listening and talking to him without being face-to-face. It was actually quite nice having company on the run. She usually listened to music, but enjoyed hours of solitude as well. Having someone to share what she was seeing on the trail was . . . nice.

Though they might allow an hour or so of silence, there was something immensely comforting knowing Derek was never more than a whisper away. Then he'd break the silence to point out an ob-

stacle to watch for, or tell her to look to the right at the next bend to
see a bird's nest at eye level.

It pleased her that he wasn't hesitant to ask for her advice when he
needed it. He'd only run two races, and she was more experienced.
At least in this instance. He'd put on a good burst of speed after the
last stop, and was ahead of her by about fifteen minutes. Not much.
She'd catch up and then wave to him over her shoulder as she passed
him.

Lily had taken a precious twenty minutes to shower and put on
fresh clothing at the last stop. Some people stayed unshowered for the
entire race. She wasn't one of them. She didn't mind *getting* dirty, but
she had a big problem with *being* dirty. Apparently so did Derek.
She'd learned he'd been in the shower just ahead of her. As if she
needed to be told. She had recognized the signature scent of his soap
and the hint of his shaving cream the instant she'd stepped inside the
makeshift stall.

It was amazing and more than a little disconcerting to realize just
how familiar he was to her—how many intimate details regarding
him were stored without authorization in her consciousness.

Odd that she couldn't summon a single intimate memory of her
late husband but she had a vivid catalog of her awareness of Derek.
She didn't even need to close her eyes to remember the feel of his
hands on her body.

She gave herself a mental slap and came back to reality. He was
staying just ahead of her all the way. Annoying man. She needed to
catch up and pass him soon.

"I had to leave Ajax at the food drop," she told him absently, keeping an eye out for . . . anything. Still a little spooked by the shooting
that morning, she constantly had the sensation of being watched. Even
though she'd convinced herself the hunter, or whoever, wouldn't be
following the Iditarod trail, a small corner of her mind worried. When
she'd stopped to check the dogs earlier she'd been tense the entire
time, waiting for the *someone* to start taking potshots again.

Nothing had happened. Of course it hadn't. She felt a little silly
for her paranoia. But a spot between her shoulder blades continued

to itch, so paranoid or not, she kept her nine-millimeter within easy reach. She'd also removed her rifle from the scabbard in the sled, and kept it close at hand. Better safe than sorry.

"The dog okay?" Derek asked, his voice a low rumble in her ear.

"He will be."

Ajax had somehow managed to tear a nail and had been limping badly. Glad she'd stopped, Lily had loaded him into the sled and dropped him at the next checkpoint. He'd be flown back to Anchorage. People had won the race with fewer dogs, but Rio was as dependable as the sunrise and had a strong back and a determination to one day be lead dog, Lily could tell. Just as she knew her lead dog Arrow had a thing for Derek's lead dog Max. The animals were always nuzzling each other and had even slept curled beside each other last night. Maybe they were in love. She laughed at herself. Lust was more like it. Max and Derek had that much in common.

"What?" Derek's voice sounded smoky and intimate, and almost right inside her head.

She'd forgotten he could hear her. "Dad always complains because I anthropomorphize—if that's even a word—the dogs."

"Since you practically live with them, I don't think it's strange you give them human characteristics," Derek said easily. "You probably know them better than you do most humans."

"I like them better most of the time, too," Lily told him dryly. She narrowed her eyes. Was Opal limping now too? She'd keep an eye on her for another mile or two.

"Is that why you became a vet?"

Lily smiled. "That and all the money I make." What she earned had always been a joke to Sean. He'd told her she'd earn more waiting tables at the Dipsy Diner on Main Street. Their county wasn't big enough to support three full-time veterinarians.

Still, she loved what she did. Matt and her dad actually handled everything but the Flying F. The ranch, and the breeding and training of her dogs, kept Lily busy. Her marrying Sean had worked for all of them. She'd supervised the breeding program to increase the herd. In fact, she'd named Diablo when Sean and Derek had brought the vicious-looking, three-and-a-half-million-dollar bull home. She'd had to authenticate every vial of Diablo's sperm that sold. Clearly Sean had forged her signature on the fake vials.

Of course she hadn't known anything then. Other than she'd found Prince Charming, he adored her and she was going to marry him. She'd loved the way he teased her, and the way his brown eyes warmed when he was with her. She'd loved his flirting and the way he made her feel like a woman, even when she was dressed in jeans and work boots.

She'd been blind and naive. Stupid and trusting.

Not anymore.

"I don't see you taking your loot and heading off to Fiji."

"I'm not big on traveling," she said, admiring the way the light struck the snow, making it look like whipped cream.

"You went to Montreal on your honeymoon."

"We didn't get out much," she fibbed, feeling the remembered weight of fury and humiliation tighten her chest. Sean had flirted with a sleek redhead in the bar. The second night of their honeymoon, he'd come back to the room at midnight, smelling of expensive perfume and reminding her that men weren't programmed to be monogamous.

Lily had tipped the room service tray that had sat there untouched for five hours onto his expensive suit. Then she'd told Sean that good manners suggested that he at least wait until the honeymoon was over before screwing some French hooker he'd picked up in the bar.

Devastated by his betrayal, she'd immediately moved to another room. She despised liars.

Sean had quickly learned that his loving country wife had reached her saturation point and had an intolerance for one more ounce of bullshit.

Furious with herself for being oblivious to all the clues, Lily was also disgusted with herself for being blind to Sean's faults. And God only knew, there were a lot of them.

Hurt and bewildered by the sudden change in a man she believed loved her, Lily was at a loss. She was on her honeymoon. The beginning of their lives. Together. And now that life had gone up in smoke right before her very eyes.

Hurt. Angry. Confused. She was all of those. And worse. She felt stupid. And, damn him to hell, *used*.

She'd spent her honeymoon exploring a city made for lovers. Alone.

That had been the beginning of the end for them. The scales had fallen from her eyes and she'd seen Sean for the man he really was. And in hindsight that had only been the tip of a very large iceberg. She should've run like hell then, because the minute they got home, she was stuck.

Sean had returned from the doctor's office a week later. The same day, in fact, she'd gone into town to see their lawyer, Barry Campbell. They'd faced each other in the impersonal, overdecorated dining room with a dinner neither of them wanted to eat laying between them.

Lily, filled with righteous indignation and a deadly calm, told him the marriage was over. Sean, somehow shrunken and not so self-confident anymore, told her he had terminal cancer. She'd discovered later that he'd been seeing the doctor for months.

The doctor had given Sean six months to live.

Of course she hadn't believed him. Not for a moment. But a visit to his doctor the next day confirmed the grim prognosis.

Lily couldn't leave then. Sean was a shit but she wasn't. Regardless of what had transpired between them, she couldn't bail on a dying man, not even one she could no longer love. She wanted to, God, how she'd wanted to, dreamed of it, in fact. She didn't want anything from Sean, especially not the guilt of leaving him to die alone.

Maybe that had been a mistake. Maybe she should have left him despite his illness. She might have had she known the six-month sentence would turn into three long, agonizing years.

"Lily?"

"What? Oh, um—travel. I took a cruise to Mexico when I graduated from college."

"I'll take you to Bora-Bora. The water's the most amazing translucent turquoise, and the sand is so fine it squeaks underfoot. You'd love it. Have you ever snorkeled?"

Despite the frigid cold, and her breath hanging visibly in the air, Lily felt a surge of heat at the thought of being anywhere *near* Derek scantily clothed. A picture superimposed itself over the whiteness of the winter landscape. Of a beach, the white sand hot underfoot. Of crystal-clear turquoise water. The sound of gulls. And Derek, wearing nothing but a white smile and a golden tan.

"Are you having trouble breathing?" he asked, sounding concerned. "The altitude—"

"We aren't that high. I was pushing the kids a bit too fast and got distracted," Lily lied through her teeth. Thoughts of Derek were better than a thermal blanket. "Where were we? Oh, yeah. Snorkeling. The closest I've ever gotten was last year when Zephyr kicked me into the water trough. And believe me, what was floating in there had nothing to do with tropical fish."

Derek laughed in her ear and she smiled at the deep, rich sound of it. "Is Fiji where you're always going off to?" she asked, curious.

"Not as often as I'd like," he said absently. What the *hell* was he? A moron? Derek asked himself furiously. Why bring up her and Sean's honeymoon? Dumb ass. Of *course* they hadn't gone out much. Jesus. Sean had wasted no time on his return telling him every erotic detail of their Canadian honeymoon. The couple had spent every second in bed. And very little of that time sleeping. Damn it to hell. Even after all these years Derek still had pictures in his head of Lily and what she'd done on her honeymoon. Only he always transposed himself for Sean.

He saw one of the Iditarod's famous yellow-diamond highway signs ahead that stated WATCH YOUR ASS. He stomped on the brake to slow down the team, and proceeded with caution, reminding himself to concentrate on the task immediately at hand.

"I appreciated you not going on so many trips after Sean got sick," Lily said in his ear.

T-FLAC hadn't exactly done the Snoopy dance about it, that was for sure, but he wasn't about to leave Lily with the burden of nursing

Sean and worrying about the ranch. He had damn good hands in place, and a ranch foreman he paid an obscene amount of money for two reasons: one, he was that good, and two, Derek didn't want anyone stealing Ash away from him. His old T-FLAC buddy was indispensable, and he knew it.

"I wanted to be there, Lily. For *you.*"

Lily sighed and the sound rippled through the mic right into Derek's ear and then slipped into his soul. He frowned, waiting to hear her brush off his concern, as she had so many times before. But she didn't. Maybe it was the anonymity of being able to speak without looking into his eyes, but she seemed to be more comfortable speaking honestly with him now than she had been in years.

"Maybe I didn't say it in so many words," she said, her voice soft, wistful, "but I did appreciate it, Derek. I don't know if I could have handled it all without knowing you were nearby."

It pleased him to hear her say it, but he knew that with or without him, she would've made it through. One of the things he loved best about her was her spine. Sure, she could be stubborn as hell— but she was loyal to the bone. Even when she shouldn't be. Sean had had her loyalty and he hadn't deserved it. But Lily lived by her own code, as Derek had learned over the years. The core of her was solid steel. She could bend when she had to, but she'd never break.

It had torn a hole in his heart, watching her struggle to take care of her practice, the dogs *and* Sean. But there'd been no stopping her. "Yeah, you would," he said. "You're the strongest woman I've ever known, Lily."

He wasn't insensitive. Sean's death had been goddamn hideously protracted. He'd been given six months, and had fooled the doctors by lasting three years. Derek knew it had been hell for the man he'd once thought of as a friend. That said, Sean had milked every step of his slow decline for everything it was worth. He had been neither brave nor stoic. And he'd dragged Lily down the painful path every step of the way.

She'd eventually become pale and drawn herself, tending Sean without a word of complaint. She'd never suggested by word or deed that she felt anything other than total devotion to her dying husband. Yet Derek was pretty damn sure that Lily must've been aware of Sean's transgressions, even that early on. She was smart as a whip. How could she *not* have known about the other women?

The question was, had she continued to *love* Sean? Really love him, despite what she knew? He didn't think so, but how the hell could a man be sure? Still, it would've been hard for any woman to forgive the womanizing, the lies, the wheeling and dealing. *If* she'd known about any of that.

Why hadn't she kicked the son of a bitch in the balls and walked away?

Because she was who she was, Derek thought with equal parts frustration and admiration. Lily was a loyal, strong woman who refused to shirk even the most ghastly of obligations once she'd made a commitment. Come hell or high water, she *would* stick out something like Sean's illness. To the bitter end. If she'd been the kind of woman to skip out on Sean—even though he'd deserved it—she wouldn't have been the woman Derek loved.

That's what made her who she was. And as much as Derek wanted to shake her for wasting those years on a man who couldn't, didn't, appreciate her, he also had to admire the hell out of her for her unshakable loyalty.

And mingled with his admiration for her was an ache, a persistent yearning to be loved completely. By her.

"You know," Lily began, caution flags dangling off every syllable, "it would have been easy to turn my back on Sean. You, too. We have that in common."

"I wouldn't have left you to go it alone," Derek assured her. Somewhere deep in the recesses of his mind he wanted to make damned sure that Lily knew she had been and was his only concern.

"You helped make a horrible situation tolerable," she continued. "And it wasn't just Sean's illness. It was . . ."

"Was what?"

He heard her long sigh in his ear before she spoke. "Nothing. He was your friend and he's dead. Let's leave it at that."

While Derek had no intention of ever telling Lily the truth as he knew it about Sean—what was the point?—what she knew, if she knew anything, was enough. There was such a thing as overkill. No. He'd leave sleeping dogs to lie, as it were.

Lily was the kind of woman he needed. Unconditionally supportive, strong, independent. God only knew, his life wasn't normal. He needed a partner who could deal with his chosen profession. Cope with the separations and not being kept in the loop. Quite simply, Lily possessed everything he could ever want from a woman.

The one thing he knew Lily despised was being lied to. He was going to have to tell her about his association with T-FLAC. He'd left that disclosure too long alrea— "Jesus Christ!"

He and his team had been dropping gradually down toward the valley below and zigzagging through forest as he and Lily talked. Suddenly he was plunging down a very steep hill; directly in front of him was an unnecessary warning sign; DANGEROUS TRAIL CONDITIONS.

No shit. You'd have to be blind and stump stupid to miss the trail vanishing over the edge of the cliff.

Even Lily's warm laughter couldn't chase away the chill of foreboding as Derek stomped like hell on the brake and hung on for dear life.

"Reached the entrance to Happy River steps, have you?" Amusement rang in her voice.

He grunted, said a quick, silent prayer, then proceeded carefully and gently over the lip to plunge diagonally down the face of an extremely—God Almighty—*extremely* steep slope. It took nerves of steel not to look over the drop.

"Stay in the ruts." Lily's voice was calm.

His heart pounded as badly as it had when faced with eleven fully armed tangos in a backstreet Bangkok alley. "No ruts to speak of," he told her flatly, pulling up on the dogs. There hadn't been enough teams over this trail yet to *make* any ruts.

"Keep the brake on," Lily told him, "and trust the dogs. They've done it before."

Hell, *he'd* done it before. Last year. But it still scared the bejesus out of him. Give him a lunatic terrorist armed to the teeth any day. Then, he could at least shoot back. Here all he could do was pray and hope his dogs were feeling confident and fleet of foot.

Fifty yards later the path doubled back; he and the sled were almost lying on their sides. The muscles in Derek's arms and back pulled and bunched as he fought to control the downward momentum of dogs and sled. His heart pumped, and his vision and hearing blurred, then sharpened.

At the bottom was a flat area. It seemed like a hell of a long way away right now. But he kept that in mind as they crept along at a snail's pace.

"At the bottom yet?" Lily asked ten minutes later.

"Did you hear my sigh of relief?" Derek asked with amusement as he brought the team to a stop so they could all gather themselves for the next switchback. There was still a long way to go before hitting the safety of the bottom of the ridge. But saying a "thank you, Jesus" and taking time to wipe the sweat from his brow were in order.

"Make that a prayer." She sounded out of breath herself as she started the same downward climb several minutes behind him. "And don't look down!" she warned unnecessarily. The drop to the gorge on his right was fifty feet. Straight down.

"Stop worrying about me and *concentrate,* damn it," Derek said more harshly than he intended. He was scared spitless. Lily was sixty pounds lighter than he was, and as strong as she was for her job, as much practice as she'd had over the years, this bit of the trail was a ball buster.

He realized he was holding his breath, reliving each step of the descent, every bit of protruding underbrush, each bend, each—
"Watch for a broken branch as you come across the top edge," he remembered. "See it?"

"Yeah. Thanks."

"Stay in my ruts."

"Believe me. I am."

He imagined her gloved hands tight on the handlebars. A fierce look of concentration on her face. Until he saw the whites of her eyes and the pink of her cheeks, he wasn't budging.

"I'm. Coming. Down. Very. Slowly," Lily assured him, amusement lacing her words.

Derek glanced up and behind him, waiting for her to come round the bend so he could breathe again. There was no sign of her yet, but the clouds were now low enough to touch, a dirty white, heavy and ominous. It was about to snow. And snow big. Damn.

Hey, God, Derek mentally prayed. Can you just hold off until Lily is on flat ground and safe? Amen.

"I'd kill for a cup of c— What the heck!" She was cut off by an ear-splitting *screeeech.*

Sounded like something enormous tearing.

One of the giant pines ripping from its moorings?

The earth shook. Derek's dogs started barking crazily.

The thought flashed into his mind even as he listened— Jesus. *No way*— A split second before the roar—*another* sound. A detonation. A small one, but a detonation nevertheless.

And up here, that was all kinds of dangerous.

He released the brake so the dogs could run for it if necessary, then jumped off the back of the sled and raced up the switchback.

"Lily? Where are you?"

What he saw as he tore around the upper bend stopped his heart in his chest and caused an icy sweat to film his entire body.

Half the hillside was breaking away from the mountain and tumbling to the gorge below in a giant plume of fast-moving snow and rock.

Avalanche.

Eight

"*L*IL-EEEEEE!*"*

Heart in his throat, Derek rounded the curve at a dead run, just as a rumbling wall of white hit the back of Lily's sled with the thundering force of a bullet train.

Jesus.

Running flat out, he ripped off his restrictive coat one-handed, not feeling the icy bite of the cold as he tossed it to the frozen ground and lunged for the center line between the heads of her lead dogs. Made up of thick rope, and reinforced with steel, it ran the length from the leaders to the sled. And Lily.

His hands closed around cold steel; his fingers immediately turned white with the strain of the downward drag. The muscles in his arms and back bunched as he focused everything he had on keeping hold of Lily's team.

Her dogs barked and howled, frantic, answered by his own team down the path behind him. The cacophony of sound jolted the air and filled every crevasse of space across the narrow canyon.

In the flash of a second before everything went to hell, Derek's gaze collided with Lily's, and he saw shock and fear in her terror-wide eyes.

Then in a heart-stopping fall, Lily and the wheel dogs closest to the sled went backward over the edge of the mountain, followed by an enveloping blanket of white and brown.

Derek's breath staggered and his heart lurched as he watched the terrifying now-you-see-me, now-you-don't disappearing act.

Jesus— Prayer, not a curse.

"Hang on," Derek shouted into the rising wind. "For Christ's sake. Hang on!"

He didn't know if she could hear him through the mic. He prayed she could. And prayed she was alive and conscious enough to know he'd find her.

Barking manically now, aware of their peril, the thirteen tethered sled dogs slid backward. Feet struggling for purchase in the relentless and inexorable pull of the backward slide of the snow-enveloped sled.

Putting their shoulders into it, the lead dogs, Arrow and Finn, battled to keep the rest of the team from plummeting to the gorge below under the onslaught of the debris bombarding them from the hillside above.

"Good dogs. Good kids," Derek rasped, gripping the gang line and digging his boot heels into the trembling earth in an attempt to help them. Damn it, *he* needed help to pull this out of the crapper.

"We can do this. Good dogs. Come on. Another step. And an-other. Yes!" The dogs dug in; brave, strong and willing to fight for life, they made a little progress, then fought the slide backward. "One more. Good dogs. One more." Opal's and Deny's heads emerged over the lip. Derek grabbed the line between them, hand over hand, straining every muscle as he pulled them up to flat ground. "Good dogs. Good dogs. Lily? Can you hear me?"

He kept up the litany of praise to the dogs as he worked desper-ately to get them onto stable ground. He couldn't see Lily in the billowing clouds of white. "Please be okay," he muttered between determined, clenched teeth. "Let me hear you, Lily, sweetheart." He reminded himself she was there, roped to the sled, hanging on and doing what she could to help. Which was nothing, save encouraging the team. He had to think of something else to do. Something to halt the slide of the entire team down the mountainside. If that happened they would all die.

Derek closed off the fear compartment of his brain with a loud clang.

Don't go there, he warned himself, cold with fear. Don't, for Christ's sake, go there.

He put his full body weight into helping the dogs pull. The animals worked with him. They knew help when it presented itself. But they were wide-eyed with fear as their feet slithered and slid and they struggled to find firm footing on the constantly shifting ground.

With his help, they fought for each step as the earth continued to groan and rumble. Spumes of snow and rubble shot out as if the ground itself were trying to shake them loose.

He managed to help/drag them, inch by agonizingly hard-fought inch. His back screamed. The muscles in his arms begged for mercy, but he didn't let up. Couldn't let himself or the dogs surrender. And more by will than strength, he pulled them to the far side of the trail, as close to the left-hand side of the drop-off as he could get them. Protected some from the tumultuous fall of snow and rock, nevertheless they again slid back another three feet.

Four.

Six—

Derek held on for dear life, sliding along with them, skating on the snow as if wearing skis. "No," he shouted, digging his heels in, dragging furrows through the loose snow and rock. "Hike." Like they weren't trying? The dogs were giving it everything they had. Chests heaved, tongues hung out with exertion and their sides expanded and contracted like bellows, their breath mingling with swirling snowflakes.

Failure was *not* an option.

With almost superhuman strength he dragged the dogs forward again, reclaiming lost ground. Rio and Grady scrabbled up onto the path. He wouldn't let them go. Wouldn't lose Lily or the team. Wouldn't stand on the edge of oblivion and stare down at her broken body, by God.

Finn's and Arrow's front feet lifted completely off the ground as Derek pulled with every ounce of his strength. He felt each muscle and tendon do its job, and he thanked God for his physical ability and relentless training. He'd need every gram of strength today.

It took a precious five minutes for the earth to quit dancing enough for the dogs to be able to stand still. He had them. Safe. No more sliding.

Now Lily. *Please, God, Lily.*

"Extra chow for you guys tonight," he told the dogs grimly, releasing the line and pausing to make sure they weren't still being dragged backward. Satisfied, at least for the moment, he stepped back. "Hang tough. Stay."

There was a mandatory shovel on his sled. But he wasn't going back down the trail to fetch it.

Not a second to waste, he practically threw himself over the path's ragged edge.

Slithering. Sliding. Hands. Feet. *Keep low to the ground for better balance. Where—* A quick glance to get a bead on the position of the dangling, snow-loaded sled. He lowered himself over the side of the steep cliff. The only reason he did it with more caution than his screaming internal alarm required was that if *he* fell to his death, then so would Lily.

He meticulously maneuvered, crablike, until he neared the lump of snow indicating a sled and its precious human cargo buried in the hillside, a precarious forty feet above the gorge.

Ten feet away, he yelled, "*Lily.* Talk to me!"

On one of his first T-FLAC assignments many years ago, Derek and a small team had been inserted into the stronghold of a small terrorist cell holed up in a high-mountain retreat in the Andes. He'd been suitably scared shitless then, too. But he'd never experienced anything as close to pure terror as he was right now.

Fear for himself wasn't even close to the fear he had for Lily. It would be like comparing a tadpole to a killer shark.

Back then, the avalanche that had covered him and his teammates had killed three of the seven men, incapacitated one with frostbite and a broken leg, and given Derek a healthy and terrifyingly realistic knowledge of just how long Lily could survive covered by tons of snow.

"Lily?"

As he scrambled to her position, he gauged the texture of the snow covering her and the sled. Light and fluffy. She had a higher chance of survival because she'd be able to breathe. Heavy, wet snow, as some of this was, could lead to suffocation. He remembered not being capable of even flexing his fingers when *he'd* been buried. That was the first time he'd realized his own mortality.

God only knew, it sure as hell hadn't been the last.

He kept talking to her, shouting nonsense as he scrambled the last few feet. He needed to believe she could hear him, was plotting cutting comebacks to everything he was saying.

"You're going to a lot of trouble to slow me down in this race, Lily," he shouted, scanning for a sign, any sign of her. "If you think this is going to keep me from winning, you're nuts. I'm going to save you first, then beat your ass."

Nothing, damn it. Nothing. "I'm willing to give you a half hour to rest up, but after that, no more Mr. Nice Guy." *Please, God, let me find her.*

A speedy rescue was imperative. Most avalanche victims lasted about thirty trapped minutes before— "Answer me, goddamn it!"

"Maybe I would if you'd stop yakking away long enough to hear me!" Lily's muffled, annoyed voice responded in his ear without missing a beat.

Relief was a drug. It swept through his bloodstream and made his head swim and his heart leap up into his throat. He laughed. "That's my girl."

"Talk, talk, talk." Her voice was barely audible, but fierce. "Get me out of here, would you? I'm freezing my— I'm so co— Derek?" The bravado leaked out of her voice. "Please. Make it *fast*."

There was no word in the dictionary for cold like this. It burned and bit and clawed at her exposed skin; it sneakily seeped into every seam, every buttonhole, every crevice until she was shuddering so violently she couldn't tell if it was her moving or the sled carrying herself and the dogs to their spectacularly gory deaths in the canyon below. Somehow, she'd managed to curve her elbow over her nose and mouth as they fell, so at least she could breathe. But it was as mercilessly black and icy cold as a crypt— *Oh, shit. Don't go there.*

"Don't move, okay, kids?" she told the unseen dogs soothingly. Melba whined; Dingbat, confused as usual, gave his I-haven't-a-clue-what's-going-on bark. "We're going to get out of this mess," she promised them grimly, terrified that she couldn't hear the rest of the team. "*And* beat the pants off Derek and his team, you got that?" She hoped that sentence wouldn't go down in history in the category of famous last words.

"Don't waste air talking," Derek said calmly into her ear. "Everyone is clear except you and the wheel dogs. Hang tight. I know where you are. I'll have you out in a few minutes."

Her right arm was tight at her side, her left over her face. The blood wasn't pooling in her brain, so she figured she wasn't hanging upside down like a terrified bat in a black-ice cave. She wiggled the fingers of her right hand. See? she thought optimistically. It wasn't all bad.

Using her full strength she jerked her arm upward; it moved about an inch and a half. No point wasting time being terrified. Plenty of time for that later. She had to help Derek rescue her and the dogs. Oh, God. The poor dogs. Melba had been around the block a few times, she'd be okay. But Dingbat must be a quivering mass of terror.

"Damn." She tried to move her arm again. It moved up a few more inches. "Hang in there, kids. Things are looking u— Aaargh!"

Sled, dogs, snow . . . *her*, jerked down. Backward.

The dogs yelped in terror.

So did she.

Her heart jumped up into her throat and beat there like a trapped bird.

OhGodohGodohGod.

"Jesus Christ, Lily!" Derek's voice was muffled, but his tone was crystal clear. "Stop moving!"

"Not a problem," she whispered back without moving her lips. Were her eyes closed? She wanted them open, but she couldn't tell.

Derek was close. She knew without a shadow of a doubt he was digging her out as fast as humanly possible. And as independent as she was, there was not a darn thing she could do to help him or herself but wait. She wasn't good at waiting. No patience, her mom used to say.

Oh, great, Lily Marie! Think about Mom now, why don't you? Because the last time her mom had laughingly said that was the last time her mother had spoken to her.

Lily and her parents had flown in her dad's twin-engine plane to Billings to buy Christmas presents the year Lily turned eight. Her father was an excellent pilot, but he didn't take the family with him very often when he flew. The Cessna 172 was for veterinary business when it was too far to travel by truck. So this was a special occasion. She and her mom had dressed up in their best dresses, and then bundled up in thick down coats and heavy boots because of the cold. The snow had been especially pretty that year. Soft and pristine white.

Lily wanted a Barbie camper, and she was pretty sure it was one of the things they were going to be picking up in town.

Her mom smelled so good. She'd even let Lily dab on a little perfume for the trip. The inside of the small plane smelled of Carolina Herrera, and antiseptic from her dad's emergency medical bag, which was on the floor in back where Lily sat. There was also the faint stink of horse manure. Lily couldn't decide which of the three smells she liked the most.

She'd fallen off the roof and broken her leg the summer before and didn't like heights so much anymore. So when she felt the vibration of the plane as it taxied down the runway, Lily squeezed her eyes shut and pictured Ballerina Barbie riding in her new camper.

Her stomach did that weird dippy thing that made her want to throw up as the plane took off. Because she knew closing her eyes wasn't very brave, she forced them open and made herself look down on the red roofs of their house and outbuildings as they circled. Her stomach wasn't happy. But she did it anyway.

There was Cinnamon, a copper-colored blob near the barn. She should be inside where it was nice and warm, but her horse loved the snow for some reason. Holy camolie, they were high. Cinnamon got smaller and smaller as they rose.

Lily's eyes dried out because she was determined not to close them, not even to blink. Her eyeballs were dry, her mouth was dry and her heart was thumping really, really hard in her chest. Out of the corner of one dry eyeball she could see the lace on the front of her dress bounce up and down with her heartbeat as she tried not to panic at how high up they were.

She shifted uncomfortably in the seat. The lacy dress itched; she'd rather be wearing her favorite jeans, but they were going to a nice dinner after shopping and she was a *girl*.

Maybe the stupid price tag was sticking her neck; she tried to twist around to check, tangling herself in her coat and the seat belt.

"Sit still, honey." Her mom turned her head to smile back at Lily. "You have absolutely no patience, do you, Princess Pea? Well, I don't blame you, but we'll be there soo— Oh! What's that noise, John?"

The engine coughed and gagged like Piewacket with a hairball. Her father swore. Her father never swore. Lily's gaze shot from her mom's pale profile to the back of her dad's head. "Daddy?"

"Jesus," Derek said, scowling down at her through the opening he'd made in the snow. "Did you hit your head?"

Dazed and disoriented, Lily blinked. "What?"

"You just called me Daddy."

She scowled. "Did not."

It'd taken her eyes a moment to focus, but she appeared lucid enough. Derek bit back a smile. She looked like a ruffled baby owl popping out of her nest. But this was no time for levity. Her position was precarious as hell. The sled hung over the edge of the hillside, anchored, thank God, by a fairly sturdy-looking outcropping of saplings.

But that anchor could change in a heartbeat.

Digging his way through to her had been laborious and frustratingly time-consuming. He hadn't wanted to jar anything loose, and he'd had to dig with his hands while braced just as precariously as she was on an unstable hillside.

Narrow-eyed, he'd watched for the small telltale escape of steam to pinpoint exactly where she was under the pile of snow covering her, the sled and two of the dogs.

She was still buried shoulder deep. But other than looking a little dazed and confused, she was alive and well.

"Ready to get out of there, or are you enjoying the view?" The drop was spectacular, and hair-raising. She hadn't even glanced behind him to look; her eyes were fixed, to his very real amusement, on his crotch, which was at her eye level.

He would've enjoyed her position a hell of a lot more if her expression wasn't quite so glassy and scared and she wasn't neck deep in snow. "Lily, are you all right?"

She licked her lips. A quick swipe of a pink tongue over her mouth. A nervous gesture she'd deny emphatically. Nevertheless, heat shot to his groin.

"I will be when you get me out of here; my butt feels like it's in a deep freeze." Her answer was a little shaky, but vintage Lily. She wasn't blinking and kept her attention on him, not the drop, and he didn't have to wonder if her flying phobia affected how she felt about heights as well.

He made short work of clearing the rest of the snow around her. As soon as she had an arm free, she helped.

"Slow and methodical. Slow and methodical," Derek cautioned as she started bailing frantically.

"Yeah." She cast a worried look up to where she could hear but not see her team on the ledge above them. "Right. Are the others all okay?"

"Worried but maintaining," he said dryly. "Keep digging." Thank God her coat was Gore-Tex and waterproof; she was sensibly dressed for the terrain and climate. She'd be cold, but he'd fix that soon enough. "Can you shake off the rest of it?" he asked when he could see her lower body.

"You betcha, Bubba." She did just that, carefully kicking away the thick snow encasing her lower legs, and brushing away what she could with her gloved hands.

"Anything hurt?" He gave her a top-to-toe once-over.

"No," she said dismissively, her attention focused now just beyond the snow-covered sled to where the two dogs should be. "Let's get the kids now."

He held out his hand. Without hesitation, Lily grabbed it and used his leverage to climb from the back of the sled. The entire lump of snow, sled and dog, creaked and slid back several feet as she did so. "Oh, God."

He twisted both hands into the front of her coat to steady her, curling his fingers into the thick damp pile and jerking her flush to his body. She grabbed on to his coat to regain her footing, and for a moment they stood unsteadily together.

From above them came a long, sharp howl from one of the buried dogs. "Dingbat," Lily said, recognizing like a mother would which dog was calling. "Hang in there, buddy." Her brow pleated in a quick worried frown. "Get the snow out of the sled, I'll liberate the kids."

"Go up top and wait. I'll take care—" At her narrow-eyed look, he grinned and gave her a salute. "Yes, ma'am." She wasn't hurt, just scared and cold. Waiting for him to do the job wasn't going to change that. Freeing her animals would. He put a large hand on her butt to help her up the hillside. She yelled a disgruntled, "Hey!" but it didn't have much heat.

"Climb *above* them before you start messing with the snow," he told her unnecessarily. Lily knew what she was about. She wouldn't endanger the dogs any more than she'd endanger herself.

Listening to her talking to her animals in a quiet, calm voice, he put his back into unveiling the heavy sled, and considerably lightened the drag as he dumped yards of snow and rock from the sled bag with nothing but his cupped hands.

"They're cold and scared but okay!" Lily yelled down.

Not *How are you doing, my hero?* Derek thought dryly. It was all about the dogs. "Ready to hike?" he yelled up, giving the handlebars a shake to be sure everything was free.

"What about those little trees holding— Oh! Wow, how macho of you," she said with gratifying awe as he hefted 350 pounds of sled and equipment up and over the saplings holding it in place. They then served to stabilize it so it didn't slide downhill again.

He considered digging up the small trees that had saved her life, and having them bronzed. "Let's do it."

"Hike!" Lily yelled to the dogs, and, with happy yips and barks, all fifteen laboriously started pulling the loaded sled back up to the trail. It might be slow-mo, but it was progress nevertheless.

Derek climbed up to where Lily stood, one leg straight out behind her bracing her body, the other bent uphill as she pushed and shoved the back of the sled to help the dogs.

Her face was pink with exertion and cold, her mouth a serious line. Admiration filled him. She didn't waste time feeling sorry for herself. Or giving into hysterics over being buried by an avalanche. She just got up, brushed herself off and kept moving. God. Was there any other woman in the world like her?

Now, if he could just get it into her thick head it wasn't *Sean* she loved—

Finally, finally they were up on the trail once again.

Derek reached up and brushed snow off her hat.

He captured her eyes with his. More gold than green when she looked up at him as if unable to look away. He cupped her face in his other hand, allowed himself the perverse pleasure of seeing surprised awareness before he crushed his mouth down on hers.

She gave a small *ompff* of surprise.

Thank you, he thought, spearing his tongue into the warm sweet cavern of her mouth. Thank you, God, for keeping her safe for me.

He wasn't gentle. Digging her out had taken that ability right out of him. He cradled her head in one hand to support her, and ravished her mouth, not taking time to savor her never-forgotten taste. No, this time was all heat and flash. Surging blood and pounding pulses.

Heat flooded Lily, banishing the bone-deep cold she'd experienced moments ago. The warning bells were drowned out by the thundering sound of the blood rushing to her head.

His hands—she swore she could feel the heat of his hands right through the thick fleece of her coat. His breath on her face felt warm. The pressure of his body aligning itself to hers felt hot. Steam was probably erupting from the top of her head.

"You idiot." Lily clung to him with her hands fisted in the front of his coat. "We could have fallen."

"But we didn't."

"Pure luck."

"Not a chance, honey. I worked too hard to earn that kiss."

"Yeah?" She smiled up at him, because damn it, he *had* earned it. "What'd I do to earn it?"

"Born under a lucky star, I guess."

"Egotistical ass," she said without heat.

"I know when a woman wants me." He looked into her eyes. "And I want you. I've never made any bones about that, Lily. I'm done pretending otherwise."

Like a fish wriggling at the end of a hook, she tried, "Sean—" It was halfhearted at best. But she gave it a shot.

"Is dead." Derek cupped her head in his large hands so she couldn't look away. "I'm not. Get used to the difference. Get very used to my mouth on you. And my hands. Hell—start giving some serious thought to what it's going to be like when we're both naked."

Lily's heart did a dip and roll. "God. You're amazing. You say you want me as if that gives you entrée to *having* me. Okay. You want me. For how long?"

"What are you expecting me to say? 'For as long as it takes us to tire of one another'?"

"That would be the honest answer, yes."

"But it isn't the answer I'd give you."

"Isn't it? What's the longest relationship you've ever had with a woman?"

"That has noth—"

"A month? Two months?"

"I was in love with one woman for four years."

"Really? And still no commitment?" She *tsk*ed. "I rest my case. I don't do temporary, and I'm not interested in permanent. Fortunately for both of us, even though Sean is gone, I still consider myself *married* to him, so get it into your head that I still love my husband, and leave me alone."

Oh, Lord. She was going to go to hell for lying like this. But it was better than leaving an opening for Derek to sneak into her heart. She wondered if she had really *ever* loved Sean. Sadly, she didn't believe Sean had ever really loved *her*. His best friend had wanted her, and Sean had moved in and snatched her up from under Derek's nose like a prize at the fair.

More fool her for believing his lies. He'd been a sucky husband. The least he could do in abstentia was let her use him as a shield against Derek.

Sean was probably sitting in that hot place laughing his vain head off at this turn of events, Lily thought a little desperately.

Derek bent his head and brushed his mouth over hers again. This time in a light kiss. It should have been unthreatening, but it wasn't. He gave her an assessing look as he stepped back from her. "Keep telling yourself that bullshit, Lily, if it makes you feel better. You're too smart to be pining over a memory—a not-so-great memory at that. One of these days you're going to have to face the reality of the chemistry between us.

"When Sean was alive I did the honorable thing and stepped aside. When Sean was sick and dying, I did the honorable thing and gave you space to cope with what was happening. Well, Sean's gone now and as far as I'm concerned, honorable is pretty much out the door."

"The door isn't open for you, however."

He shook his head ruefully. "Stubbornness is one of your more annoying traits."

Just because he appeared to be capable of reading her mind, Lily thought, didn't mean he really *could*. She hoped. "Really? I consider it one of my best assets."

He laughed, and touched her cheek briefly before saying with real amusement, "You would. Right, let's get the hell out of Dodge before the mountain does a nosedive again."

As soon as she was able, she stepped out of his hold. He wanted to grab her up and squeeze her until she begged for mercy. He wanted to wrap her in cotton batting and keep her safe.

He wanted—

Hell.

He *wanted*.

Nine

THE FUCKING WOMAN HAD TEN LIVES.

What the hell was he supposed to do? Go up to her, tell the stupid bitch to stand still, then shoot her point-blank between the fucking eyes? How would *that* look like a goddamn accident?

He'd told them, *told them,* that one little stick of dynamite wasn't going to do anything but make a little bang. But they hadn't wanted an avalanche big enough to bury Alaska. Just big enough to take out the bitch. Who would have guessed she'd be lucky enough to survive going over a fucking cliff?

A man could only work with the tools he was given. One fucking stick of dynamite? He needed to bring down half the fucking mountain to kill her.

Fuck, he thought, scratching at the hives on his neck, they were going to be pissed. *He* was pissed. Not to mention sick to fucking death of this unrelenting fucking *cold*. Hell wasn't hot. Hell was fucking icicles. Hell was snow, miles and miles of snow and frozen feet and a running nose and knives of ice scratching your lungs with every fucking breath. And he wanted the hell out. Except he couldn't *get* out until the bitch was dead.

To make matters worse, there was some other dude skulking around again. He'd caught a glimpse of him this morning up on the ridge. Not part of the Iditarod madness. The guy wasn't even making a pretext of pretending to blend in. He looked like a goddamn albino ninja. Dressed completely in white and tooling around in some high-powered and eerily quiet ski mobile the likes of which he'd never seen before. The thing was like a ghost zooming in and out of the trees, just out of his line of vision. But he *knew* the guy was out there.

Watching. Waiting.

Had they sent someone *else* to do what they figured he couldn't do? He'd take care of this dickhead just like he'd taken care of Croft. Fuck. Had they brought in an outsider?

It was important that Lily die before she could make any more inquiries about the bull cum. He was dreading having to report in at the next stop that not only was the bitch still breathing, but she and macho man had been sucking face out there on the trail. Everyone had liked it just fine when the two of them were barely talking. Now?

Would they want him to off Wright as well?

Fuck shit damn. It was hard enough to kill one person, let alone two. And Wright didn't look like he'd die quick and easy. Not that Lily was a cakewalk either. The annoying bitch from hell.

Never should have taken this damn job. Honor schmoner. Hadn't wanted to do it, and sure as shit didn't want to be here now. Unfortunately, there'd been no saying no. Not to the suits. They wielded kick-ass power, and could and would make his life a living hell if he didn't come through.

If they'd sent the white ninja in to do his job, then he might as well kiss his own sweet ass good-bye. He was dead meat.

He shot a nervous glance over his shoulder.

Nothing there but trees and snow.

But suddenly he felt as though he had a fucking bull's-eye painted on his back in neon.

He smelled the stink of his own fear-sweat and he wanted to puke.

THEY TRAVELED SEVERAL HOURS IN RELATIVE SILENCE, THE KISS THEY'D shared an unmentioned elephant in the middle of the room.

Derek hadn't been flirting.

God, Lily thought, that was even scarier than falling off the side of the mountain. Derek always flirted. It was in his DNA to flirt. He did it with devastating effect, too. If it were an Olympic event, Derek Wright would have the gold. And knowing that, she'd found it relatively easy to ignore the looks and innuendos for the past few weeks.

Relatively. God only knew, she wasn't going to let him know just how affected she really was.

But he hadn't been playing games up on that cliff. Not this time. The look in his dark eyes had riveted her in place. He'd been dead serious. There hadn't been a glimmer of amusement there. He wanted her, that look had said, and nothing and nobody would stand in his way. And then, in case she hadn't got the message loud and clear, he'd said the words out loud. And taken the relationship to a whole new level.

I want you.

Flat out. No frills. Unequivocal,

I. Want. You.

She'd felt as though a guided missile had locked onto her, and was prepared to shatter her into tiny atoms when she least expected it if she didn't surrender. And Lily knew, God help her, that throwing Sean up to Derek every time he got close wasn't going to be a deterrent for much longer. The thought made her heart race and her palms sweat with equal parts fear and anticipation.

Still shaken by just how close she'd been to death, receiving that soul-shattering kiss had rocked her to her toes. Now, Lily had to force herself to focus and concentrate, which was proving more difficult than she'd thought possible. Usually from race start to race finish, she kept her mind clear of everything and anything not pertaining to the trail ahead and the welfare of her dogs.

Derek had been in the race before. She'd barely noticed. He'd been no more to her then than a fly in the ointment. A minor annoyance.

But this year was different.

Now he was a *major distraction*.

Damn it.

Using the brake often, and spending a lot of time balancing up on her runners, Lily forced herself to concentrate and get to the next checkpoint as fast as possible. Forget about the kiss, she told herself firmly. Forget all about it and the power behind it. Forget about the man and his strong arms and broad chest and hard— *Oh yeah.* Scolding herself had only made the memory more vivid. Good job forgetting.

"Tell me how you and Sean met," she said into the lip mic, keeping her tone cool and casual with effort. Good idea. Talk about Sean. She wondered if she'd be struck by lightning for using her dead husband as the proverbial bucket of cold water.

"You know how we met," he said flatly in her ear.

"Sean's version." Which knowing what she did now was probably as much BS as everything else he'd told her. Lily didn't give a damn how the two most annoying men in her life had met. Lightning or avalanche. She wanted to put the memory of Sean *the husband* between her and Derek. Unfortunately it was starting to feel like a piece of flimsy cellophane between herself and a wild tiger, as opposed to the nice comfortable shield it had been before the start of the race.

When had the balance of power shifted?

"Why do you care how we met?"

"Hey, it's conversation, okay?" She bit her lip. More lies. It wasn't just chitchat. It was holding Sean up and waving him at Derek to remind him that she wasn't available. She hoped to hell he believed that more than she did.

"Right," his voice grumbled in her ear. "You want to talk. When I'm far enough away for you to feel safe?"

"Hah!" she scoffed. *You betcha, Bubba!* "The words *safe* and *Derek Wright* don't belong in the same sentence."

He hummed, low and throaty in her ear, and she felt the vibration pulsing through every blasted cell in her body like a warm caress. Dangerous, dangerous man.

"I think I like that," he said softly.

"You would," Lily countered. She wished Derek had stayed in Montana as she'd asked him to. Then she wouldn't be traveling along this dangerous trail wondering about the ramifications of kissing the infuriating man, the equivalent of giving an inch, when she should have 100 percent of her concentration on what she was doing.

Of course if he hadn't been nearby she'd probably be dead now. Lily shivered at just how close she'd been. Twice. A cold chill snaked along her spine and it had nothing to do with the snow drifting silently through the air on gusts of wind. Derek had turned into some sort of strong, completely too attractive guardian angel. And she wasn't entirely sure what to think about that. A more unlikely angel would be hard to find.

"If you don't want to talk, I'll listen to my music. Are you going to tell me how you two met or not?" she said, more to break the disturbing electronic silence than anything else. Music, of course, would be a hell of a lot safer. Since when, Lily wondered, had she decided to live a little dangerously?

"Yeah. I'll tell you," he said, his voice suddenly soft and lethal. "Ask me whatever the hell you want about Sean and our relationship. Ask now, or forever hold your peace. Because, God help you, Lily, this will be the last damn time I'll discuss a dead man with you."

Her hands tightened on the handlebars. "The fact that you don't want to talk about him doesn't make Sean disappear." This was like poking a tiger through the bars with a sharp stick, Lily thought, unable to stop herself and not knowing why.

"How long are you going to let the memory of your dead husband dictate your life?" Derek asked in a hard voice. "There's respect for someone's memory and then there's using a tragic event to justify putting your own life on indefinite pause. Any idea when you'll be giving yourself permission to enjoy life again?"

"I enjoy my life just fine, thank you," she told him with every ounce of conviction she could muster.

"You *work*."

"I love my job."

"There's more to life than working." The nerve-wracking silence stretched out again.

Lily could see her shield crumble right before her very eyes, but she mentally held on to it with a tight-fisted grip. "Sean's only been dead six months. Hardly a lengthy mourning period by anyone's standards."

"Your marriage was over long before Sean died."

You have no *idea,* Lily thought, getting a panicky feeling in the pit of her stomach as her safety shield cracked even further. Did Derek know that she and Sean hadn't had a physical relationship after the honeymoon? She sure as hell hoped not. He'd be like a bloodhound for sure.

God. She hadn't had sex in more than three years. That was probably why Derek's kisses affected her so deeply. Lack of nookie could do that to a girl, Lily decided. She stared at the unending vista of snow and trees that stretched out on either side of her for miles and miles. Lonely. Cold. Barren.

Much like her life right now, she thought, feeling restless and alone. It would be so easy, so very, very easy, to fall into Derek's arms and take what he wanted to give her. No matter how little, or for how short a period of time. But Lily knew she'd be worse off after than she was now.

Just because she didn't know what she wanted to be when she grew up didn't mean she could or should use Derek as a stop-gap measure now.

Changes had to be made in her life. She knew that.

But putting her hand into the flame to assure herself it was really as hot as she'd been told would be beyond stupid.

"Fine. We'll play it your way one more time." He inhaled sharply and blew the air out in a rush and Lily could have sworn she *felt* that hot breath brush against her ear.

"I have another ranch in Texas." He spoke softly, intimately, as if they were sitting across from each other at a candlelit table. She could almost *see* the wavering flames dancing in his dark eyes. She could hear the sigh of his breath and almost convinced herself she could smell his cologne on the icy air.

Lily's fingers tightened on her handlebars as her sled tilted and then bounced down onto both runners as she lost concentration again and just . . . felt. *Focus, Lily Marie. Focus.* He'd dropped back a little, but she felt him there, protecting her back, watching out for her. Keeping her safe. It was a strange, unfamiliar sensation. She didn't want to like it this much. Damn him.

"Sean's father—"

"Tossed him out on his ear and disinherited him," Lily inserted, fighting to maintain control. "I know that part of it."

"He'd had ranching experience. I hired him as a hand. Worked for me off and on for a number of years. Then he heard of his father's death, and that the ranch was being sold off by the bank. He asked if I'd be interested. I was."

"Why?"

"Why not?" he asked mildly. As if everyone could afford two multimillion-dollar ranches in two different states. Why not indeed? "I was interested in expanding my breeding program with the Red Brangus," he continued easily. "Montana was as good a place as any."

Lily remembered Sean's father, Vern Munroe. A more cantanker-ous, judgmental, *unforgiving* man she'd never met. He'd regaled any-one who'd listen about his no-good, ne'er-do-well son. The details of just why father and son had never seen eye to eye had been lost in translation. Sean's mother had disappeared after going out to buy cigarettes when he'd been a teenager. The last anyone had heard, she'd gone off to Hollywood to break into movies. She'd never been heard from again.

Lily'd heard the stories for years, and vaguely remembered Sean from grade school. But she'd gone on to boarding school in San Francisco, while Sean had gone to high school in Billings. By the time she got back home after graduating from Texas A & M, he and his father had had their falling-out and he was gone.

Lily had found him amusing, charming and open when they'd first met. Sean wasn't nearly as smooth and sophisticated as Derek was; she'd loved that about him. He was still a small-town boy. A small-town boy who'd made good. When she talked, he listened with his undivided attention, watching her features, paying attention. He remembered things she'd told him. And God help her, she'd been flattered and dizzy with delight. He was her Prince Charming. Good-looking and clearly mad about her. He spoiled her with small gifts and bushels of flowers. He held her hand at the movies, and never pressed her to give anything she wasn't ready to give him.

Lily thought afterward that the reason Sean Munroe had married her was because she wouldn't sleep with him before he put a ring on her finger.

In retrospect, holding on to her virginity had been a damn stupid thing to do. She should have slept with Sean and got it out of both their systems. The relationship would probably have lasted five minutes.

In the beginning, when they'd first started dating, she'd used the loss of his mother and the estrangement from his father as excuses for his bad behavior.

Unfortunately, he'd never done anything to move forward and get on with his own life. Everything he said and did was always someone else's fault. He'd been "born under an unlucky star." He'd had "bad breaks." And, starting with his parents, people were out to screw him.

She should have paid attention to the signals. She hadn't been used to dealing with that kind of negativity and instead of running for the hills, she'd tried to fix him. The only thing wrong with that theory was, Sean hadn't wanted to be fixed. Sean *liked* being a victim. It was comfortable for him and a role he'd perfected over long, agonizing years of practice.

Sean never took responsibility for his own actions. His father had hated him. His mother had walked out. Derek hadn't pulled his weight, and Lily wasn't supportive. It had gone on and on, until Lily had turned a deaf ear.

The town of Munroe—if a gas station, a Piggly Wiggly and the Methodist church could be called a town—had been named after Vern's grandfather. The ranch, started in the early fifties, was the largest in the area, and when Vern's health had started fading and he'd gone off to Billings to the rest home, a lot of people had been put out of work.

The nursing home had eaten up his savings, throwing the ranch into receivership to pay off the rest of his debts. As far as anyone knew, he hadn't had contact with his son in years.

Lily couldn't imagine bearing a grudge that long. Sean hadn't wanted to talk about it, and at the time she'd imagined the hurt had been so deep he hadn't been capable of discussing it. Apparently Sean's bad habits and even worse behavior had started early.

"So you came to Montana and bought Vern's ranch. Did Sean contribute *anything* to the purchase?" Lily asked curiously. Sean had told her he had. That as soon as he left his father's spread he'd bought his own place in Texas and made a killing in the cattle market.

"No."

"I should have known." Why would Sean tell the truth about anything when he so clearly preferred the elaborate lie? Lily frowned. "Then why on earth did you allow him to tell everyone you worked for *him*?" Sean bragged about his holdings, about how many head of cattle he ran, about his prize bull—he'd let Lily name Diablo, for heaven's sake!

"I wasn't around that much."

The fact that he had another ranch in Texas explained his many absences. "True."

"I figured if Sean wanted to play big man in Montana, what did it matter to me? We both knew the truth," Derek said in her ear, sounding as close as a breath.

It was considerably easier talking to Derek without seeing him. Lily bit her lip. Should she ask him about the bull-sperm sales now? Matt had made her promise not to talk to Derek about it until their investigator had more information. It made sense, she knew. But the bull belonged to Derek. Didn't he have a right to be apprised about what was happening?

Unless he was the one in charge of the illegal sales.

She wondered if the investigator had contacted Matt with any new information. Even now, Sean was making her responsible for cleaning up his messes. Knowing Sean's illegal scheme would have long-term legal and financial ramifications, she had a sudden, and surprising, fear that Derek would just wash his hands of the whole situation. She didn't want to confront the possibility of living without Derek in her life. How scary was that?

God. What a mess.

As far as she knew, the sperm sale was the last bit of Sean garbage she needed to clean up before she could go about the rest of her life. Derek was right. She'd been on "pause" for way too long.

"How do you feel about taking a long break when we get to Rainy Pass?" Derek asked, closing the gap between them just as the trail emptied out on a bushy plateau at the other end of Squaw Creek. They were required to take two eight-hour stops, and one twenty-four-hour stop. As impatient as Lily was to skip those rules, a) it wasn't permitted, and b) at a certain point her body would shut down if she didn't take all three of those lengthy mandatory rest stops. But until they reached the Yukon River it was too soon.

She glanced at Derek out of the corner of her eye as he came up alongside her team. He looked like a wild Cossack with his bulky coat and black fur hat, the earring winking as blue as his eyes in the sunlight.

"Four hours'll do me," Lily said absently as her stomach did a little flip-flop. With *hunger*, she told herself firmly, trying her damnedest not to think of how smooth and firm his lips had been when he'd kissed her as they'd balanced precariously on the cliff side. Or how hot he'd tasted. Or how her heart had hammered and her knees had

gone weak when he'd ravished—and that was the only word for it—
ravished her mouth.

Turning her attention back to the trail before she tipped over the
sled while fantasizing about his mouth, she controlled the dogs as
they smelled food and put on a burst of speed. They were all hungry.
A nice long stop was just what the kids needed. And she could get a
few solid hours of much needed sleep. The adrenaline rush had left
her a little shaky and a lot exhausted.

The kiss had left her with the inability to concentrate. A couple of
hours of oblivion would do her good.

"Don't let me hold you up," she said casually as they pulled left
onto Puntilla Lake for the last stretch before reaching the lodge
checkpoint up ahead.

"Nothing's going to hold me up, sweetheart," he said with a
chuckle of amusement, clearly seeing through the cellophane for the
puny shield it was. "I'm a man on a mission."

THEY CHECKED IN, THEN STARTED A FIRE TO HEAT THE DOGS' FOOD, THEN
took their bales of straw to a sheltered spot under the trees to spread
for their animals. Derek smiled inwardly at how perfectly synchronized
he and Lily were as they each performed their tasks and finished up
at the same time.

There was one other team there already, the musher inside enjoying a late lunch, his dogs sleeping in the winter sunshine on their bed
of straw.

Just as they finished up, two more teams pulled in.

"I want Matt to look at Dingbat's shoulder," Lily told him absently.

"Don't be long. Remember, you're a competitor out here, not a
vet. Let Matt take care of the pack. You need to rest as much as they
do."

"And I will," she said over her shoulder, wandering off to talk to
her stepbrother, who'd already finished inspecting Derek's dogs.
"Catch you later."

She had no idea how soon later would be. Derek stuck his hands in the pockets of his coat and strolled over to greet the two other teams as they pulled out of the check-in area.

"Glad to see you made it through the pass okay," he said easily, speaking to Don and Jeff. He scanned the people milling about. Was the shooter here? He kept an eye on Lily and Matt.

"Crap. As if getting through the Happy River steps wasn't hard enough," Don groused, jumping off the sled. "Were you the one who cleared the trail?"

Derek smiled as they shook hands. He didn't much like the guy, and although he always trusted his instincts, he knew that a good portion of his dislike was because Don had dated Lily briefly. Derek tried to see him as a woman might. He just looked like a ballplayer gone to fat to him, but a woman might find his Nordic look appealing. "Pretty much dumped its load on Lily," Derek told the men, "then cleared itself. I reported it when we checked in. You made it through okay?"

"Yeah. Is Lily all right?" Don glanced over to where she stood talking to several of the volunteers.

None of your damn business. "Shaken. But not a scratch."

"Thank God," Don said easily. "Man, I was buried in an avalanche a few years back when I was up here trainin'. Scared the hell outta me, I gotta tell you. Glad she wasn't hurt."

Lily could've been a lot more than hurt and all three men knew it.

Jeff shuddered. "I don't want to do that again in a hurry."

"Not until next year, anyway," Derek said with a smile. Mushers had notoriously short memories for the danger. It was the exhilaration of the race, and the challenge, they remembered year after year.

Don chuckled, rubbing a gloved hand across the back of his neck. "Man, I'd kill for a decent cup of coffee."

"I'm sure they're ready for us inside," Derek told him.

They chatted about the trail conditions for a few more minutes, and when the two men went into the lodge, Derek went to collect Lily.

SHE WALKED LIKE A TODDLER—EVERY STEP A CONSCIOUS, WOBBLY EF-fort. Balancing on a sled for hours on end made for some pretty tight thigh muscles.

"You're making good time," Matt commented as he knelt to ex-amine the first in a line of energetic animals.

The checkpoint was in stark contrast to the hours spent on the trail. Memories of snow and solitude were lost in the bustling activity of busy volunteers and curious bystanders. Automatically, her head turned in the direction of the scent of coffee. As if predestined, her eyes found Derek in the crowd.

His profile was ruggedly handsome, more so when he offered an easy smile as he shook hands with a couple of the other competitors.

"Earth to Lily!" Matt called.

"The trip was . . ." She paused, realizing she didn't really want to rehash her misadventures on the route with Matt. "It was fine," she lied.

"You and Derek seem pretty evenly matched this year."

"I'm taking it easy on him," she returned with a mischievous grin. "I don't want to humiliate him this early in the race. That would be unkind."

"God forbid you ever be unkind," Matt muttered.

"What does that mean?"

He shrugged as he ran his hands along a dog's leg, massaging the joints at the shoulder and knee. "I'm just worried about you. The last few years have been tough and I'd like to see you start to enjoy life again."

Lily gave him a startled look. "You, too?"

Matt cast her a sidelong glance. "Me, too?"

Lily frowned. "Derek accused me of the same thing this morning. Not true. I enjoy my life just fine. I have our practice, I have my dogs, I have friends—"

"You've forgotten how to enjoy yourself. Which is completely

understandable," Matt added quickly. "You've had a very intense burden to carry, but maybe it's time to move on."

"I am moving on," Lily insisted, though her brain was suddenly
racing in a zillion directions. Eventually, though, all points converged
on the blatantly obvious. There was some truth to Matt's comments.
Was her life that bland?

She tried to think of how she might describe herself to a stranger.
A vet? No, that's my job, not me as a person.

*A widow? Nope, even worse. That means Sean gets to define who I am
even in death.*

Lily looked around the tented area, afraid for a minute she'd find
people staring at her and pointing. Here she was in the wilds of Alaska
having possibly the most important moment of self-realization of her
life. It was like being in a bad Fellini movie.

"Something wrong?" Matt asked.

Yes! I don't know who I am anymore. She shook her head. "I'm
whipped," she answered with a smile. "And I can, too, be unkind.
Ask anyone who gets between me and a hot meal."

"Trail food doesn't stay with you long, huh?"

She glanced over and caught Derek's eyes for a second. "You have
no idea how hungry you can get out there."

Ten

"THERE'S A FIRE UP AHEAD," DEREK SAID IN HER EAR. "TIME FOR a few hours' rest for both us and the dogs. We're stopping."

Lily didn't protest his high-handedness. She was exhausted, and absolutely starving. "Fine with me."

They hailed the camp as they approached. Three teams were gathered beside a roaring fire in the shelter of the trees. The mushers rose to greet them, and the dogs loudly barked hello.

They knew Bob Thompson, but introduced themselves to the two mushers they didn't know, Stan and Dave, and then split up to do what had to be done so they could eat and get some shut-eye.

The snow was coming down a little more densely now. Lily took care of her dogs, then liberated Derek's, and spread their sleeping mats. Then started the paw inspection. Derek, she noticed, was setting up a small tent. It made sense. They were six hours from the next check-point, and the predicted snowstorm was making good its promise to dump a few inches on them tonight. Even for a few hours' rest, the shelter made sense.

"No point pitching two," Derek said, coming up behind her.

"Knowing you, you'll be out of here the second your eyes pop open. One will save time." He paused as if waiting for her to argue.

She didn't. "Okay."

She was too tired to argue something that made perfect sense. She'd crawl into her sleeping bag and be fast asleep before he was. And be up and gone before he was awake. Lily planned to get herself and her dogs up after four hours. In the meantime, spending a few hours in the relative comfort of his tent would be welcome. It wasn't big, and she knew it would be a tight fit. But she was an adult, not an adolescent. Derek was too clever to attempt to jump her bones just because they were both prone in a small space. And if he could keep his hands off her, she most certainly could do the same with him.

Once she was done tending the animals, Derek had their coffee and food heated and had spread a sleeping bag beside the warmth of the fire. By the time they sat down to eat another of Annie's wonderful homemade meals, several other teams had arrived, and a party atmosphere built as greetings were shouted over the ruckus of a hundred excited dogs barking and howling to one another. Once the animals were fed, they'd tuck their heads beneath their tails and be dead to the world, but for now it was a madhouse of sound.

The campsite was a hive of activity as everyone took care of their dogs before coming back to the fire. Five small tents were pitched on the lee side of a small hill under the shelter of towering pines. Gather a group of mushers on a cold night beside a fire and the party was on, even though it usually lasted only an hour so. Everyone was equally tired and needed their rest. But it was pleasant to talk about trail conditions and shared experiences.

Somehow Lily found herself leaning back against the solid strength of Derek's chest as she stared into the dancing red and gold flames of their fire. Letting the conversation ebb and flow around her, she leaned her heavy head against him, finding a perfect spot in the curve of his shoulder as, only half awake, she listened to the conversation.

Barb had had a run-in with a moose just that morning, and between her and Derek exaggerating their stories, there was much laughter and teasing before everyone trundled off to their respective sleeping bags with full tummies and smiles on their faces. Lily closed her gritty eyes and let the firelight play on her lids.

"Ready for bed?" Derek asked softly, brushing bare fingers against her cheek in a warm caress.

Lily was too sleepy to move. "Hmm," she answered noncommittally. The sweet sound of a harmonica drifted over the chilly darkness. Holding her so she didn't fall over, Derek rose, then reached down and took her hands to pull her to her feet. Without missing a beat, he drew her body flush to his. There were too many bulky layers to feel anything but safe. Lily looked up at him. "What are you doing?" she whispered when he didn't release her.

"Enjoying a quiet moment with you." He tucked her head against his chest and started moving his feet.

Lily had to hold on to him and follow suit or stumble. His clothes smelled of wood smoke and damp leather. Lily turned her head to rest her cheek against his chest, and let her eyes drift closed, just savoring the moment. "We have quiet all day long." Her voice was muffled against his chest.

"Not like this. Not when I can hold you."

She realized they were dancing slowly. In the dark. Softly falling snow swirling around them. She slipped her hands inside his coat and wrapped her arms around his waist. He was warm, and Lily felt the overwhelming desire to curl up against him and draw that warmth deep inside herself. His utter masculinity emphasized the contrast between them. She'd never felt more female, more aware of her *self,* than when she was with him. The hard strength of his arms holding her made her feel more feminine. She spread her palm against his chest, feeling the steady beat of his heart beneath layers of clothing. She ached to touch his bare skin and called herself all kinds of fool for enjoying this so much.

Even though he was a foot taller, Lily fit right against his heart as if she'd been made to fit right there, as if they'd danced this way countless times, and knew each other's rhythm. Powerless to resist, her body rested against his. He was hard and strong, his arms like steel bands around her, keeping her safe, making her feel safe. Which was illogical, since he represented everything that was dangerous right now.

"God. I ache, I want you so badly." He tilted her chin up with his finger and brushed a kiss across her forehead. She waited for him to kiss her; wanted him to kiss her. Instead he tucked her head against his chest again.

"It's good to want things," Lily told him, feeling cheated and trying to be flip as her knees literally went weak at the unequivocal statement. "Doesn't mean you always get them."

He trailed cool fingers across her nape. "In this case we both want the same thing."

She looked up at him, hot and cold shivers dancing up and down her spine as he caressed her neck with gentle fingers. Flip was replaced with a shiver of premonition. For a moment they stared at each other, barely breathing. Lily felt a chaos of emotion fluttering inside her chest. "And do you always get what you want?"

His gaze dropped to her mouth briefly then rose to capture hers again. "Yes."

"Thanks for the warning." She needed to put a stop to this. Soon. She really did. Her breasts felt achy, her insides hot and liquid.

Derek swayed with her as the harmonica played a sweet, haunting melody that would've been more familiar coming from a fiddle. He wrapped a large hand around hers and held it against him so Lily felt his heartbeat echo in her own body. Her knees weakened further, and she wondered rather vaguely how long they'd hold her.

"I've always wanted you. Never stopped. This is going to be our turn." He and Sean had always been competitive. Derek had met her first, then she'd gone and married Sean. Was this his way of coming full circle?

She struggled to untangle emotion from physical awareness. It wasn't easy. "I'm not interested in having a casual affair with you, Derek. That's not my style." No, getting married was, she thought wryly. And look how well *that* had turned out. She should have had an affair with *Sean*. That would've worked out better, and been a whole lot less painful.

She felt the brush of his warm lips against her. "Maybe a casual affair isn't what I want."

Her eyes narrowed suspiciously. How long was a *serious* affair, according to Derek? A year instead of a couple of months? His women friends were legendary, but none of them seemed to last long. "Well then, maybe you'd better spit it out." She tilted her head so she could see his face, but it was all shadows and firelight and impossible to read. "Because I'm not sure just what it is you *do* want. Sex?"

His eyes darkened. "Hell, yes. I want you in my bed. In my arms. In my life." His voice was low, beguiling. He brushed her jaw with his fingertips and drew in a breath as he stared down at her, the sapphire earring winking in the firelight.

Her breath stuttered. Interpretation, she reminded herself. It was all in the interpretation. "You have to slow down."

"Maybe it's time you speeded it up and got with the program." Impatience throbbed in his voice. "You refuse to listen to what I'm telling you, you won't let me tell you how I feel—"

"This is neither the time nor the place." An ache spread in her chest. "Everything out here is magnified unrealistically. *Especially* with all this other stuff going on."

"This started long before the race and you know it."

"I don't trust it," she said flatly, finding it hard to draw a breath as she damned herself for a coward.

"Why not?"

Because I'm terrified that, like Sean, the illusion of you will be nothing like the reality. "I just don't."

He caught her chin in his hand and pressed a kiss to her mouth. "A few more days won't kill me," he groaned into her mouth. "*Much.* God. I love the smell of you. Snow, wet wool and the lemon fragrance of your hair."

"You're nuts."

"I like dancing with you like this. Look how well we fit together," he murmured, his voice thick. He stroked her cheek with his thumb. Back and forth. Back and forth, until her skin became hot and her body ached. "We have to do it on a real dance floor sometime. I want to see you in a slinky dress, something thin and clingy and short enough to show off your truly spectacular legs."

Only their bodies moved now. Gently swaying from side to side. Lily felt breathless and giddy. High on cold air and hot Derek. "You've never seen my legs."

"Yeah, twice. Our movie date, and then that day I came over to see Sean and you'd just taken a shower, remember?"

"No." She'd walked out of the bathroom rubbing her hair dry, dressed only in her shirt and panties because she'd forgotten her jeans on the bed. Sean had kept her talking to him in the bedroom, almost intentionally delaying her while Derek sat beside the bed, his face impassive. His look had told her that he'd seen hundreds of pairs of bare leg and hers were no big whoop.

"He wanted me to want you, you know."

Lily stared up at him, trying to read his expression by the glow of the flickering fire. The dancing reflection in his eyes made him look slightly demonic. "What?"

"He enjoyed knowing how much I wanted you."

"You told him?"

"No. But one of Sean's most remarkable traits was knowing how to read people."

Sean's remarkable trait had been noted and despised by his wife. Because he read people so that he could con them, and the people he'd conned never knew they'd been hit. Herself included.

"He was good at manipulation," Lily said flatly.

"He's the last person I want you thinking about right now," Derek said dryly, brushing his mouth across her forehead again. "Just close your eyes and rest against me for a few more minutes while Rob plays. You need to rest tonight if you want to kick my ass tomorrow."

"I'm beat." She tried to move out of his arms, then flushed hot and embarrassed when she realized that he'd let her go immediately. It was *her* arm about his waist holding them together.

"Are you going to be an octopus in there?" Lily asked, jerking her chin toward the small tent.

"I've never been an octopus in my life. Doesn't mean I won't want to hold you."

Lily gave him a considering look for a fraction of second. "I'm really exhausted. Let's go to bed."

Derek gave her a brilliant smile. A smile that shot straight inside her chest like a bolt of sunshine warming her from head to toe. Oh, God, Lily thought, feeling panicky inside, I am in such big trouble here.

"Bless your heart, sweetheart," Derek said, still smiling. "I've been waiting for you to make that offer for years."

"Dream on," Lily whispered back. Not exactly brilliant, but the best she could manage right now. *Yep. Big trouble.* She scrambled into the tent. It was going to be a tight fit. It did, however, give her pause that she was far gone enough to sleep beside the man who'd told her flat out that he *wanted* her.

"Take off your boots," he told her, crawling in beside her feet first.

"No way. My feet are already freezing."

The firelight bathed the top of his dark head in a red halo. How fitting, Lily thought with amusement as she closed her eyes. Angel and demon. Two for the price of one.

She listened to him zip up the entrance of the tent, enclosing them in a bubble of darkness. He settled down beside her, and pulled the sleeping bag more tightly around her head. "Warm enough?"

His breath fanned her face as he leaned over her; she smelled the coffee he'd drunk with dinner and the toothpaste he'd just used.

"Toasty."

His knuckles brushed her cheekbone. She felt the warmth of his fingers trailing along her cheek, leaving a path of heat to her mouth.

"I'm always amazed at how soft your skin is. Soft, and silky. The only time I've ever seen skin like this is on my nieces and nephews as babies. You glow as if you have a light on inside you."

"Derek—"

"Your skin should be as tough as old leather, but instead it's as fine-grained as a baby's." His thumb brushed down to her mouth as his fingers cupped her cheeks.

He turned her face up to his, and Lily couldn't help the lazy drift of her lashes as she opened her eyes. He was going to kiss her, and she wanted him to with every fiber of her being.

The fire lit only the very tips of his black lashes, leaving most of his face in darkness. Lily shivered as his thumb rasped over her lower lip.

He leaned over her. Their eyes met. *Kiss me.* Her heart trip-hammered in her chest. Plenty enough time for her to jerk her head away and be sensible. *Kiss me.* Lily watched him approaching until her eyes strained. She closed them as he lowered his mouth to hers. At first he merely brushed his lips back and forth over hers. His mouth was warm, and firm and smooth. She felt a hint of stubble as he grazed his mouth against hers in a languid sweep that made her breasts ache and her breath catch.

His tongue, hot and moist, teased the corners of her mouth. Lily was surprised to hear her own ragged breathing as his tongue stealthily pried her lips apart. The taste of him was intoxicating. Hot and sweet.

Oh, God. How could any woman resist this? How could she?

He raised his head and her mouth felt cold. "Sweet dreams," he told her softly. He dropped an avuncular kiss on the tip of her nose, then rolled over.

Lily stared at the back of his head and realized he'd cleverly never fully answered "What is it you want?" when she'd asked earlier.

HE NEEDED SLEEP, GODDAMN IT. THESE PEOPLE MOVED AT THE DROP OF a fucking hat, but at least *they'd* gotten a few hours' shut-eye. More than he could do, he thought bitterly as he kept Lily in his sights as she trundled along in the valley below him. He had to stay awake to keep an eye on her until he could get close enough again. What the fuck had they been doing last night? Dancing? He'd like to have been a fly on the wall of that tent after they crawled in there together.

Imagining what they'd been doing to each other had kept him warm for the first hour. The next three had been fucking purgatory.

Fuckshitdamnittohell. They'd barely stopped to rest the dogs before they were off again. Didn't they ever fucking get tired? And as for food— Ten grand burning a hole in his pocket didn't make up for smelling their food from a mile away when he'd had nothing to eat but jerky for hours. He wanted pizza. Hot. Spicy. Dripping with gooey cheese. And a beer.

The next stop, he promised himself. The very next time they stopped, he'd do her. *Hell, fuck. Why not* them*?* He'd kill 'em both.

Then he'd go back home and take a nice long vacation. Somewhere tropical. Somewhere where the chicks wore string-bikini bottoms and went topless. Where their white teeth glowed against their tans. Yeah. Somewhere nice and hot. Somewhere with hot babes and cold beer.

He scratched the back of his neck. They'd been traveling for fourteen boring fucking hours. They'd have to take a decent break soon. And when they did, he'd be ready.

SIXTEEN GRUELING HOURS LATER AND DEREK FELT AS THOUGH HE'D never slept. He had planned ahead and made a reservation for one of the four guest rooms at the lodge at the next checkpoint. Even though at the time he hadn't been sure if he'd even want to stop there. If nothing else, a hot shower and a meal he didn't have to defrost first held great appeal. Now he was glad he'd done it.

Lily's face was pale. She was running on empty, and desperately needed a few uninterrupted hours' sleep. Naturally, she'd never admit it. Especially to him. And damned if a part of him didn't admire that stick up her ass, even if he did want to yank it out. A few hours in a warm bed would go a long way to revitalize her. Hell, revitalize both of them.

Especially if he could talk her into sharing a bed.

Not that he'd planned on that before. But now, with her here and the memory of the kiss still rattling through him, it was hard *not* to consider it. But first things first.

He wanted Lily rested. Safe.

Keep it casual and nonthreatening, he reminded himself as he fed his team. All he wanted to do was snatch her up in his arms, carry her upstairs and tuck her into his bed. He tamped down the clawing need.

After the dogs got clearance from the volunteer vets, Derek checked in while Lily went to the bathroom. When she came out he handed her a key. She took it automatically, then frowned as she looked up at him. "I can't take your room."

"I'm not that altruistic," he told her dryly. "We're both exhausted. I'm willing to share. And before you get all bent out of shape, there are two beds. I promise to behave."

She looked suspicious, but the fatigue dragging at her was helping him make his point. One last temptation. "How does a nice hot shower sound?"

"Like heaven." She eyed him warily, but the glance didn't have any of her usual heat. "And that would be a *solitary* heaven."

"Hey," he said, giving her a grin that had been known to bring women to their knees, "no ego problem with you, is there? Did I *mention* showering with a friend? I don't think so."

"Okay then," she said with a slow, sweet smile that confused the hell out of him. "As long as we're clear on that, I'd love to take a shower."

"See?" He quirked an eyebrow, and felt that smile through his body like a warm caress. "Wasn't so hard to be nice to me, was it?"

"I can be nice," she said sweetly. "If you could be trusted."

He gave her a wide-eyed-innocent look that didn't fool either of them. "Me? I'm harmless."

She snorted.

People milled around them in the lobby, but it was as if they were in their own private little bubble.

"Why are you so skittish around me, Lily?" he asked softly. "Have I ever done anything to make you think I'd take advantage of you? Or done anything you don't want me to do?"

Her eyes narrowed. "Skittish?"

"Like Cosmos."

Lily just stared at him. "Oh, please. You're comparing me to a *mare*? How flattering. And I suppose you think you're the man to break me to bridle?"

Oh, he'd like to *ride* her, no doubt. But as to the other . . . "No. I'd never break you."

She looked up at him, humor now glinting in her eyes. God, she was pretty. "But you consider yourself a stud, don't you?"

"Now who's being flattering?" he teased. "I wouldn't exactly call myself a stallion."

"I didn't say *stallion,*" Lily pointed out with a laugh. "But now that you mention it, you consider yourself the biggest, baddest stallion of all, don't you? Fortunately *I'm* totally immune to your charms."

"So you've mentioned. About ninety-nine times." He reached out and gently brushed her cold cheek with his fingertips. "Wonder who you're trying to convince?"

Eleven

THE ROOM WAS UTILITARIAN, CLEAN AND WARM. THEY EACH, RATHER symbolically, Lily thought, dumped a duffel bag at the foot of each full-size bed. "Dibs I shower first," she said, swamped by the overwhelming need to lie down and close her eyes. She pulled off her fur hat and tossed it onto her bed. Derek did the same.

And they stared at each other.

Lily realized, with frighteningly little alarm, that she was trapped between the two beds, a desk at her back, and a very large, very potent Derek Wright just two feet away.

"Go for it." A wicked gleam lit his eyes and a small smile curved the lines of his mouth. He stood far too close. Damn him. He wasn't going to back up.

"Go for what?" *Him?*

"That shower?"

Right. The shower. She'd just called it. One look into his eyes made her forget everything. *Oh boy.* This was going to be harder than she'd thought.

Lily tried to look away, and found she couldn't. "Oh, yeah," she whispered. "Shower. I'm looking forward to it." His blue eyes were almost black as he observed her. God. Those x-ray eyes again. And, God help her, she was sure she felt the heat of his large body through both their sheepskin coats. Ridiculous, she assured herself. Pure fantasy born of serious sleep deprivation. But her pulse pounded in places she hadn't felt a pulse in years, and her breasts tightened.

She'd woken in the early hours of this morning cradled in his arms, her head on his shoulder, his warm breath ruffling her hair. She pretended to be sleeping when she sensed he was awake. *Coward.* Instead of jumping up and beating him out of camp and getting on the trail early, she'd lain there in his arms. Content to drift and dream.

Now hours and hours later, it was as if they had gone directly from the snug, warm intimacy of the tent to this pristine, well-lit bedroom.

Holding her gaze, Derek slowly started unbuttoning his coat. He had beautiful hands, Lily thought. Broad palms, long fingers . . . Her mouth went dry, and her throat closed up with longing. She wanted his hands on her. God help her, she wanted his mouth on her, too. Her brain was frostbitten. Why else would she even think like this?

Lord, it was hot in here! Lily started unbuttoning her own heavy coat, realized what that might look like and stopped, her hand on the top button.

"Think I'm going to jump you?" he asked silkily, a wicked glint in his eyes.

Unconsciously she licked her lips as he shrugged off his coat, unveiling jeans and a heavy-knit navy blue sweater. He tossed the coat on the bed beside him. His chest was broad and solid. He smelled of damp wool and man, and Lily's internal organs did the happy dance at the delicious combo.

She looked up into his smoldering blue eyes and shook her head. "Don't be ridiculous. Of course not." She was losing her mind here. This was Derek Wright, for God's sake. A woman, a sensible woman, didn't hold the gaze of a cobra moments before it struck. She shot it or ran like hell.

There was nowhere to run. Her gun was in the duffel at the foot of her bed. Three feet behind Derek.

"I need to go to the bathroom," she lied rather desperately.

He smiled knowingly. The rat. "You went downstairs."

Lily scowled. "So what? I have to go again."

"Fine. I'll go down and see what I can rustle up to eat while you take care of business." He didn't move. "Any preferences?"

"Lots and hot."

Unfortunately, "lots and hot" could refer to a number of things that had nothing to do with food. Besides, she had something a lot more immediate to contend with than hunger. How had he gotten so close? The room was small but it suddenly felt like a closet.

Of course he *was* enormous. Tall, broad— Oh, God, and they were supposed to sleep in this room? The beds were only a few feet apart. She couldn't do it. She really couldn't.

Lily was willing to bet there wasn't a woman alive who could survive a night with Derek Wright and walk away unscathed. Physical impossibility. Even a *nun* would find herself tempted and Lily was no nun.

Her body swayed toward him. As much as her instincts urged her to press closer, self-preservation ordered a retreat. Now if only there was somewhere to go . . .

It was as if he could read her mind. Oh, Lord, she hoped he really couldn't. "Okay," she said and winced at how loud her voice sounded, even to herself. "You get food, I'll take a shower—" She inhaled sharply and blew the air out in a rush. "Then we'll get some sleep and hit the road bright and early."

"Uh-huh."

"Seriously." She took a step forward, holding out both hands to ward him off just in case. "You food. Me shower."

"Deal," he said, his gaze locked on her mouth. Suddenly she yawned, a huge, unaffected, jaw-popping yawn. Derek's laughter broke the spell. "Okay, go shower, then food, then a nice nap. Hit the bathroom, I'll be back before you know it."

That's what she was afraid of. As soon as the door closed behind him Lily rifled through her bag for clean clothes, then stumbled into the bathroom, legs still shaky and pulse pounding. She locked the door behind her, which provided a flimsy sense of security. Not that she imagined Derek would rudely come in when she was showering, but she also felt certain that if he was so inclined, a mere standard lock wouldn't stand in his way. There was something moderately thrilling about the thought. For just a brief second—a flash of a second, really—Lily imagined Derek kicking in the door, scooping her into his arms and carrying her to bed. In her mind's eye he was more dashing than Rhett Butler, and the scene way more erotic than the constraints of a 1939 film.

Chicken, she scolded herself as she turned on the shower then stripped. So much for trying to become proactive. *That* had all the earmarks of a woman not willing to make a difficult decision, and hoping the man would take that choice out of her hands. Shame on her.

She shook her head at herself.

The hot water felt wonderful on her cold skin, but she didn't linger. If she stayed under the spray she'd be asleep in minutes. Her tired brain extrapolated from there. Derek would have to come in and haul her comatose body, naked, out of the shower. Lily wasn't sure she could resist him right now. Even if she was in a coma. Trust didn't come into it. Her body and her brain weren't in sync on Derek Wright.

He'd saved her life twice in as many days. Yet she still wasn't sure she could trust him. Unfortunately, she could deny it till the cows came home, but Derek turned her on. He always had. She touched her wet lips, remembering his kisses, and felt the tingle all the way through her body.

She purposely turned the stream of hot water to cold and yelped as the first blast struck her breasts and belly. "Take that, you dimwit," she whispered, but she turned it quickly back to hot again. She'd been in the *snow* with him for days, for God's sake, and that cold hadn't kept her from feeling the attraction. A short blast of cold water didn't stand a chance. She wasn't immune to Derek's charm. And, God help her, she wasn't completely vaccinated to prevent reinfection either.

"But," she argued with herself, "why should I be so worried? So I want him. Big deal. Sex isn't a lifetime commitment, for pity's sake. It's just sex. Chemistry." Lily climbed out of the tub and grabbed a towel. Was she that much of a coward? Derek couldn't hurt her emotionally unless she allowed him to. She put her foot up on the edge of the tub to dry her leg.

She was a mature woman.

Not a young girl.

She enjoyed sex.

It wasn't illegal to want a man when his—*her*—affections weren't involved. Was it?

She'd tried love. It hadn't worked out for her. So what? She didn't want to *marry* Derek. All she wanted was to sleep with him. Sex without love could—she assumed—be just as good as sex while in love.

Lily yawned as she dressed, another jaw-cracking yawn that brought tears to her eyes. She was torn, and all her instincts of self-preservation were in conflict as far as Derek was concerned. She wanted him, but she didn't *want* to want him.

Fact was, her chemicals were strongly attracted to his chemicals. Pheromones hard at work.

But you don't trust him, her brain reminded her.

Why, though? she asked herself. Sean had been the liar. She'd already established that. So why was she so determined to cling to some of those obvious lies he'd told her about Derek?

Because those lies were the only things preventing her from falling into Derek's arms and making a complete fool of herself. That's why.

All the things about him that attracted her, attracted legions of *other* women, too. And when a man was presented with a banquet, why make a commitment to eating one peanut butter sandwich for the rest of his life?

That was reality.

She had nothing to offer a sophisticated man like Derek Wright. The novelty of her would eventually wear off, and he'd move on to greener pastures.

"But on the other hand," she murmured, "I'm not *expecting* a commitment, am I? And if I control the situation, we both win. He wants sex. I want sex." Boy howdy, she wanted sex. With him. Only with him.

Right now she was a challenge for him. The one that got away. Lily suspected women rarely told Derek no. So she'd become his Moby-Dick.

Oh, God. Her brain was going to explode.

Too much thinking, not enough sleeping.

That's all this was. Exhaustion overriding common sense.

She opened the bathroom door, expecting to see her nemesis, but the room was still empty. Her stomach growled long and pitifully, reminding her she was starving for more than just Derek's touch. Walking to the window, she brushed aside the drape to look down at her team lying stretched out, sleeping in the late afternoon sun.

Volunteers and observers still milled around out there, checking in a few teams, inspecting dogs, drinking steaming mugs of coffee and apparently oblivious to the cold. It was freezing, but they didn't seem to care. Of course they slept well at night, somewhere enclosed and warm. And most of them traveled by snowmobile, vehicle or plane from checkpoint to checkpoint.

They should try a sled and team for real excitement, Lily thought, her gaze touching on each of her dogs. She grinned as Dingbat rolled onto his back—legs folded over his barrel chest, mouth open, tongue lolling as he slept. She didn't need to hear him to know the little monster was snoring. Her Arrow and Derek's Max lay curled together, their doggie breath mingling over their heads.

"Sweet dreams, kids." She let the drape drop over the window. "Me next." She removed her duffel from the bed and tossed it on the floor, then lay down with a gusty sigh. A flat surface had never felt so good.

"Come on Lily," she whispered drunkenly, "at least stay awake long enough to eat." That was her last conscious thought as her eyelids drooped.

DAMN IT. GETTING THE FOOD, WITH A LODGE FULL OF PEOPLE, HAD taken Derek longer than he'd planned. When he returned to their room, Lily was fast asleep, curled up in the middle of her bed.

He nudged the door closed behind him. She didn't even flinch in her sleep at the noise. Shaking his head, he set the loaded tray on the table between the beds.

The room smelled of Ivory soap and steam, and the faint, subtle fragrance of Lily herself. Derek took a moment to skirt his bed and lock the door, then shoved a straight-backed chair under the handle. Not as a defense, but as a habit. A puny chair couldn't stop someone from entering, but it would make enough noise to give him that millisecond of advance warning.

He considered the imminent danger, and dismissed it as negligible. For the moment. There were too many people around for his half-assed assassin to make a move here and now. Coward he appeared to be, he'd rather strike when there was no one else around.

And that suited Derek just fine. He planned on giving the bastard enough rope to hang himself. But for now, he was safe. And he'd keep Lily safe, too. He'd let her enjoy another day on the trail. A short one. And at the next checkpoint his team would be in place and she'd be airlifted back to a safety zone. Whether she agreed or not.

This wrinkle with Milos Pekovic's Oslukivati couldn't be helped. National security had to take precedence. But not even for his country would Derek put Lily in danger.

Considering how scared she was to fly, man, she was going to be pissed when he tossed her into a helicopter.

But better pissed than dead.

She'd get over pissed. Dead was forever.

He looked down at her. She was, disappointingly, fully dressed after her shower. But he'd had an enjoyable time downstairs waiting in the chow line fantasizing about coming back upstairs to find her waiting for him. Naked. In his bed. As he'd envisioned so many times before.

Her hair would be wet, tangled in sweet-smelling skeins down her back, clinging to her damp skin. Her nipples would be the same soft pink as her lips, begging the touch of his hands. They'd be hard because the bedroom was cooler than the humid heat in the bathroom. She'd raise her arms to welcome him—

Derek shook his head and ruefully smiled down at her sleeping form. Not his Lily. She'd be more likely to raise her fist at him than open, willing arms.

She just didn't trust him.

Never had.

But she would, by God. Lily Munroe would learn to trust him. And soon.

Of course, shipping her unwilling butt home was going to set his goal back a step or two, he thought wryly. But what was life without a challenge?

And God only knew, Lily Munroe was challenge personified.

She'd pulled the covers back, but hadn't had the energy to pull them over herself as she laid down. She was curled on her side facing him, the sheet and blanket crumpled at her feet. He studied her face as she slept. The long dark lashes resting against her cheeks, the snake of her braid leaving a damp trail across the front of her pale yellow sweatshirt.

He rose quietly and pulled the covers up over her. Indulged himself by letting his palm glide over her damp hair, over the sweet, warm contour of her cheek. His eyes lingered on her soft mouth and he ached.

He tucked the covers up around her neck, and she shifted slightly in her sleep. The covers rustled as she snuggled against the crisp sheets. She gave a little whimper of pleasure, and the sound shot directly to his groin. *Ah, Jesus, Lily—*

"What are you dreaming about, little hedgehog?" he asked, voice husky and soft so as not to wake her. "What's going through that agile mind of yours when you watch me with such distrust? When will you feel safe enough with me to stop using Sean as a smoke-screen? And when the hell are you going to admit that you want me as badly as I want you?"

He brushed his fingers over her lips as he sighed. "Sleep easy, sweetheart. I'll be right here keeping you safe." *From everything. Including myself.*

Ignoring the sandwiches on the tray, and the Thermos of coffee, Derek grabbed up his duffel and went into the bathroom to shower.

AN HOUR LATER, HIS HEART JUMPED WHEN HE SMELLED HER CLEAN, damp skin as she came out of the bathroom. She'd woken about ten minutes ago and gone into the bathroom for a second shower. The room was almost dark; just the faint glow of the lights outside illuminated it and lessened the shadows. Hands stacked beneath his head, Derek kept his eyes closed, feigning sleep.

He heard the soft pad of her bare feet across the carpet as she walked past the foot of his bed to the window. Checking the dogs. She stayed there a few moments. He heard her turn, and imagined the warmth of her gaze on him.

He kept his breathing easy, and with difficulty, his libido in check. "I know you're awake."

So much for stealth. He opened his eyes and smiled at her. She didn't smile back. "Shit. Now what? No way could I have pissed you off already," he said softly. "I was sleeping. I'm an innocent man."

She wore shiny black athletic leggings, the pale yellow sweatshirt and a scowl. She spread her feet as if getting ready for a fight, and folded her arms over her chest as she glared at him. "You're a lot of things," she countered. "Innocent isn't one of them."

"What's the problem now?"

She narrowed her eyes. "Let's just have sex and get it over with."

His heart stopped dead in his chest and he came up on his elbows. "Say what?"

"Sex." Her head tipped to one side and her long rope of damp hair swung gently against her breast. "You want it, and I like it just fine. So what do you say? Let's just do it and get it out of your system. All this sexual tension is distracting me from the race."

"Jesus, Lily." Derek choked back a laugh. "What happened to foreplay?"

"You started foreplay in Anchorage, didn't you?"

He swung his legs over the side of the mattress and rose. He towered over her, but she stood her ground, still glaring at him. It was the least loverlike stance he'd ever seen. He bit back a smile. *Ah, Lily.* A rapid pulse beat at the base of her throat as she tried to stare him down. The familiar shaft of longing cut through him, this time so deep he almost snatched her up in his arms.

"Yeah. I did," he said evenly. "Even though I usually prefer my foreplay to be a bit more proactive. I didn't think you noticed."

"I noticed." Bright flags of color burned in her face, and her eyes, very bright, and more green than hazel, settled levelly on his face. "Well?"

"Are you positive this is what you want? Here? Now?"

She shrugged. "If I wasn't sure, I wouldn't say so. You've been trying for years to get me naked. So here's your chance. Let's see what you've got." Brave words for a woman who could barely make eye contact.

Derek bit back a sympathetic smile. *How far will you take this, sweet Lily? How far can I let you take this before I internally combust?* A test then. He hooked his thumbs into his front pockets to keep from grabbing her. *Down boy.* "Quite an invitation."

She reached for a sandwich from the tray and took a bite. "Just make it relatively quick, okay?" she said, mouth full. "I really would like to get going."

Ah, Jesus, he thought, wanting to laugh. He hoped to hell they could laugh about this one day. Right now he felt as though he was dying a slow, painful death of anticipation, with a very real chance of grave disappointment as the payoff. "Never say quick to a man."

She swallowed, then shrugged. "Whatever." She took another bite, her eyes on his face as she chewed. "I don't have all day. Take it or leave it."

If he didn't "take it," he was afraid she'd choke considering how fast she was chomping down on that sandwich.

Sweet, precious Lily. So nervous. So brave.

He reached out and brushed crumbs off her chest and she jumped. Her nipples showed beneath her sweatshirt, hard little buds that made him ache. "Easy. Easy," he whispered to her, but telling himself *very* sternly that as much as he wanted it, this wasn't the night he'd be sleeping with Dr. Lily Munroe. She was too jumpy, and clearly running on pure bravado. Still, she'd offered to bring him a step closer to his eventual goal.

He gave her an assessing look. Didn't mean he couldn't play along. "Fine." He pulled his T-shirt over his head and tossed it behind him on his bed. "Take your clothes off and lie down."

The pulse visible at the base of her throat hammered, and Lily shot him a startled look over the crust of her second sandwich.

Derek mimicked her earlier careless shrug. "I'd rather make love to you slowly the first time at least. But hell, I'm more than willing to accommodate you if you just want down-and-dirty sex. Get naked and lie down."

"You sure know how to set the mood."

"The mood will be long past if you don't hop to it, sweetheart. Strip."

Lily tossed the half-eaten sandwich back on the plate and wiped her hands, then licked a crumb off her lower lip. The movement shot directly to his groin. Jesus. He was ready to jump out of his skin here. He thought for a minute that she'd chicken out and change her mind as she hesitated. But damned if she didn't cross her arms and grab the bottom of her shirt.

Either she was prepared to drive him to drink by the slow-mo striptease, or she was even more nervous than he'd thought and was having a hard time baring herself to his avid gaze. Either way his mouth went dry and his body rigid as each delectably pale inch of skin was revealed as she tugged the soft yellow fleece up her body.

He leaned down and brushed his mouth against the still-damp skin of her chest. She froze. "Keep going," he told her, his voice thick as he dropped kisses across the gentle mounds of her breasts. "I'm just getting a head start while you get undressed."

He kissed the silky skin of her underarm, and let his hands learn the gentle slope of her midriff as she remembered halfway through that she'd been removing her shirt.

She got it over her head and tossed a flutter of yellow onto the bed behind her.

With leisurely appreciation his gaze traveled down her body, then up again. "Worth the wait," he told her reverently, letting his eyes feast. Feverish, balanced on a knife edge of desire, he already felt crazed with lust, but forced himself to take slow, easy breaths.

Her skin was creamy pale in contrast to the black leggings she wore. No sexy, lacy underwear for his Lily. Hell no. Just a plain, un-adorned, utilitarian white cotton bra. Not a shimmer of ribbon or a ruffle of lace, just the soft swell of her breasts for decoration. Derek had never seen anything as sexy in his life.

Her nipples poked through the thin fabric as if reaching for him. Her breasts were small, plump and ripe for his touch, and flushed rosy with desire. He cupped her through her bra. Her lashes fluttered, but she gamely watched his face as he ran a thumb over the hard points.

"How's that pressure feel for you?" he asked politely.

"F-fine."

"Only fine?" He frowned. "Damn. I'm losing my touch." He bent his head and brushed a kiss to one nipple through the fabric of her utilitarian bra. She speared her fingers through his hair. *Good. That's good.* He drew the hard little bud into the wet cavern of his mouth and sucked until he felt her knees give. *Better.*

"Hard-and-fast sex can be excellent." He blew gently on the wet fabric, and she whimpered, her fingers tightening in his hair with a muffled little moan. "I have absolutely—like that? Terrific—no problem with making it hard"—he brought one hand up to cup her breast as he suckled—"and fast. If that's what you—oh, this succulent morsel feels lonely—want." His mouth clamped down gently on her other nipple and he had to hold her upright as her knees wobbled.

He licked down her cleavage, and murmured, "That's what you want, right? Instant gratification?" He skimmed his hands around her rib cage, and felt the falter of her pulse beneath her soft skin like a swarm of butterflies beating their wings to freedom. "Lily?"

Eyes glazed, lips parted, she mumbled, "Ah . . . I . . . sure. Yes."

"Then it's the do-it-your-way special coming up." He smoothed a hand up the satiny skin of her back and clicked the fastening of her bra, then brought his hands up to her shoulders and skimmed the straps down her arms. She shivered.

Electricity came off her skin in waves. For a moment he thought she'd renege as she held her arms clamped to her sides, holding the flimsy garment in place. But after a small hesitation, Lily relaxed and the bra fell to the floor.

The outside lights glinted in her eyes as she said impatiently, "Are you going to kiss me again anytime soon?"

"Hmm?" he asked absently, letting his senses fill with the sight of Lily topless. "Perfect."

"I'm too sma—"

"Absolutely perfect."

Watching her, looking into those heavy, dazed eyes, he reached behind her head and brought her braid forward over one breast. He picked it up, and painted her pale pink nipples with the paintbrush at the end of her plait. Then he unwound the rubber band at the end and used both hands to spread the golden brown, Raphaelite mane over her creamy shoulders.

Her pupils dilated as she whispered, "I don't know what to do with my hands."

His penis leaped in anticipation. "Anything you want." He took her hands and put them palms down on his chest. Her fingers curled against his burning skin, as she stared up at him, lips parted. "Kiss me."

Hooking his thumbs into the silky spandex leggings encasing her hips and legs, he gave a tug. He'd kiss her until the earth's light died. He'd kiss her until she didn't know where she stopped and he began. He'd waited so damn long for this that he didn't want to skip one infinitesimal step.

"Yeah, sure, in a minute," he told her dismissively. Oh, he'd kiss her all right. But not until her mind and body were on the same page. "If I have time. Damn, these things are tight," he gritted out. "How did you get into—ah, just like Christmas."

He skimmed the leggings down her legs, taking an interesting-looking white thong with them. Not so utilitarian after all, sweet Lily.

She was naked.

Pale and naked.

Pink and naked.

Beautifully, gloriously naked.

He wanted a portrait painted of her just like this.

Her skin was satin smooth, flawless, lickably silky, begging to be tasted. He was so hard he was in pain.

Was quick sex really what she wanted? No emotion? She'd held him off for . . . hell, forever. And now she wanted it fast and dirty? "Are you sure this is what you want, Lily?" he asked, watching her eyes darken and lose focus.

"I'm standing here naked, aren't I?" She reached out and hooked her fingers into his belt loops, jerking his hips toward hers. "One of us is overdressed for this party." Her fingers went for his fly. She was going to have a tough time getting his zipper down over his erection, but he let her fight it for a while.

She was trying damn hard, but he was harder. He pushed her hand aside. "I'll do it."

He was primed as a pistol, and so ready for her, her desire to have fast-and-dirty sex might become a reality.

When she reached for him again, he kicked off his jeans and

shorts and sat down naked on the rumpled bed. He reached out and pulled her between his spread knees before she could back away. She gave a startled yelp as he held her in place, implacable hands bracketing her hips, thighs clamping around hers.

"There's fast," he murmured, leaning forward to place his open mouth on her smooth belly. "And then there's *mm-mm* good."

Twelve

MM-MM GOOD? LILY THOUGHT VAGUELY. SHE'D GONE FROM SIM-mer to boil before she'd taken her top off.

Oh, God. Don't seduce me. Don't make this perfect, she thought desperately, fisting her hands in Derek's hair as his mouth, warm and firm, glided across her stomach on a slow path designed to swamp her defenses. She squeezed her eyes shut. *Don't make me feel as though this could be forever when I know, for you, there's no such thing.*

Wham bam, thank you, ma'am would scratch both their itches, and allow her to emerge unscathed. But Derek wasn't letting her have her way in this. He seemed determined to take his sweet time tormenting her.

No fair! This was her party. She should be allowed to dictate which sensations received invitations.

But, as always, Derek had his own agenda.

She shifted, and his hard fingers tightened implacably around her naked hips. Did he think she was going to call uncle *now*? Her head felt unbearably heavy as he held her against his mouth, as though she were a particularly juicy ear of corn he wanted to savor.

The analogy was spot-on accurate as she felt herself melt like butter under the slow, hot onslaught of his mouth. Her head fell back and she gave a little moan.

"I love the feel of your skin," he said, lifting his head as his thumbs brushed her hips. "Just as I imagined. Smooth and silky as it looks. And Christ. Soft. So soft." He trailed burning kisses across her belly button, then made her body tighten when she felt the hot lave of his tongue on her skin.

Lily's knees buckled; only his strong hands held her upright. "Derek—"

"I'm not doing this the way you think you want it, sweetheart," he murmured thickly as his hands curved over her hips to stroke her bottom. "I've waited a goddamned eternity for this moment. Nobody's going to rush me. Not even you." He brushed a heated kiss across her left breast, then took her nipple into the hot cavern of his mouth.

Lily's bones melted. His strong arms held her upright. Every nerve and cell in her body felt alive and alert. Head back, eyes tightly shut, she felt each silken strand of his hair between her fisted fingers. She felt the hairy rasp of his legs against the smooth skin of her thighs as he clamped her between his knees to keep her where he wanted her.

His hands were lightly callused, erotically so, as he skimmed them slowly up her back, tracing the indentation of her spine. "Once," he said with a dry chuckle, "I lived for months on one sighting of your bare feet."

"Bare feet?" Lily asked vaguely. There were no words to describe the sensation of him suckling her nipple. It felt . . . sharp . . . sweet . . . frustrating . . . blissful as he curled his agile tongue around and around in a maddening caress that left Lily jumpy and aching for more.

"When we went to the movies. You wore high-heeled sandals. Your feet were bare. You always wear work boots. It was the first time in my life I realized I had a thing for feet. Your feet."

Lily felt a bubble of amusement fill her chest. Silly man. She ran her hands down his skull, feeling his hard head cushioned beneath the silky weight of his hair. He needed a haircut, she thought, as she cradled the back of his head and at the same time exerted enough pressure for him to suckle her nipple harder.

Laughter, lust, some other *L* word bubbled up in her chest as she said weakly, "My feet are bare now, too."

"Hard to imagine," he said, voice muffled, "but I found something I like even better." He kissed the side of her breast. "But hold that thought."

Her fingers trailed down the back of his strong neck and then she had to spread her hands on top of his broad shoulders as he moved with exquisite care across the hill and valley from one breast to the other.

This so wasn't what she'd had in mind, Lily thought with one of her few remaining brain cells. But then, how could she have imagined anything like this? Her experiences with men were pitifully few, and Sean . . . she wasn't sure Sean even *counted* as an experience.

Oh, Derek Wright was in a league all his own.

And oh boy.

"Are we thinking—ah—of taking this to a flat surface soon? Or are we doing it where we stand?"

He peppered the dip between her breasts with kisses. "No hurry."

"This from a man whose—" erection was so hard and enormous Lily felt it move impatiently against her thigh as if it were alive and knocking for entrance. Saliva dried up in her mouth; her heart pounded painfully against her ribs. She felt both hazy and preternaturally alert. Her skin felt too sensitive, all the pleasure nerves exposed. Her breasts felt hot and tender; her skin buzzed as if electrically charged.

His hand came up to stroke her breast, sending hot shivers all the way down to her toes. "Whose?" he asked huskily, breath hot and damp against her skin, dark head still bent over her breast. Hands still on his shoulders, Lily dropped onto the bed, her knees on either side of his hips. She brought her hands up to cup his face, then tilted it up so she could see his eyes. Clear. Steady. Hot blue.

A part of her wanted to push him away. Making love with him

would bring her more unhappiness in the long run than she'd ever known.

Run. Now. Don't look back!

But, God, how could something that felt so right be wrong? Hadn't she dreamed of this—even on her wedding night? Hadn't she imagined her husband's arms to be those of the man she'd fled because she'd been too afraid of the strength and power of her attraction to him?

Yes, she thought. She had. She'd wanted Derek even then and the time for running was long past. That was then. This was now. And now, she wanted to sink down on him, take his entire length inside her and ride him hard and wild. Her body shuddered with longing, with the primal urge to mate with this man. To stake her claim. "Please tell me you brought condoms?" she said, a desperate hitch in her voice.

This was just sex, she reminded herself. *Just. Sex.*

It helped matters that her body was having a damn good time in the process, that her brain was on vacation and her lips had gone numb.

But it was just sex.

"I did, sweetheart, and I'll certainly use one if that's what you want. But I haven't had sex in six years, and got a clean bill of health at my last annual ph—"

She stared at him, eyes wide. *"Six years?"*

"Yeah."

"How could a man like you not have sex in six *years?*"

He raised a dark brow. "A man like me?"

Speechless, Lily waved a hand to encompass him from head to toe.

His eyes crinkled. "Maybe I was waiting for my Princess Charming?"

"Do you want mayo with that baloney?" Lily asked sweetly. "The rubber isn't for me anyway. It's to protect *you.*"

"You've never slept with anyone but Sean."

True. "And everyone *he* slept with. Please?"

"You did know."

"Yes."

"How long?"

She didn't misunderstand him. "We didn't have sex after the first night of our honeymoon."

He did a double take. "Never?"

"Never."

Stunned, he looked at her. "You're practically a virgin."

Her lips twitched. "I don't think *practically* would count if I wanted to become a nun."

He touched her warm cheek with his fingertips. "I'm thinking you don't."

"Not right this very moment. No."

"Fortunate."

"Isn't it?"

He shifted her body as easily as if she weighed nothing at all, and grabbed up his duffel from the floor. He reached inside and pulled out a handful of foil packets.

"I'm not worried, Lily. It's been years for both of us. But I'll wear the rubber—unless you'd like us to make a baby tonight."

God, she'd forgotten. How stupid was that? She'd been so worried about possibly contaminating Derek with whatever Sean might have left in her, she'd never considered the possibility of pregnancy. But a baby . . . Her heart hurt at the temptation.

"No," she said achingly. "I don't."

He nodded, glanced at her and asked politely, "Two or three? Or do you only have time for one quickie?" Pretending not to be horny enough to gnaw off his own hand was stretching his willpower paper thin.

"One should do it." She gave him an uncertain look as she casually pulled the pillow onto her lap to cover herself. "Shouldn't it?"

The white cotton pillow looked like coarse hemp against the creamy silk of her breasts. Her nipples were still hard little points of the palest pink, and just tempting him into another taste.

"Do what?" Derek asked, tossing the handful of rubbers onto the tray on the table between the beds.

"Get all this sexual tension out of your system."

"Mine?"

Her face flushed hot. "*Ours,* then."

"One definitely won't do it, sweetheart. But it's a start."

He saw the flicker of apprehension cross her face, which she quickly hid with a flutter of her lashes. Then she tilted up her chin and met his eyes steadily. "Let's do it." The telltale throbbing pulse at the base of her throat showed how hard she was trying to be nonchalant about sitting on the bed naked with him standing over her.

Good. *He* didn't feel the least bit nonchalant. He'd waited for this moment for six years. And God only knew, he was more than ready. But he was damned if he'd be rushed.

"Come on," she shot a little taunt in her words, "let's see what you've got."

Derek watched her face. What was she up to? Why was she in such a damn hurry? Why now? Was sex for Lily merely scratching an itch, as she was trying so damn hard to convince him?

Hell no, it wasn't.

She'd loved Sean, and had made *him* wait for their honeymoon before she'd allowed him to make love to her. God, he thought, trying not to beat his chest and yell from the rooftops. She was, for all intents and purposes, still a virgin. A mere technicality.

He let his gaze drift down to her bee-stung lips, up to her heavy-lidded, feverish eyes. No. She'd been startled when he'd kissed her. He'd felt the electrical buzz of her skin as he touched her, and the way her heart pounded beneath her creamy skin. Lily wasn't impervious to his lovemaking.

Then it dawned on him: she thought sex would be yet another barrier between him and her heart. She believed, bless her misguided and flawed logic, the mechanics of quick, medicinal sex would put him off the hunt and sidetrack him.

He grabbed the shielding pillow from her lap and tossed it on the other bed, his eyes on her face. "Any preference?" he asked graciously.

Her pupils were enormous as she watched him. "N-no."

"No problem." He gave her bare shoulder a gentle shove and had her flat on her back. "I have plenty."

"Plenty of what?"

"Preferences. I'll teach you every one. Then you can teach me yours." He stroked a path from thigh to belly, entranced with the way her skin flushed at his merest touch. "No, never mind. Maybe I'll just try and figure out what yours are. Yeah. I like that idea better. For now."

He sat down beside her and splayed a hand on her stomach, then lowered his head to brush a kiss across her hipbone. Satisfaction blossomed when her muscles contracted beneath his lips. "I like this spot right here." He trailed a string of open-mouthed kisses between the edge of his hand and her silky hair.

"Your skin's as smooth as satin right here." He inhaled the fragrance of her arousal as he let his mouth travel from hipbone to hipbone and resisted going into dangerous territory—by a breath. Lily moved restively beneath the onslaught of his mouth.

He braced one arm on the bed beside her hip for better balance, and trailed the fingers of the other hand up the inside of her right knee. "Let me know if I'm doing anything you don't like," he told her, tasting her skin with the tip of his tongue. Her entire body shuddered, and he smiled a tiger smile against her quivering stomach. "Well?"

"Y-you're doing just fine."

"Need a book?"

"A bo— What?"

"Apparently you're unfazed by the foreplay part of our program. I wondered if you'd like to read while I do this?"

Lily started laughing. "Very funny." She propped herself up on her elbows. "If I liked it any more I'd be nothing more than a puddle on the sheets."

"Hmm. Is that so?" He trailed his tongue through the silky hair at the apex of her thighs, and followed with his hand. Her skin fluttered, and she dropped back against the mattress and combed her fingers through his hair and held on. He dipped his tongue in for a taste.

She was wet, slick and swollen. His heart tripped and hammered with desire. This was like nothing he'd known before. He'd wanted other women, but not like this. Christ, not like this. The disparity of what he'd had with other women and this here, now, with Lily, made those experiences pale in comparison. They didn't even come close.

Starving, he controlled the raging hunger, taking only the smallest of licks. He ached, but he pushed away the clawing, craving beast of need to gentle her with his lips. He wanted her wild for him. Needed to feel *her* need as well as his own. Wanted to know she was as overwhelmed as he was.

There would never be another first time for them. This had to count.

He shifted her legs farther apart with his shoulders and Lily felt the hot spear of his tongue enter her slick heat. She was so ripe for him that every movement sent a million small electrical shocks ricocheting through her body. The feeling was sudden, and too intense. She fisted her hands in his hair. His mouth on her there was so intimate, so invasive and personal, she felt as though she had been hit by a tidal wave—

Her brain went white, and she was nothing more than sensation. She felt high on him. Giddy with want. Delirious with need as his mouth ravished her with a hunger that would have astonished her if she'd had any brain cells left. This was torture. Her head tossed from side to side. "I'll confess."

He pressed his thumb against the hard bud to hold his place as he mumbled, " 'Fess what?"

"Anything," Lily panted. "Anything. Everyt— Oh, God—" Her hips arched off the bed as he put his mouth back on her, holding her firmly as he ravished her with lips, teeth and tongue. And that magical thumb seemed to be everywhere at once.

There wasn't enough air in the room, she thought frantically as she tried to suck oxygen into her starving lungs. Her heart pounded deafeningly in her ears.

The roller coaster took her higher. Higher. Higher.

"Derek . . ." This couldn't be happening. How could she stand it another moment? How could she stand it if he stopped?

"Let go."

She shook her head, reached for him. "Come into me. Now!"

"Not yet." He tilted her hips, opening more of her to him. She thought she couldn't climb any higher.

He took her to the summit.

And pushed her over the edge.

It took several years of her life for Lily to come back into her body. She felt as limp as an overcooked Chinese noodle. She couldn't move a muscle if she tried.

"How was that for you?" Derek asked thickly, head on her thigh.

Lily tried to lift a hand to touch his face. She was paralyzed. *Hmm. How interesting.* "Pretty damn amazing, thank you." She sounded drunk.

"Yeah, *I* thought so." He lifted his head, and shifted his large body up between her thighs like Poseidon rising from the sea. He hovered over her. Big and sweaty, muscles and tendons gleaming, mile-wide shoulders limned by the light from the bathroom. A pagan god claiming his woman in a ritual as old as time.

She found a bit of much needed energy, hooked her ankles over the lean muscles of his butt and pulled him closer. The hard, silken length of his penis brushed her damp opening. Lily slid a hand between their bellies and wrapped her fingers around him, feeling the raw strength of him, hot and throbbing in her fingers. "*Mm-mm* good, indeed."

Derek chuckled.

"Come to me."

He reached over and grabbed one of the foil packs beside the bed, then tore into it with his teeth. Lily choked back a laugh at the speed with which he liberated the rubber. She snatched it out of his fingers with her free hand, then squeezed her hands between them to roll it down his impressive length.

He was a large man and, how fabulous for her, had the body parts to match.

She lingered over her assignment—this was a first for her and she wanted to get it *juuuust* right; he squeezed his eyes shut, and every muscle in his body tensed as he held his hips away from hers to give her access. The tendons in his neck stood out in sharp relief as he pushed words out of his mouth with apparent difficulty. "How's the fit?"

Lily slid her hands up his chest, loving the feel of his springy hair over solid muscle. "Snug." She started sliding one hand down the steps of his abs. "But I can always check again—"

He grabbed her hand and threaded his fingers through hers, then anchored it above her head. Eyes hot with anticipation, he lowered himself to his forearms and plunged inside her like a hot knife through butter.

And Lily, greedy for him, held on for the ride of her life.

Later, much, much later, Lily gave passing thought to starting a conversation. Speaking would require more strength than her body had managed to recover. Besides, any chitchat would belittle the experience. Words simply couldn't convey the breadth and depth of emotions still churning in her depleted cells. No, this was too special for a verbal play-by-play. It was too special to be merely special and that scared the hell out of her.

EVEN FIVE HOURS LATER, FOR DEREK, IT WAS AS THOUGH THOSE FEW precious hours had never happened. "You're not out of my system yet, my sweet little hedgehog," Derek had told Lily with a satisfied smile as he looked down at her sleeping face moments after they'd made love for the third time, while she'd slept like an exhausted puppy cuddled against his side. "Guess you'll just have to try harder."

The thought made him smile now, but hell, he'd lost the post-coital glow hours ago. It was no wonder many of the contestants hallucinated along the trail, Derek thought, listening intently to a barely there noise as his sled swooshed across the snow.

A full moon played cat and mouse with low, heavy, scudding snow clouds. The landscape went from brilliant, blinding white to inky black in undulating waves that made visibility damn difficult. Fortunately, the dogs could follow the trail markers with no difficulty, and Derek didn't bother turning on his headlamp. He'd enjoyed the dark and the quiet, enjoyed the soft rasp of Lily's breathing in his ear for the past several hours. But now he was on full alert.

Danger hovered just out of sight.

Someone was out there in the darkness. Tracking him.

Dog teams could use trails high-speed snow machines couldn't, but he'd heard the low throb of a powerful engine for several hours up in the higher elevations. Following him? Keeping pace just out of sight?

Part of the Iditarod support team or the mysterious sniper?

Sound was distorted between the mountains and thick trees, but the vehicle appeared to be several miles away, not yet attempting to close the gap. *Not yet.*

He'd change that.

He didn't enjoy being the mouse in the game. Time to turn the tables.

He smiled a tiger smile. He was ready.

He'd weighed the risks of being separated from Lily. But since it was him they were after, if he put himself directly in the assassin's path, he'd be an easy target. And Lily would be miles ahead and safe.

He wanted Lily as far the hell away from him as possible, no matter that he wanted to hold her tightly in the shelter of his arms to keep her safe. But being with him right now was the most dangerous place for her to be.

The sat phone vibrated. He clicked channels so Lily couldn't hear him. "Talk to me." It was Dare. Derek filled him in on the avalanche.

"Could've been triggered by the movement of your sled, or the dogs barking—"

"I heard the detonation a few seconds before it blew," Derek said harshly. "It was just bad timing that I'd moved ahead faster than they anticipated, otherwise I'd've been the one buried." Just thinking about Lily under all that snow made his gut clench. "It's one thing for those sons of bitches to target me, quite another to harm Lily. Find out who the hell knows I'm here."

They talked a few more minutes, both baffled by the way this was playing out.

"Perhaps Pekovic is sending his grandkid in as a training exercise?" Dare suggested.

"God only knows it's low-scale enough to be someone without a whole hell of a lot of experience. Still, even a screw-up can kill. Look at what our guy did to Croft. This person knows his way around a knife. Several of those cuts were postmortem. Not only was the son of a bitch enjoying himself, he wasn't afraid that I'd be there any minute and find him. He lingered.

"I'm not taking chances with Lily on this. Feed in what data we have and give me a face."

"I'll do what I can. W-ch -ou -k. Int—"

Derek frowned as Dare faded out, but he kept the line open.

Who the hell *was* after him? And why? His T-FLAC cover was airtight, had been for twelve years. Nobody but family and fellow operatives knew he was anything other than a rancher. How the hell had this intel leaked? And who had it?

The reality of the situation was, it didn't matter the who or why. He had to cut Lily loose to keep her safe. Damn it to hell, he didn't want to believe that he couldn't keep her safe. But the avalanche had changed all that. It chapped his hide that he couldn't protect her in this. The wilderness was just too vast, filled with just too many natural hazards and hiding places.

His problem was twofold. He was sure the sniper and Oslukivati weren't connected. Hell. He had to be more than sure. He'd have Dare check out the possibility of a connection.

Would Lily be safe apart from him right now? The possibility that they'd try to get to her to get to him gave him pause.

"Damn it to hell." I didn't protect her from a sniper or the avalanche, he told himself, adjusting the reins as Max and Kryptonite pulled him a little off the trail to bypass a fallen tree. If the sniper had been halfway competent, Lily *would* be dead right now. If the explosion had been the correct velocity, half the damn mountain would've catapulted Lily and her team to their deaths.

Both times he'd been within shouting distance. How had he helped her? And why the hell, if they were that close, had they targeted Lily instead of him? Ineptitude? Or strategic planning? Jesus, he was at a loss for the first time in his life. The people he worked with took care of their own asses.

But not Lily. Lily was an innocent.

She had no business being anywhere near the scum of the earth that Derek and other T-FLAC operatives had to deal with daily. He hoped to God whoever had set the explosive hadn't seen him *kiss* her. Who knew what would set the guy off? No. From now until this was resolved he had to treat Lily circumspectly. Show no affection at all. She was in danger. Christ.

Leave her behind and she'd be defenseless against the assassin. Keep her with him and he doubled her danger. Send her ahead, she might be safe. With him nearby she'd at least have his expertise for protection.

Darius wasn't back on the line. But he would be soon. "Chiku is having problems," Derek told Lily after clicking channels. "I'm going to stop to rest the team."

"He checked out okay in Rohn." He imagined that endearing little worry frown between her brows. "Want me to turn around and take a look?"

"No. I think he pulled a muscle. I'll put a heat wrap on it, and let them rest for an hour or so. Don't worry," he told her lightly. "I'll catch up with you in Nikolai."

Lily laughed. "In your dreams. I'll be long gone by the time you get there."

"Keep your mic on in case I need advice." So that he could hear if she was in trouble. She was only about ten minutes ahead of him now. Close enough to get to her if there was any sign of trouble, and just far enough away to attract attention only to himself.

The faint hum of the snowmobile engine beat against his temper.

"Will do. Check Eyota, too, when you stop," Lily instructed. "She looked constipated."

Derek choked back a half laugh. "Constipated? And if she is, I do . . . what?" *Yes, I can hear you. Come and get me, you son of a bitch.*

"Toss a couple of those frozen pumpkin treats in with her food when you heat her snack," Lily told him cheerfully. "She'll be fine."

"Will do."

He heard her click the mic, and smiled. She thought she was turning it off, but all she was doing was changing channels. Wherever she went, he'd be there.

The sat phone buzzed. Still smiling, he flicked off Lily's audio so she couldn't hear him, and clicked in to HQ. He could hear her breathing softly in the background.

Thirteen

W HAT HAVE WE GOT?" DEREK DEMANDED.

"Hey, don't bite my head off," Dare snarled in his ear. "I'm not the one touring the tundra and going through the mountains." He didn't like being control and stuck in the office; he wanted to be in the field. But Dare was babysitting someone and wouldn't leave her, not even to do a job he loved.

"I've still got the guy riding my ass. I thought I'd stop and have a word with him," Derek told him. "Fill me in while I wait. And while you're doing that, have someone check again the possibility that my friend isn't an Oslukivati operative."

He heard Darius typing away on his keyboard as he spoke. "Doesn't sound competent enough for the connect, but we'll see. . . . Now to the meat. Homeland Threat Advisory and the National Security Council have agreed to finally admit we have an 'installation' up there, and they would 'have reason for concern' if said facility were breached. Pretty much, it means we should all be shitting ourselves until Oslukivati's contained."

"Hell." Derek rapidly put up a mental map of the area. It made sense that the United States would have some sort of installation way the hell up here in Alaska.

"What kind of facility?" he asked Darius. "Too far for a DEW? Or did they stick another one up here somewhere we don't know about?" Distant early warning observation stations were strung across the Aleutian Islands. It was possible—hell, probable—they'd added a few without advising T-FLAC. The anti-terrorist group didn't work for the government. They were freelance. And therefore frequently the last to know, as well as often the last resort for an efficient cleanup.

"Could be. They're not talking. But we have *our* best people in on this. Possibly a critical energy infrastructure?"

"Are you asking me or telling me?"

"You are one cranky ass lately, what's up with you?" Dare asked, his tone amused. "Woman troubles?"

"Out here?" The faint sound of the snowmobile engine changed. Infinitesimally. The guy had made a turn. Which way?

"Your lovely widowed lady vet partner is there, isn't she?" Of course Dare knew Lily was here with him. It was the loaded implication in the observation that made Derek frown.

The man hadn't left HQ in a year; how did *he* know Derek's feelings for Lily? "Nobody likes a smart-ass," Derek said absently, listening to the faint sound of the approaching engine.

"Better than being a cranky ass," Dare countered.

Derek checked the clip of the Baer, then returned his weapon to the outside pocket of his coat, where he could reach it quickly. "They'd better work on plugging that leak while they're at it. It pisses me off that the bad guys know what's up here before we do."

Dare's voice was dry as he said, "They'd better tell us where the hell we're headed before it's too late."

That was a given. "*Any* coordinates?"

"Michael's in D.C. putting pressure on the president as we speak. Kinda hard for us to go in to help the Marines if they don't tell us where the hell they are."

Derek thought of his ex–Navy SEAL brother, Michael, and smiled.

They'd have those coordinates within the hour if he knew his brother.

"I'll be in Nikolai in about four hours," he told Darius. "Have a snowmobile and my equipment ready, and have someone there to take Lily back to Montana, where she'll be safe. This asshole blew up the mountain to get me, and almost killed her. Until this situation is contained, I want her—"

"It's not that I regret having sex with you," Lily spoke directly into his ear, cutting off the feed from Darius. Clearly she'd been chewing on the subject for hours. "Now that I've had time to consider my actions, I'm wondering if I wasn't a bit . . . rash."

"Rash?" he parroted, opening his mic to her. "It was incredible! You did things with your body that are forever imprinted on my brain. And I sure as hell am not going to let you slip away now."

Derek switched gears easily as he keyed Dare back in. "Get back to me on those details ASAP," he told his control, then clicked back into Lily's audio channel without her being any the wiser.

Of course she'd try to diminish the intensity of their lovemaking. Safer for her that way. "Nice try, sweetheart."

"We weren't thinking clearly."

"And I took advantage of you?" he asked dangerously.

"No," she said honestly. "If anything it was the other way around."

Derek laughed. "It was exactly as it should've been. Mutual. Don't analyze it to death."

"Sean—"

"Don't," Derek said tightly. "Do *not* throw Sean up to me now. It won't work, and frankly, Lily, I'm damn sick of pretending it ever did. You might lie to yourself about him. But you will not lie about what's going on between us."

"I'm not lying about anything, Derek. For your information, I was about to say Sean had never touched me the way you did in those few hours—"

He inhaled sharply, taken off guard, and lost his chance to talk.

"But now I'm not feeling quite so *friendly*." Lily's voice tightened, then dropped a notch as she asked, "Derek, I have to know. Are you

involved in the bogus bull-sperm sales? And don't lie to me, either.
Please."

Derek frowned as the hum of the engine got closer, staying parallel instead of closing in. He removed the Walther from his pocket and held it in readiness against the handlebars. The Baer in his right, the Walther in his left.

Come and get me, you bastard. "Say what?"

"Someone is selling sperm overseas and claiming it belongs to Diablo."

"And you know this—how?" Derek asked softly into the lip mic, as his eyes scanned the darkness. Definitely closer. No visual. But within range.

"I was in the birthing shed about six weeks ago and overheard two of the hands talking about it."

Christ. Exactly what he *hadn't* wanted to happen: Lily knowing about the illegal activity going on at the ranch. He'd insisted on keeping her out of it. It didn't take a rocket scientist to realize just how dangerous Lily's discovery was.

The sale of prime bull sperm was a multimillion-dollar business. Hell, Diablo's sperm went for upward of a million dollars a vial. The main objectives behind Sean's scheme were to develop and refine various biotechnical applications related to the in vitro production of bovine embryos on an industrial scale.

Good DNA, which Diablo had in spades, was essential. A high-genetic merit bull could produce thousands of viable offspring. The fact that Diablo's sperm had also been successfully sexed before sale made it much more valuable.

Derek suspected the article about sexing in the *Cattleman's Weekly* last year had started the ball rolling internationally.

"Who the hell were they?" he demanded, keeping his voice low so it didn't carry. The custom, handcrafted rosewood grip of the Baer Ultimate combat pistol fit comfortably in his hand like an old friend. The Walther was backup.

Come on. Come on. Come on.

"And *exactly* what did they say?"

"One was Sam Croft." She sighed and her voice sounded ghostly, whispering through the mic. "I didn't recognize the other guy's voice. They said it made no difference whether Sean was around or not, it was business as usual, and another large order from their buyer in Japan had just come in."

His heart shuddered in his chest. Croft. Dead. Bloody. Brutally murdered Sam Croft. On a snowy Alaskan mountainside.

Not Oslukivati.

Closer to home.

Much closer to home.

Who the *hell* was the second man? Who? "Jesus Christ, Lily. Did they see *you*?"

She huffed out an insulted breath. "Of course not."

"Are you positive?"

"Yes, I'm positive. It was well after midnight, and I'd fallen asleep in Clementine's stall waiting for her labor to intensify. I woke up when I heard their voices."

"What were they doing in there?"

"I didn't get up and ask them, for Pete's sake! I stayed where I was and kept quiet, and hoped like hell they didn't have reason to round the wall. They stayed about five minutes, then left. Clemmie didn't start her contractions, and I eventually left, too. I stayed at the main house and went back the next morning. I'm sure they didn't see me."

She didn't sound as sure as he'd like her to be. "It was dark. They could've watched you cross back to the house." She only spent the night at his house when he was gone. He'd change that, of course. But first things first. His blood chilled at the ramifications of what she'd just revealed. She'd known about this for weeks.

He'd had his own investigation going for the past eighteen months. Sean had been eyebrow deep in the mess. And even with him gone, the rest of the cartel involved was cleverly evasive, covering their tracks well. Nevertheless, his people were closing in on the top men now.

But, Jesus Christ, he'd had no idea Lily knew about it. "Why didn't you tell me weeks ago?" he demanded.

"First of all, because you weren't *there,*" Lily said with asperity. "Second of all . . . damn it, Derek. How do I know *you* aren't involved?"

The accusation was a brutal punch to the gut. "You think *I'm* involved?"

"Sean was. It's easy money and extremely lucrative," she told him, her voice flat. "And it is your ranch."

"What if I were involved? Do you realize how damn stupid it is to ask me about this *now* considering the circumstances? We're alone out here. Miles from help— Jesus. *Jesus.*"

"I'm armed, and a very good shot," she reminded him, then paused before saying quietly, "But you didn't know anything about this, did you?"

"As you say, it's my ranch. Damn straight I knew," he told her shortly, and with a sense that he'd been given a reprieve. "But set your mind at rest. In this case," he said bitterly, "I'm one of the *good* guys. It was *you* I didn't want to know. Christ, Lily, you have no idea who these people are, and what they could do to you if they knew. You should have contacted me and told me what you'd overheard. My staff always knows how to reach me."

"Your staff. But not your partner," she said flatly. "Trust goes both ways, doesn't it?"

Damn it, they shouldn't be having this talk now. Where the hell was the snowmobile? Closer? "I wanted to protect you. A shitload of money has been changing hands. In the *multi*millions—"

"The money's in my name in the Caymans," Lily said flatly. "Just tell me who and where; I can't wait to get rid of it. The bastard. I had no idea until I went through his papers that he'd opened an account in my name."

"Gambling was one of his biggest vices. All from the comfort of his sickbed."

"I don't think so, Derek. He hadn't left the house or gone out of town in years. How—"

"*Online* gambling."

"My God." Her breathing sounded in his ear, harsh with anger as she added, "No wonder he had that damn computer on his lap night and day. I thought he was scouring the medical sites for any new cures or treatments."

"He was keeping in touch with the overseas buyers, brokering the sperm sales and then gambling with the proceeds," Derek told her flatly. "Heavily. It's a wonder there was any money left at all. He wasn't that lucky." The only luck the sorry bastard had had was Lily. And he'd screwed up there.

"Between the sperm sales and the gambling, he made and lost millions of dollars at the click of a button. We're talking about a lucrative enterprise generating multimillions of dollars here. Makes no difference if Sean is around or not. Clearly the operation is still viable. And the pie has one less piece to be split," Derek said, still listening for the engine.

"Do you think for a moment they'd let you walk away if they thought you knew anything?" Derek asked.

"You didn't bother telling me about it either. So I figure we're even."

"The difference," he told her grimly, "is that I was protecting you." He put on a burst of speed, feeling an itch of apprehension crawl up his neck even though the snowmobile was still running parallel. Still about three clicks away. Not getting closer. Not going away. "I've had an investigative team working on it for over a year."

Come on, you son of a bitch. Come get me.

"Maybe they could get together with the one Matt and I hired," Lily told him dryly.

His fists clenched over the handlebars. "Matt knows?"

"I trust him."

So did Derek. He let the fact that she didn't trust *him* pass. For now. "Sean formed a cartel years ago. He was smart enough not to involve too many people. We've already apprehended several of them, and turned them over to the appropriate authorities. It won't be long before we have them all."

"Oh my God, Derek." She paused and took a breath. He could almost see the stunned realization in her eyes. "*That's* why someone was shooting the other day, isn't it? It wasn't some kid, or a poacher or someone out shooting at the Iditaroders. It was someone deliberately shooting at *me.*"

He'd gone there several minutes ago.

And damn it, now he didn't know *who* the sniper or avalanche starter had been after.

Him? Or Lily?

"The sniper the other day was Sam Croft," he told her flatly. He paused to listen. Nothing but the breeze zephyring through the tops of the trees.

"How do y— You found him up there, didn't you? My God . . ."

"He was sliced and diced," Derek told her brutally, the time for subtlety over. "Murdered. I suspect by the person who started the avalanche."

"It doesn't make sense." Derek heard the bewilderment in Lily's voice. He could practically see the small frown between her brows as she tried to sort through the new information. "Why are they killing *each other?*"

She was a vet. A woman who healed the sick. Violence had never been part of her life before now. And thanks to Sean's greed, and Derek's own belief that the killer was after himself— "Be quiet a moment . . ."

The sound of the powerful engine was all but indistinct.

"Can you hear a snowmobile close by?" he asked Lily urgently. *Jesus Christ—*

A long silence throbbed between them as she listened. Finally she said softly, "No."

"Well, he's there," Derek told her, not ready to believe the guy had merely moved on. "I want you to clear your weapon and have it in your hand. *Now.* Unstrap your knife and keep it close, too." The little whittling knife in her boot wasn't going to stop a bullet, but if the guy was close enough . . . Derek put on another burst of speed.

"You're scaring me."

"Good. Scared will keep you alive. Where are you? Is there anything you can use as cover?"

"You mean like a fortress with a moat and drawbridge?"

"I mean like trees growing close together, or a rock formation."

"Plenty of trees. There's a nice stand about fifty yards ahead. Unfortunately I'm smack-dab in the middle of the river right now." He heard the wobble in her voice and cursed. "Yeah," she said weakly. "I'll ditto that. I'm heading for the trees on the bank as we speak."

He imagined her out there on the frozen whiteness of the wide river, spotlit by the moon. Her dogs and sled dark against the brilliance of the ice. A sitting target.

He wanted to warn her about suck holes, frozen whirlpools, some of them large enough for a whole team and driver to fall into. Covered by snow, they were hard to see. But of course Lily knew about them.

He listened intently for the hum of the engine. Didn't hear a damn thing. But his mouth was dry as a desert and his heart pounded hard and insistently, warning him of danger.

"Hunch over the handlebars to make yourself a smaller target and *haul ass.* I mean it, Lily. Get the hell off the ice as fast as you can." Jesus. Was that the throb of the snowmobile closing in, or was it the blood pounding in his ears? "*Go. Go. Go!* I'm six minutes beh—"

"I hear i—"

A loud retort of a high-powered rifle followed by a piercing and gut-wrenching *crrraaaaack* split the air and cut her off midword.

Derek got the chilling sound stereo, through the air *and* through the mic. "Lily? Talk to me. *Talk to me, goddamn it!*"

Her high-pitched scream cut him to the bone.

No way. No fucking, *fucking* way! She'd done it again!

He'd hidden the snowmobile and walked to the tree line ahead of her. She'd been a thing of beauty tooling down the center of the frozen river on her own. A living, breathing target.

He'd fix that.

The moon was now playing nice, and shone down on the bitch, full and bright as day. The only way she could've made it any easier for him was if she'd stopped to wave.

Hidden by the trees fifty yards away, he'd waited, a shit-eating grin on his face. Man, this made up for all the times she'd managed to slip his freaking noose.

He lined up the lead dog in the crosshairs, his finger gently squeezing the trigger, just waiting for the right moment. The right second. "Come to me, baby."

He paused on the inhale. Shoot her—easy—but he was being paid for an *accident.*

Aiming for the ice just ahead of the dog, he squeezed the trigger, already spending the ten grand they'd promised him.

Even from here the ice made an impressive noise as it cracked, sounding like a giant plate glass window breaking. Through the scope he watched the spread of the cracks: veins of black running through the white ice like in some weird alien sci-fi movie. Cool.

"Open. Open. *Open!*"

For a second he watched his life go up in smoke. The cracks kept fucking spreading, but the dogs raced around them unharmed.

He lined Lily up in the crosshairs, the barrel of the rifle following her as she came directly toward him. Sweat stung his eyes despite the fucking frigid air. He blinked back the sting, a half a heartbeat, just as he squeezed off another shot.

The shot went wild.

Fucking hell. He was going to go down there and club her to death with the stock of the rifle. Just pound it into her face until she looked like hamburger meat.

His heart raced at the thought. Yeah. Fuck *accident.* Now it was personal.

The noise startled him but good. "What the f—"

Ruptured open by the force of the bullet, the ice fragmented in a spectacular crash and thunder to expose black water glistening beneath its deadly surface.

A nice *big* hole. "Oh, yeah."

He lowered the high-powered rifle and grabbed the binocs from around his neck. Damn things weren't focused— *Yes. There!*

Damn. The fucking dogs did a mad zigzag to avoid the fragmenting ice breaking away beneath their feet. Fuck. Little shits were running flat out. *Damn fuck shit hell!* They were over the cracks and, like the goddamned Energizer Bunny, still going.

She was going to do it again—

They were taking her *away* from the break. *Turn around, you little shits!*

No. Wait—

Fucking perfect.

The dogs, freaked by the noise of shattering ice, hauled ass at breakneck speed for the shore, barking their fool heads off. The sled tipped, and Dr. Munroe was flat on her face, spread-eagled, and sliding toward the nice big hole in the ice he'd shot up for her. She wasn't even screaming or nothing as she careened, helter-skelter, toward the gaping mouth of death.

"Have a nice trip, see you next fall." He laughed as she nose-dived into the water with a splash.

"Now *that's* an accident," he said as she went under. "Am I good or am I good?"

ONE SECOND LILY AND THE TEAM WERE GLIDING ACROSS THE FROZEN river as fast as possible toward the safety of the tree line, the next, she'd been flung off the sled and crashed onto the hard, slick surface of the ice.

The deafening noise of the shattering ice beneath her made her heart stop, and she went sliding at the speed of light face-first across the slick ice. God. Was she going to die here? Crash through the ice and drown? Just like that? She spread her arms and legs wide, trying to flatten herself and find some sort of purchase. But there wasn't anything to hold on to and the slide built momentum.

She slithered and slid inexorably toward an inky hole up ahead.

It happened too fast to control. She had a moment, a nanosecond, to be grateful the dogs had escaped harm before a giant slab of ice tilted like a trapdoor and plunged her headfirst into an icy hell. The only thing she remembered was to *exhale* as she went under.

It's not so very cold, she thought with detached surprise as she plunged down and down through watery black as thick and viscous as honey.

And then it hit her with the impact of a wrecking ball to the lungs, cold so freezing it took her breath away, paralyzed her limbs and made her mind go white.

OhGodohGodohGod.

Disoriented, too terrified to panic and incapable of swimming, Lily flailed herself upright in the inky depths. Arms and legs leaden, visibility nil, lungs screaming, her prime directive—to clear the surface for a gulp—God, a small *sip* of air.

Up-up-up-up-up-up!

But which way was up? Wildly, she looked around and spotted the air bubbles rising toward a surface looking no brighter than the black currently freezing her to death.

Her clothing weighed a ton, but contained enough air to help her rise to the surface in an ungainly, uncoordinated way that was nevertheless effective. Every inch of her body felt as though it were being sliced by pitilessly sharp razor blades as she popped through the opening in the ice.

She sucked great drafts of freezing air into her aching lungs.

"—o me!" She heard in her ear. And realized she still wore the lip mic tucked securely under her hat.

Derek. As close as a voice. Warmth. Light. Hope.

Tears froze on her cheeks. "C-come—" *And get me the hell out of here!*

Eye level with the moonlit frozen river, Lily saw nothing beyond a few feet in front of her. She made a grab for the edge of the ice, but her gloved hands were useless, slapping at the frozen perimeter of the hole with no hope of finding purchase. Where had she fallen in? The ice would be more stable in that direction, she knew. She turned her head and saw where she'd cracked the ice on her way into the water. It looked a million miles away.

"I'll be there in less than a minute," Derek said urgently in her ear. "Are you hurt? Did he shoot you? Jesus, Lily, talk to me!"

His voice, she told herself. Listen. Concentrate. Cling to the warmth of him and the promise of the cavalry on its way. Lily clamped her lips between her teeth when new pain sliced into her skin as she started swimming to the other side. Shudders racked her body, and her face felt numb and so sore, more tears welled. "F-fe-fell in—"

"Christ. You fell into the water?"

She nodded, realized he couldn't see her and managed to mumble, "C-c-c—" *Cold.* God, it was beyond cold. So cold, she felt almost warm with it and she knew the dangers of that. She had to get out. Now.

Her brain filled with snow. White and blank. "Cold," she tried again, more to prove to herself she still could than anything else.

"Lily, sweetheart," Derek said urgently. "Stay with me— Where ar— I see you! I see you. I'm coming."

Her leaden arms smacked the water in a clumsy attempt to keep swimming. Beneath her, the current moved, tugging at her like a lover, leading her off to a frozen bed. She refused to go. Wouldn't give up. Couldn't give in to the numbness dragging her down, making her so tired, so bone weary all she wanted to do was close her eyes.

"Lily!" Derek's voice again. And as if he knew what she was feeling, he insisted, "Stay awake! Fight, Lily. Fight hard. I'm almost there, sweetheart. I'll get you but you have to fight the cold."

Fight. Lily knew all about fighting. She could do this. She'd never quit before. She wouldn't quit now. Not with Derek so close. So-please-God *close*. She bobbed in the icy water like a cork, but finally managed to hook her elbow onto the jagged rim of shattered ice and hold on. Pain in wracking paroxysms flooded her with agony and convulsed her muscles. Her lungs labored to drag in a breath, as if her chest were too frozen to allow it. Her body ached, her mind spun. There was something important she needed to do. Something . . .

She rested a heavy head on her wet, crystalline-covered sleeve, realizing with no alarm that her intellect was fading in and out. Something . . .

"Hey there, gorgeous. Look at me, come on. Look over here."

With a superhuman effort, she lifted her head, forced her eyes open and there he was. Derek Wright, her nemesis, her lover. Her savior. Larger than life, hot-blooded and sexy as hell. Come to rescue her from a fate worse than death— No, that wasn't right. She stared at him blankly.

Twenty million feet away, he lay flat on his belly and slithered toward her like a polar bear on the ice.

"You'll g-get wet," she told him thickly. Silly man. "Where are your d-dogs?" she asked crossly, breathing in raw agony as the frigid poison of the arctic water squeezed at her lungs. *Tired. So cold. So tired.* "Bye . . ."

"Saf— What do you mean, *bye*? Shit!"

Boneless, she slithered right off the edge of the ice and went under the water again. There was peace hidden in the black cold. Peace and sleep and a slow warmth crept into her bones, reaching for her soul. It's not so bad, she thought.

Then her survival instinct kicked in, splintering the peace and demanding she rise again to the surface. Blindly, she followed, kicking against the pain of her frozen limbs until she breached the surface. Her skin burned like fire as she gasped for air, throat raw.

"Jesus, woman!"

Tears fell hot on her cheeks, quickly freezing into crisp little icicles that stung. Shards of sharp pain shot into her skin like hooked claws. About eight feet away she saw the bits of scuffed and jagged ice where she'd fallen off the sled.

The unstable ice was directly between her and Derek. He'd fall in— She wanted him here with her. Big. Warm. Safe— She frowned. No, that wasn't right. They'd both die. "D-don't, D-D-Derek—"

Stop, she thought. He was too heavy to come any closer. She tried to tell him, but her lips were numb and too thick. "S-st-"

He swore a blue streak. "I'm not stopping, Lily. I see the bad ice. I'm going to try to go around. Just hold on. That's all you have to do. Just hang on. I swear to God, I won't let anything happen to you. Just. Hang. On."

Easy for him to say. Oh my God. I'm going to die here, Lily thought, hearing Derek's voice as if in a dream. In the middle of Alaska. In—bullshit, Lily Marie! Get out of the water. Now!

She needed something to anchor into the ice, something she could use to pull herself out. Something . . . her knife!

She jackknifed her right leg up, and fumbled with uncoordinated fingers to feel for the small whittling knife in her boot. Her face went into the water as she struggled to pull the knife from the scabbard attached to the outside of her boot.

She choked and gagged, but managed to liberate it, then used both hands to bring it to the surface, terrified she'd drop it into the water because she had no feeling left in her fingers.

She looked across the white expanse of moonlit ice. Derek was gone. Had he really been here, or was that wishful thinking? Had her imagination conjured him when she needed him most? Was her brain dying and firing off last-minute hallucinations?

Fourteen

LILY SOBBED WITH FRUSTRATION AS SHE ATTEMPTED TO GET BOTH hands high enough out of the water to plunge the knife into the ice to get purchase.

"Clever girl," Derek said from behind her as she hacked into the solid crust. "Kick your feet like you're swimming. Harder. Yes! Keep at it, sweetheart. You're amazing."

His voice. God, his voice. Yes. She could do it. She'd help him help her. Lily anchored the knife to the hilt with all her strength, then used it to drag herself, inch by agonizing inch, up over the lip of the hole. Her arms strained, her chest screamed, her mind went blessedly blank. And at last, she made it. Out of the water. But not out of danger. She lay there panting, muscles stiff and clumsy, vision blurred, wheezing for breath.

"A little more. You're almost to me," Derek encouraged. She turned her head and could just see the top of his head. He was *miles* away. She'd be an iceberg before she ever reached him. "Come on, sweetheart. Get cracking. It's cold as hell out here."

Well, yes, it is, Lily thought crossly. But he didn't need to sound so darn cranky about it. She was the wet one. She stabbed the knife in the ice again, and dragged herself across it with both hands.

Derek eyed the thirteen feet or so separating them. The ice was thin enough here to see the shadow of deadly water beneath. He dared not go another inch. He'd flattened himself as much as possible, spread his limbs out to distribute his weight, but he wasn't able to get any closer.

And somewhere on the riverbank, a sniper could be watching them right now. His shot hadn't offed Lily as planned. But it had scared the dogs and caused Lily to fall into the water.

Although his blood boiled with rage, he couldn't worry about the sniper right this second. If he didn't hurry, hypothermia would finish what the sniper had started.

The shot could prove fatal after all.

He slowly reached down into his pocket and took out the belt he'd stuffed in there while running. "Lily. Grab on to this." With a flick of his wrist he tossed the buckle end to her.

Chin on the ice, she gave him a blank look from under her ice-encrusted lashes. The metal clicked inches in front of her hand. She didn't blink.

Shit.

"Grab the belt, Lily. Grab it and hold on," he told her calmly while his heart pounded inside his chest at how close he was to losing her. "Come on, sweetheart. Grab it and let me pull you to safety."

"D-don't n-n-need you t-to watch out f-for me. Saved mys-self."

Derek chuckled. "Hardheaded as always. Yeah. You did. Finish saving yourself so we can get you warm." He was seriously considering risking it and going in to grab her.

The only way she could've moved faster was if she were in reverse. Hypothermia had set in, she was uncoordinated, her breathing was too slow and she was clearly disoriented.

"Lily, see the black belt right there in front of you? *Other* right in front of you, sweetheart . . . Yes. There. I want you to put out your right hand—okay, that one will do, too. That's a girl. Now grab hold of the belt. Hold it tight. Now bring your other hand up and hold on tight with that one too— Leave the knife. Leave. The. Knife."

She lay there staring at him blankly through glazed eyes, the belt held limply in one hand, her whittling knife in the other. She blinked uncomprehendingly at him.

"Goddamn it, Lily Munroe," Derek yelled, fury masking his terror. "Drop the fucking knife and hold on to the belt with both hands. Do it *now.*"

She gave him a wounded look, but she managed to get both hands firmly on the end of the belt. He gave an experimental little tug. She slid forward. "Hold tight." He tugged again. Another precious few feet. And again. And again.

The second she was close enough, Derek grabbed Lily's wrist. Without wasting time, he hauled her toward him, sliding her parallel against his body. Clasping her tightly in his arms, one hand cradling her head, legs entwined with hers, he rolled away from the fragile edge of the hole as quickly as he dared. The danger was still too real. The ice was thin and now with both of their weights combined, they took a risk with every roll. But there was no other way.

Jesus. *Jesus.* So close. A heartbeat later and—

Hypothermia had sapped her strength, willpower and problem-solving ability. Thank God she'd had enough wherewithal for those few moments to use her knife to get out of the water, because there'd been no way to get close enough to grab her. A few more seconds and it would've been over.

He held her saturated body tightly against his, legs and arms tangled, and rolled again. She didn't make a sound as he crushed her between his weight and the unyielding surface. Water sprayed off her clothing as he rolled over and over and over, until he was positive the ice was rock solid, and wasn't going to give beneath them.

"Hang on, Lily." His voice came swift and soft, hushed in the night, but he wanted to keep her conscious, aware. "We're almost safe, sweetheart. Almost there. We'll have a fire. Get warm."

"*Warm,*" she repeated, her voice a ghost of its usual strength.

That scared him. She was bone white and damn near frozen. But that wasn't all he had to worry about. Somewhere out there was a sniper who might just be itching to finish his job.

Blinding white shimmered and glittered in the moon's light. Every second they were out there on the ice was another second closer to a bullet in the back. Or the head. Or— There was no cover. Not even a cloud across the moon.

Eventually they hit the bank. Derek realized he'd been holding his breath, waiting for the sudden impact. He staggered to his feet, taking Lily's dead weight up with him. Water streamed down her body; her head fell limply against his chest as he swung her up into his arms and ran.

Both teams of dogs waited up the bank in the shelter of an outcropping of rocks and shrubs. They moved restively as he carried Lily toward them, barking insanely and watching him with anxious eyes.

Derek carefully lowered Lily down his body until her feet touched the ground. Her knees buckled. Bracing his knee between her legs to keep her upright, he held her upper arm firmly as she swayed.

Skin ashen, eyes unfocused, she gave him a puzzled look under lashes crusted with ice. "I'm a little p-penguin s-s-short and s-s-stout," she told him solemnly, voice slurred.

"That would be a teapot, sweetheart. I'm going to have you warm in a moment. Hang in there." The dysarthria worried the hell out of him. But slurred speech was going to be the least of her problems if he didn't hurry. He ripped off her wringing-wet hat and tossed it aside, took her long braid in his fist and squeezed out the water, then yanked his scarf from around his neck and wrapped it around her wet hair. Minimizing heat loss, especially from her head, was the top priority.

Limp as a rag doll, she was conscious, barely, as she stood swaying in his hold. If he didn't have such a tight grip on her arm she would've crumpled at his feet.

"Stay with me, sweetheart," he told her roughly, as he yanked off his own hat and tugged it around her face and neck. The scarf would keep the inside dry while giving enough bulk to hold it on. "In a minute you're going to think you're lying on the beach in Hawaii."

Bullshit. She wasn't shivering. Bad sign. The most important thing was to warm her torso first.

She frowned up at him. "Know w-who you look like?"

"Who, darling?" He ripped open her water-heavy sheepskin coat as she watched him with dazed eyes, cheeks pale, lips tinged blue.

"Derek." She lowered her voice to a slurred, conspiratorial whisper. "I d-dream about him, you know."

"Do you?"

Her eyes fluttered closed as she sagged against him. He made a grab for her and gave her a little shake. "Stay with me, baby. Tell me what you dream."

Her coat off, Derek grabbed the hem of her sweater and tugged it over her head. She slapped ineffectually at his hands, ataxia making her clumsy. "N-no way, b-b-buster. S-stop!"

"Just trying to get you warm." He found the buttons on her icy shirt, ripped them open and tugged the heavy wool off her shoulders and down her arms. Then he yanked her silk thermal undershirt over her head until she stood before him, shuddering, half naked in the moonlight, her skin marble pale and gleaming wet.

He briskly started rubbing her upper body with the extra scarf he carried in his pocket.

She scowled. "Th-this does *not* feel like m-my—n't hot and s-s-steamy—t-this h-hurts! Ow! S-stop it!"

"Good. Good that it hurts, Lily," Derek muttered, keeping his movements brisk and his words soft. Jesus, she was cold. He kept up the friction. Waiting in vain for her skin to warm.

"Derek h-hurts m-me, t-t-too." She wiggled halfheartedly, trying to escape. Damned if he'd let her.

"Derek hurts you?" he asked, and told himself he was only keeping her talking because it kept her awake—aware.

"H-h-he w-wants m-me."

"Yeah," Derek muttered, still rubbing her fiercely with his scarf. "He does."

"B-b-but on'y now."

"Now and always, sweetheart."

"Uh-uh." She wagged her head drunkenly, shoving at his hands with her frozen fingers. "D-der'k n-n-not an al-ways m-man."

Those few frozen words punched at him and felt like dozens of icy knives piercing his flesh and scraping at his heart.

"He's not?" Don't engage, he told himself as he scrubbed at her skin with the scarf. Don't pay attention. She's half out of her mind.

"N-n-not f-f-for m-m-me," she whispered and gave a sigh that tore at him. Then she tried to pull away. "H-h-hurts."

She was so weak, her attempt at escape was pitiful. He continued rubbing her dry as quickly as he could despite her protests. "I know, sweetheart. I know it hurts. Almost done. I have to get you dry. Ah, hell. Don't cry."

Trying his damnedest to ignore the tears running down her ashen cheeks, he tossed the thick wool scarf aside and yanked off his coat, which he'd kept on to retain some of his own body heat before transferring it to her. Stuffing her arms through the armholes was like trying to corral an octopus, but he finally succeeded and zipped it closed, then snugged the collar up around her face. He brushed the tears off her cheeks with his thumbs.

She looked so forlorn it tore his heart. "God, Lily." Her name ripped from his throat like a prayer tossed to an unaware heaven. He pulled her close and wrapped his arms around her briefly, more for his sake than hers. He needed this moment. One moment, to hold her. To assure himself she was alive. Safe.

But even as he thought it, he knew she wasn't safe. Not yet.

"T-think I'll t-t-take a lil n-nap now."

"I know you're tired, sweetheart," he assured her, heart twisting. "I know." Blocking emotion from his brain, Derek knew he had to raise her core temperature. Fast. She wilted in his grip and he swung her up in his arms again and ran to her sled.

The sled was totaled from being dragged and bounced, first across the ice, and then up the rocky bank, most of it on its side. Her gear was strapped to what was left.

"I'll get you guys unstrapped soon," he told the dogs. "Lily first." One-handed, he unclasped the straps and started ripping out what he'd need.

Sleeping bag first.

He snapped open her tarp, spread the bag on it and lowered her gently. With a deft economy of movement he slid his hands under the coat she was bundled in and yanked down her soaking-wet pants and long underwear, and pulled two pairs of thick wool socks onto her feet. He rolled her, unzipped the thermal bag and stuffed her inside it. Then he zipped it up to cover her head and face.

Jesus. He wasn't moving fast enough. He scraped his hands roughly up and down her length, rubbing the sleeping bag and the frozen woman beneath.

"Shiver, sweetheart. Come on. Start shivering. Please." He desperately wanted to crawl into the bag with her and warm her. But there were things he needed to do first. He just hoped to God he could do them fast enough to keep her alive.

"Arrow. Come." Derek arranged Lily's dogs around her in a tight circle. Arrow, her lead dog, rested her head on Lily's shoulder and watched Derek with trusting eyes. Dingbat huffed worriedly as he settled his chin and one paw on Lily's belly, watching his every move as Derek scavenged enough bits of wood to start a fire and put a pot of snow on to boil.

Next, he unstrapped his tent and sleeping bag and set up camp as fast as he'd ever done in his life. By the time the tent was up, the water was boiling merrily in the pot. He found Lily's hot water bottles and filled them, wrapped them in several of his T-shirts and tucked them into his own sleeping bag inside the tent and close to the fire.

Next he grabbed his duffel, the large Thermos off his sled and his rifle, and tucked everything inside the tent.

There was a chance the sniper hadn't stayed to watch his arrival. A chance, slim, but a *chance* the bastard thought he'd done what he'd come for, and was gone.

Derek didn't like the odds. Not when Lily was part of the equation.

Didn't matter how much he wanted to go after the son of a bitch, she was his top priority right now. Still, he placed both his weapons near the entrance to the tent. Ready.

"Okay, kids," he told the dogs softly as they looked up at his approach. "I've got her. Good job."

He picked Lily up, sleeping bag and all, and carried her the few feet to the tent.

Once inside he held her upright as he unzipped her from her sleeping bag. She emerged like a butterfly from a cocoon. Knowing skin-to-skin contact would warm her up the fastest, he hesitated. He wasn't about to chance having to haul ass after the bad guy buck naked in the snow at a moment's notice. He opened his shirt and pushed his pants down, then quickly unwrapped her from his heavy coat and climbed into the bottle-warmed sleeping bag with her.

Jesus. She was cold as ice. But at least she'd started shivering—a good sign. Derek tucked her hands under his armpits, curling his body around hers to have as much skin contact as possible. He sandwiched her legs between his own, then wrapped his arms around her, spreading his hands on her icy back and butt, and pulled her tightly against him, her face tucked into his neck.

He immediately started shivering himself.

She moaned as he moved his arm out of the bag to reach for the Thermos close by.

"F-freezing."

"I know, love. But you're going to be okay."

"Hmm. C-cold. N-n-not w-wet."

"Right. Now, let's get you warm from the inside, sweetheart." One-handed, he managed to uncap the large Thermos, then poured half a cup of Annie's minestrone.

The soup steamed gently as he put the wide-mouthed cup to her mouth. "Soup. Open."

She managed to part her lips, but her teeth chattered so hard she couldn't unclench them. "S-sorry."

Derek stared at the cup, then took a sip, concentrating on the liquid and leaving the vegetables in the cup. The soup was savory and hot enough to burn his tongue. He touched his mouth to Lily's, and when she opened her mouth, transferred the soup from his mouth to hers.

She moaned with pleasure as the hot liquid slid down her throat. He took another sip and repeated the process until the cup was empty. "More?"

"Nuh-uh. N-nuff. S-s-still c-c-cold!"

"I know, sweetheart, you'll be warm soon."

"N-never."

Concerned, he nevertheless chuckled. "Yeah. I know it feels like it. Think hot thoughts. Think Hawaii. Sun. Heat. Making love on the beach."

"*Mm-mm* g-g-good?"

Hypothermia 101. Moving muscles provided body heat. He crushed her cold mouth with his. Nothing gentle now. Beside the urgency he felt with her naked body pressed against his length was the imperative urgency to get her warm.

Slowing down, he grazed her mouth with a light-as-a-feather touch. Tilting his head from side to side at the same time to seductively brush her lips, he then sucked her lower lip inside the wet cavern of his mouth.

Her mouth opened readily under his and she invited him in, her tongue a full participant.

Heat rose in Lily like a distant memory. She wanted to touch him, but her hands were clamped tightly beneath his arms. She pressed her breasts against the hard plane of his chest, brushed her nipples against the crisp hair there and shuddered, not from cold, but from the sharp, sweet sensation shooting from the tips of her breasts to deep inside her. Not even an iceberg stood a chance against the rising heat she felt inside as he laved her mouth with kisses, deep and wet.

She drew in a deep, shuddering breath as he brushed warm fingers across her cold cheek, then held her face cupped in his large hand as he continued kissing her as though to stop would be the end of the world. His other hand ran up and down her back, pressing her tightly against him to the furnace heat of his body with spread fingers.

He kissed her in as many ways as Eskimos had for saying snow.

Slow kisses. Fast kisses. Hot kisses. A hot breeze as he blew gently on her damp mouth, then heated her beyond boiling as he ran the tip of his tongue slowly along the middle of the roof of her mouth, then softened it to explore her teeth and gums, causing Lily to moan with pleasure.

He was an excellent kisser. He didn't just kiss, he made love to her mouth as if nothing else mattered in the world than giving her sublime pleasure through their seeking lips. He drew away slightly to give her a moment to draw in an uneven breath, two, three— Then, as if he couldn't wait another heartbeat to have his mouth on her, his tongue delved deeply into her mouth with long, sure strokes. Heat poured through her veins like hot champagne, her breasts ached, her nipples felt almost painfully erect.

The hard, silken heat of his erection brushed against the cleft of her thighs and she shifted restively, her legs firmly sandwiched between his so she couldn't move but a scant, suggestive inch back and forward.

He hummed with pleasure. His mouth moved from her swollen lips; Lily murmured a protest, but he'd already found her next favorite place for him to kiss as he placed the furnace of his open mouth against her jaw, taking small, stinging bites along the way. Lily's throat arched and she hummed low in her throat as he skimmed his mouth between her neck and collarbone, then laved damp kisses along the ridge.

A slow, deep burn started in her belly, as he tasted the cool skin of her throat, then took stinging little bites back up to her ear. Her breath hitched as he laved the outer swirls, around and around, before he speared his tongue inside.

The hand on her cheek smoothed down her throat, callused fingers rasping her ultrasensitive skin. His knuckles skimmed down her breastbone, and then his fingers spread to cup her breast as his mouth traveled back to hers.

Lily's legs shifted restlessly as he rubbed her nipple to a sharp, aching point.

He brushed her eyelid with a kiss, murmuring, "You seem to be warming up nicely."

"F-foreplay is very effective that way." Lily managed to angle her head enough to kiss his jaw, her skin leaping with pleasure. "But I'm still cold." It was a blatant lie; she was hot enough to start a forest fire. She rubbed her hand across his chest, loving the tensile strength of muscle and bone beneath the crisp hair.

"Are you now?" He ran a finger slowly up and down the crease of her butt until she arched into him with a shudder.

Spontaneous internal combustion made her pant. "Freezing," she told him solemnly, slipping her legs from between his, this time without difficulty. Their faces were inches apart, and the sustained eye contact made the experience intensely personal and exquisitely intimate.

The outer rim of his iris was almost black as he said softly, "I can fix that," and slipped inside her.

"I was sure—*oh!*—you could."

Two halves of a whole.

"I HAVE TO GO OUT FOR A COUPLE OF HOURS," DEREK TOLD HER, brushing a kiss somewhere in the region of her left eyelid. The man was clearly distracted, and not by having a warm, naked woman mere inches away. "I'll bring your duffel in."

"You think he's still out there?"

He crawled out of the bag, letting in a wash of refrigerated air and giving her a brief yet lovely view of some very manly parts. Lily jerked the warm bag around her throat as Derek started the contorted process of righting his clothes while bent over in the close confines of the tent. "I sure as hell hope so." He picked up his weapon and tucked it into his belt, then snatched up his coat from the ground.

Lily shivered. This time from fear. Not since childhood had she been so close to death. Yet in some weird way she'd never felt more alive, either.

"I know I heard a shot just before I fell into the water."

Derek nodded, his expression fixed and taut. "More than one. I heard them, too. The guy's missed so far. I'm not going to give him another chance."

Lily grabbed his forearm as their eyes met. She saw something cold, calculating and determined in the depths of his midnight blue eyes. "You're a rancher and I'm a vet. We need to get to the next checkpoint to alert the authorities and the other mushers. Let them hunt this guy down like the sniveling animal he is."

"My problem, my solution."

She fumbled with the edge of the bag; she was not going to let him go after some lunatic with a gun, a mission and questionable aim. Cold air clawed at her bare, love-warmed skin. This time she ignored the cold, shivering as she rose up on her elbow. "I don't think we should tempt fate, but if you're going, I'm coming with you."

"Not just no, but hell no." He picked up his rifle. "Stay where you are. If he's around I'll find him. Then I'll be back."

"Pretty damn arrogant of you," Lily said quietly. "I can help you. You know I'm a terrific shot."

"Yeah." He bent to cover her up again, zipped the bag to her throat and then brushed her cheek with his finger. "You are. Which is why your rifle is right here, and why I'm confident you can take care of yourself while I'm gone." He rose to fasten his coat.

"But—"

He cut her off. "He could circle back and kill the dogs. We're already screwed with only the one sled. All yours is useful for about now is kindling."

Lily sucked in a shaky breath. "God. You're right. Sorry. I didn't think about that. Still, I'm getting dressed. Damned if I'll sit here like an ice cube just waiting for him to show up." She snagged her duffel and grabbed some fresh clothes.

"I'll take care of the dogs before I go."

"No. I'll do it."

He looked torn. "Damn it. You need rest. You can barely keep your eyes ope—"

"I'll chug some of my special vitamins," she assured him, trying to look more alert than she felt. "Just go and get it over with. And Derek? If you won't be smart, at least be careful."

"I will." He unzipped his duffel and withdrew a large, lethal-looking knife.

Lily's eyes widened as he strapped a sheath onto his right thigh and inserted the weapon with the deftness of someone who knew exactly how to use a deadly, seven-inch blade on something other than a nice piece of steak. He dropped his pant leg to cover it and Lily blinked back a sudden clutch of fear.

Who was this man? Everything she'd thought she'd known about Derek mere hours ago was suddenly wiped out by this grim-faced stranger with cold eyes who was armed to the teeth.

Fifteen

Mouth dry, Lily asked calmly, "Is there anything you want me to do while you're gone?"

His eyes narrowed. "Keep a sharp eye open for anything out of the ordinary. If our shooter knows he blew it again, he could become really dangerous. And if he gets close enough, a bullet from an incompetent's gun is just as lethal as one from someone who knows what the hell he's doing."

"Should I break camp?"

"Yeah, but keep the fire going so you can stay warm." He scraped one hand down his face and Lily knew he was torn between going out to do what must be done and staying behind with her. Safety won. "Pack up, but leave any duplicates behind. I'll have someone come and get what we leave."

Who someone? Lily wondered, but gave him a sharp salute without asking. "Yes, sir. I'm right on it, sir."

"Too bad I can't ask you to stay here naked waiting for me. It would sure as hell be an incentive to hurry back."

"Here's an incentive to hurry back." Lily pulled his head down to hers and sank her teeth into his lower lip, then sucked it into her mouth before kissing him seductively.

He cupped her face as they broke apart. "*Damn* good incentive." Then he put on his game face again. "Stay vigilant. Trust no one. I mean it, Lily. We have no idea who we're dealing with here. Shoot first, ask questions later."

"The next person through will be an Iditaroder."

"Or the sniper," he reminded her.

"I'll make whoever it is identify themselves before I blow dem avey, hokay, Arnold?"

He didn't smile at her bad impression. "This is someone you know, Lily. Someone you've talked to, and probably laughed with. Someone who's blending in with everyone else. I'm serious. Trust no one. This person wants you dead. He won't keep screwing up. Eventually everyone gets a break." His eyes darkened. For a moment Lily thought he was going to kiss her again. But he just stood there looking at her, mouth grim, eyes shadowed. "We haven't even begun to explore our possibilities. Stay safe."

"While I respect the take-charge attitude here, what makes you think you know what some crazy is thinking?"

Derek paused briefly and something unsaid passed across his face. He didn't offer any explanation. "I don't want anything else happening to you. Take care of yourself until I get back." He pulled her up for another quick kiss before letting himself out of the tent and zipping it closed behind him. Lily listened to the crunch of his boots in the snow as he strode away.

She dressed quickly. She'd been lucky, really lucky, Derek had been there to help her, and in time. Nearly drowning had been a terrifying experience, and one she'd probably have more than a few nightmares about in the years to come. But at least she was alive to *have* those nightmares. She rummaged around in her bag for more layers since her coat was somewhere out there, soaking wet. Then she went to take care of the animals, her mind whirling along with the flurries falling from the moonlit sky.

Derek had chosen the campsite well. On one side was a pile of large boulders that reflected the fire and made the heat stronger, on the other a dense clump of shrubs backed by a thick stand of trees.

The fire was still crackling, and she put on a large pot of the dogs' food to heat up. Then, grabbing up her rifle, she went down to the river. Ears alert for any sound, gaze scanning her surroundings, she retrieved the clothing Derek had stripped off her.

Derek was making her crazy and more than just in the physical sense. When had he gone from rancher to Lone Ranger? Over the years she had interpreted his behavior as arrogant self-assuredness. Now, those same traits were cast in a new and different light. His decisiveness and intellect far outshone anything Sean had been capable of. He easily took command of situations, so how come he'd been so hands-off? Lily's life was suddenly equal parts confusion and excitement. Hadn't she come to Alaska to plot and plan a simple, quiet life?

Adrenaline coursed through her veins. While she didn't relish having some loony arbitrarily shooting at her, she had to admit there was something exhilarating about her circumstances. The blend of impending danger and raw sex was a heady combination.

Dawn was still a distant promise, blending land, water and sky into a dark gray watercolor wash with no delineating markings to show one surface from the other. Lily shivered. From where she stood, she couldn't see the hole out on the river where she'd fallen in. But it was out there. She felt it. Terrifying. Deadly. Almost her own watery grave.

She looked at the bits and pieces of her sled scattered about. No point trying to gather them up. There was no way they could reconstruct it and make it trail-worthy again.

The race was effectively over for her, Lily thought, walking back up to where Derek had made camp. But considering that life had almost been over for her, the race didn't seem quite as important as it once had.

She wrung as much water out of her coat as she could, spread it close to the fire, sheepskin out to dry, then started taking down the tent. Her rifle was within easy reach at all times.

THE HUNTER WAS BEING HUNTED.

Derek followed the running steps in the snow leading away from the river. He found where the guy had stood to take his shots at Lily. Saw the three twenty-two shell casings on the ground, and glanced up the hill through the trees where the man's deeply shadowed foot indentations in the snow looked like a slashing black marker leading away in a zigzag pattern up the hill.

The wind came up, blowing its icy breath against his face. He repositioned his goggles and pulled his scarf up to cover the lower half of his face as he slogged through the deep snow.

The guy had slowed here. Derek turned around to see what the sniper had seen. A good view of the river with the moon so bright. He'd stood here. Watched Lily go in. But had he seen her climb out? Had he seen Derek's arrival?

He read the position of the man's booted feet. The guy hadn't stayed long. Long enough to gloat perhaps, but maybe not long enough to make sure his shots had been successful.

The snow up here was calf deep, which made it heavy going. Derek paused as a wisp of sound reached him. A coughing engine? Yeah.

Got ya!

He closed his eyes to pinpoint the sound in the thin mountain air, then changed direction slightly and headed north. The stupid son of a bitch was flooding the engine of the snowmobile. With any luck at all the idiot was going to strand himself and become an all too easy target.

The sat phone vibrated against his chest. Damn. "What?"

"Love talking to you. You're always so cheery," Dare said in his ear.

"Make it fast," Derek said, sprinting through the trees, following the footprints in the snow. "I'm hunting."

"Ash made contact. Your bull-sperm bad guys are all in custody," Darius informed him, cutting to the chase. He rattled off half a dozen names Derek was familiar with; a couple of them were hands Sean had brought in when Derek had been away on one of his trips. And Barry Campbell, their lawyer. Figured. "Oh, yeah. And your stalker is one Clay Barber," Dare said. "Tell him hello when you see him. I'll send the garbage detail out to pick up the body."

The line went dead. "Thanks," Derek said dryly to dead air. He disconnected, pausing to listen for the faint bass hum of the engine, then started running again. Like Sam Croft, Barber was an employee, although Derek couldn't bring the man's face to mind. Between the two ranches, hundreds of people worked for him.

He ran the next mile guided by the sound of the coughing engine. Easier going under the trees, where the snow wasn't as thick, and the rocky ground made traction better. Cresting the hill, he saw a man bent over a vehicle, his back to him. Derek rested the rifle against a tree trunk and stealthily made his way down to where the guy, who was swearing a blue streak, tinkered with the engine of the Polaris.

The other man didn't know he wasn't alone until Derek had one arm jerked around his throat, and Derek's weapon in the small of the coward's back. "What the fu—"

Derek dug the barrel of the Baer combat pistol into the guy's spine and tightened his arm around his throat to cut off any other attempts at speech. "Barber."

Clay pulled at Derek's arm, and found enough air to gasp, "Hey, man. Am I glad to see y— Fuckit, Wright." He forced a laugh and shook his head, holding both hands up, palms out. "You oughta calm down, man."

Derek was in no mood for this. "Cut the crap. I know you're the one who tried to kill Dr. Munroe."

"Kill? No fucking way, man."

"How much they pay you to off Dr. Munroe?" He pressed the barrel of the Baer hard against the mastoid process behind Barber's ear, and applied upward and inward pressure.

"Ten grand," Barber said quickly.

"You think ten grand's worth dying for?" he asked conversationally as Barber struggled in his hold. "Just for the record, you didn't succeed." Derek tightened his forearm against Clay's throat again.

"Fuck. You're choking me. Le' go."

Spreading his feet, Derek tightened his grip and jerked Barber off balance. "In your dreams, asshole," he hissed into the younger man's ear. Smelling the guy's anger. Smelling the stink of bloodlust. Derek leveled the pistol at the larger man's head.

"I'm not the one about to die, dickhead." Surprisingly light on his feet, Barber spun around and ducked under Derek's arm. Derek gave him a hard chop to the back of the neck. Barber laughed as he danced away.

He turned and charged Derek, head down. The man was unarmed, and as much as Derek craved shooting the bastard point-blank, that wasn't his way. He waited until the man was close enough then swung his fist in and up, nailing Barber in the solar plexus and dropping him like Shamu diving into his pool.

Barber doubled over, staggered, then straightened with blood in his eye. "I should've killed you first."

"You should've tried." Good, Derek thought, widening his stance as Barber started dancing from foot to foot in a half circle around him. Shooting the son of a bitch would save time. But, Jesus, he *wanted* a fight. Mano a mano. He hoped the guy was good and fought dirty.

"You took how many shots at Lily?" he taunted. "And not one hit? Tsk, tsk. You're one piss-poor sniper, Barber." Derek watched the man's narrowed eyes. "Hope you're better with your fists than a gun. I'm in the mood for a little exercise." Derek wiggled his gloved fingers in a come-and-get-it taunt.

Barber came up swinging, as enraged as a drunken sailor. Derek jerked his head back a split second before Barber's meaty knuckles connected.

He was strong.

Perfect.

"I know you work for the cartel selling the bogus sperm, so don't bother shitting me. Who's next up the food chain? Who's paying

you? Give me a name." Just in case anyone had been missed in the
sweep.

"Fuck you."

"Wrong answer." Derek spun him around and delivered a powerful uppercut to the chin. Barber staggered backward, eyes wild. "We
have all your associates in custody," Derek told him grimly, grabbing
him by his jacket front. "You might as well give it up."

The man wiped blood off his mouth with the back of his gloved
hand, his expression murderous. "Fuck you." He put his head down
and charged again. With a derisive snort Derek stepped aside. The
other man staggered past him yelling obscenities, his arms windmill-
ing for balance.

Blood pumped hard as adrenaline rushed through Derek's veins.
He spread his feet in a defensive stance as Barber turned. Every cell
in his body *screamed* to beat the bastard until he was just a bloody
mark on the snow.

Shooting him would be too damn easy. Instead of putting a bullet in him, he'd rather pull the son of a bitch's balls out through his
nose for what he'd done to Lily. Derek tucked the Baer back into the
shoulder holster as Barber charged again, shoulder down.

They came together like two bulls locking horns in a fight for supremacy. Equal strength. Equal desire to be the last man standing.
Equal adrenaline rush with no place to go.

Screaming like an animal, Barber staggered back, arms flailing.
Derek used his own momentum and jerked him by the arm, then
swung him in a half circle and shot out a kick, hard, to Barber's mid-
section. The man grunted; air pushed out of his lungs with a great
whoosh. He crawled to his hands and knees, gasping for breath.

Derek waited until he staggered to his feet, then dropped him
again using a snapping karate side kick to Barber's knee. Barber howled
with pain, but this time he only staggered, then came at Derek full
tilt, again screaming obscenities.

Derek did a half side step and tried to twist his body, but Barber's
thick head hit between belly and rib and they both crashed to the

ground. The younger man on top, Barber straddled Derek, pummeling whatever he could reach. Derek jackknifed, got a booted foot wedged securely against Barber's kidneys and thumped him with his heel. Barber screamed and twisted around. Derek rolled, taking the younger man with him. Sweat flew like confetti as they matched punch for punch, both panting, gasping for air as they rolled, beating the crap out of each other as they went.

"I should've offed you first," Barber gasped, face red.

"You could've tried." They circled each other, a macabre duet. While the wind howled through the treetops, their breath came hard and fast, then frosted in the icy air.

Locking his gaze with Derek's, Barber reached down and pulled a Tarpon Bay hunting knife from a sheath on his left thigh.

Derek smiled, all teeth, already tossing his KaBar from hand to hand. "Your weapon of choice, is it?" Derek asked dangerously, remembering Croft's injuries and the relish with which they'd been inflicted.

"Slice and dice, asshole. Slice and dice. I'm gonna have me a little fun with you, and when I'm done, I'm gonna go find me a pretty lady doctor to play with."

Derek keep his feet moving, his right arm relaxed, as he cut and thrust, cut and thrust. Barber did the same. They circled, clearing a ring in the snow at their feet.

"Look around you, asshole. This will be your last sight. Me with this knife in your gut," Derek told him, feeling a familiar eerie calm settle over him as he feinted and parried.

To the death.

Only one man could leave this hilltop alive. And it had to be him. Anything else was unthinkable. Barber would never get another chance to be within a thousand miles of Lily.

There were three major target groups in a knife fight: muscles and nerves, blood vessels and vital organs. Severing the muscles and nerves would disable Barber's limbs. Eventually. Severing blood vessels and vital organs would ultimately cause death, the last deterrent for any attacker.

Barber did a high thrust and his knife skimmed Derek's throat. First blood. Derek shot out his left arm and closed his fingers around Barber's thick neck. His reach was only marginally longer than the younger man's, and he kept his arm extended as Barber danced around cursing as Derek squeezed.

"Fuck you, Wright. Fuck you."

"You have a limited vocabulary. I'd love to send you to prison to get a higher education, but time's a wasting and I have to book."

Clay gave him a narrow-eyed look. "You think you're gonna leave me here?"

No. Darius will send a garbage detail. Eventually. "It's a straight shot to McGrath—only about a hundred fifty miles. Better start walking."

Barber came at him with a front kick, which Derek blocked with an X block. He grabbed Barber's leg behind the ankle and pulled it to one side, then delivered a quick, sharp groin kick with his knee that had the younger man doubled over and shrieking like a girl.

"Fuck you." Barber ran, half crouched to protect his balls, heading toward the snowmobile, where the rifle's butt end jutted up from a scabbard. Derek ran and did a low tackle. Their bodies hit the side of the snowmobile with a loud *thunk,* Derek on top. Move, block, strike. Strike again. Blood poured from Barber's nose. He heaved upward, lunging to his feet, staggering, sweat and blood pouring down his face. Derek rolled out of the way of Barber's size-thirteen boot as it slammed down inches from his head. Barber turned, his sniper rifle in his hands.

"Like I said, fuck you, Wright."

"No." Derek threw the KaBar in a gleaming arc. Seven inches of partially serrated, tool steel, clip point blade with epoxy coat and blood groove sank into Barber's throat right up to its carbon steel guard. "Fuck you."

LILY HEARD THE THROB OF A SNOWMOBILE APPROACHING THROUGH THE tree line above camp. Grabbing her rifle, she climbed the small outcropping of rocks and laid down flat to watch its approach. Just because she wasn't planning on shooting the next pair of eye whites she spied didn't mean she wasn't ready.

Lifting the rifle to her shoulder, she peered through the scope crosshairs for a better look. Damn it. The glass was shattered. Must've happened in the fall.

She watched the dark speck get larger and larger as the vehicle approached, weaving expertly through the swaying trees. Snow flurries made visibility difficult. Now she saw him. Now she didn't. Frustrating. Maddening.

Friend?

Foe?

It was barely dawn. Possible, but unlikely the rider was part of the Iditarod's auxiliary volunteer team. If it *was* one of the crew, he'd be on the marked trail, not high up above the tree line. Besides, no one would be traveling between checkpoints at this time of the morning. He'd be there already.

No. This wasn't anyone involved with the race.

The question was, was this the shooter, or someone else? She flattened herself on the rock to wait until he was closer.

WHERE THE HELL WAS LILY? DEREK THOUGHT AS HE CAME DOWN THE hill on the Polaris and saw the camp up ahead. The fire glowed against the shadowy gray of densely falling snow. Tent down. Dogs agitated and barking. His eyes scanned the area. No sign of her. He suddenly realized the head mic was stuffed in his pocket. Damn. Not smart. By the time he got the thing out and installed it in his ear, he'd be in camp.

Had the bastard had yet another accomplice? He shifted the throttle and aimed for the center of the clearing, his brain filled with images too hideous to imagine.

Hurry. Hurry. Hurry.

THE DOGS WERE BARKING LIKE CRAZY. LILY WATCHED THE SNOWMOBILE approach, heart in her mouth. It crested the hill and made straight for camp without slowing down. Lifting the rifle, she tried to take a shot. Just a little warning, which Derek, wherever he was, would hear.

The rifle snicked.

Oh, hell. Jammed.

WITH RELIEF, DEREK SAW LILY PERCHED ON THE ROCKS ABOVE CAMP. Clever girl. If she wasn't sure of his identity she would've fired off at least a warning shot. But she waved the rifle to acknowledge him. Thank God, she was okay. He lifted his arm in a wave, bounced on a knoll, and had to grip the bars with both hands and concentrate on slowing the vehicle down.

AS THE SNOWMOBILE WHIZZED CLOSER, LILY TRIED TO SEE THE FACE OF the man rapidly approaching. She couldn't identify him. The coat he wore was similar to those worn by dozens of the men on the trail, including Derek. His face was covered by a hat, goggles and scarf.

Suddenly he was too close for a warning shot anyway.

Lily swung the rifle like a club.

The man tumbled off the machine, falling like a rock. The snowmobile kept going. Down the hill, *bump, bump, bump,* and then skated with a hideous screech across the river on its side.

Lily jumped down off her low perch and ran over to where the man lay on his back.

He wasn't moving, but she approached with caution, rifle raised so she could give him another solid whack if he looked dangerous and tried to move.

Oh, hell . . . "Derek?"

His eyes were closed, his face dead white. But it was the bright red blood welling from the cut over his eye that made Lily drop to her knees in the snow beside him. "Oh my God, Derek. I'm so sorry. Wake up. Please, wake up."

He was out cold. "Wake up and yell at me, would you?"

After a few minutes she realized he wasn't going to be chatting with her anytime soon. Lily ran back to camp and unharnessed Arrow and Melba.

With the help of the dogs, she managed to roll Derek's long body onto a tarp, and then the three of them dragged him back to the fire.

Sweating, she rummaged around in Derek's gear for a first aid kit and the sleeping bag roll she'd just packed. Damn it. She wished the tent were still up as snow blew wildly around them.

She unzipped the bag. With much huffing and puffing and cursing, she eventually rolled all two hundred pounds of solid muscle onto the bag, and then zipped it to his chin.

He still hadn't moved. Not good.

She carefully removed his shattered goggles and winced at the sight of his face. Fortunately the bleeding had almost stopped. But his eyebrow and eyelid were already discoloring and swelling. He was going to have one hell of a shiner, and a monstrous headache, Lily thought, feeling sick to her stomach as she cleaned the wound and then got out a butterfly bandage.

She heard a soft buzzing sound and paused to listen, heart in her throat. What—

Band-Aid stuck on the tip of her finger, she looked around, searching for the cause of the incongruous sound.

A phone? Out here? No way. It buzzed again.

She looked down at her patient. Reaching inside the bag, she patted him down until her fingers encountered a small black phone in Derek's top pocket. "Well, I'll be d—"

biiiizzz

"Hello?"

Silence. Then, "Who the hell is this?"

"Dr. Lily Munroe."

"Put Wright on."

"He's, ah, sleeping. Can I take a message?"

"Wake him."

"I'm sorry. As much as I'd like to, I can't. Leave a message and I'll te—"

"Is he alive?"

"Yes. God, yes."

"Then wake him the hell up. This is an emergency."

An emergency? Hell. Is everyone having emergencies these days? "He's unconscious," Lily told him flatly.

"Uncon— What happened?"

"I hit him rather hard."

"*You* hit him?"

"Yes," Lily told the anonymous man with asperity. "*I* hit him. Hard enough to knock him out cold. Would you like to hear the gory details, or do you want to leave him a message, which he'll receive as soon as he wakes up?"

"Wake him now," the man told her urgently. "Even if you have to dunk his dumb ass in the snow. Get him conscious and on his feet, pronto. Then have him call me. You've got two minutes." He clicked out. He didn't bother telling her who to say called.

Hey, Derek? A guy just called, said it was an emergency. Call him right back. Who? I have no clue. About what? Ditto. Lily shook her head. She frowned as she put the phone down on the bag by Derek's head.

Probably his stockbroker. Yeah. Microsoft or IBM dropping a few points was cause enough to call Derek in the wilds of Alaska in the middle of a race. It would be nice if Lily even remotely believed her own interpretation of the call.

"Why don't I believe that for a minute?" she asked aloud. "I feel as though I've fallen down the damn rabbit hole."

She checked his wound. Still seeping. Lily used another disinfected swab, then closed the gash with several butterfly bandages. He'd have a scar there to remind him of today. But knowing Derek, it would look rakish rather than gruesome. "It won't spoil your looks a bit, cowboy. But you're probably going to be a little cranky with me when you wake up. So what's new?"

"Jesus. What hit me?" Derek grumbled, raising a hand to feel his forehead. Lily grabbed his fingers before he could poke at the wound.

"Unfortunately, *I* did." She checked his pupils. "God, I'm sorry. You were on the snowmobile, and coming so fast—"

" 'S okay. Would've done the same thing. What in God's name did you hit me with? A two-by-four?"

"The stock of my rifle. Why are you sitting up? You probably have a concussion."

"I don't."

"I'm the doctor," she told him firmly, taking his face between her hands. "Look into my eyes."

"Beautiful."

His pupils looked normal. But she'd keep an eye on him for several hours anyway. Not hard to do. He was easy on the eyes, this lover of hers. "You're delirious."

"And that makes you smile?"

"The fact that I didn't break open your head like a melon is cause for celebration," Lily told him, leaning forward to give him a brief peck on the lips. "Lie down, I'll get water for you to take some aspiri—" The phone buzzed.

Derek patted his chest pocket. She pointed to the phone on the sleeping bag. He ran his hand over the creases searching for it, then picked it up and barked, "What?"

"Feel the warmth. Nice of you to join the land of the living," Darius said sarcastically. "I'm filled with confidence that you, and you alone, are now responsible for getting the bad guys and saving the world. Especially knowing you were flattened and vanquished by a girl."

"I've got a headache, and I already have my own pain in the ass right here." Derek grinned at Lily and touched her cheek. "Do you have a point?"

"How bad's the head?"

"Since I just woke up, I'm not sure yet, but I'm anticipating a lollapalooza of a headache. Thanks for asking."

"Be sure," Darius said, all humor gone. "Because you're the only game in town, and we are seriously in the crapper here. I have good news and bad news."

Darius's pause had Derek's full attention. "Start with the good news," he told him dryly, taking the ibuprofen Lily handed him and chugging it down with water. "I could use some."

She frowned and mouthed silently, "What's going on? Is it about your dad's wedding?"

He'd almost forgotten his father was getting married at his place in a couple of weeks. He frowned and shook his head, which caused his vision to dance. Then made a hand gesture, silently asking for a cup of coffee. The pot steamed gently several yards away on the fire.

Lily grumbled a bit at having her question ignored, but went off to get the coffee. The view of her spectacular ass would've been much better if Derek could have observed it through both eyes. Unfortunately his left eye was not only throbbing annoyingly, it was swollen shut.

"Sat pictures indicate large vessels where they shouldn't be on Norton Sound," Darius told him. "And in case you didn't study your geography before your trip, like a good little Eagle Scout, the sound would be the big blue blob on the left of your trusty map, indicating an inlet off the Bering Sea. The location of our fan for the shit to hit, as it were, is north latitude sixty-four degrees, west longitude one hundred sixty-three degrees.

"Nome, the place you were heading eventually anyway, is on the north shore and the Yukon River flows into the sound from the south. Following me so far?"

"Loud and clear." *Thanks,* he mouthed to Lily, who'd brought two mugs back with her, handed one to him and then folded her long legs tailor fashion to sit on the foot of the sleeping bag.

Since she looked so damn cute sitting there, a scowl between her pretty eyes, he blew her a kiss. The frown eased a little and she reluctantly smiled back.

"Is a geography lesson my good news?" he asked Dare. "I was much better at biology."

"I'm sure you were. No. The good news is those coordinates are our target."

"North latitude sixty-four degrees, west longitude one hundred sixty-three degrees. Got it. And our friends are doing what to whom?"

"Our friends are planning to detonate a dirty bomb. A *very* large, *very* dirty bomb. Which will not only seriously compromise the river and inlet, but will effectively take out Uncle Sam's ultrasecret DEW installation south of Nome. Not that we know anything *about* a top-secret facility there, but if we *did*—which we don't—it would be toast."

"As would the people living there," Derek pointed out reasonably. "Doesn't sound like terribly good news to me."

"Hell, Derek, the good news is we've got the intel. The bad news is a front has moved in," Darius continued. "Impossible to mobilize aircraft for the next twelve to sixteen hours. You, my fine dog-loving friend, are *it*."

"Jesus." A prayer.

Sixteen

ILY HAD ABSOLUTELY NO IDEA WHO DEREK WAS TALKING TO, BUT he looked grim, his mouth taut as he listened and responded. She was done being mystified by the calls. Now she wanted answers. Real answers.

She winced as he touched a finger to the side of his face, distracting her for a moment from the mysterious conversation. Oh, God, she'd *hit* him. Just because it was unintentional didn't make her feel any better. Her stomach hurt just looking at his poor face. His left eye was completely swollen shut, and his face was black and blue, not to mention several other painful colors, from his eyebrow to his cheekbone.

Feeling absolutely horrible, she pulled the clean sock that she'd dug out of her bag out of her pocket, set her steaming mug down and filled the heavy wool with snow.

"Have arrangements made for my cargo pickup at the next checkpoint," Derek demanded, then paused to listen. "The most precious cargo I've ever ordered transported. Pack and ship accordingly." Derek closed his eyes—*eye*—in pain.

"Shit. That's right. No flights of any kind . . . Yeah. Yeah. I do."
Pause. Frown. Glare. "I know you will."

Lily handed him the snow-filled sock. He stared at it as though
he'd never seen a sock before. She held it up to her face. He ignored
her.

She refused to be ignored. Leaning in close, she laid the freezing
sock alongside his face and Derek hissed in a breath as he instinctively
tried to escape her. She moved with him, holding the ice pack firmly
in place.

Shooting her a glare, he asked, "Do we have an educated guess
when our friend's little party is scheduled to start?" He tilted his mug,
tossing scalding coffee down his throat as if it were an antidote to the
ice nestled close to his face.

"Of course they will," he said sarcastically, glancing at his watch,
having to angle his wrist to see it properly with his good eye. "I'll
keep in touch. Let me know when there's someone there to make my
pickup, and my merchandise is secure. And Dare? This request is
nonnegotiable." Once he clicked the phone off, he tried again to
dodge the snow sock.

"Don't be such a wuss," Lily chided. "Keep this on your face or
your eye will swell closed permanently."

"You're a vet, not a people doctor," he reminded her, apparently
feeling as surly as he looked.

"Fortunate," she quipped, "since you're acting like an ass."

"Stubborn, aren't you?"

"Hello, have we met? I'm Lily." She motioned toward the phone.
"What was that all about?"

Derek rose and held out a hand to pull her to her feet, even as he
clapped the snow sock to his face with the other. "We've got to get
cracking. This storm's moving in faster than anticipated. They're pre-
dicting snow, gale force winds, all followed by a severe ice storm."

"Don't worry about it," Lily said with more confidence than she
really felt. "We're well equipped for that kind of weather." While
they had all the dogs, her sled was toast. She was rapidly reaching the
point where if she didn't sleep soon she'd slip into a coma of exhaus-

tion, and Derek was swaying on his feet and had a pretty serious head injury. Things weren't looking good right now.

This big storm was going to complicate the next leg of the trip.

"Trust me," he said tightly. "It's a bad one."

The lover was gone, and in his place stood a grim stranger Lily almost didn't recognize. He dropped her hand and turned to the fire, which he proceeded to cover with snow. The flames fizzled and died, then gently steamed.

What wasn't he telling her? "Okay, ice storm. What else?"

"Nothing."

The dogs, sensing something, milled around looking worried. Dingbat huffed anxiously and Lily went over to rub his ears. "It's okay, baby." Still squatting beside the dog, she looked up at Derek. "Talk to me. What's really going on?"

The wind started picking up, swirling small flurries around their feet. Derek scrubbed his battered face with one hand. "I want you to continue on to Nikolai on your own."

Lily tried to read his expression, but it was like trying to read a closed book with a blank dustcover on it. She had exactly the same sensation in her chest now as she'd had that night on her honeymoon when Sean said he was going down to the bar for one drink while she primped for a romantic dinner in their suite: a hard, taut band of foreboding squeezing across her chest. Dingbat nudged her cheek with his icy nose. She kept her eyes on Derek. "Why?"

"Would it be possible for you to just do what I ask without asking questions?"

"Yes. I'm sure the time will come. But this isn't it."

"Lily—"

"Something's wrong. Don't shut me out. I know. I know," she said quickly when he gave her a one-eyed glare. "I can see you're in a hell of a hurry. Tell me quickly so we can be on our way."

He paused long enough for her to think he was going to blow her off, then said quietly, "I was going to tell you this anyway. But this was neither the time nor the place I would've chose—"

"Yeah, yeah. Fine. *What?*" Lily said impatiently, getting to her feet and trying not to wince at his poor prizefighter face. She wondered briefly what she'd do if he told her he was a serial killer, wanted in fifty states. Or a bigamist—

"I work for an organization called T-FLAC," he told her, watching her face intently. "It's a privately funded black ops anti-terrorist group."

It took her brain a couple of seconds for it to compute. "Are you telling me you're a . . . spy?"

"Anti-terrorist operative."

"Holy crap." She shook her head as if she couldn't quite believe what she was hearing.

"Lily, I wanted to ex—"

She cut him off. "That is *so* cool."

Surprised, Derek just stared at her. "You think it's—cool?"

"Hell, yeah. Don't you?"

"Actually, yeah. I do." His smile was a bit lopsided because of the swelling. "Whoa." He put up a hand as she opened her mouth. "I can see the questions bubbling over. I'll tell you what I can about my job—when we get back home, okay? Right now I've got to haul ass."

"You're on a mission *now*?"

"Right now."

"Wow."

"We gotta move."

Right. She and James Bond had to get a move on. Holy crap, she thought again, sliding him covert glances as she helped him break camp. Lily stuffed the million and one questions down with difficulty. *An anti-terrorist operative. Wow.* Bore some thinking about. She threw equipment into its storage compartment as she asked, "Was that your . . . person who sends you out on jobs? Don't tell me anything if you're going to have to kill me afterwards!" she added quickly, not sure if she was joking or not.

He smiled. "Control. Yeah. I have less than ten hours to reach a location south of Nome." He touched a finger to the lip she was biting to prevent herself from blurting out a string of fascinated questions. "I can tell you this much. We've known of a terror attack somewhere in the vicinity for several days, but not the exact location. Now I have it. Now I go."

"For heaven's sake, Derek, you can barely *see*." Terrorist attacks were something she read about in the paper or watched on the six o'clock news. Not something someone she lo—*cared* about was involved with.

A clutch of panic closed her throat. Spy types were sexy and fun to watch—in movies; she suddenly realized it wasn't fun finding out Derek was one of the people who put themselves on the line every day to keep her country safe. She swallowed the metallic taste of fear. "Let them send someone else."

Packing and getting on with business, he didn't even spare her a glance. The snow flurries whipped around their legs as the wind got stronger, and the sky darkened accordingly. "The storm has already closed the airports where our people were waiting for the coordinates. Getting that intel, even half an hour ago, would've made the difference. But now . . . There is no one else, Lily."

He wasn't grandstanding or being arrogant. If he said there was no one else, then there was no one else. He stumbled over the coffeepot lying on the ground at his feet, turned slightly, then bent to pick it up.

Oh, God.

"Forget the next checkpoint." Lily snatched the pot from him and emptied the last few inches of coffee on the ground. "I'll have to go with you. Be your eyes."

"Jesus." He looked appalled. "Are you out of your mind? You'll go to Nikolai, where I know you'll be safe."

Yes. She was out of her mind. For even *thinking* about going into danger. She'd had more danger in the last few days than she'd had in a lifetime already. But she was also out of her mind worrying about *him*. Under normal circumstances she presumed he was capable of doing whatever he was supposed to do—and doing it well. But how could he do when he couldn't *see*?

She fisted one hand on her hip and stared him down. "How will you know I'm safe?"

"I'll have people waiting there to take you back to Montana."

She thought about it. Frankly, with some relief. She was tired of being scared. "Fine. Come with me, and let them go with you wherever you're going. You need the help. I can see myself home."

"You can't," he said, face grim. "There aren't any flights out for the next twelve to sixteen hours. The storm—"

"So you aren't even sure if your people will be waiting for me when I get there, are you?" she asked.

"They will be."

"Before either *I'm* dead or *you're* killed by these bad guys?"

"Lily, we don't have time for this."

"And you were just going to pull me out of the stupid race like I'm a child needing a time-out? Without a damn explanation?"

"There'll be another race next year. Win that."

She wanted to hit him. She helped him fight to hold down the tarp as they tried to cover the sled and secure the gyrating canvas. It felt as though it were alive and fighting for its life. "Damn it, Derek," Lily snapped. "I don't give a rat's ass about this race. I'm thinking about Mr. Super Spy, who just tripped over the damn coffeepot."

"I didn't see it."

"My point exactly."

"Just do this for me, will you, Lily? Cut me a break here? Take pity on the blind?"

"Fine. Say I do it your way. Who says I'll be safe between here and the checkpoint? I lost my gun in the water, and my rifle's jammed." She paused, gathering ammo. "Did Barber tell you who'd sent him?" Derek shook his head with a wince. "No? I rest my case. So far we've had both Croft and Barber after me. What if there's someone else just waiting for us to separate?"

Beneath the bruises, he actually paled and Lily knew she'd scored a direct hit. It didn't make her feel any better.

"Jesus, Lily—"

"No. Listen to me. I understand you don't want me to come with you. And frankly, I'm not real happy at the thought of getting in the middle of some terrorist plot to overthrow the world. But the reality is, you don't have twenty-twenty vision right now. And that's my fault."

"Lily—"

She pulled her goggles on because the blowing snow was starting to sting her face, then jumped as a huge chunk of snow dropped from the swaying branches of a nearby tree with a loud *thwack!* God. She was already spooked.

"The storm is almost here," she told him, keeping her tone even with effort. "We don't have time to debate this, do we? I'll be safe traveling with you until we get to wherever it is you have to go. And once we get there, I can take the dogs and find a safe place until the danger is past. You can do whatever you have to do. Don't look at me like that. You know there isn't any other way to do this. Someone has to be there to take care of the dogs. I'm your girl there. And if push comes to shove, in a crunch you could use my shooting ability."

"I don't want you anywhere within a five-hundred-mile radius in a freaking *crunch*."

"Well, that makes two of us. Believe me." Lily threw both hands wide, then let them drop. "Contrary to the last couple of days, I don't have a death wish. Finish up with the packing and culling of our stuff," she told him briskly, turning around. "I'm going to pick our fastest dogs and reharness them."

"No."

"Talk to yourself," Lily told him. "Time's a wasting."

In the end Derek acknowledged Lily was right. He couldn't do it on his own. His vision was seriously impaired. An ice pack wasn't doing much for the swelling. Not only was she a necessary adjunct to his sight, but in this case, it was Lily who was the expert. She'd put together the fastest dogs with the highest endurance levels. Eighteen of the best-trained sled dogs in the country. Not only were the dogs the best but Lily was acknowledged as one of the best mushers around. She'd get him where he had to be a hell of a lot faster than he could do it on his own.

She'd trained in the worst weather possible. Hundreds and hundreds of hours of trail time. This storm was going to make her experience invaluable to him. Torn between needing her and desperate to keep her safe, he weighed the pros and cons.

What if Croft and Barber weren't the only ones they'd sent? How safe *would* she be on the trail? Eventually there might be other mushers nearby to give her some semblance of safety. But they couldn't protect her if the next shooter was more efficient than the last.

Matt would see she got home safely. But when she was back in Montana, who knew who was waiting for her there?

Christ. He scrubbed a hand across his jaw. Take her into the kind of danger he was anticipating? It was insanity.

Should he trust her and her well-trained dogs to get him where he had to go in the fastest way possible? The truth was, he needed the dogs' speed and Lily's expertise. And more than that, the only way he could be sure she was safe was if *he* was with her.

No way in hell did he want her out on the trail, alone, in this storm. Any musher with any sense would've already battened down the hatches and found shelter. She'd be alone out there.

Jesus. A catch-22.

If she were with him he wouldn't have to stop, other than to snack and rest the animals, and they could travel through the day and night to reach the location quickly. As much as he loathed putting Lily in danger, she was right. He wondered rather ruefully if he'd ever live this down.

And then realizing, like it or not, that he had no choice, he hoped like hell they both lived to tell their grandchildren about it.

DEREK REPACKED HIS SLED, KEEPING ONLY WHAT HE DEEMED ABSOLUTE necessities in a bid to hold down the weight. Then he cleared a space in the cargo bed for a passenger. They were traveling light and fast.

Lily opted for writing a note to Matt, which she attached to Finn's collar, telling her brother she and Derek had decided to go off on their own for a few days. Matt would put a romantic spin on it, which was fine.

With blurry eyes Lily watched the dogs they weren't taking with them disappear over the rise as they followed the trail to the checkpoint, alone. In seconds their tracks were covered by wind-driven snow.

Derek wrapped his arm around her shoulders and gave her a squeeze. "They'll be fine."

"They don't need anyone telling them where to go." She rubbed her nose with her palm, watching until the last tail disappeared over the rise. "They know the trail better than we do."

"Damn straight." He herded her to the team, who by this time were practically jogging in place and singing the Hallelujah Chorus in their eagerness to get going.

"Don't worry. They'll be with Matt this afternoon," Derek told her. "This is one of the times you're going to agree to do as I ask. I want you to ride in the sled for the first four hours. Try to take a nap. Close your mouth, please. Because, thank you," he continued when Lily snapped her mouth shut, "because you're still in shock after your dunking, and I'd feel better if you rested. Will you do that for me? Please?"

"Yes, sir. Just don'—"

He brushed her mouth with his. "Nothing is going to happen to either of us. Actually, I just want to be able to take a nice relaxing nap on *your* watch."

He helped Lily step into the basket of the sled. "I love watching you sleep," she told him as she sat down with her legs extended. "You make a cute little snuffling noise just before you drop off."

Derek chuckled as he went to the back of the sled. "I do not. Maybe something manly like a good rib-cracking *snore*—but a snuffle? No way."

"Very sweet. Quite endearing, really." She looked in the direction her other dogs had taken. "They'll be okay, won't they?"

"Matt'll get them home safe and sound and have them waiting

for us when we get back. Lip mic on?" he finished, directly in her ear.

Lily spread an unfolded sleeping bag over her to keep her warm since she wouldn't be doing much moving in the next few hours, and nodded. "Hit it."

Even though she could practically feel Derek standing directly behind her, the lip mic made it possible for them to communicate without shouting.

It was a beautiful day for a run. Crisply cold but windy. And that wind was picking up speed at an alarming rate. The dogs, eager to stretch their legs, let out assorted happy yips as they crested the hill. Derek steered them expertly away from the marked trail their little friends had taken, and with only a brief hesitation they streaked along as if they were on greased wheels.

Lily felt a pang as they left the trail behind. She was going into uncharted territory, and that always made her a little nervous. She coped better when things were predictable. Her heart lurched at just how unpredictable the past few days had been. Other than falling into the water, leaving the race, abandoning her dogs, blinding Derek and joining a supersecret organization out to save the world from terrorists, it had turned into a pretty good day, Lily thought with a grin.

THE BLIZZARD HAD STARTED JUST MINUTES AFTER LEAVING THE RIVER. Bundled up, taking her turn on the back of the sled, Lily's head ached from trying to see beyond the snow-dancing yellow beam of her headlamp. Her fingers were stiff on the handlebar from gripping it so tightly as the sled slid and slithered from side to side where there was no traction.

The night was horror-movie eerie, she thought, licking dry lips beneath the heavy protection of the wool scarf. The bright moonlight of the night before was just a memory. She could almost feel the low clouds brushing her shoulders in the oppressive darkness.

The only sound was of the runners gliding across the frozen snow with a high-pitched *sssssssshhhhheee,* accompanied by the crunch of the dogs' feet breaking into the icy crust as if stomping on cardboard with every step.

Across open plains, over small frozen tributaries and through deep forests, she, Derek and the dogs seemed to be the only creatures on earth.

And the snow kept falling, and falling and falling. Covering their tracks as if they'd never been. Very *Twilight Zone*-ish.

Kind of spooky.

And kind of thrilling, she thought, correcting a left-hand skid with a flick of the brake. She loved the challenge of the Iditarod. But this wild race through unmarked territory, this anticipation of an event people sleeping safe in their beds didn't even know about—this made her heart race and her pulse leap. She felt . . . *alive*. Terrified. But alive.

To fight the bad guys, they first had to triumph over the elements. This was something she could do. Something she was good at.

She felt almost heroic.

Who knew she would have made a great spy?

"Need to stop?" Derek asked softly in her ear. He'd been very quiet for several hours since their last stop and she suspected he'd dozed off and on. Just as he'd stayed silent when it was her turn to be in the cargo bed, she'd left him alone, too. He hadn't gotten much sleep lately. The black fur of his hat and the sleeping bag covering him were mounded with snow and shiny with ice.

"I'm fine, and the kids are loving it," Lily assured him, brushing a small mound of snow off the top edge of her goggles. "You could pour me a cup of coffee, though."

"Sure." He found the Thermos and carefully poured a steaming mug of coffee, then handed the half-filled container back to her, over his head.

Lily pushed down the thick scarf covering the lower half of her face and took the mug. Her goggles fogged up, but she didn't care. She took two sips, enjoying the burn all the way down to her esophagus before she murmured, "Elixir of the gods."

"Isn't it, though." He drank from his own cup. All Lily saw was the steam coming from beneath a snow cap and floating up to her in the dark. "I could get used to this," he told her, his voice melting over her like thick, rich chocolate. *Hot* chocolate, Lily thought fancifully.

"What?" she asked lightly. For some reason, hearing his voice after so many hours of silence made her heart actually ache. "Traveling at the speed of dog in the snow?"

"Me sitting here while you do all the work. This is what it'll be like when we're really, really old."

"Don't tell me." Lily laughed; the wind hurt her teeth and she quickly took another gulp of rapidly cooling coffee. "Me pushing you around in your wheelchair?"

He chuckled, and the deep, rumbling sound rolled around her like a warm breeze. "Or me pushing you in yours. Or both tooling around in our high-powered, state-of-the-art chairs together."

"I think I'll get a fluorescent-red racing stripe on mine," Lily said, keeping her tone light. Just idle chitchat as they traveled. Not a commitment to a future together. One thing could be said for Derek Wright, she thought, ignoring the ache in her chest: when he had his attention focused on a woman, she felt as though she was the *only* woman in his world.

It was a heady sensation, and one she'd remember with heat long after their affair was over. In the meantime, they were out here together—perhaps not romantically at this very moment, but sharing an adventure together—and she wasn't going to spoil one precious moment with him by taking a reality check a second too soon.

There'd be plenty of time for that later.

"Racing stripe, huh?"

"You bet," Lily said, forcing lightness into her tone.

"Uh-huh." Derek paused and in that moment, a world of time ticked past. "Doesn't matter how fast you go, Lily," he said softly, "I'll always catch you."

THE PREDICTED ICE STORM WAS EVEN WORSE THAN DEREK HAD ANTICI-pated. Within hours, tree branches and shrubs became encapsulated inside cocoons of crystalline ice.

They now stopped every half hour to check the dogs' feet, change booties and give the animals a few minutes' respite from the layer of solid crust frosting the top of the snow.

As much as Derek hated to take all these stops, he realized if Lily wasn't with him, the trip would've been much more difficult. No, he admitted honestly, he wasn't at all sure he'd've made it. She shouldered more than her fair share of responsibility without comment or complaint. And she knew her dogs' strengths and weaknesses and drove them accordingly.

"Can you tell me a little about what we're heading into?" Lily asked in his ear. Her voice shook, partly from the cold, and partly, he was sure, from fear. She sat in the sled bed, muffled from top to toe. She'd still be cold, though. It was almost easier standing on the back of the sled and using one's legs to help propel the sled forward.

"The bunch we're after is called Oslukivati. A Serbian terrorist group," Derek told her, blinking to get his headlight focused back on the dogs. "They're on the top terrorist lists around the world. Somehow they've discovered an early warning installation up here, south of Nome. If this installation is taken out, they could bring in missiles and the United States wouldn't know about them until they'd taken out a major city."

"My God."

"Our intel shows they plan to eliminate the early warning facility with a dirty bomb, and then come in guns blazing. A one-two punch. All carefully coordinated with one of the biggest storms to hit Alaska in seventy-eight years."

"How—" Lily's voice caught and she had to start again. "How can one man possibly do this alone?"

"I'll have backup," he assured her. "Don't worry." Christ only knew, he was worried enough for everybody. Dare had assured him nothing was going to be in the air for at least twelve hours. Plenty of time for Oslukivati to blow up half the free world. *"Gee!"* he shouted to the dogs.

"Where's backup?" Lily demanded. "I don't see the cavalry racing in to help you. I want cannons and flamethrowers and atomic weapons of our own, damn it!"

T-FLAC operatives were a resourceful bunch. If they couldn't fly in, they'd find another way. Derek forced a chuckle. "I'd kinda like to see you operating a flamethrower."

"Hey. Get me one. I'll do on-the-job training."

Derek shifted his weight as the lead dogs curved around a clump of frozen bushes before straightening out again. Lily wouldn't be within five miles of the action. Once he located where he needed to be, he'd head her and the dogs toward Nome and safety. She'd make it. She had to.

"I'll consider giving you a flamethrower for your next birthday, how's that?"

"Seriously, Derek—"

"Seriously, Lily. My people will be there to greet us with open arms." *Please, God.*

"Are the bad people ever stopped?"

God. He considered lying through his teeth. "Occasionally."

"Crappy odds. Why do you—" She cut herself off with a sigh. "Because that's just who you are."

Derek checked his GPS in his headlight, and adjusted the heading of the dogs slightly. Yeah. That's who he was.

He'd never before doubted his role in life. He thrived on his work with T-FLAC, and even when it occasionally didn't feel as though they could ever make a dent in the terrorists that kept sprouting around the world like a cancer, he knew that he, and others like him, did make a difference. The world was a safer place because men and women like him did everything in their power to make it so.

It was the big picture that had always kept him focused, and sane in the middle of chaos. But suddenly the picture was pinpointed down to this small, slender woman, and there weren't enough T-FLAC operatives, not enough Marines, or Rangers or even freaking Navy SEALs, to circle the wagons and keep her safe.

Big picture. Small woman. The bottom line was he was heading, hell-bent for leather, *with Lily,* into danger.

And there was absolutely no assurance that he wouldn't have to go in alone.

"The dogs have to have a break." Lily cut into his thoughts. "Sorry."

"We'll stop for half an hour. Enough time?" He knew she wanted to beg for a couple of hours. No can do, he thought, slowing the dogs gradually.

She was a trouper, and his heart swelled with emotion when she said quietly, "Fine."

They pulled off under a thick stand of trees, taking time to light a small fire to heat coffee and soup and food for the dogs. Derek did kitchen duty while Lily meticulously went down the line checking and rechecking the dogs' feet and legs for ice cuts.

"Everyone's good except Rio," she told him through the lip mic. "I'll take him up in the basket for the next leg and then see how he does." She came to stand beside him, muffled so that all that showed were her eyes behind her goggles. "I hate to delay us more than necessary, but they have to rest and eat."

"I know. The break won't hurt us, either. We've been making good time, all things considered." He glanced up at the lowering clouds and the never-ceasing fall of snow. If anything the storm was worsening. As were the chances of the good guys being at the location when he arrived.

Ground teams would be coming up from Anchorage. They'd have to stop for gas to fuel snowmobiles. No, Derek acknowledged to himself, there was now only a snowball's chance in hell of him having backup. His eye throbbed in protest.

There wasn't a damn thing he could do about his vision. Or this storm.

Jesus.

"Coffee done yet?" Lily looked longingly at the blackened pot over the fire.

"Another couple of minutes. The pot's so cold it's taking longer to heat up. How are you holding up, sweetheart?"

"I'm peachy. Frozen-daiquiri kinda peachy, but peachy all the same. How's your poor eye?"

"Doesn't need the sock anymore."

Her eyes crinkled, but he couldn't see her smile behind the scarf. "I'm so relieved. It would spoil the whole James Bond image if you had to chase the bad guys with a gym sock pressed to your face."

"I love you, Lily."

Her eyes widened behind the goggles. Shock? Surprise? Pleasure?

"I, ah, love you, too," she said, voice muffled. "I'll go unharness the kids while that brews. Be right back."

And she was gone.

That went amazingly well, Derek thought ruefully, shaking his head as he watched Lily working with the dogs through a veil of falling snow. He hadn't meant to blurt it out like that. But just looking at her had made his heart swell with love and pride. He'd felt it for so long that saying he loved her sounded natural. *To him.* The timing sucked, of course, as did the location. But she'd taken his declaration in stride. Too much in her stride. He was sure she'd repeated the words back to him more by rote than from the heart.

He shook his head.

It wasn't like him to blurt out something that important. Clearly she'd heard the words, but not the passion nor the sincerity behind them. Or if she'd heard it, she sure as hell didn't *believe* it. Bless her stubborn little heart.

No. His fault.

She deserved better than a blurted declaration in a *place* like this, and at a *time* like this. He turned his libido down to a slow simmer, and promised himself the next time he told Lily Munroe he loved her, they'd be somewhere romantic, there wouldn't be a dog in sight and he'd be holding her hand—so she couldn't run away.

Seventeen

*D*ON'T EVEN THINK ABOUT IT. DISMISS IT. TREAT IT AS CASUALLY *as Derek did.* Lily closed her eyes, and snuggled down in the sled to stay warm while Derek fed the animals, and the falling snow turned to ice again.

When a sophisticated man like Derek told a woman he was sleeping with he loved her, that didn't mean he *loved* her. She got it.

"Move over," he instructed, looming over her.

"Geez, Louise, there's barely enough room— Whoa!" He climbed in and in one quick move twisted her up and over so she was sprawled on top of his body. "Okay. That'll work."

He chuckled as he pulled the insulated sleeping bag up to cover their heads.

Toasty.

"Hi," he said, pressing a hot, yearning kiss onto her mouth.

Lily touched his face in the darkness, mentally cursed her glove and managed, between biting the fingertips and sheer desperation, to get it off her hand. She cupped his rough jaw with warm fingers. He needed a shave. She rubbed his prickly cheek with her palm, loving the feel of him. "Hi, back," she whispered against his mouth. She wished they were naked instead of bundled from head to toe and smothered by a sleeping bag. She wished—

She wished.

"One day," he told her, nibbling her jaw, "we're going to make love outside in the sunshine. Take a blanket down to the pond, spread it out on the grass and get naked. How's that sound?"

As if he imagined her still with him in three or four months. Her heart jittered and she forced it to behave with difficulty. There was no point wishing for something that wasn't even close to the realm of possibility. If she'd imagined this man out of her reach before, knowing he was a spy type put him over the fence and locked the gate. "I'd settle for a nice wide bed right now," Lily told him, arching her throat to give him access.

"I've thought of making love to you ever since we made love." He rubbed her lips with his. A sweet, yearning gesture that made Lily ache inside as soft, silky ribbons of emotion unfurled inside her. "I need to touch you." He paused to kiss her as though he had hours and hours to devote to learning the shape and texture of her mouth instead of a few stolen minutes. "Skin to skin."

Lily's breath quickened as she trailed her mouth across his strong jaw. "As lovely as that sounds," she nibbled at his mouth, "not even for great sex am I going to get naked right now." She ran her tongue across the seam of his lips until he welcomed her in.

Despite the many layers of clothing separating them, Lily could feel his hard length pressed against her thigh.

"We'll liberate the essentials," he rasped against her mouth as he managed to unbutton his jeans with one hand. "How 'bout that?"

"Hmmm." She twisted her upper body so he could unbutton her coat while she fumbled through his layers at the same time.

The sled bounced and creaked as he pushed the fabric around his hips down and out of the way; the sleeping bag slipped off the top of her head, letting in a knife-sharp sliver of freezing air. Lily started giggling at how ridiculous this was, and Derek chuckled as he nuzzled her cheek.

But his hand unerringly found her breast. "Jackpot," Lily said breathlessly, laughter still effervescing in her chest as his clever fingers slid through multiple layers of heavy clothing to find bare skin. She whimpered with pleasure when he played with her erect nipples.

"Were you doing something with that hand down there?" he asked politely, shifting his leg to give her hand better access.

"This one?"

He dragged in a shuddering breath as her fingers closed around his turgid length. "Jesus," he said on a choked laugh, as his body reacted to the cold. "Your hand's like freaking *ice!*"

"Suck it up," Lily told him, feeling saucy and sexy, and ridiculously happy. She hadn't known until this moment just how much she had to offer, desperately *wanted* to offer. To him. She wanted to give him everything she was, everything she hoped to be— Her heart lodged high in her throat as emotions engulfed her.

Either she had to fight this, or she had to let go and surrender to the inevitable.

Lily slipped under.

She took his mouth and used her tongue to demonstrate how her body felt. Hot. Yearning. Needy and willing to give everything.

He jumped beneath her fingers, growing and warming to the touch. It didn't take long for him to return to hot and hard in her hand, and her body ached to feel him deep inside her.

The bed of the sled was narrow, there was absolutely no room to maneuver, and they both had on so many layers Lily couldn't imagine how on earth they were going to do the deed. Laughing, frustrated and giddy with desire, she stroked Derek until he groaned into her mouth in frustration.

She used her tongue and teeth on his mouth, biting, nibbling, loving the power, the heady rush of knowing he was completely focused on her. On her mouth and on her hands.

His fingers tightened briefly on her breast. Lily whimpered as his hand fell away. "Hey! Come back! I was enjoying——" His large, impatient hands tunneled under the open wings of her coat, yanking up layers, and rolling her onto her side so that she bumped the edge of the sled and the sleeping bag slipped.

She didn't notice.

His hands were still busily trying to get her naked.

Hot. Burning. Eager. She shifted her legs to grant him access to her zipper. Good old Levi's sewed their buttons on really well. There would be no pulling this one off in his hurry. The heavy-duty stitching made him take his own sweet time, as he fumbled one-handed to undo the button and unzip her jeans at the same time.

"You've done this before," Lily accused, smiling against his mouth as the zipper went down millimeter by millimeter. The recalcitrant button remained stubbornly in the buttonhole.

"Graduated from unfastening a bra around——damn it, is this button superglued shut or what?——a pillow, one-handed, mind you, to button-front jeans and—— Ah . . ."

"Ahhh," Lily echoed as Derek's hand slid across her stomach and his fingers delved into the flattened curls waiting for him. She shifted as best she could to give him better access.

He caressed her until her laughter tangled with desire. Heat surged through her, making their cocoon steamy and filled with the fragrance of arousal.

"Can we——?" she demanded, trying to wiggle her jeans down over her hips.

"Now this is a position I can enjoy," Derek murmured wickedly as her movements opened her up even more and he slipped several fingers inside her slick heat.

"H-hold that thought," Lily told him grimly, using both hands to shove her jeans as far as she could without rolling off him. Not that there was anywhere to go. "Could you lift——the other way——now the other——no. Yes!"

Four hands, impatient and clumsy, finally managed to push aside enough fabric. Lily threw her knee over his hip, then slid her open body, verrry, veeeeery s-l-o-w-l-y across his until he begged for mercy in a hoarse, unrecognizable voice.

He slid his fingers between her taut body and unerringly found the hard little nub nestled in her damp curls. "Wright," he drawled brokenly in sexy James Bond British. "Derek Wright." And he slipped inside her.

Lily's back arched at the sharp, sweet, exquisite sensation of being filled to the hilt. Heart pounding loudly enough to hear, she ran her hands down his flanks, then gripped the clenching muscles in his lean backside and dug in her short nails to bring him closer.

A slow roll started low in Lily's loins and gained momentum until she grabbed his butt and held on as her body bowed and arched under his. It took only seconds for them to climax. Together.

They lay panting, unable to move, snow falling where the sleeping bag had slipped off.

Inches away, a dog huffed and growled.

"Dingbat's confused," Lily said, groggy and satiated.

"When he's a little older," Derek brushed her hair off her damp cheek, "we'll sit him down and give him the talk about the birds and the bees."

CRYSTAL CHANDELIERS OF ICE DRIPPED FROM EVERY BRANCH. FORTUnately the snow had slowed. Unfortunately the wind had picked up, whipping snow and ice in violent swirls across the ground.

Hell wasn't heat and flames, Derek thought, bent double in the strong arctic wind. It was snow, frozen sharp as a pick, with wind driving the cold deep through half a dozen layers of clothes, searching for skin.

He pushed back the discomfort.

He'd tried contacting Dare off and on for the past three hours. The line was dead. Nice knowing backup was ready, but not worth an ice cube to a polar bear since no one would be able to fly in. Not for several hours at least.

He'd left Lily two miles away from the coordinates Dare had given him, sheltered beneath a dense stand of trees. Unfortunately they couldn't risk a fire. She'd taken three of the dogs up into the sled with her, and they bundled beneath as many layers of insulation as they had with them: sleeping bags, a tarp and the extra clothing in the duffel bags.

"How you doing?" he asked softly into the mic.

"F-freezing my adenoids off, thanks for a-asking."

He put his head down against the gale, and smiled. "Kids not keeping you warm?"

"Sure they a-are. Did the g-good g-guys sh-show up yet?" she asked hopefully.

Nothing was going to show up in this weather. Whatever, whoever, wasn't here yet, and was going to have to wait out this storm. "Not yet." But he was praying as he'd never done before. "But the good news is I've found the facility I was looking for."

He'd also found a de Havilland Beaver in a snow-covered Quonset hut behind the main building. The best news he'd got all day. The Beaver was one of the most dependable aircraft around, and was there for the use of the Marines staffing the installation. It would be in top working order. He was depending on it.

"Don't g-go anywhere without backup!"

Like he had a choice? Adrenaline pumped hard and fast. He didn't answer the question, or address the worry he heard in her voice. "Lily?"

"I'm here."

"See the two tall trees south of you?" he asked through the mic. At her affirmative he gave her instruction on how to get to the plane.

"Hook the dogs to it—it's on skis—then drag it all the way to the other end of the runway and turn it back the way you came. Hopefully this snow will keep up long enough to cover the tarp. You'll be able to hide it in plain sight. Can you do that?"

"Ah— Of c-course," Lily assured him, teeth chattering. "I'm presuming you know it'll f-fly, and it has gas and all that good s-stuff?"

"Yeah. This puppy is old, but well maintained. It'll fly. Not until we get a break in the weather, but it's sound. Load the dogs in it when you have it situated. It'll give you better protection from the elements. I'll meet you there when I'm done."

As casually as if he were calling from work to see if she needed a quart of milk on his way home, Lily thought. She eyeballed the two trees up ahead, reluctant to leave the dubious protection of the trees under which she'd stopped to wait for him to reconnoiter the installation.

"I'll take care of it," she told him, striving to sound calm and competent. "Go do your thing. We'll be fine. *Hike,*" she told the dogs quietly, and they moved forward. The headset went silent.

She'd go and find the de Havilland, she and the kids would drag it wherever the hell Derek wanted it, and then they'd climb aboard and wait for him.

But there was no way, no way in hell, she was flying *anywhere.*

DEREK HAD TO BLOCK LILY OUT OF HIS MIND. HE NEEDED FULL CON-centration on the job at hand. He'd practically fallen over the plane, and that was only because the Quonset hut was large enough to slam into. It had taken a little more time to find the cement building he was looking for. And then only because he had precise coordinates.

The snow reflected a little light, and his night-vision goggles provided enough definition to see shapes. Pretty much everything looked like a snow hill.

All that was visible was a wide door, cracked open a few inches; the rest of the small, shedlike structure had been buried in wind-driven snow.

He walked the circumference, found two snowmobiles backing the building, both half covered with snow, but clearly there'd been no attempt to hide them. Not the personnel manning the station. They'd used the de Havilland.

Each vehicle could potentially carry six men. But there was no sign of anyone. No visual. No sound.

"Am I allowed to talk?" Lily whispered in his ear.

"Go," he told her barely above a whisper as he pulled the distributor wires from each vehicle and tucked them into his pockets.

"I found the plane. I'm hooking it up to the gang line now."

"Be careful," Derek told her, scanning the area for footprints or anything else indicating how many men had entered the building.

"You, too. I— Just be extra careful, okay?"

"Make sure the tarp's covering the entire plane when you get it situated, get in and lock the doors," he told her softly, blocking out the tremor of fear he heard in her voice. He doubted anyone who didn't know Lily well would've picked up that she was scared out of her mind. "I'll be there before you know it," he told her gently, and then added, "Radio silence unless you have an emergency."

He clicked off before she replied. Lily may be afraid, but she'd do what he asked of her, and she wouldn't take any foolish chances. She was aware of how volatile the situation was. Still, when he'd packed for this last leg of their trip he'd transferred most of his weapons and ammo to her. An arsenal. Keeping several weapons for his own use, he'd given her the Walther and his rifle, both fully loaded, and ammunition to spare for each. She was an excellent shot. And he knew she wouldn't hesitate to shoot should the need arise.

He circled back to the front of the building. It was hard to tell how long the door had stood open, but a knee-high pile of snow indicated some time had passed since anyone had stepped inside.

Loaded for bear, weapons ready, Derek slipped sideways through the opening and paused to let his eye adjust to the deeper darkness inside. Usually he had superior night vision, but one eye, no matter how good, was no match for pitch black even with the nvg's.

The anteroom he was in measured ten by fifteen. Cement block. No windows. Door at his back. On his right a narrow elevator without a door. On his left, steep cement stairs leading down.

He took a moment to jam the elevator simply by stuffing his heavy fur hat into the crack between the cement floor and the floor of the elevator. It wouldn't be going anywhere. And in the dark, the hat would be damn near impossible to see—unless one was specifically looking for it. As added insurance, he used the KaBar to wedge the fur good and tight into the chink.

He removed his coat and tossed it behind the door. Next he carried cupped handfuls of snow across the room to the top of the stairs; after several trips, he crouched to spread the soft mounds into a thin frosting across the width of the landing and the top two steps. Then he poured water from his flask until the snow melted and started setting up nicely.

He paused to listen. There was a faint sound from far below, echoing like a memory up the stairwell.

Derek's heart leaped in his chest with anticipation and his concentration focused tightly. Razor sharp. All his senses went to high red alert.

Keeping close to the left-hand wall, his blind side, Derek stepped over the rapidly forming ice on the floor and started running lightly, soundlessly, down the stairs.

Eventually the black receded; he pushed up the goggles as the golden glow of lights from below became brighter and brighter. He paused on the landing five stories below ground level. One level above the action on the main floor.

The steady, low-grade hum of electronics.

Booted feet scuffing on bare cement.

Voices.

And the sharp, fetid stink of death.

DRAGGING A PLANE IN THE DARK—AS IT PROBABLY WOULD IN BROAD daylight as well—proved to be quite an adventure. Fortunately, the snow gave off a faint gleam, which was the only way Lily could see where she and the team were going. Derek had told her not to use her flashlight.

This spy business was proving very interesting. Nerve-racking, but interesting. The heavy plane slid with ease on its skis, and the team pulled it along as if it weighed no more than a loaded sled.

The runway—if the narrow clearing between the trees was the runway—wasn't long. It only took about twenty minutes to get the plane where Derek wanted it. Having worked up a comfortable sweat helping the dogs, Lily went to the leads, her Arrow and Derek's Max, and coaxed them to make a wide circle to turn the plane back the way they'd come. Their tracks had already been obliterated by the gently falling snow and the soft gusts of wind, sweeping the clearing as effectively as a broom. While there was no way on God's green earth Lily was going to go up in the plane, it was going to make a decent shelter from the bitter cold.

"Derek's spy pals will be here soon," she whispered to the dogs as she walked them into the wide turn necessary at the end of the runway. "What's the bet they're on their way as we speak? In nice fast snowmobiles. What, Rio? You'd prefer a *truck* with a *heater*? Good thinking. Me, too."

With the plane turned, Lily focused on getting inside. No easy feat. First the tarp had to be pulled aside; already half covered with snow, it was heavy and unwieldy. Using the sled as a step, she opened the door and shone her flashlight inside, her cupped hand directing the beam and subduing the light.

It would be a tight fit. There were eighteen dogs, plus herself and, in a while, Derek. There was room for two up front, and six passenger seats in back. God. Just *looking* at those bucket seats in the close confines of the cabin made her mouth go bone dry and her heart pound erratically. She hadn't been anywhere near a plane in years. Not since she was a child, in fact.

Think of it as a doghouse, Lily told herself firmly. Just a shelter. Nothing else.

"You kids are going to have to double up. So behave." Fortunately the dogs, once liberated from the line, were able to jump inside the plane unaided, except for Dingbat. Lily picked up all sixty pounds of wet, shaking fur and lugged him to the plane, then heaved him inside. "There you go, big boy. Find a nice spot for a nap."

She grabbed the essentials from the sled, then, coffeepot in hand, clambered into the doorway, tugged down the tarp and closed the door.

God. How could her nose bypass wet dog and only smell *plane*? Leather, dust, jet fuel—blood.

No. No. No. "Ow!" Lily pinched the back of her hand to make herself snap out of the impending panic attack, then sat there listening to her own harsh breathing echo in her ears in time with her manic heartbeat.

Doghouse. Shelter. On the ground.

It was dark as a tomb without her flashlight. She shone the narrow beam around the interior to check the dogs. They didn't care what was going on around them. They were in shelter and a lucky few lay on padded seats. Noses tucked under their tails, they were asleep in minutes.

Dingbat curled up on the pilot's seat with his head on his paws and huffed. Lily leaned over to rub his soft ears. "It's okay, boy. Everything is okay. Close your eyes now and take a little nap. Nothing's going to happen to Derek. He'll be here soon, and then we'll all go home, safe and sound. Good boy, that's it, close your eyes."

Clicking off the flashlight, Lily closed her own eyes on a little prayer. "Please, God. It's bad to lie to animals. Back me up here. Keep Derek safe. Amen."

THE STATE-OF-THE-ART COMPUTERS ON THE VARIOUS WORK CENTERS were dark, the vast underground room dimly lit with what was clearly emergency lighting. Derek counted heads.

Five men standing. Bad guys?

Only five? His first thought flew to Lily.

Of course, it was *possible* only five people had come to do whatever they'd come to do. But what if the other men were up there?

He resisted the overwhelming urge to hear Lily's voice, but clicked into her channel, just to hear her steady breathing.

Sleeping.

Safe.

He clicked off, scanning the room, this time counting the dead Marines slumped over their workstations. Six head shots.

Bad guys, five. Good guy, one.

Not bad odds, Derek thought, flattening himself against the wall in the stairwell and taking aim.

Pop.

Head shot. Make that four bad guys, he thought with satisfaction as the man closest to him dropped, soundlessly, like a shattered watermelon. He shot the next man right between his startled eyes as he turned to see what the *thump* was. He shot the next in the throat before he could draw his weapon.

Two to go.

Derek hit the floor running. A moving target, with the element of surprise on his side, he wasn't wasting time. Two bad guys, or two hundred. Whatever they were doing here had to be stopped.

He was it.

"Góspadi! Amyerikányets!" Shots went wild as each man ducked behind a workstation for protection.

"Hell, yeah, assholes," Derek yelled back in Russian. "Pray. This American's here to stop your sorry asses!"

Where the hell was the bomb?

"Èb tvoju mat'!"

Ignoring the curses, Derek got off another shot, which shattered a monitor in a spray of glass and plastic near one guy's head. Bleeding, the man screamed and ducked again.

Out of the corner of his right eye, Derek observed the first guy moving closer. *Good, stay on that side of me, asshole.* He got off a shot, released the magazine and slammed in another clip, moving forward in a crouch.

The second guy, small and agile, moved with the speed and stealth of a cat. A woman? Moved in around his left side. He lost sight of her for a moment as he concentrated on the man, closer to him. A loud *pop* as a bullet winged him on his blind side, causing Derek to stagger as the bullet went through his right bicep. *Jesus.* His arm immediately went numb. He switched the Baer to his left hand, and despite the blood on the grip, got off a volley of fast shots. *Pop. Pop. Pop.*

The woman spun with the velocity, then dropped to the floor out of sight. Derek edged his way toward her in a crouch, leaned over and felt under her jaw for a pulse. There wasn't one.

Sorry about that, ma'am. Four down. One to go.

They circled each other like tigers in a small cage.

"Khuem grushi okolatachivat', khuilo?" Derek taunted, closing the gap.

The last remaining man, not happy with being told he was a lazy son of a bitch, came up from his hiding place with a vengeance.

Derek fired off a series of rounds in rapid fire. The man, looking surprised, fell to his knees, then crumpled, slow-mo, on his face and lay still.

Derek reloaded, then went to inspect the damage. He quickly felt for pulses, then looked around for the detonation device.

There.

Christ. The countdown had started.

22:31:56

Pulling the webbed belt off a dead Marine lying staring at the ceiling, he wrapped the fabric about his upper arm to staunch the blood flow. The pain made nausea rise to the back of his throat. He'd felt worse, and blocked it out. He managed a clumsy tie, then yanked it tight with his other hand and his teeth. Pain bolted through his arm directly into his brain. He ground his teeth together until it ebbed.

He crouched to see what he had to deal with.

Right arm useless, he used his left hand as best he could; he undid the screws in each corner of the outer casing, then carefully laid it on the floor beside him. Ignored, blood ran down his arm as he tried to figure out what was where inside. *Ah, shit . . .*

22:02:01

Derek wiped his bloody palm on his pants as he angled his head so he could see better. The wires jumped and blurred as he turned and tried to focus sideways.

21:48:06

Then—

21:01:35

Jesus. He tightened the tourniquet again with his teeth. It didn't help. Blood welled, saturated the cloth, then dripped on the floor between his spread knees in an ever-widening pool. The fingers on his right hand went numb.

And goddamn it! He couldn't *see* well enough to do a damn thing.

20:56:54

He reached for the tangle of colored wires again. They blurred. He withdrew his left hand.

Defeated, Derek stared at the red numbers inextricably ticking off the seconds on the computer monitor. He could see *those* just fine.

But he needed two eyes.

And God help him, two hands. His heart thumped arrhythmically. He was screwed.

20:04:21

Lily . . .

"Jesus. *No way*—" Despair pressed icy fingers against his rib cage as his brain scrabbled for alternatives. *Please God. Don't make me need Lily here. Not Lily. Please.*

"Focus, goddamn it! Focus. I can fucking *do* this!" He tried reach-

ing for the wire again. His vision blurred and jumped. He saw double out of his good eye. Blood pulsed out of his arm.

He wanted to yell. Kick something. Shoot something. Kill—

20:00:00

No. No way in hell was he bringing her down here . . .

No choice. No freaking choice. He couldn't do it alone. Bile rose
up the back of his throat. "Goddamn it." He keyed the mic. "Lily!"

"What? What happened?" He'd clearly woken her.

"I need you, sweetheart; hell, hate to sound like a cliché here, but
your country needs you. Are you in the plane?"

"Yes, you sa—"

"Get out now. Run like hell down the side of the airstrip, keeping to the trees. I'll meet you halfway. Take your gun and your rifle
and keep an eye out for— Shit! Just be careful, you hear me? And,
Lily? Run like you've never run before."

"I'm on my way. *Stay*," she instructed the dogs. He heard Dingbat cough, the snick of the door, then the rustle of various materials
as she climbed out of the plane.

19:58:08

"Keep the mic open," he told her grimly, as he ran full speed up
six flights of stairs.

Nineteen minutes, two seconds.

Eighteen minutes, thirty-one seconds—

Jump sheet of ice on the top three stairs. Grab coat. Slam through
door. Haul ass.

He checked his watch.

Fourteen minutes, fifty-nine seconds—

The snow had stopped, he noticed absently. He pushed his arms
through the sleeves, and followed the fog of his breath as he ran flat
out toward the landing strip, his strides long and deep in the snow as
he made a sharp left and practically flew. The pain kept him focused.

Reminded him there was more at stake than a bloodied arm. He glanced down to make sure there was no dripping through the thick sleeve of his coat to leave a trail. Seepage, yes. Dripping, not yet. He melted into the trees, and saw the shadow of her coming toward him, recognized the long legs churning up the snow.

Glanced around. Snipers? Gun man? Tango?

Nothing. No one. All clear.

Less than fourteen minutes—

"What?" she asked, not quite out of breath. She'd made good time.

"Need your eyes." *And your steady doctor's hands.* Derek grasped her arm with his bad hand. Pain, like freaking fire, consumed his arm. Teeth clenched, he turned on a dime, taking her with him. "Run."

Eighteen

S HE RAN. NO MORE QUESTIONS.
Thirteen minutes—
Back into the small structure. "Wait," he said, vaulting over the icy steps and landing. He held out his arms.

She jumped.

A leap of faith.

His heart soared and his arm screamed. He grabbed her hand in his left, and half pulled her down. Flight one. Flight two. Three, four, she was starting to pant. Five.

Eleven minutes, two seconds.

They smelled death before they hit the bottom floor.

"Oh my God." Staring at the bodies, she looked at him with part horror, part ferocity. She yanked off her coat and tossed it over a computer monitor. Looked around again and shook her head. "Where the hell do I start?"

He grabbed up her hand again. Pulled her. "They're all beyond help. This way."

She followed, only because he was dragging her by the hand like a reluctant child on the first day of school. She was a healer. Blood and body parts splattered floor and furniture and she couldn't tear her eyes away from the carnage.

9:57:04

"Then what am I doing here?" Lily demanded, turning to face him at last.

"I need your help to defuse that."

That was a black metal box about the size of a Tourister suitcase, attached to a computer by a spaghetti of multicolored wires. The outer casing lay beside it like an overturned black turtle.

"Looks like something some kid made in shop," Lily said dryly. "Just unplug it."

"Remote-controlled detonation. Those wires have to be cut. In the correct order."

Her eyes went wide. "It's a bomb."

"Under normal circumstances," Derek told her grimly, his entire attention on the numbers changing slowly and inexorably on the black screen. *Seven minutes, nineteen seconds.* "There'd be an ordnance team here, which in turn would dispatch a robot with cameras. Then the ordnance expert would go in, in full body armor, and with extensive backup, and defuse the bomb."

His ordnance team was Lily.

Shit on a shingle. He handed her the tweezers and a pair of wire cutters he'd scavenged from one of the desks, then pulled her down to crouch in front of the computer monitor. "I'll talk you through it. I can't see well enough. Here." He handed her the tools.

Christ. Tweezers and a pair of small wire cutters. And he prayed. Prayed as he never had in his life, that his T-FLAC counterparts were approaching right this second. That any nanosecond now he'd hear their footsteps racing down the stairs.

6:02:57

Lily shot him a worried glance. "You've done this before. Right?"

"They're all different," he evaded. Bombs weren't his field of expertise. But they were both going to get a lesson in a hurry.

5:00:01

"Very gently," he instructed, "pick up the yellow wire. Yes. Just like that. Slowly . . . slowly. Hold it right there. Now carefully move the white one under it, and pull the white to the side out of the way. . . . Good."

There was a loud crash and a scream from the stairwell as someone fell down the stairs. Then whispered voices carried down five stories. Reinforcements had arrived.

Not his guys. They would've checked for the ice.

Damn it to hell.

"Don't worry about them," he told Lily calmly. Her surgeon's hands, used to doing delicate surgery on her patients, were rock steady as she played pickup sticks with the wires.

Hurry. Hurry. Hurry. "Okay, now take the top red wire—no, the one next to i—yeah, that one, and pull it through between the white and the yellow."

"Derek?" Lily said mildly, not looking at him, "could you just cut to the chase instead of giving me the blow-by-blow? There're a zillion wires here. We clearly don't have all day. Which wire am I trying to get to, and what do I do with it when I have it?"

The newcomers had reached the third-floor landing by the sound of them. Quiet they weren't. Derek hefted the Baer in his left hand, and half turned on his haunches. He couldn't watch the stairwell and Lily's hands at the same time. He tuned into the men approaching, and focused his eyes on her delicate hands.

"See the short black one right there on the left in back?"

"Cut it?"

Jesus. I think so. "Yes." *Unless there's a sequence-delay firing relay—* He'd tried to see if there was a dual firing system. He hadn't detected it before but . . . hampered by his Cyclops vision, he looked again.

4:01:45

How long would it take her to move each wire aside without triggering the firing mechanism to get to one, short, freaking wire near the back? More than—

Three minutes, forty seconds.

And, God help him, what if he was wrong?

"Okay. I'll do this," Lily told him as calmly as if she were cleaning one of her dogs' teeth. "You go check to see who's making all that noi— Holy crap!" A shot went directly over their heads, ricocheting off the wall and sending shards of cement in all directions.

3:08:32

"Are you su—"

"Go!"

He went. Guns blazing.

Blocking out the noise behind her, Lily focused on the mess of wires in front of her. She had nothing to draw on to help her, other than doing her own oil changes and tune-ups on her ancient truck twice a year. Somehow she didn't think that counted here. She took a moment to swipe both sweaty palms down the sides of her pants. She drew in a shuddering breath to calm her nerves, which were jumping like fleas on a barn cat. *Oh, God. Oh. God. One more breath. In. Out. In.*

The red numbers on the dark computer monitor beside her left knee blinked.

2:42:01

She used the tweezers to pick up and move another yellow wire. What would happen if she cut them all? It might work—if she could get them in one slice. She looked at the way-too-small wire cutters. Not a chance in hell.

Derek hadn't told her what kind of bomb this was. But any bomb was a bad bomb. She really, *really* didn't need the details.

"This," she whispered to herself, tuning out the grunts and thumps and flying bullets around her, "is a poor sick little puppy. If I don't immediately do this surgery, this sweet little guy is going to die, and the little girl who owns him will be heartbroken, and have to go into therapy for the rest of her life."

She took a breath.

"All I have to do is cut that black artery, and this sweet little puppy will live to romp another day."

Nothing but a fat-bellied little pup, Lily told herself.

Cut the damn wire.

01:09:00

"Let's go," Derek said, coming up behind her. Lily's head was bent over the bomb. Prayer or desperation? Didn't matter now. Her steady hand hovered above the device and he silently applauded her, but his heart squeezed with emotion. If he hadn't brought her here, she'd be safe. How much time did he have to regret his decision?

He leaned down to take the wire cutter out of her hand.

She muttered, "Na-ah," and snipped the wire, then bowed her head. The silence was profound.

After several tense seconds, and when they didn't blow up as expected, Derek put a hand on her shoulder, and she turned to look up at him, pale-cheeked and bright-eyed. She put out a hand so he could haul her to her feet.

"I think I just defused a bomb," she whispered with awe as she stood beside him. "How amazing is that?"

"What?" He stared at her. Afraid to believe. Afraid not to. Damn it, he'd never been afraid before.

01:07:58

He looked at the computer clock, waiting for it to click over.

01:07:58

"You did it." He turned back to stare at her, impressed as hell—amazed she'd tackled a task he'd seen buckle the knees of most rookie T-FLAC agents.

She grinned and he recognized the thrill of victory shining in her eyes. "Well, duh! Wasn't that why you brought me down here?"

"Jesus, Lily." He laughed. "You'll probably get a commendation from the president."

Her grin widened. "Cool. I'll hang it in the barn. I'm sure all my patients will be impressed." For all her bravado she swayed on her feet, and her face was so pale he prayed to hell she wasn't about to pass out. He put his right arm around her. He couldn't feel her; the entire arm was a dead weight. But she leaned against him for a moment, before saying brightly, "Now what?"

"Now we split. I think there are more of these guys out there somewhere. I'd like to be gone before they get back."

"No argument from me ther— What's this?" she demanded, picking up his bloody right hand where it hung limply by his side. He couldn't feel her hands cupping his. "Where were you hit?"

"Upper arm. It looks worse than it is." And that was bad. The blood was bright red and fresh, which meant the wound was still bleeding. Not a good sign. "There'll be time to play doctor later, sweetheart. Let's get the hell out of Dodge before more outlaws show." If he'd thought she was pale before, it was nothing compared with the way the blood drained from her face now, leaving her freckles in sharp relief. "Blood bothers you?"

"Not usually. But seeing *yours,* and this *amount* concerns me a great deal," she told him worriedly. Her eyes rose to his face. "Are you squeamish?"

"No. But my sister Marnie loses consciousness at the sight of it."

"Good thing she isn't here then, isn't it," Lily said briskly. "She'd be in a coma seeing this. Can I—"

"No." He tugged the edge of his coat out of her frantically searching hands. "Stop trying to undress me, woman. You can look at it when we're somewhere safe. Come on." He dragged her to the stairs.

WHAT IF HE HAD SOME SORT OF CLOTTING PROBLEM? LILY THOUGHT, running beside him toward the shelter of the plane at the other end of the runway. Would he even realize how bad it was with all that adrenaline pumping through him? Probably not.

And if he was a bleeder, every running step he took would only pump the blood out of his body faster.

The second she could, she was going to rip off that coat and look for herself.

Dawn lightened the sky to a faint milky blue. The snow had stopped, and even though Lily knew where she'd left the plane, she couldn't see it. Cool camouflage.

It would make a great shelter until the cavalry arrived. She hoped that was damn soon. She wanted Derek in a sterile hospital room immediately. Mentally she went through what she had on hand in her own medical bag.

She pointed to the mini snow mountain about three hundred yards to their right. "Over there," she whispered, although they were out in the middle of nowhere and there was no one to hea—

A shot cracked and whooshed over their heads.

"Oh, for God's sake!" Lily said at the same time Derek shouted, "Run!"

She didn't need to be told twice. She ran. Heart pumping pure adrenaline, legs pistoning flat out. Bullets whizzed overhead in lightning flashes, and her breath sawed painfully in her lungs. Her boots kicked up clods of snow as they zigged and zagged between the trees.

Lily stumbled. Fell painfully to one knee, and was jerked up by her upper arm, and set back on her feet all in one motion. He gripped her arm, pushing, pulling. Helping her move faster. Faster. Faster.

He turned, still running flat out, to fire off a volley of shots behind him. The cordite smell stung her nostrils, and her eyes teared. She wanted to help, and turned slightly to get in a few shots of her own; her steps faltered, but Derek yanked her along with him, making her shot go wild.

"Go. Go. Go!" he shouted above the noise of weapon fire and the mechanical roar of vehicles fast approaching behind them.

The sounds filled Lily's consciousness from edge to edge. There was nothing but noise and terror. What was ahead—white snow, black trees—seemed to come at her as fast as a freight train, blurring endlessly as they ran.

Tree bark shattered with a reverberating crack, spraying sharp shards as they passed, racing through the bitter twilight of predawn.

The sound of the vehicles got louder and louder. Loud enough for Lily to hear clearly over the frantic beating of her own heart. She shot a glance to their right. Shit!

Several snowmobiles raced down the center of the wide swath, weapons firing.

Derek fired off another round. Lily did the same. She was a good shot, although she'd never tried hitting a moving target while running for her life.

They reached the plane, and the dogs immediately started barking their heads off. "Grab—yes." She and Derek each grabbed a handful of tarp and tugged. Hard. It slid off the plane with a loud *thwump*. "Get in," he shouted.

Blood, black in the half-light, saturated his sleeve. Seeing he couldn't open the door and fire at the same time, Lily grasped the door handle and tugged it open. "Get in, I can hold them off."

Derek gave a quick but heavy glance. "*You* get in, for chrissake!"

Lily wasn't going to argue. She hauled herself into the plane. "Off, baby!" she told a sleepy Dingbat, giving him a rude shove to get him out of the other front seat. All the dogs started barking.

"Get in!" Lily yelled at Derek over the cacophony of barking and gunshots. She leaned over and grabbed his collar and pulled. She was so scared he'd get shot again she didn't realize she was throwing off his aim.

The shot went wild, missing the wing of the plane by mere inches. "Now!"

He scrambled in and over to fall into the seat next to her. Lily slammed and locked the door.

"What the hell do you think *that's* going to do?" he asked dryly, starting the plane.

Mouth dry, palms damp and heart in her throat, Lily shrugged. She couldn't take her eyes off the three snowmobiles coming straight for them. Explosions of light indicated the bad guys were still shooting. And the gap between safety and wetting her pants was closing rapidly.

The plane vibrated, then moved slowly forward. Lily's eyes went wide. Her head jerked around to face him. "No! No freaking way—"

"We're sitting ducks."

"We've got plenty of ammunition. Oh, God. Derek. Please, please, *please* don't—" Lily felt lightheaded with fear as the plane taxied down the snow-covered runway straight for the three vehicles bearing down on them.

Bile rose in the back of her throat as the nose went up and the ground dropped sickeningly away beneath them.

Lily went blind and deaf with sheer, unadulterated terror.

Didn't matter if she knew it was illogical. She'd just come from a building where she'd stepped over dead bodies and defused a bomb, for God's sake, but flying in a small aircraft plunged her into a quagmire of terror.

Her brain flashed a series of chilling pictures—her mother's broken, mangled body. And blood. All that blood. Her stomach lurched. Decades hadn't dulled the all-encompassing helplessness that had paralyzed her and haunted her for all these years.

"It's okay, sweetheart. It's okay," Derek assured her soothingly as he banked the plane.

"It's not okay, you bastard!" Lily said through the constriction in her throat, not capable of tearing her eyes from the nose of the plane and the rapidly lightening sky beyond. Her heart wasn't beating, and she'd lost all sensation in her body.

He put his hand on her thigh and gave her a reassuring squeeze.

"I know you're scared, sweetheart. I know. I wouldn't've done this to you if we had any choice at all. Nome is just a hop, skip and a jump away. We'll be landing before you know it."

"And when we land," Lily told him through stiff lips, "I'm going to make sure you're sewn up and healthy—and then I'm going to kill you." Ah. *There* was her heart. That galloping, racing wild animal charging around her chest so she couldn't breathe.

He had the nerve to laugh. "Jesus, honey. I know you're scared to fly. But you just defused a bomb, and outwitted some of the worst terrorists in the world. So a little plane ride shouldn't faze you one bit."

She wanted to turn around and punch him. Hard. And many, many, *many* times. But since Lily was positive that only her full concentration on the nose of the plane was keeping it airborne, she resisted. Her teeth ground together.

"The snow has stopped. Where are your little friends?" she asked sarcastically. So much for being saved by the cavalry.

He grabbed up the headset and put it on. "I'll call in and fin—"

Lily waited. She could almost feel the weight of the vast, open air beneath her. A big, deep *blank*. God, they were high up. Sick to her stomach, she tried to inhale and get herself centered. Derek wouldn't be flying the plane unless he believed it to be safe. And God only knew, this situation was completely different from the last time. He was injured, bleeding and must be in a great deal of pain. She wasn't helping matters by freaking out. He shouldn't have to worry about *her*.

She turned, leg tucked under her, to apologize—and almost fainted.

Derek was slumped against his door.

Unconscious.

"Oh, God. Don't even joke!" Lily whispered hoarsely, her voice a counterpart to the dogs howling and barking behind her. "That is so not funny." Even though she *knew* it wasn't a trick, her brain couldn't wrap around the ramifications that the only person in the plane capable of flying it was freaking *unconscious*.

Well, she'd just have to make him freaking *conscious* again.

She'd be more than happy to do something if she just had a freaking clue what that something *was.*

The first thing she needed to do was switch places with Derek. She couldn't fly the plane from where she was. Of course, she thought hysterically as she crouched between the two seats to tug and shove his large body, she couldn't fly the plane no matter where the hell she was sitting.

Gentle wasn't an option. Lily had no idea where or how she found the strength, but somehow or other she shoved, pushed and hauled Derek halfway into the space between the two seats as the plane continued to pitch forward. She couldn't drag him out of his seat completely. The angle and his weight made it impossible.

Breathless, Lily struggled out of her heavy coat, pulled her sweater over her head and tossed both behind her seat. Right now she'd welcome a cool breeze. She was sweating as though she were in a sauna. She shoved up her sleeves, took a shuddering breath and climbed over him, careful not to kick, bump or jiggle anything on the instrument panel as she did so.

"The president should give me a freaking Medal of Honor for this," she muttered as she wedged herself between Derek's large body and the wall. It was a tight fit. She thought of all the movies she'd seen with just this scenario. Somehow or other, even dumb blondes were able to land 747s with just a little help from a cute air traffic controller on the radio.

Radio.

Okay. She took a deep breath and tried to remember where Derek's hand had been the last time she'd glanced at him. She rested her hands on the U-shaped steering wheel. Like this?

She screamed as the nose dipped below the horizon. "Move your hands, move your hands!" *Oh, God, oh, God.* She adjusted her hands and the nose came back up.

One-handed, she snatched the headset from Derek's head. *Thank God.* She heard a man talking in a monotone.

"Help— Shit! Mayday. *Mayday!*"

Fast.

She grabbed Derek's shoulder and shook him. "That's it? After all we've been through?" She shook him harder. "After I survived the damn crash that killed my m-mother, we're going to die here in Alaska before I get my letter from the president? How is this fair?" Her chest squeezed painfully, as though she were having a heart attack, although she knew it was a manifestation of her fear.

"Derek!" Nothing. Not even a flicker of an eyelash.

"God, Derek. *Please.*" She leaned over and slapped his cheek. "You have to wake up now. Really, you do." The poor dogs were going ballistic barking. "Lie down! *Now!*" she yelled at them. God. She knew her own fear was scaring them, but there wasn't anything she could do to calm them right now. Like a mother with a screaming child in the supermarket, she blocked out their alarm.

Oh, God. What to do? What the hell to do? She had nothing to bring Derek around. No sal volatile or ammonia.

She slid her eyes toward the dashboard, not wanting to move her head. Hell, not wanting to move, period. Like a rat in a maze her brain was screaming: *helphelphelp!*

"Shut up," she scolded herself. "Save the panicking for later. What do I do *now?*" The last time she'd been in a small plane was her dad's Cessna. Nineteen years ago. She'd been too young and carefree to pay attention to the instrument panel. As a child, it was simply magical to float among the clouds. Until the crash, when she learned there was no magic in tons of metal slamming into the ground.

This plane was probably just like her father's. As far as she knew, planes still flew based on the principles of stick and rudder. She couldn't begin to comprehend all the dials and knobs.

She looked down at the floor. Derek's large feet had fallen off the pedals. Accelerator? Brake? She vaguely remembered reading somewhere that a plane's foot pedals weren't like that of a car. Was that true? Oh, God. She imagined touching the wrong thing and the plane coming to a screeching halt midair, then dropping, at the speed of light, like a ton of bricks to the ground a million feet below.

He continued talking. Oblivious.

She searched frantically on the dash for a button to press that wouldn't plunge them into oblivion. There, an unmarked button. She pressed it until her thumb went white. "Mayday? Hello?"

No answer.

Was everyone in Nome asleep?

"Wake up, people!" Lily shouted into the mic on the headset. "I'm a disaster about to happen. I need some help here!"

She scanned all the dials and lights and *things* on the dash. The black numbers meant absolutely nothing to her. If one of them told her how high she was off the ground, she really, *really* did not want that information. Nor did she want to know how close she was to the ground. She kept depressing the button and calling in the Mayday. Eventually someone had to wake up and hear her. She hoped to hell it wasn't after she'd crash-landed into their control tower. But if she had to crash then that's where she wanted to hit. "Serve the slackers right, huh, kids?"

Dingbat huffed.

One instrument showed a little plane. Cute. Useless, but cute. She didn't know if having her hands on the yoke was doing anything or not. She was too scared to remove them.

She heard a loud mechanical noise as she stared at the horizon straight ahead with fierce concentration, as if her will could keep them up in the air. How much gas did they have? How long could the plane stay up if she didn't do anything at all?

Would the plane coast slowly down, or would they—

Wop-wop-wop-wop.

The noise got louder. And louder. And louder.

Something was broken.

Like miscalculating a last step in a staircase, the plane dropped like a rock. She bit her tongue. God almighty. They were going down. Fast.

Wop-wop-wop.

Her hands tightened on the wheel and the nose dipped when she pushed it down. She pulled up. The nose went up. Way up, slamming her back into her seat. Every muscle group in her body strained, and her heart pounded like a sledgehammer on speed.

The dogs howled, then started barking manically, scrambling over one another and banging against the back of her seat.

Wop-wop-wop-wop—

She pushed down on the yoke—just a little—and the nose evened out again, leaving her shaking and sweaty. The noise was getting on her last nerve. "Mayday, damn it! Don't you people go to the movies? I need *help here!*"

The nose dipped and no matter what she did, no matter how hard she pushed, it refused to come back up.

"Help!"

Wop-wop-wop-wop.

Oh, God.

"Damn you, Derek! Wake up!"

Nineteen

WOP-WOP-WOP-WOP.

"Dr. Munroe? Lily?" The voice saying her name in the headset startled her. "If you'd take a look over here at three o'clock? Help has arrived."

Lily swung her head. Her eyes took a little longer to get there. "Oh." She stared, uncomprehendingly for a moment, at the shadowy figure barely visible inside a large black helicopter hovering on her right wing. The origin of the *wop-wop-wop*.

She wasn't alone. "H-hi." And *thank God*.

"Is he dead?" the pilot sounded only mildly curious.

"Is—?"

"Look on the top of the left handle of the control yoke, that's the steering wheel in front of Derek. See the small toggle? Press and release it several times so I know you can hear me."

She did.

"Good. To talk, press the toggle left, to hear me again, release it."

"Not dead. Unconscious. Sho—" The nose dipped. She screamed, and grabbed the yoke in a death grip as all the blood drained from her head. "Shit!"

"Easy does it." The pilot's voice came to her calm and quiet. Doing nothing whatsoever to stop Lily's heart from choking her. Sweat beaded her hairline, ran between her breasts and glued her to the seat. If the yoke were a neck it would be strangled to death, she was gripping it so hard. Each bone-white finger joint ached. The harder she held on, the better chance she had of holding this damn plane up here.

Why was there no damn *air* in this thing?

"*Push* for down," he said into her ear as she gasped for oxygen like a beached fish. "*Pull* for up. It's sensitive, so pull up sl—"

Beep-beep-beepbeepbeepbeep.

Palms slick with sweat, heart hammering, Lily felt the blood drain from her head. "Oh, God! What's happening? What's happening!"

"You're pulling up too fast," he said calmly in counterpoint to her agitation. "Easy does it. There you go. All right. I'm going to talk you down nice and easy. Just do everything I tell you to, and in fifteen minutes you'll be safe and sound on the ground."

Good. Very good. "I'd like that. A *lot!*"

"You'll be there in no time. You're doing great."

Not breathing, but haven't crashed. Yet.

Yeah, great.

"I'll contact the tower and let them know what's up," he told her. "Mayday, Mayday, Mayday, Nome Tower, this is Bell, November four-one-two-hotel, Long Range, request emergency landing, have fire and rescue on alert, over."

Lily's muscles went lax with terror. Fire and rescue? Oh, God— *Pleasepleasepleaseplease. Get me out of here. Now.*

"Roger that, Bell, November four-one-two-hotel, state your emergency, over."

Listening to the two calm male voices, Lily blurted out, "Where the hell were you a few minutes ago, Ace? Reading a freaking book in the john?"

"That's enough, honey," Mr. Helicopter inserted smoothly. "Let's get you down on terra firma, and Derek in the hospital. Then you can ream us a new one, okay?"

"Okay, yes, sure. Fine," Lily said through dry lips. *Please, oh, please. I want to be on the ground now.*

He was right. All that mattered was getting down safely, and getting Derek to the hospital.

"This is Bell, November four-one-two-hotel, we are on an intercept and escort with de Havilland, oscar one-niner-three, Beaver. Pilot incapacitated, civilian at controls. Nome VORTAC, heading one-one-zero, VFR, altitude two-four-seven-five, two-five minutes out, over."

"Bell, how do you wish to proceed? Over."

Yes, Lily thought, too terrified to look at anything but her white-knuckled hands on the yoke. *Tell me. How the hell do we proceed?* There wasn't a drop of spit in her mouth, her eyeballs were desert dry and sweat ran down her temples.

"We are in visual contact, aircraft is on your frequency, passenger on headphones, will talk her down, over."

"Bell, emergency vehicles en route, runway twenty-seven, monitoring transmission, over."

"Hi, Lily." She looked at the darkened windows of the helicopter. The man inside was nothing more than a darker shape at the controls. "Huntington St. John—friend of Derek. I'll be your guide this afternoon."

Her half laugh sounded more like a sob. Equal parts humor and horror. Thank God, he seemed to know what he was doing, which made her believe that she, Derek and the dogs might just get out of this after all. Swallowing her fear, she asked, "What's first?"

"Let me clarify what's what, and we can get this show on the road." He calmly walked her through the operation and function of the instrument panel, the foot pedals and the yoke. "Ready?"

"As I'll e-ever be," Lily told him with a noticeable tremor in her voice. "Let's d-do it."

"All right. Now we begin your descent. Pull back—gently now—on the throttle. Reduce power by about one-quarter cruising speed.

See the nose drop? Don't panic. It's supposed to be about four inches below the horizon. You're doing fine."

If *fine* was sweaty palms, and severe heart palpitations, and wanting desperately to puke, she was better than fine. She spared a quick glance at Derek. Still unconscious. *Don't you dare die.*

"See the airport down to your left?"

It was far, far, *faaar* down. Her mouth was so dry her "yes" didn't make it past her lips.

"I want you to make a pass over the airstrip. Just a pass. You've got plenty of fuel. Just go around once so I can tell them we're coming in and get you lined up."

The plane dropped with a teeth-jarring jolt. Lily screamed. Her vision blurred. Sick to her stomach, saliva flooded her mouth. *OhGodohGodohGod—*

"It's okay. You're okay. Hold her steady."

I am not *okay.* She tried to swallow, but found her throat constricted with sheer, unadulterated terror. "A-around?"

"One pass, you can do it."

"You don't know me. How the hell do you know if I can do it or not?" Lily demanded furiously. She didn't *want* to be the one in charge, damn it.

"Because," he said coolly, "nothing else is acceptable. Now concentrate."

Coming in, Lily thought grimly. One way or the other, the plane would get down on the ground. She only prayed that they wouldn't need the fire trucks lining the runway so far below her.

White-knuckled, Lily did as instructed. Every curse she had ever learned streamed through her brain as she guided the plane in a circle above the airport, following St. John's instructions to the letter.

Beep-beep-beepbeeeeep. *"No!"* Lily adjusted her grip. The annoying and horrifying beep stopped. But the sound of it echoed in her brain, making her sweat even more. Once again bile rose in the back of her throat as wind buffeted the plane and it rose and fell like a dinghy on the sea. "I c-can't do th-this."

"Sure you can," St. John told her. "You're doing fine. Look for the altimeter, a red dial in the middle of the instrument panel. See it?"

"Y-yes."

"The small hand indicates feet above sea level in thousand-foot increments, the large hand in hundreds."

Lily swiped a dry tongue across arid lips. " 'K."

"Line up the landing strip when the altimeter reads one thousand feet . . . which should be about . . . now." His voice seemed eerily calm to Lily, who was shaking so hard her vision jumped and shimmied. "See the airport down there off your right wing tip?"

No. She'd just have to believe him that that's where the hell it was. She had too much else going on now to look at anything.

"Reduce power by pulling back on the throttle— No, that's too much. You're okay. Easy. Easy. There you go. Don't let the nose drop more than six inches below the horizon— Good girl. All right. Almost on the ground."

Oh, God. It was close enough to *touch*. Lily pulled on the yoke and the nose rose.

"Other way, honey. Pull back. Now don't panic when you hear— That's the stall. It's supposed to do that. Pull the yoke all the way into your stomach, until you're on the ground. Gently does it."

The plane bounced and shook as the skis hit the tarmac. Right ski. Then left ski. The plane started to porpoise—

"Ease back toward you— Hold it. It'll level out by itself."

"How do I stop this thing? Isn't there a brake?"

"Yeah, but I don't want you to use it," he said dryly. "Just let it roll out. You have plenty of runway. Slowly pull back on the throttle and the engine will stop."

THE DOGS HOWLED BEHIND HER, THE SOUND ALMOST AS MUTED AS though it were underwater. In a daze Lily stared uncomprehendingly at the yoke as St. John talked her to a wobbly taxi along the runway.

By the time the plane shuddered to a stop, Lily's jaw ached from clenching her teeth, her fingers were fused for posterity to the yoke and perspiration glued her shirt to her back.

The helicopter landed as lightly as a dragonfly beside her. A tall, dark-haired man with a ponytail leaped to the tarmac. Even as the blades rotated above his head he stalked toward her.

Several hundred feet away, a door to the terminal slammed open, and a herd of people stampeded out like cows running in front of Diablo at his horny best. An ambulance raced down the runway, siren wailing, revolving lights flashing red across the snowy ground. Personnel raced around like busy ants doing things with hoses and foam and God only knew what else. The area was a hive of activity. But none of it mattered to Lily.

She turned to Derek and cradled his head on her shoulder, her arms around him. "We landed safely, you can open your eyes now," she said, her voice shaky. But he remained still.

She felt for a pulse beneath his jaw. Thready and weak. His skin felt cold and clammy, and when she lifted a lid, his pupils were fixed and dilated. Everything she knew about medicine told her he needed help, *now*. Everything she knew about *him* told her he was too stubborn to die. But just to make sure, she whispered in his ear, "Don't you leave me, Derek. If you leave me, I swear I'll find a way to make your eternity *miserable*."

The sound of the siren grew closer and closer. On the ambulance would be doctors, medicine, blankets, supplies. She lifted her head and glared out the window. "Hurry up, damn it!"

The man from the helicopter pounded on the window, and Lily strained to reach around and unlock the door. She almost fell out, Derek in her arms, when he yanked it open.

"Derek needs help now," she told him urgently, unwilling to let go of the man she still clasped desperately to her. "I'm fine, but Derek needs help. He's been shot and—"

"It's okay now." St. John reached out a hand. "Easy, love. You did a spectacular job of it. Hop out, I'll get him. Here, take my hand. There you go."

The next half hour flew by in a blur as medics bundled Lily into the ambulance carrying Derek and they were followed by a convoy of people to the small hospital down the street.

It all seemed surreal to Lily as they took Derek off to surgery, and she lost sight of everyone as she was wheeled off to be checked by the doctor. No matter, she kept telling anyone who'd listen, the blood on her clothes was Derek's, and she was just fine.

Ten minutes later, her completely fine self was on an exam table. Her shirt was off and a serious-looking third-year medical student was stitching up the graze wound on her shoulder. It didn't take long for the three sutures and the dressing, then Lily was allowed to dress and leave.

She pushed her way out of the examining room and stalked down the crowded corridor. She stood at the waiting-room door unobserved for a minute. The man who'd saved her butt—St. John—stood by the window talking to a petite, dark-haired woman. He was a good-looking guy in a room filled with hunks. The Wright brothers had arrived, Lily thought, impressed. The room was chockablock with muscle and testosterone.

"Lily." Geoffrey Wright, Derek's father, came toward her, arms open wide. She'd only met Derek's father twice before, but she walked straight into his embrace, her throat tight with emotion. Geoff gave her a tight hug, which for some stupid reason made Lily want to cry. Resisting laying her head on his shoulder and holding on for dear life, Lily stood dead still in his embrace, and when his arms relaxed some, she stepped free.

She felt a blush climb her cheeks as all conversation stopped and everyone turned to stare at her. Geoff kept his arm about her shoulders and casually walked her farther into the room.

"Everyone," he said, his voice a low rumble demanding attention from his gathered family, "this is the very brave Dr. Lily Munroe. How's the shoulder?"

She shrugged. "I didn't notice it when it happened."

Geoff smiled. "I'm sorry you were hurt, but I'm glad it wasn't anything serious. And since I know the first question she'll ask is

about Derek, the answer is: he's out of surgery, in recovery and is expected to be fine. So while he gets his beauty rest, let me introduce
you to the rest of the family."

Fine.

Safe.

Alive.

Lily felt a smile curve her mouth even as her heart began to beat
in a regular rhythm again. Not usually shy, she was still grateful for
the solid presence of Derek's father beside her. She met Derek's twin,
Kane, and his extraordinarily beautiful redheaded wife, A. J. And although the brothers looked alike, Kane wasn't nearly as commanding
a presence as Derek.

Marnie pushed through her much taller brothers. "Give her a
break, you guys!" She practically snatched Lily from her father's side
and wrapped her own arm about Lily's waist. "She's just lived
through a harrowing experience. Let her at least sit down."

"I don't need to s—"

"Michael." A tall brother—good Lord!—wearing an eye patch introduced himself with a kiss on her forehead. "Thank you for saving
my brother's butt. We owe you."

"You're wel—"

"Hey, my turn." The petite woman at his side muscled in. She
grabbed Lily up in a tight hug, difficult to do since she looked to be
about eighteen months' pregnant. "Thank you. Oh— I'm Michael's
better half, Tally." She patted her enormous tummy. "And these two
are Sarah and Jason. They only look full grown," she said dryly, stepping back. "They have four months to go before they hatch. And not
a moment too damn soon, I say."

"That's—"

"Huntington St. John. Call me Hunt," her hero of the hour said
smoothly, breaking in. The helicopter pilot was as tall as the Wrights,
with an austere face and cool, light eyes that seemed to see everything. God. Another mind reader. "You were extraordinarily brave
up there," he told her, his eyes gleaming with sincerity. "*And* you
kept your head. Derek's a lucky man."

Lily felt the sting behind her eyes, and almost lost it. "Thank yo—"

Another brother stepped up to hug her. Lily managed a wobbly smile as she caught Hunt's eye, and he winked at her. The next brother, one she'd never met but who was easy to identify as a Wright, grabbed her up in a careful bear hug. God, she hadn't had this many hugs in her entire lifetime.

"Kyle," he told her with a smile as he set her down. "And this is my bride, Delanie." He introduced his pretty blond wife, who was also pregnant.

"I can't *tell* you how impressed I am that you landed that plane without knowing how to fly. You're my new hero." Delanie gave her a brief hug and a big smile. She patted her little round pooch under a red sweater with an arrow pointing down. "Fee and Fo. No names as yet." She grinned engagingly. "Three months along, and we already know they're going to be giants. Okay, okay. I'm moving!"

Lily had a growing sense of unreality and found it hard to focus on the voices coming at her. She sensed the blood draining out of her head, and swallowed the pool of saliva, praying she didn't pass out like a rock at these nice people's feet.

Someone else came up to hug her. Lily started to feel a greasy, cold sweat break out at her hairline; nausea rose in waves, making her skin prickle, and the lights in the room sparkled and shimmied.

There seemed to be a million people in the room all wanting to hug, pet, pat and kiss her. Lily didn't feel like a hero. She felt like a piece of saltwater taffy being pulled and pulled and—

"Absolutely fine," she answered someone's question automatically, for what seemed like the hundredth time, as she forced down some serious nausea. "Yes. *Really.* Excuse me a moment. Have to go to—" She gestured vaguely down the hall. Giving the room in general a confident smile, she made a dash for the door before anyone else could hug her.

Shoulders stiff, Lily walked quickly down the hall, past one bathroom and then another, past the nurses' station and an empty gurney. Her mind raced, her heart pounded and her stomach did a slow, sliding spin ending in a sickening lurch.

Far away from the waiting room filled with pregnant women, Wrights and assorted other strong personalities, Lily knew she wasn't far enough. The adrenaline—which had kept her going, kept her sane, kept her able to land a stupid plane when every instinct inside her had wanted to run screaming into the darkness—had now dissolved. And without the rush of heart-pounding fear, there was nothing to hold her up anymore.

Her knees wobbled as she kept moving, kept walking. Her feet moved in time to her erratic heartbeat. Her mind raced, her breath quickened and her stomach did another pitch and roll.

She'd survived the plane.

Her oldest fear conquered.

But now there was a new fear.

Living, breathing inside her.

Derek was safe.

Their adventure was over.

And so was her special time with him.

Practically on the other side of the small hospital, Lily spotted the next bathroom sign and kept her attention focused on the letters until she could slap open the door beneath.

The bathroom door opened on hydraulic hinges. Stepping inside, Lily pushed at the enormous handle with both hands. The door was closing, but not fast enough. She pressed her palms and full weight against it as panic clawed at her.

Her breath caught, strangling her.

Stomach spinning wildly, she stumbled across the small room and fell to her knees and immediately emptied her stomach into the toilet.

She wanted to blame what she was feeling on fatigue. But that wasn't the problem. Sleep deprivation was par for the course during the race, and also in her profession, and it had simply been amplified by the conditions of the race.

The race. It seemed a lifetime ago. That was someone else—someone she didn't know anymore. Or rather didn't feel.

She'd come to Alaska to find herself, yet she now felt more lost and confused than before. She couldn't fathom what would come next. Was she supposed to just go back to being a vet now? Forget the sniper, the bodies, the bomb?

Forget Derek?

The thought settled over her like a cement cloak. Was this it?

Maybe, maybe she could forget the thrill of her adventure. Not. She could live a hundred years and she would never forget the onslaught of adrenaline that had driven her through these last hours.

She shook her head, hoping her jumbled thoughts might fall accurately into place like pool balls landing in their pockets. It didn't help. She was a mass of conflicting emotions. Her whole life was askew.

Just days earlier she had thought the only thing she really wanted was peace and serenity. But she had tasted life with Derek and she was greedy for more.

But more wasn't an option and less made her want to scream.

Her whole body quivered as she clung to the cold porcelain and when she was finally finished throwing up, she curled weakly on the floor. It was cold and smelled of antiseptic. But she didn't give a damn. A sob crested and broke, followed by another, and another.

Fist pressed against her mouth to muffle her sobs, Lily didn't hear the door whoosh open behind her.

"Ah, sweetie. Of course you're crying," a woman's soft voice said from close by. "No. Don't try holding back because I've invaded your space, baby, cry it out."

She couldn't have stopped the tears if someone had pointed a gun at her and demanded silence. Nothing could stop them now that they'd finally begun. Lily had never felt so alone. So empty. So . . .

Somehow, she found herself sitting up and gathered against a maternal chest without quite knowing how it happened. She vaguely recognized the woman as Sunny, Geoffrey Wright's bride-to-be. And she was pitifully grateful for the warm embrace and the comforting sound of her voice.

"That's right." Sunny rocked her while smoothing a hand up and down her back. "Cry it out, sweetie, just cry it out. I'm right here."

Lily's throat felt raw, her chest hurt, her head ached—and the tears kept coming. Great wracking sobs broke like crashing waves, one after the other, from an endless well deep inside her. She wrapped her arms about Sunny's waist and buried her wet face against the woman's soft shoulder and continued blubbering like a baby. And through it all, Sunny sat on the floor rocking and stroking, stroking and rocking.

Derek was safe.

They'd survived everything by working together.

She'd found more than she'd ever expected to find in the shelter of Derek's arms—and now she had to give it all back.

She had to return to her life. Alone.

If she'd imagined a man like Derek far beyond her reach before, that reality was now magnified by his secret life. What could she possibly have to offer a man whose life was filled with events like this?

Danger. Adventure. Excitement.

She'd never had any illusions. The only comfort she could derive from the last few weeks would be that Derek genuinely seemed to care for her. Not *love* her, no matter what he'd blurted out in the heat of a terrifying race to get to the bad guys. No. She understood where those words had come from. Not from the heart, but from the heat of the moment.

She understood. She really did.

But it didn't make the weight in her chest any lighter.

How could she live without him?

"A little better?" Sunny asked when Lily pulled away. She reached out and snagged a long strip of toilet paper and handed it to her.

"Not better, but calmer, I hope. I feel like an i-idiot," Lily told her thickly, wiping cheeks that felt sunburned.

"Blow your nose, sweetie." Lily honked and Sunny smiled. "And again, that's a good girl. There's nothing to be ashamed of. You've had an action-packed few days of it. Anyone would cry after everything you've been through."

Sunny, a slightly overweight, middle-aged woman with the prettiest skin Lily had ever seen, and a smile as understanding and cheerful as her name, got to her feet. "Let's get you feeling more comfortable." She flushed the toilet and turned on the tap.

Pulling a small plastic cup free from the dispenser, she filled it and handed it to Lily. "You need to replace all the liquid you lost. Keep refilling this bitty-little thing while I go and find a nice washcloth. I'll be right back."

"D—" Lily couldn't make her throat work, but Sunny seemed to understand.

"I'll check on him and report back. Drink." The door slowly swooshed closed behind her.

Lily leaned against the wall beside the sink and let the water run. She gulped down the contents of the paper cup and refilled it. Over and over again. She was parched; her throat felt as though she'd been screaming for days. Raw and dry. And her eyes were painfully swollen. Bending over the sink, she splashed the icy water against her face and didn't feel the slightest bit better.

"Pathetic fool!" she told herself in a husky croak. She didn't even have the energy to mock herself for her outburst.

She had absolutely nothing to cry about. Derek was safe. And she barely had a scratch on her. Her eyes welled all over again.

The door whooshed open. "Oh, sweetie . . ." Sunny wrapped her arms about Lily and hustled her out of the bathroom and a short distance down the hall. The next thing Lily knew, she was lying on a bed, and Sunny was pulling the covers over her.

"Now let me put this nice cold cloth over those poor swollen eyes of yours, and I'll tell you all about your mule-headed man."

"How's she doing?" Marnie stuck her head around the door.

Derek waved his sister in. "Still sleeping," he whispered back.

"The doctor allowed you to come in here because you promised to lie on the other bed." His sister didn't look the least surprised to see him sitting beside Lily in an uncomfortable plastic chair instead of flat on his back. She shook her head. "Don't you have a crick in your neck sitting like that?"

"I'm fine." This was the only way he could sit and hold Lily's hand at the same time. He wasn't letting go, no matter how awkward it was.

"Our plane's been refueled," she told him quietly. "Dad's getting everyone over to the airport, then he'll send a car back for you guys— Hang on a sec." She went back into the hallway, and Derek could hear her whispering to his brothers.

She stuck her head around. "Michael says do you want a wheelchair? Don't roll your eyes at me, pal. I'm just the messenger— Hang on." She popped out again—and back. "For *Lily,* numbnuts— Hey!" she complained, realizing what she'd just parroted. "You guys! Talk to each other. See you on the plane." She blew Derek a kiss, then disappeared.

Huntington, Michael, Kyle, Kane and their brother-in-law, Jake, all crowded into the room. "We'll hang with you until it's time to split," Kane told him softly, leaning against the wall with his arms folded for the duration.

It's what he would've done for any of the men standing there like sentinels guarding the door, Derek thought, feeling a rush of love for the combined Wrights. Family. Nothing like it.

"Where are the wives?" he asked, leaning over to brush strands of hair off Lily's cheek. Even after several hours, her face was still flushed from crying. When Sunny had come to find him, he hadn't been able to get to Lily fast enough.

"Dad and Sunny are taking them to the hotel to collect our stuff," Michael answered, watching him with his good eye. He hadn't bothered with the prosthetic. Probably because of the cold. The patch suited him. "They'll meet us there."

He checked out Derek's face. "I knew you were always jealous of my patch. You just have to copy me, don't you? What'd you do? Beg some tango to sock you one, sissy boy?"

"Actually," Derek grinned, "Lily did the deed. With the stock of her rifle. I'm grateful she didn't shoot me."

The other men glanced at the bed with new respect. "Oh, I like her already," Kyle said, his blue eyes alight with laughter. "And here we all thought you were going to make a few bucks by winning this race. You've certainly had an exciting couple of days, haven't you?"

"You don't know the half of it," Derek said soberly.

"The second we were cleared for takeoff we were on our way," Hunt told him. "We passed in flight, us going, you coming. That's how I intercepted Lily. I hailed you. You were clearly taking a nap, and I turned around. You owe me an exciting mission sometime soon, old son."

"Talking a beautiful woman down wasn't enough excitement for you?" Derek mocked.

Hunt's lips twitched. He rarely smiled. "Not if I'm not the guy who ends up with the girl, it's not."

"What's the word on our target?" Derek looked from one to the other. "Everyone rounded up? Did we save the world?"

"Hell, yeah," Jake told him. "You didn't leave many bad guys to clean up. Selfish of you."

"Got the job done," Derek told them modestly.

"With a little help from a friend," Lily mumbled groggily from the bed.

They all turned to look at her.

Shooting a dispositive glance at his brothers, Derek said mildly, "Get lost."

Within seconds they were up, out and the door was closing behind them.

"How's your arm?" Lily asked, voice raspy.

"Good." He cupped her hot cheek in his hand. "I'm sorry I made you cry."

She shrugged, avoiding his eyes. "Too much stress. Adrenaline overload. I'm a doctor. I know these things." What was going on in that active brain? Not happy thoughts, Derek saw with a painful twist to his heart. *Oh, Lily.*

He crooked a finger under her chin to turn her face up to his. Her head moved, but she refused to look at him, effectively slamming a

door shut between them. Derek's heart literally ached. After everything they'd shared, she still refused to accept this magical thing between them. How could she pretend not to see it? Feel it? He knew
with every fiber of his being that they belonged together. He was
sure she felt it, too; now he just needed to get her to admit it.

"Look at me, Lily." Her lashes fluttered upward until her hazel
eyes fixed on his face. "I'm sorry as hell that you had to go through
everything that happened there at the end, but I'm not sorry for
everything that happened before."

"Me, neither," she assured him in a too bright voice. "Business as
usual is sure as hell going to be dull after defusing a bomb and flying
a plane."

His arm ached like fire, and he shifted in the hard plastic chair.
She shifted at the same time, and his hand dropped from her face. He
sat back, missing the contact, feeling the gulf between them widen.
"That's not what I was talking about."

A frown pleated her brow. "Oh. You mean the sex? That was
spectacular, too."

Derek closed his eyes, feeling as though someone had punched
him in the solar plexus. "Jesus, Lily."

"Well, it was."

"Is that all we had? Spectacular sex?"

"I wouldn't say *all* so dismissively," Lily assured him, keeping eye
contact, but not able to hide the flash of vulnerability he saw in her
eyes. "Spectacular, toe-curling sex is nothing to be sneered a—"

"Shut up," he said furiously. "Just shut the hell up." He rose and
looked down at her. Small, belligerent and so afraid she could barely
make eye contact. *Jesus, Lily, what the hell am I going to do with you?*

He started walking toward the door. She didn't say anything, and
he could tell she was holding her breath. He turned with his hand on
the door handle. "Everyone said how brave you were. But you know
what, Lily? You're acting like a damn coward, because you won't believe me and you sure as hell won't believe your heart. And rather
than take a risk that what we're feeling couldn't last a lifetime, you'll

play it safe, never knowing how long we'll last because you won't take a chance on happiness." He yanked open the door. "Maybe, just maybe not everyone you care about will end up abandoning you."

She frowned. "Nobody's abandoned me. What are you tal—"

"Your mother—"

"Died," Lily said in a small voice.

"*Abandoned* you by dying," he want on ruthlessly. "And your father *abandoned* you by remarrying and focusing his attention on his new wife and son."

Her chin tilted even as her eyes filled. "I don't feel that way about them."

"Don't you?"

"No. I love my father, and adore Matt."

"Nice to know. But you still took your father's defection as being abandoned, Lily. I know you."

"No, you don't."

"Sean abandoned you by cheating on you. Do you want me to go on?"

"I want you to go and get yourself a shingle and start practicing for real. *You* seem to believe the nonsense you're telling me."

"Haven't you wondered why it is you refuse to believe how much I care for you?" He shook his head when she didn't answer, fury and frustration vying for first place. Infuriatingly stubborn woman. "You won't risk all we can have because you think that like everyone else in your life you've loved, I'll walk. Isn't that right?"

She turned her head on the pillow and closed her eyes. Closed him out.

He ached to go to her, to grab her up and shake some sense into her. To hold her in his arms and assure her that he was in it for the long haul. The hard metal doorknob bit into his fingers as he clenched his hand around it.

This was something Lily was going to have to figure out on her own. For once the sheer force of his will wasn't going to fix it. He swallowed regret, and felt the sting of disappointment blur his vision.

Battle forfeited.

But he hadn't lost the war.

"I'll send someone to get you when we're ready to leave." He shut the door quietly behind him.

Damn it to hell.

Twenty

YOUR PROBLEM IS, YOU BOUGHT INTO SEAN'S BULLSHIT AND LIES
instead of trusting Derek," Matt told Lily, bringing two mugs
of his truly awful coffee to her as she sat at his kitchen table on
a bleak Friday night.

It was more than a week after they'd returned home, and Lily felt
as though someone had performed open heart surgery on her with a
dull spoon. And forgotten to close.

"What's this? A very lame attempt to apply theories you learned in
ten weeks of Psych 101?" She took a gulp of scalding-hot coffee and
pulled a face. "Ew! How can anyone screw up with a Mr. Coffee?"

"How can anyone screw up when a decent guy loves her?"

"I know he *wants* me." She turned the mug in the wet ring on the
Formica table, before looking up at her brother with a scowl. "As
your older sister, that's not even *close* to the same thing."

Matt seated himself opposite her and shook his head. "Listen to
yourself, for God's sake, Lily. You're splitting nonexistent hairs. The
man's clearly nuts about you. Shit, I'm just nuts trying to get through
to you. I'm a guy. If I can see it, why can't you?"

"Because you are a guy," Lily told him dryly. "It's that whole Mars-Venus thing."

"It's the whole Sean bullcrapola thing. That slugbelly never told a word of truth in his miserable life. I can't begin to understand why, knowing what he was, you'd believed *him* and not Derek."

"I don't," Lily said quietly, feeling miserable down to her toes. "I don't believe the things Sean told me about Derek, but if I let go of that illusion—"

"What? What'll happen if you allow yourself the happiness Derek so clearly wants to give you?"

"I—"

"Shit, you're like a pane of glass," her brother said, clearly exasperated. "Not to be confused with a *pain in the ass,* which is also true. You keep wondering if he's going to let you down—note, I said *if,* not even *when,* right?" He shook his head, gulped coffee and grimaced as he slammed down his mug. "You think he'll do what Sean did and cheat on you. You think if you give him all you've got he'll eventually walk away and leave you with nothing in reserve. Admit it."

Lily stared at this brother of her heart. "Yes," she whispered, chest aching. "That's exactly what I think." She rubbed the ache behind her eyes. "No— Okay. No. That's *not* what I— Damn it. I don't know what to think anymore."

"Well, start thinking something," he said with brotherly candor. "Because we guys have fragile egos—we can only stand to hear so many no's before we turn tail and run like hell."

"My point exactly."

Matt rolled his eyes and pushed off the table with both hands. "Want some brandy with that?"

"No."

"Good thing. I don't have any." He fell back into his seat. "You drive a sane man to drink."

"Sorry." Lily's throat ached and her chest felt tight. "How can I make my head believe my heart, Matt?" she asked achingly. "How can I make myself trust on just blind faith that he won't break my heart?"

"How's that heart feel right now?" he asked quietly.

"Point taken."

He rolled his eyes. "I rest my case. There's a cure."

"But what if it's a case of what doesn't cure me will kill me?"

"And what if it's the best damn thing to happen to you? Prepared to risk never knowi—"

Her phone rang. She whipped it out of her breast pocket so fast she almost got whiplash. *Derek*—

"Derek?" Matt asked as Lily read the text message.

She shook her head. On the Wrights' plane, coming back home, she'd told Derek she needed space. Time to think. It was hell getting what she'd asked for. "Joe. He needs help with a cow's early delivery. Back to normal." She rose from the table and carried her mug to the sink and dumped out the coffee. "Thanks for dinner and the pep talk." She walked back, leaned over and kissed the top of Matt's head. "You're a good brother."

"If I was that good you'd listen to me." He rose to hug her. "Don't give up everything because you're afraid, Lily. Some things are worth fighting for. And some things have just got to be taken on faith alone."

FAITH, LILY THOUGHT, PULLING HER TRUCK UP OUTSIDE THE BARN. HER heart, her body, her soul, had faith in Derek. It was her damn brain she was having a problem with. And even that was yearning to take the leap. Unfortunately, there was a last, infinitesimal part of her that held her back.

She tugged her knit cap down over her ears and unsnapped her seat belt, staring off into the darkness. How could a broken heart feel worse than this? How could she possibly miss Derek more than she did right now? How could the pain of being without him from now on be as bad as the pain of having him and losing him?

"And when," Lily said out loud, exasperated with herself, "will I know? *How* will I know? How do I make that leap?" She grabbed her medical bag from the seat beside her. When that door had closed behind him in the hospital up in Nome, she thought her heart would stop beating. For a full five minutes she'd stared at the closed door, praying for it to open, feeling as though the air was being sucked from the room. Sucked from her life.

The truck door pinged when she opened it. And sitting here, half in and half out of the truck, wasn't going to resolve that part of her life. She stepped out onto the snow-crusted ground. She had a patient waiting. One thing at a time.

Back to normal. But nothing *felt* normal anymore. In fact, being back home felt weird. The trip to Alaska, and her experiences there, had knocked her world off its axis. Her life just didn't seem to quite *fit* anymore. She slammed the truck door and ran to the barn through a flurry of snow. A week ago she would've felt the chill in the air; not now. Now she knew what real cold felt like.

She ignored the square amber glow of light coming from the main house's kitchen a few hundred feet away.

Even from out here, she could hear the raised voices and laughter from Derek's friends and family, probably gathered around the kitchen table to enjoy coffee after one of Annie's excellent suppers.

To be fair, she'd been invited. She'd been included in the various activities of Derek's family all week. She'd been far too busy to attend any of them. And even though it killed her to say no, it was better this way. A clean cut was easier to stitch, quicker to heal.

Better to get back to normal as quickly as possible. Maybe someday normal wouldn't feel weird anymore. Maybe then her memories of this past Iditarod would be wiped out and replaced by different memories.

Better to be content with what she had, Lily decided, rather than miss what she didn't. But oh, God, how she missed Derek.

Instead of lingering outside between the house and the barn like the Little Match Girl, Lily tugged at the barn door with both hands. The door was locked. "Geez, Joe!" She pounded a couple of times. No answer. Tugging up her collar, she started walking around to the other side of the enormous structure, wishing she'd grabbed her flashlight from the glove box.

She'd attend Derek's father's wedding in a couple of days because it would be rude not to, and she'd make sure she didn't stand too close to Derek. Didn't look into his eyes. Didn't smell his familiar, know-it-in-the-dark fragrance. She'd hear him talk, but she wouldn't listen to the timbre of his voice. And she would *not* touch him. Under any circumstances, Lily promised her heart, she would absolutely, positively not touch him. She wouldn't get close, because one touch from him would make her melt like snow in a microwave oven. And after his father's wedding—she wasn't sure.

So much had happened recently. Even the race had been anticlimactic. It had felt odd not finishing. Odd driving through Nome in the wrong direction, and seeing the crowds waiting for the first team to ride under the banner, through the rearview mirror.

Still, parts of the journey had been breathlessly exciting as well. Derek kissing her. Derek making love to her. Sharing a sleeping bag. Hearing his voice in her ear for mile after mile. Defusing a bomb and landing a plane had just been the cherry on the sundae. But during that time with Derek, she'd learned something—not just that she loved the man, which she hadn't expected at all, but that she was more *fearless* than she'd ever guessed.

She'd defused a *bomb,* for Pete's sake.

She'd landed a *plane.*

And she'd fallen in love with a man who was probably destined to break her heart without even trying.

She shook her head at herself as she pulled open the enormous barn door and slipped inside, inhaling the familiar fragrances that never failed to ground her. Animal and straw. This, *this* is what she'd miss if she left Montana. She was doing a job she loved, which was more than most people could say. Surely, she told her aching heart, surely this would eventually become enough.

Lily stripped off her coat, hat and scarf, and called out, "Hey, Joe? I'm here. Front door's locked."

"In back," he called, sounding worried.

Lily hastened her steps, boots crunching in the straw as she followed his voice to a back stall. "What's the prob— Don?"

She saw Don Singleton first, simply because he was the only face she recognized. Lily looked around uncomprehendingly. Out of the corner of her eye she saw Joe lying on his stomach against the far wall. Dead or alive? *He* hadn't called to her.

"*Run,* for chrissake!" Don yelled, struggling in the hold of a man as big as a sumo wrestler.

The stall was filled with men. "What on earth—" Her words ended in a scream as a beefy arm, coming out of nowhere, wrapped about her throat from behind and pulled her half off her feet. Her medical bag thudded to the floor.

The arm around her throat tightened and Lily was pulled hard against the person behind her. She made a sound like a cat with a hairball, and grabbed the beefy forearm with both hands, trying to yank it from her neck as she choked. Instead of loosening his grip, the man held her more tightly, cutting off her air. She gagged again.

Another man stepped out of the shadows. "Give the good doctor a little more air, Serg." The arm loosened fractionally, and light-headed, Lily sucked in a gulp of oxygen. "Good evening, Dr. Munroe."

She had no idea who he was; she'd never seen him before in her life. She noted he was medium height. Solid build. Eastern European accent. And most important, he had a handgun. A *large* handgun. Pointed right at her.

Lily's blood ran cold. Lord, the thing was looking bigger every second. One shot from it and she'd be nothing but a messy spot on the straw at his feet. She didn't think there'd be time to feel any pain. Small comfort.

She struggled against the stranglehold around her neck. "Let me go this instant. Who the hell are you gu— Oh my God!" At a nod from the man with the gun, the sumo wrestler behind Don reached up and casually slit his throat. Horrified, unbelieving, Lily stared as, eyes open and startled, Don crumpled to the straw. Blood pumped from the obscene wound in his neck. Her gaze darted to the man in charge. The man whose gun didn't waver by so much as a hair. Bathed in a cold sweat, Lily felt her heart jerk and stutter as he stepped closer.

"He served his purpose by leading us here. Now I have a small request of *you*, Dr. Munroe."

"I'm not doing you any favors if that's how you repay them," Lily snapped, mouth dry. She stuck her hand in her hip pocket.

The gun jerked as he said impatiently, "Please to remove your hand from your pocket, Doctor."

"Sorry," she muttered, buying time and not immediately following his command, feeling for the flat little numbers on her cell phone. "I'm going to do exactly what you want. Look, I'm scared." Fear could actually *focus* the mind, she thought. And besides, once you've stared down a bomb, the muzzle of a pointed pistol just didn't have the same impact.

She pushed what she hoped was number one on her speed dial. "See, no problem here, just emptying my pockets to show you all I have is chewing gum." She pulled her hand out, palms facing outward, gum clutched in one of them in what she hoped was a conciliatory gesture.

"See how cooperative I am? There's no need for any more bloodshed. Want some?" She offered a stick of gum. Keep him talking, and hope that Derek picks up his phone in the middle of supper with his family. Pray he hadn't left his cell upstairs, or in the car or—

He jerked the barrel up to indicate she could go ahead. Lily took her time unwrapping the strip of gum she didn't want, then stuck it in her mouth. "Who are you guys and what do you want?"

"My name is Milos Pekovic." He stepped closer. He stood four feet away, and Lily could smell his too sweet cologne and old sweat. "I am an old friend of Mr. Wright's," he said smoothly. His brown hair was slicked off his face. His eyes were dark and dead-looking and he had terrible teeth. Heroin or bad dental hygiene, Lily thought. As if she'd ever get the chance to identify him in a line-up.

It didn't take a brain surgeon to realize these men were completely

out of their element in a barn in the depths of a Montana winter.
From their accent she figured they were Slavic—Derek's terrorists?
Could they be? Her entire body went hot, then numbingly cold.
Could be. *Were.*

"I would like for you to contact Mr. Wright, and request he come
here to the barn."

Fear was replaced by a spurt of something hot and ferocious. *No.
No way!* "He's out of town."

"No, Doctor. He is in the house. Give her the phone," he instructed one of the shadow men on Lily's periphery. A man thrust a
cell phone at her. "Make the call," Pekovic said coldly.

Lily ignored the man beside her, and didn't reach for the instrument. She was banking on Derek hearing the conversation and being
warned. "I don't know the number."

"It is preprogrammed. Hold the phone for the good doctor,
Demitri."

JAKE MANNED THE PHONE IN THE HOUSE, READY TO FIELD LILY'S CALL.
But he'd let the phone ring for a while. Headset on so he could hear
what was going down, Derek ran lightly across the wide-open expanse separating the house from the barn.

They'd split up. Derek, Kane, Kyle and Hunt to the barn, Jake on
the phone, his dad, Michael and several of the other guests, many of
them T-FLAC operatives, getting everyone out of the house to safety.
No easy task with a houseful of women, many of them pregnant, and
half a dozen small kids. How the hell had Pekovic found him? Derek
wondered as he approached the south door of the barn and watched
the others melt around the building as planned. *Followed someone from
the race.* There were only four people it could possibly have been:
himself, Lily, Matt and Don Singleton.

Immaterial at this point. Derek was chilled to the bone imagining
Lily within a thousand miles of the Butcher. The only thing that kept
him marginally sane was that Pekovic could easily have killed her already. But that wasn't his way. He'd play with her like a cat with a

mouse. Teasing and taunting. Waiting for the person he *really* wanted to show up.

He'd been praying Lily would call him all freaking week. This wasn't exactly the joyous reunion he'd envisaged.

"There's no answer," Lily said, her voice only slightly muffled.

"He will answer eventually." Pekovic's voice. Straw rustled loudly. Derek heard Lily's breathing. A little fast. *I'm on my way, sweetheart. Hang tough.*

"You must be pretty scared of Derek to bring—what? *Twelve* guys with you?" Don't push him, sweetheart, Derek thought, grateful for the information. He knew his brothers, circling the building, had heard. They'd already eliminated seven men outside.

There were more somewhere. Pekovic never traveled without an army. He let the others do their jobs and concentrated on his.

The straw was as noisy as walking on broken glass. Grateful he wasn't wearing his heavy work boots, Derek walked as lightly as he could, keeping to the side wall and the deeper shadows. The swelling in his face had gone down. But he was still having problems with his vision. His twenty-twenty was shot to hell. The barn was dark except for the glow in the stall up ahead.

"I can't breathe. Tell this guy to let go of me," Lily demanded, her voice a little high with fear. Derek was proud she was maintaining her composure nevertheless. He heard the faint tap in his ear, indicating Kyle was in. Kane and Hunt would stay outside until needed.

"Better—" Lily. "Still no answer."

"He will answer. Bring her to me." Pekovic.

Derek moved faster.

Lily's indignant, "Hey!" Then a small, "Oh my God. Don't cut me, please don't cut me."

The Butcher held her at knifepoint.

Derek tapped out a quick code alerting the others he was going in. *Now.*

He vaulted over the six-foot wall separating him from the action. In the air he calculated where everyone stood. Then he completed the jump and was over the barricade in a flurry of motion. He executed a roundhouse kick to the guy closest to him, taking him down expediently with a foot to the jaw. A second later he got off two shots in quick succession, hitting two more men.

"Hold your fire!" Pekovic shouted into the chaos. He had Lily tucked under his chin and was using her as a shield. He held a small, razor-sharp blade to her arched throat. A thin line welled red against her pale skin. Derek blocked out the sight of Lily's terror-wide eyes.

"Hold your fire," Pekovic demanded, pulling Lily even more tightly against his body. "Or I will kill the doctor."

The Serb's men unwillingly stopped firing, but kept their weapons trained on Derek.

"Hurt her, scumbag," Derek told his old enemy dangerously, "and I'll give you a run for your money with that fucking knife."

"An eye for an eye, my friend. An eye for an eye. You killed my Irena, I will accept the life of Dr. Munroe in exchange."

Irena? The woman at the facility? "Not acceptable." Derek kept his attention on the Serb, but knew exactly where his men stood and to a bullet the strength of their firepower. The Oslukivati leader wanted him to watch him gut Lily, and when he was assured Derek was insane with rage and pain, he planned to slice him. Slowly.

Not gonna happen. Derek spread his feet in the straw. "Irena was part of our war," Derek told the other man coldly. "Dr. Munroe isn't. It's me you want. Let her go."

Pekovic laughed. "You are the fly in the ointment of my life, Mr. Wright. Always butting in where you are least wanted. Today you do not—how do you say? Call the shots. Throw down your weapons. It is finished."

A dozen weapons snicked around him.

Keeping eye contact with his nemesis, Derek lifted his arms away from his body, as though he were about to toss both the Walther and Baer aside. The Serb kept Lily's body between them. But the Serb was at least a foot taller. In a lightning fast move, Derek lifted the Baer and shot Pekovic square between the eyes. Lily screamed. A nanosecond later he hit the man closest to his nemesis with a bullet to the cheekbone from the Walther. Lily dropped to the ground, still in the Serb's arms. Derek didn't know if she'd been hit, but couldn't stop now. Two men came at him at the same time. One got off a shot that missed his head by a hair. He ignored the brush of death and fired again. Two-fisted. He got them both as they charged.

The next guy was on him before the dust settled. Derek dipped his shoulder and hefted the guy aside, then chopped down with the Baer until the oaf's gun hand went numb and his weapon flew across the stall and thudded against the wall. Another man charged him, fists raised like a prizefighter's. Derek stepped in with his right foot and let the man's momentum spin him around. Before the Serb regained his footing, Derek grabbed the back of the man's head by his hair, and thumped him hard against the back wall. A crunch indicated the guy was down for the duration.

He could hear gunshots and screams from outside the barn. His reinforcements were busy with problems of their own. Another bullet skimmed his forehead by a hot breath; he lunged for the man, doing a flying tackle that took them both down. Straw and chaff flew as they rolled.

Lily screamed. Derek took his eye off his opponent for a split second. Was Pekovic still alive? Jesus Christ—

A blow, stunning in its force, jerked his head to one side as the man used the butt of his pistol to strike his temple. A shower of bright lights peppered Derek's vision. He flipped the man, and pressed his forearm into the guy's beefy throat.

The man's eyes widened. He gagged, fighting for air. Derek pressed harder. The Oslukivati operative's eyes bulged as his face turned purple. Another deep press and it was over.

Derek raced over to where Lily and Pekovic lay entwined like lovers. Neither was moving. He shoved the Oslukivati leader off her. The man was quite dead; hard not to be with half his face blown off.

Derek wrapped his arms around Lily. She shook like a leaf in the wind as she rolled over and grabbed the front of his shirt in both hands. She buried her face against his chest. He tightened his arms around her, cupping the back of her head in one hand. Close. Too freaking close—

"I–is it over?" she demanded, voice wobbly.

The gunshots and yelling outside had diminished somewhat. Every now and then he'd hear a pop. Pekovic couldn't have chosen a worse time to come calling. The ranch was thick with T-FLAC operatives here for the wedding.

He separated a little way from Lily to scan her face. "Are you cut? Shot? Hurt?"

She blinked up at him, her eyes a little dazed, mouth trembling. "No. No, I'm f-fine."

She was covered with blood, her face and hair splattered. Pekovic's. Derek rose with her in his arms. She was going to put up a fight, but screw it, he needed her as close as possible . . .

Unpredictable little hedgehog. Her head flopped to his chest and she wrapped her arms about his neck. Her damp breath tickled his throat. He tightened his arms around her convulsively. Jesus. Close. So close.

"Okay, Musketeers," he shouted to his brothers, "get your asses in here. All clear at the house?" he barked into the lip mic to Jake.

"Secure," his brother-in-law responded in his ear with his usual calm.

Suddenly the barn was filled with noise and light as reinforcements arrived.

"I can walk," Lily told him, voice raw. She didn't try to move.

He dropped a kiss to her hair and tightened his arms. "I like you just fine right where you are. Get the garbage out of here," Derek told Hunt and Kyle as they strolled into the stall.

"How come you always get to have all the fun?" Hunt demanded, not a hair out of place as he stripped weapons off bodies. Bad guys had been known to come back to life at the most inopportune moments.

"Just trying to impress my girl," Derek said, holding Lily against his heart. "Kane? Check on Joe and Singleton back there while you're at it."

He strode through the chaos of the barn as men came and went. A siren sounded. The local police. The feds would get involved, as would several other agencies. But things were contained. He strode across the wide area between barn and house, the snow and gravel crunching underfoot.

Every light was on in the house as he ran up the shallow front steps, crossed the wide back porch and kicked open the kitchen door.

"Marnie," he yelled at his sister. Couldn't see her, but he knew she was somewhere around. "Close your eyes, and keep 'em closed."

His sister stepped into view. "Why? Oh! Ick!" She flopped into a kitchen chair and covered her pale face with both hands.

"Jesus." Jake crouched beside his wife's chair and wrapped an arm about her shoulders, his attention on Derek and Lily. "Shot? Where's Kane?"

"She doesn't need a doctor. All the red's Pekovic's," Derek assured them, his steps not slowing as he crossed the huge crowded kitchen and started for the stairs next to the pantry. "Get a report from the guys."

"What can I do?" Tally demanded, waddling after him, hand on her belly.

"Keep everyone out of my way until morning." He gave his sister-in-law a smile, which she returned.

He bounded up the stairs, down the long upstairs hallway and into his bedroom, kicking the door closed behind him.

"Like they don't know what's going on up here," Lily grumbled into his chest, face flaming.

He strode into the sumptuous master bathroom. "A shower, you mean? Crank that handle, would you?" He shifted her so she could reach over and turn on the water.

"That won't take 'until morning' by any stretch of the imagination," Lily told him as he released her legs and let her body slip down his. She held on to his neck, brushing her lips across his on the way down.

"I don't know. Might," he told her, yanking off her coat and tossing it to the floor. "You're very dirty." He ripped the buttons on her shirt and stripped it off before she could squawk. Her soft, pale skin was stained an obscene red.

Steam billowed from the room-size shower stall as she toed off her boots, and he finished stripping her at the same time. "Is this going to be a spectator event," she asked politely, "or are you coming in here with me?"

"Oh, I'm coming. With you. In," he instructed, chucking his clothes at the speed of light and leaving them in a pile on the black marble floor.

Lily stepped into the glossy black stall and adjusted the temperature, then lifted her face to the spray as Derek stepped in and closed the door. Her hair darkened and sheeted down her body like a second skin.

"You lead a very dangerous life," she said, eyes closed as she tilted her head back under the water.

Derek poured shampoo into his hand. "Not all the time." He rubbed up a lather between his hands and massaged it into the long strands of her hair. "That was damn clever of you to use the cell phone."

"I know." She grinned up at him through runnels of water.

"You must have nine lives," he told her ferociously, as he found the soap and started washing the blood off her precious body. He kept it as clinical and impersonal as possible. For now.

"Hmm . . ."

He laved her breasts; her nipples peaked and poked through silken strands of her long hair. Okay. He wasn't feeling as impersonal as he needed to be right now. He arranged her hair to expose her lovely breasts. "You've been very brave." He rubbed a soapy thumb back and forth across the pale pink buds. So pretty.

She opened her eyes and shot him an unloverlike glare. "Hang on. Aren't you the one who called me a coward?" She put a hand on his hip to steady herself.

"No." He couldn't resist the small pout on her succulent mouth, and leaned down to sip the water from her lips. The maneuver took several minutes as he had to have a quick taste to refresh his memory. There was a little battle of the tongues for supremacy. He let her triumph so they could both win. "I said you were *acting* like a coward," he whispered against her mouth. "Not that you *were* one. There's a difference."

She rolled her eyes, but didn't move away when he ran the flat of his hand down her midriff. She reached up and used her teeth to tug at his bottom lip. God. She loved to live dangerously. He sank into the kiss even as his fingers tangled with the down at the apex of her thighs. She wouldn't let him in. "The only time I've ever seen you act that way is when you're trying to make me think you don't care about me."

"I care about you." She wound her wet arms around his neck and pressed her body flush against his.

The physical play was clouding his brain; he struggled valiantly to stay on topic. "Not enough," he told her, wanting to laugh despite the seriousness of the conversation. No wonder he loved this woman. She'd fight him to the bitter end until she finally *got* it. "Not the way I want you to."

She leaned her body away from him a few inches. "I had wild and crazy sex with you several times. In the snow, no less. What more do you want?" How could a woman with such bravado in her voice still have so much vulnerability in her eyes?

He pushed the soaking strands of her hair back over her shoulders, then cupped her face and tilted her chin up so she had to meet his eyes. "I want your heart, Lily. I want your love. Damn it, I want it all."

"Oh, God—" She shook her head.

"No?" Derek asked. He dropped his forehead to hers, his voice a deep rumble. "Why not?"

Lily's throat felt raw and tight, and when she cleared it, she might as well have been trying to swallow ground glass. "I—I just can't." *I can't give up that last little piece of me that will keep me marginally sane when you leave.*

"I don't believe that, and neither do you. You wouldn't have had wild and crazy sex with me at all if you didn't love me. You love me, Lily. You love me with everything in you. Heart, body and soul. Admit it."

Her eyes met his. Held. Her mouth was dry, her heart pounded. Standing here naked with Derek, skin touching, she couldn't've been more vulnerable if she tried. "I'm scared," she admitted quietly, forcing herself to keep eye contact even though she'd rather be hiding under the covers in the dark. Alone.

His whole body went rigid. "Of *me?*"

His voice sounded so shocked, so hurt and even horrified at the idea, she shook her head again. "No. God, no. You were right when you insisted I have this crazy fear of abandonment. I thought you were full of it, for even *thinking* that, let alone saying it out loud. But *I've* kept thinking about it ever since Nome. Running it through my mind. I think—no. I *know.* You were right. People I love leave. And even while the rational, adult part of my brain knows that isn't logical, there's a piece of me that believes if I allow myself to love you, that eventually you'll . . . leave too."

"*Leave* you? Hell, Lily, I've been waiting a lifetime to be with you. I've told you that."

"No, you haven't."

Derek grasped her chin with a large, wet hand. Lily stood her ground, chest tight. He moved in closer, forcing her to tilt her head back to see his face.

"Well, what the hell *did* I tell you then?" he said.

"L-lots of things."

"I told you I want you." He cupped her face in his hand and made her look up at him. "Beautiful," he breathed. "I told you I need you." His clever fingers stroked her intimately, and a shudder of want zipped through her body. She held his gaze, and kept her thighs locked against him.

"That's not enough, Derek."

"Damn right, it's not," he told her, his voice thick. "I also told you I love you." He slid one hand under her hair to cradle the back of her head.

Like a fish on a hook, she mentally struggled against the wonder of it. So close. Her heart told her the truth, but did she dare believe it? She wanted to cry. She wanted to scream. God. "You didn't mean that—"

"Yes," he said firmly. "I most certainly did." He brushed his mouth over hers. "I've loved you since the first day I saw you, Lily. From the first instant I set eyes on you six years ago I knew we belonged to each other. I loved you then, and I love you more now. I haven't stopped. Not for a second. Not for a heartbeat. You're the only woman I've said those words to. Ever."

Lily found herself backed against the wall as hot water sluiced over them. How could any woman in her right mind not accept the words he was saying? How could any woman resist him when he was beyond meeting her halfway? When his blue eyes were lit by a heated internal fire, and his mouth was but a breath away from hers? He offered her everything she'd ever wanted, if she was just willing to take that leap of faith.

"I wasn't talking about just that moment," he said, his voice thick as he stared down at her. "Or for now, or for a while. For *always*, Lily. For always."

The pounding of her heart was deafening in her ears. "Always?" she said, the single word on a sigh of breath, her entire body tensed.

"Always and beyond—*ompff*," he muttered, stumbling back a step as Lily launched herself at him, jumping up to wrap her legs around his waist and her arms about his neck. "What are you doing?" he asked against her mouth.

There'd been no other choice. "That," Lily told him, resting her forehead against his, "was my leap of faith." The doubts, the fears, any small nugget of reservation, melted away as she looked into his eyes. Here was home. Safety. Love. Commitment.

He was her heart's desire.

He grinned, that seductive, sexy, charming Derek grin that she loved so much and which made her heart smile. "Good for you. You sure as hell took your sweet time about it!" He kissed her, a sweet, drugging kiss that left her weak and exhilarated at the same time.

"You are my adventure." He cupped her bottom and shifted against her. "You're my calm." He backed her against the cool marble wall. "You're my home." He pushed into her slick heat and stayed still because the sensation for him must be just as intense as it was for her. "I want to go to sleep with you at night, and wake with you beside me in the morning." He moved slowly inside her. "I want babies, and dogs and pets and chaos, and everything else that comes with a family. I want it all, Lily. Say yes."

Lily lifted her hands to cup his face. His eyes were dark, and alive with emotion. "There was a lot of talk there," she told him gruffly, "but I didn't hear a question."

His smile was slow and wicked and absolutely wonderful as he started moving inside her with purpose. "Will you marry me, Lily?"

She looked into the eyes of the man she loved, and saw there love, promise and a long, happy future. "Why, yes, Mr. Wright," she said breathlessly. "I do believe I will."

Epilogue

GEOFFREY AND SUNNY WERE MARRIED IN DEREK'S GREAT ROOM, with the double doors open wide into the dining room to accommodate all their family and friends. Derek's housekeeper, Annie, with the help of Marnie, Tally, Delanie and A.J., had decorated the house in garlands of fresh flowers and twining coral-colored satin ribbon. The fresh spring fragrance belied the gently falling snow outside the windows.

"That was beautiful," Lily told Derek as they rose to mingle with the guests heading into the dining room. The ceremony had been performed by a friend of the bride, an ordained minister they'd flown in from San Francisco. The wedding had been casual and low-key, with children of various ages and temperaments enjoying the attention of all their uncles and aunts in the same place at the same time.

Marnie's two little girls, blond angels, had monopolized Derek's lap throughout the ceremony. Lily had been fortunate they'd allowed her to keep one of his hands for herself.

An enormous five-tier wedding cake sat in the place of honor on the sideboard. Sunny, dressed in a smart cream-colored lace suit, held her new husband's hand and they stood by as each of Geoffrey's sons toasted them.

Derek took his place last at the couple's side. Despite his yellow and purple eye, he looked dashing and handsome in a dark suit. Lily felt an almost overwhelming surge of pride and, blast it—yes— *ownership.* This is *my* man, she thought, heart suddenly racing with sheer, unadulterated joy.

She wore a silky floral dress, and for Derek, high-heeled sandals, her legs and feet bare. He'd ogled her naked toes until she'd given him a little kick in the shin to get his attention off her feet and legs and back to the wedding.

Derek waited while his brother Michael topped off several people's glasses. He met her gaze and gave her a look that spiked her temperature and made her hot and shivery inside. It was a miracle they'd made it downstairs to the wedding in time as it was. They'd spent most of the past two days in bed. Talking, planning. Making love.

Derek gave her a small smile, his eyes heated with promise, the sapphire earring in his ear winking through his dark hair.

He raised his crystal glass. Held her gaze for a second, promising her her heart's desire, then looked at his father and his new bride. Lily smiled from her heart.

Everyone raised their glasses as Derek said, "A toast to my father and his beautiful bride, Sunny, whom we all welcome into the family with open arms and love. Our dad's been alone for a long time, and seeing how much he loves his new bride makes that wait all the more worthwhile." He smiled at Sunny's daughters standing near the door. All blond, all beautiful and all looking around at his T-FLAC associates with the same cool blue eyes.

"We haven't just gained a mom, we've gained two lawyers, an investment banker and a race car driver." Everyone laughed.

"Thank you all for schlepping out here to the wilds of Montana in the middle of winter like this. And while you've all partaken of my most excellent hospitality by being well fed and well watered," he grinned, "I'd like to offer you something *else* since you all happen to be here right now. And God only knows getting the Wrights and their assorted partners, offspring and friends all under one roof is a feat in and of itself. . . ."

Lily sipped the excellent champagne as Derek's voice melted over her like thick, dark chocolate. She'd never been so at peace with herself and her world as she was now. She looked around at the smiling faces of Derek's family and friends. She'd never seen so much open affection and love expressed. In a few hours the wedding party would be over. The guests would be back in their rooms at local motels and in Derek's bunkhouse, and she and Derek would be upstairs. . . .

". . . the library," Derek finished. He came toward Lily with his hand outstretched. She gave him an inquiring glance as she laid her hand in his. His warm fingers closed around hers as he smiled down at her, only at her. As if they were the only two people in the room. Lily's heart almost burst with love for this man who hadn't let her hide any of her emotions. Even from herself. This man who'd made her face her own fears and stood beside her as she'd vanquished them.

"Come with me," he said softly, leading her through the guests, who parted for them like the Red Sea. Lily barely noticed.

"Anywhere."

He led her down a short hallway, and pushed open one of the double doors into his library. Lily's heart leapt. She also wanted to be alone with him, but good grief—

"The guests—" she protested as he pulled her inside the room. She got a flash of dark leather, and hundreds of books, brilliant flickering light and the fragrance of flowers. But she couldn't take her eyes off Derek.

"Will be here in a second." He gave her a slightly uncertain look. "What are you thinking?"

Lily stood on her toes and rested her palms on his chest. Beneath her fingers his heart pounded steadily. Passion banked; she lifted her mouth to brush his lips with a kiss. She held his gaze. "I don't *think*. I *know*. I love you, Mr. Wright. I give you my heart, my body, my mind and my soul. I give you everything that I am, and everything that I can be.

"I want to marry you, and make love with you morning, noon and night. I want to make a baby with you. I want to live with you, work with you and God only knows"—she smiled—"fight with you for the rest of our lives."

"Me, too," he whispered, wrapping her in his arms. His mouth crushed hers in a soul-scorching kiss. They both moaned and pulled apart.

A loud round of applause startled her and she blinked as they broke apart. Lily looked around, slightly dazed. The library was filled with people, candles flickered on every surface, flowers spilled from crystal vases and soft music rippled over the hum of voices. "Will you make an honest man of me?" Derek asked, turning her to face the minister who stood to one side of the fireplace in her flowing robes, watching them expectantly.

Lily's smile was serene as Derek took her hand and drew her forward. Happiness and tranquillity filled every corner of her being. "You bet." Her heart swelled with emotion. "I think I've loved you forever," she told him quietly, her eyes for him alone.

"Hell, I knew that." Derek brushed her damp cheek with his thumb and gave her a blinding smile, his heart in his eyes. "Forever and a day, my love. Forever and a day."

Author's Note

I hope you enjoyed reading Derek and Lily's adventure in the wilds of Alaska. For centuries human beings have pushed boundaries, explored new horizons and challenged themselves to do the impossible; they've worked in tandem with their animals to achieve boundless glory. The Iditarod seemed to be a perfect backdrop for *On Thin Ice*. I needed a setting that could act as another character to foil T-FLAC operative Derek Wright.

In researching the history of the race, I was astonished at the bravery and the guts the participants—including the dogs—showed every year. The Iditarod committee and volunteers who staff every checkpoint make sure the participants braving the elements are well cared for.

I have taken liberties with actual events—turning a difficult and harrowing race into something more romantic. However, some of the places and people mentioned in conjunction with the Iditarod race are real. Their tireless help in answering my questions and sharing their expertise is much appreciated. Any mistakes or errors in *On Thin Ice* are mine alone. I encourage you to learn more about Alaska and the Iditarod by visiting the official Iditarod websites.

Action and adventure, love and romance—they make the world go round! See you in Anchorage in 2005!